GULF

GULF

MO OGRODNIK

JOHN MURRAY

First published in Great Britain in 2025 by John Murray (Publishers)

1

A CIP catalogue record for this title is available from the British Library

Hardback ISBN 978 1 399 81527 7
Trade Paperback ISBN 978 1 399 81528 4
ebook ISBN 978 1 399 81530 7

Typeset in Granjon LT Std

Printed and bound in Great Britain by Clays Ltd, Elcograf S.p.A.

John Murray policy is to use papers that are natural, renewable and recyclable products and made from wood grown in sustainable forests. The logging and manufacturing processes are expected to conform to the environmental regulations of the country of origin.

Carmelite House
50 Victoria Embankment
London EC4Y 0DZ

www.johnmurraypress.co.uk

John Murray Press, part of Hodder & Stoughton Limited
An Hachette UK company

The authorised representative in the EEA is Hachette Ireland,
8 Castlecourt Centre, Dublin 15, D15 XTP3, Ireland (email: info@hbgi.ie)

For my mother

I came to know myself, and this frightened me.

—JAMAICA KINCAID, *Autobiography of My Mother*

If sin existed, she had sinned. All her life had been an error, she was futile. Where was the woman with the voice? ... And what about the continuation of what she had begun as a child?

—CLARICE LISPECTOR, *Near to the Wild Heart*

Verily, Allah forgives all sins.

Qur'an, 39, 53

I.

DOUNIA

Dounia moved from one air-conditioned environment to another. Beyond weather. Post-weather. The bleak landscape of Ras al-Khair rolled by through tinted windows: power, desalination, and mineral plants lined the shore; construction sites and shipping containers littered the dust-powdered desert. The Kingdom's mineral capital would soon have the largest shipyard in the world. Slick videos promised a future of international tourism. Chinese cruise ships would dock at the port on Silk Road maritime tours, Russians and Asians would disembark to dine at five-star restaurants. Meanwhile, there was yet to be a secondary school, and the main shopping was two hours across the border in Kuwait or two hours east in Dammam. She'd never forgive Hamed for bringing her to this desolate industrial complex.

The car slowed at the security gate, and Dounia considered the green Saudi flag inscribed in white. Outside, the air was tinged with ammonia; inside smelled like leather. Raj, the driver from Kerala, loved the maroon Range Rover, treated it as his own, vacuumed it daily, and removed dust and dirt with a flannel cloth at sundown. Both car and driver had been a wedding gift from Hamed eleven months ago. The security guard waved them through, and the tires crept along the road of sand, winding through the maze of construction sites of the Dream Development. Her in-laws' compound, her new home, was the first completed. Situated on the perimeter, this prime location would one day overlook a golf course. Now it was a dumping ground for cement pilings and orange mesh.

The house was modern: two white shoeboxes stacked on top of each other with a slab of concrete slicing down the middle—a crude addition to the already harsh landscape. The ground floor enclosed a central courtyard and a fountain with koi, seven already dead. Sliding shutters shaded and cooled the interior, and while the outside had a spare formalism, the inside had the decadence of a coiffed casket. Hamed's mother, Basma, designed with a flair for purple: a majlis with lavender couches, silver tea trays with bouquets of silk lilacs on tufted plum ottomans, a dining room with violet place settings for twelve (she had yet to entertain a single guest), and a marble staircase with a grapevine of inlaid tiles winding beneath the banister. She and Hamed had arrived five weeks ago. Dounia had no friends in Ras al-Khair, and she spent her days in the compound with her mother-in-law: two women and an unborn child, all strangers to one other.

The pregnancy was the plan that backfired. Hamed vowed they would live apart from the family once she got pregnant. She'd conceived easily and was looking at homes in Jeddah, dreaming of dinner parties and schools, when Hamed's father, Ibrahim, died. Her father-in-law was a visionary who knew how to sell the future; a man who conceived and led infrastructure projects, who dedicated his life to the country he loved, whose dreams were contagious and inspired those around him; a man with whom people longed to affiliate, including Dounia. Her father and Ibrahim had been childhood friends, now each with a construction company and eyes on building commuter rails across the Kingdom—a strategic partnership, a consolidation of assets, a union.

Her father-in-law had cast a glow of possibility across her life. Now, in the clearing, Dounia considered her husband. Hamed wore wire-rimmed glasses from Japan, and his perfectionism was stifling, like fussy confections displayed in specialty shops. He'd inherited the railway line that would connect mines in Kuwait to Ras al-Khair and eventually to Riyadh and beyond, as well as shares in the Mineral City Dream Development project. What he lacked in imagination, he compensated for in reliability, and when his infirm mother, Basma, insisted the couple move into her newly constructed luxury home, one of the first on the coast between Jubail and Ras al-Khair, Hamed had agreed without consulting Dounia; a flinty silence settled between them.

Six hundred thirty square meters, three floors, five bedrooms, seven bathrooms.

Maid's room in the basement. Raj's apartment in the garage.

The foyer was the punctum, the place that bruised her. Not the foyer per se, but the red Venetian chandelier, Dounia's single contribution to the home. In Venice on their honeymoon, she'd watched an artisan expand glass with his breath. With hot irons, he stretched long tubular roses, twisted ringlets, and sculpted delicate grasses. When the pieces cooled, he gathered the glass stems into an inverted scarlet bouquet with a wingspan more than a meter. Beneath these reeds of red, she'd imagined finally making good on the promise of herself. So much seemed possible in those early days, but now the chandelier hung in the foyer of the Dream house, immobile, on the brink of shattering from the cold.

Hamed controlled the chill with a white remote. Central air consumed his obsessive nature. He called in technicians when it strayed half a degree above or below 15 degrees Celsius, a temperature requiring layers for Dounia but perfect for Basma. Sweaters and wraps hung in the entryway, on the backs of couches, beside her bed. Wool, cashmere, and cotton blends enveloped her expanding body, and when her husband returned home, it was the remote he reached for, his mother he went to see.

Dounia was a woman in revolt, majestic with pregnancy, her eyebrows and nose defiant brushstrokes on an oval face. In Jeddah, her womb had been a site of speculation. She cherished the half-formed thing and refused to know the sex; the fetus deserved freedom and she stockpiled the blessings for the child as if they were her own.

But a month ago, the new technician in Dammam announced the baby was a girl. Stunned, Dounia lay on the examination table as the nurse smeared gel across her womb and measured the grainy image on the screen for developmental milestones. As the baby's heartbeat pulsed into the room, Dounia watched her mind skid toward female stereotypes and fears. This is where the kidnapping begins, she thought. We are all guilty. I must protect her.

Without thought, the lie of expecting a boy had unfolded in sidelong glances, the lowering of her chin, the return of her gaze, the way her lips curved upward. Secrecy bonded Dounia to her unborn daughter and conjured the illusion of freedom. But it was a stupid lie. Stupid because it would be impossible to conceal and unthinkable to confess. And the lie got passed down through family phone calls, shopkeepers, emails, texts, and social media, snaking along buried wires on the ocean floor toward Paris, murmuring on winds of ones and zeros across the Gulf, and ending in a blue pregnancy announcement embossed in gold.

JUSTINE

It was a vivid afternoon in April. Justine ran up the stairs of their fourth-floor walk-up. Despite the time, she'd stopped at the pharmacy for a bright lipstick to offset her brown cocktail dress. Winded with excitement, she fumbled for her keys on the landing.

The door swung open into a vaulted darkness. An aching presence greeted her, pulsed like a call box lost at sea, and hushed her mood. Their cat, Cornelius, a devoted and portly rescue, circled her feet, and she wondered if he'd been fed. She removed her shoes and tiptoed through the galley kitchen, where white lilies had been abandoned on the counter in their plastic sheath, stems dry, bound by an orange rubber band. That morning, she'd received a rave from the *New York Times*: "Justine Willard's Curatorial Debut: *The Opossum: America's First Monster and Mascot*. Finally, an exhibition that brings the American Museum of Natural History into the current conversation, upending the racial hierarchy that's been entombed with Roosevelt at the door." The opening was in two hours. Sean was asleep.

She followed the path to their bedroom. Sunlight cracked between the shade and sill, and Sean slept, a pillow over his face, his chest rising and falling with an occasional murmur. She counted his breaths. For months she'd come home to her husband asleep in the dark. He'd been denied tenure, and after a year's grace period, he was now facing his final weeks of teaching. But tonight, she wouldn't worry about Sean, his dearth of interviews on the

American Studies job market, the notice from the Columbia housing office confirming their end of occupancy in August. She'd discovered the envelope, ripped open, on her dresser. Sean's moods, which once rose and fell with regularity, now stood flooded and inert; his bright moon gone dark. And what about their daughter, their Wren?

She fumbled for her mother's pearls in the wooden casket on the dresser and slipped into the bathroom. They'd planned to meet Wren at five o'clock at the corner of 105th and Broadway and walk through Central Park to the museum. She'd splurged on vintage lingerie and stepped into the high-waisted underwear embroidered with lavender pansies, slid her arms through the wide silk straps of the matching bra. They'd reminded Justine of the women she came from, mothers and grandmothers who packed with tissue paper and worried about unexpected trips to the emergency room in dirty underwear. The pansies spread across her belly and full breasts, displaying them with grace. She felt beautiful and sexy in them and would not allow the mirror to change her mind. She had tender skin that bruised and burned easily, and as a child, splashes of pink calamine lotion covered rashes and bites during summer months spent mostly in shade. Those Augusts under oaks morphed into dark winters in libraries and then the silence of archives, bending over specimens and reanimating the dead in her beloved dioramas. Sean had mapped her freckled skin, traced her blue veins like rivers, and named her intimate destinations with care. Her delicate plumpness as a child had settled into a grounded and zaftig appeal.

Justine removed the dress from the hanger and stepped into the brown silk folds of the 1940s cocktail dress, a nod to the original launch of the Hall of North American Mammals, a place where she'd now gathered artists and scientists from around the globe to reimagine the female opossum with meditations on colonialism, migration, and maternal care at their core. Initially the British had depicted the opossum as a monster—due to its pronged penis and double uterus—but with further scientific study, the small mammal's expanding pouch and ability to carry more than a dozen offspring on her back elevated her to the quintessential symbol of migration of the early seventeenth century. In an interview, Justine couched the opossum as "a predecessor to the Statue of Liberty." It was Sean's insight and might have led to an argument, if he'd bothered to read the press.

He tapped on the bathroom door, a new formality of their estrangement. He raised the toilet seat and released a heavy stream of urine. The smell hung in the air and settled between the old green tiles and stained water fixtures. After flushing, he sat on the toilet and watched as she tied the lavender cummerbund around her waist. She saw pieces of him in the mirror: a cowlick, a watchful eye regarding her. He reached out, and she stepped backwards into his touch and felt the comfort of his fingers slipping the silk-covered buttons through their eyelets.

"We're supposed to meet Wren."

His fingers tugged and straightened her hem. "Beautiful."

She placed her hands on his soft, sloping shoulders, but he avoided her gaze.

"You go on. I'll meet you there."

———

Across the street, Wren waved from a bench in front of a coffee shop. Justine watched her daughter register the absence of Sean and then quickly recover. She wore a brown baby-doll dress, to match her mother, with beat-up purple high-tops, and when

Justine joined her on the bench, Wren presented her with a gift wrapped in tissue paper and twine.

"What? A present!"

"Just something I made. Open it."

Wren beamed as Justine unwrapped the paper and string. Inside was a papier-mâché opossum, its narrow face intricately rendered, its body finely painted in strokes of grey and white, its long tail pink and delicate. Justine pulled Wren close and smelled the residue of chlorine in her hair. "It's perfect."

"Like the ones in your show . . . Shake it."

Justine shook the marsupial. Something rattled inside. Wren relished surprises and any form of mischief.

"What is it?"

"Open it and see."

Justine searched for a secret opening but found nothing. "I'm not going to destroy it, if that's what you think."

"It's the only way."

Justine flipped the opossum on its back and began to tear a small hole in its belly.

"Not like that. You have to smash it."

"I'm not doing that. I want to keep it."

Wren snatched the opossum from her hands and hurled it against the sidewalk. Justine watched it break on the concrete and slump at their feet like roadkill, but Wren laughed, giddy with excitement.

"Mom, it's not that big of a deal. That's what we're learning in art class: break it and break it again. Picasso's motto. Don't you want to see what's inside?"

Justine retrieved the broken pieces of the opossum and discovered two antique hair combs. Across the top of each one, Wren

GULF   11

had painted miniature scenes: one with a mother opossum alone on a snowy bank, and the other with six offspring on her back.

"Dad found the combs. I just painted them."

Justine allowed Wren to sweep back her hair with the combs, to reveal her slate-blue eyes that observed the world from a distance and confessed her loneliness when she laughed.

The sky was low and filled with mist and hyacinth as they walked arm in arm through Central Park. The forsythia glowed white beneath the streetlamps coming on at dusk, and as the darkness fell around them, Wren squeezed her arm. "I'm so proud of you, Mom. I really am." But beyond her daughter's admiration, Justine sensed anxiety, and she hooked her arm around her daughter's waist, smiled, and greeted passing strangers.

———

Live musicians animated the hall with contemporary takes on early American music. Saws and spoons accompanied banjos, gourd fiddles, and sitars in rhythms forged through migration. Stone Fence cocktails, a mix of whiskey and bitters, circulated among the artists, critics, and museum members crowded into the narrow passageways. Embraces between corduroy, spring suits, and silk dresses mingled with hushed conversations against walls. Justine searched the crowd for Sean. Wren had disappeared with a friend, probably out on the steps with stolen cocktails and napkins full of cheese.

She stood in front of her favorite diorama, *December at Midnight*. A silence fell around her as she locked eyes with the wolves suspended mid-hunt on a frozen lake, their jaws open, a freeze-frame of instinct before they tackled their prey beyond the frame. A scene where visitors always lingered, and the only diorama

from the original collection Justine had included in the show, with
the subtle addition of a witness: an opossum in the snow-dusted
branches. She'd spent hours discussing every aspect of the exhibition with Sean: the artists, colonialism, the significance of reimag-
ining the diorama. Yet here she was, alone—a pyrrhic victory. It
felt gloomy to celebrate without him.

A man with thick greying hair joined her at the glass. "Justine
Willard. I've been looking for you. What a show. A real Walter
Benjamin!"

He had a British accent and was the kind of man Justine
never used to notice but, with age, had come to appreciate. He
wore a wrinkled linen suit, no tie, and touched her dress sleeve:
"Lovely . . ."

She leaned against the wall so people could pass, trying to place
him. He bent toward her, fixing her with his gaze. "The falcon.
Abu Dhabi."

"I don't even know where that is on a map."

He laughed, sure she was kidding. "A modern-day Casablanca.
That's how I'd describe it."

"Minus the gin joints."

"Oh, no. There's plenty of that." He reached into his coat
pocket for a business card. "Callum Salter, director of the British
Museum. I sent you an email."

She sipped her drink. "I'm sorry, it's been so busy . . ."

He beckoned to a woman across the room. "We've been hired
to curate the Sheik Zayed National Museum. I want you to meet
the director. She's coming now. Brilliant. Emirati. A PhD in art
history, the material culture of the region." An elegant woman
with an air of authority approached. A black headscarf hung loose
around her thick hair streaked with grey, and she wore Justine's
favorite shade of lipstick: poppy.

"Khadijah al-Daheiri—Justine Willard. I was just telling her about you."

"Good things, I hope." Khadijah smiled warmly at Justine, but her stateliness seemed to unsettle Callum.

"I'll finish. Broad-minded and intimidating. Stalled projects are finally moving."

Justine had heard about the museum district. Plum jobs. The Louvre and Guggenheim had not yet broken ground, but they were hiring curators and sponsoring talks. Creating a museum from the ground up. The salaries and benefits were excellent.

Khadijah's dark brown eyes assessed Justine, and within moments she extended her hand in warmth: "I love what you've done with the opossum. Rare for the art world to infiltrate a natural history museum."

Justine felt flattered and wanted Khadijah to know her interests were sincere. "My specialty is in natural history archives. Their intersections with material culture and the contemporary world." She worried she sounded pretentious and vague.

"Callum wants me to hire you for the falcon exhibit. What you've done here, only bigger. More ambitious. The museum will honor Our Father Sheik Zayed. I was seven when he formed the UAE. I don't know if you're aware of his leadership? Extraordinary. His vision embodies what it means to be Arab in the twenty-first century."

Justine was drawn to Khadijah's bold aspirations, and she wondered what it would be like to leave the dioramas and dimly lit rooms, to cross the Atlantic and live thousands of miles away. People mistook Justine for a well-traveled person who spoke multiple languages, but she'd only traveled to Europe once. Latin, a dead dialect, was her foreign language. Like her opossums, she was nocturnal, but for a moment she imagined leaving the darkness for a shadeless sky, studying the falcon, giving Sean time to finish his book and Wren new experiences. Khadijah searched her face, waiting for a response, and Justine smiled vaguely.

Callum drained his glass. "The peregrine is calling."

FLORA

The storm was early, but only by hours. The wind hurled across the sea toward a southern island in the Philippines. The window for evacuation had closed, and Flora carried everything her arms could hold upstairs to where they slept. Instinct hijacked sentimentality as she neglected her grandmother's quilts, her college diploma, and photographs. Instead, she groped for cans of tomatoes and peaches, bags of rice, and, in the middle of this downpour— water. She filled every bucket and bottle with water and more water, squeezing past Joenard on the steps as he wrestled with an oversized TV. His fleshy stomach pushed against the screen, and as he struggled to hoist the monstrosity up the stairs, he groaned, "Fucking hell."

"Forget that. Just get the food."

He ignored her, his face red from exertion and beer. She gathered what remained in the refrigerator: bread, milk, eggs, butter, sticky jars of mango relish. She stumbled up the steps, bottles clanking in the bucket of her skirt, and emptied them on the bed beside her children: eight-month-old Datu in the lap of sixteen-year-old Pia. The three of them watched as Joenard struggled to wrap the television in a sheet.

"Dammit, you could help."

Wind ripped the bamboo shades from the wall and presented a terrifying view of the hurricane: the sky was white, the sea was brown, and the air was filled with water. Palm trees bent and swayed like long-haired women above a rising tub. A puddle formed in the middle of the bed, and they clung to damp pillows. Datu sucked on his fingers and clasped the corner of his blanket with his fist. A bureau slid across the room. Flora brought the child to her breast, more as a comfort to herself, and leaned back into Pia. Joenard took hold of Datu's foot for reassurance, but Flora folded the child into herself, and the man released his grip.

The gale thwacked the tin slab above them. The arms of the storm reached deep into their home. Ropes tore. Beams split. Pia screamed, and Datu began to cry. The roof ripped from the walls, waved upward, and then disappeared. Maybe into the sky, maybe into their neighbors' house, maybe out to sea.

Joenard left the bed. "We need to leave. Now."

Flora was unsure if she should trust Joenard, a man who'd moved into her home when they'd gotten pregnant with Datu, but he herded them off the bed, and they clung to the railing, staggered down the stairs, and waded out into the road, already thigh-deep in water. A large trash barrel floated by and Joenard caught it, grunting as he held on with one hand and emptied the trash with the other. He stretched out his arm for Datu, but Flora would not let the baby go.

She pointed to a blue bus on the hill behind them. "We need to go up. To the jeepney."

"That'll take too long."

Flora tightened her grip and secured the blanket around Datu. "You go."

It was maybe a minute before Joenard understood what she was saying. She could feel everything inside her harden around the child; though this man was stronger and in many ways more capable than she, a familiar distrust and hoarding took hold and revealed her misgivings about the man.

"C'mon!"

But Flora would not hand the baby over. Devastated, he climbed into the barrel without them. The bowels of homes floated past: broken beams, saucepans, and stuffed animals belly-up in the storm. Flora could not watch him float away, and instead she gripped Pia's hand and led her up the hill in a series of small lines, zigzagging toward pilings, tree trunks, and branches, grabbing anything that would propel them forward, never letting go of her children until they finally reached the blue jeepney, crammed with people waving them onward, but when Flora revealed Datu in her arms, they squeezed together and welcomed them inside. The three of them slid between the wet bodies and settled into the human nest. Flora closed her eyes. It was muggy and breath fogged the windows. It seemed impossible, but they'd made it.

For a while, they were just families packed into torn leather seats, listening to the wind pound against the glass, but then a tidal wave upended the bus and toppled it on its side, transforming them into a soggy mess of bodies, and they fell against one another like soft fruit stuffed into canning jars. Water poured through the windows and swallowed their screams. Flora clung to Datu as the chaos of legs, elbows, and stomachs tangled around her. A foot wedged her face against the glass—blocked her mouth and nostrils. She gasped for air and squeezed Datu's torso while shoving the foot off her face.

But she could feel it happening.

Datu slipping away from her.

And then gone.

Flora could never remember how it happened, how Datu disappeared, how she ever let go. She thrashed through the water, her arms sweeping and searching through knotted bodies as she wailed and groped for her baby: his thigh, his foot, his finger. Anything. She found his blanket. Her heart surged. She followed it to the end and discovered a tangled snake of absence.

"Datu, Datu. Pia! Find Datu."

———

The town ran out of body bags. Flora slept on the bare floor of an open-air church that was now an evacuation center. A crucifix hung above a pile of rice bags with Bible verses written in black marker. Flora whispered prayers into a broken wall: "Hail Mary, full of grace, the Lord is with thee. Blessed art thou amongst women and blessed is the fruit of thy womb, Jesus." She rolled over, her breasts hot and swollen, her body cold. She was not alone. Other mothers had lost their grip in the slick waters, had failed in their basic duty: to hold on. But Flora was not seeking solace. In hushed tones, she overheard relief workers delivering information. Thousands dead. Mass graves. An entire city flattened. A cruise ship catapulted onto shore.

Pia created flyers of Datu, hand-drawn pictures tacked to ripped tree trunks, walls drying in the sun. She appealed to relief workers sheltering bodies in old bedsheets, scoured the hill beside the overturned jeepney, and combed the shore. A woman led her to an area of unclaimed infants, and when she found him, she climbed up to the church and forced her mother into the sunlight, into the city where people were rebuilding their homes, past the families eating rice over open fires, candles alight in mourning within feet of the departed. Numb, Flora followed Pia through the algae of low tide, feces, and broken branches. She moved aside for people reclaiming refrigerators and couches, trailing behind her daughter through the silence of destruction.

"Joenard's here somewhere," said Pia. "He's trying to put our home back together."

Flora didn't say a word. That life was over. Their home, the store, destroyed by the hurricane. Bibles, bags of rice, bags of beans, pencils, sponges—everything gone. Gone like Datu. No, not like Datu. Datu was dead. If only she'd trusted Joenard, her baby would be alive. She could not forgive herself for the selfish claiming of their child in that downpour. Not now, not ever.

Sheets, some printed with daisies and Mickey Mouse, wrapped the dead that lined the shore. A burlap bundle lay amid broken stalks of grass. Pia had wrapped her brother the way Flora taught her, but now only a cracked window exposed his closed eyes. Flora sank into the sand and brought Datu into her arms. Her breasts leaked in anticipation; a false alarm that made her weep.

Pia dug a hole beside her mother. When she was done, she pried Datu away from Flora and placed him in the grave.

"Joenard should be here," said Pia.

Flora sprinkled a handful of dirt over Datu and prayed.

Together, mother and daughter reached into the coarse shore and filled the grave.

Their fingers touched as they patted the mound smooth. Flora found two sticks and wrapped grass around them to make a cross, and as Pia gathered stones and arranged them in her brother's name, Flora observed the devastation. The air reeked of death, wet mold, and smoke. Flattened homes littered the beach. The landscape, their neighborhood, the city—decimated. She would have to break her promise. A promise she began whispering in church when she was seven, when her mother left to work in Japan: "I'll never leave my child and do what my mother has done to me."

Flora's breasts were engorged, red and hot and hard; she needed a baby to suck that infection out. Pia could stay with her great-aunt in Mindanao and continue school. The Gulf paid a premium for Filipina workers; she'd become a woman gone, a mother sending money home.

ZEINAH

Zeinah's father stood at the foot of her bed. He wanted her to consider a marriage proposal, even though girls in Raqqa were drinking antifreeze and committing suicide to avoid marrying ISIS fighters, even though her mother's best friend, a surgeon, had fled across the border because no one can perform surgeries in a niqab. She watched her father's hands search his empty pockets and then land on his hips, his fingers searching for a belt loop, something to hold on to. She heard her mother crying at the kitchen table, tears that traveled across floorboards, down hallways, and seeped into the rug beneath Zeinah's bed. But still, the man was wealthy, her father said, and he promised to take good care of her.

In the beginning, Raqqa was the test tube for the revolution. Assad was too busy with Aleppo and Damascus, and he believed his payoff to the local tribal leaders would secure the city. Many people wanted the revolution, but few wanted to lead. Soon battalions controlled different parts of the city, policing broke down, and water and electricity were scarce. ISIS kidnapped activists and, like Assad, paid off tribal leaders for their allegiance, usurping the antigovernment forces. And initially ISIS offered relief from the chaos; they reopened the flour mill and reinstated local services. Everyone craved order and was grateful for the necessities. ISIS formed Islamic outreach centers, but they soon evolved into surveillance and spy organizations.

ISIS strengthened their mission through their commitment to family, offering bonuses for marriages, honeymoons, and off-spring. They paid local sheiks to issue decrees, and foreign men arriving to build the caliphate were demanding wives. ISIS patrolled the streets and harassed women for not wearing the veil. There were rumors of murder and then the beheadings in Al-Naim Square. The central fountain where children swam last summer was now a theater of violence. Fear gripped families everywhere—at their kitchen tables and between their sheets, in the shoes they ventured out in. Meanwhile, the Syrian regime bombed neighborhoods to reclaim the city, abandoning its people in the cross fire.

Her father, once a Raqqa government official, now worked as a mechanic for ISIS in exchange for a meager salary. The marriage promised protection and Zeinah's safety in an apartment nearby—a real concern for her parents after the kidnapping and disappearance of her brother, who'd participated in early protests against Assad. The marriage seemed impossible to refuse.

———

Zeinah clung to her mother in the kitchen and heaved against the faded flowers of her apron, inhaling the scent of onions and talc lodged between her mother's breasts.

Her father waited on the stairs. "We can't be late."

Zeinah felt the slack in her mother's embrace, felt her body recede, until she stood alone between the doorjambs.

Her mother and aunt boycotted the wedding—a legal proceeding in a beige room with broken windows. Her father and uncle were present.

A witness for the groom.

———

After the wedding, Zeinah sat on the dusty bench seat of a white Nissan pickup, a marriage certificate tossed between her and a man, apparently from Iraq. Omar, probably not his real name, had slid a ring on her finger—a ring she dared not look at but touched and twisted, discerning a considerable stone.

They drove through Raqqa. Death was in heat: groins sweating, beards growing, urine reeking. Men tucked loose trousers into flat-footed boots and patrolled neighborhoods. Wild dogs rolled in the waste, dry-humping strangers. Metal grates closed like curtains across storefronts on the abandoned streets. As they passed Al-Naim Square, Zeinah saw puppies eating from the stomach of a rotting corpse. Her favorite café was boarded up, daubed in black, tables and chairs upended in the dirt. A ransacked town square: ice-cream store closed, shelves emptied, no men on the corner comparing lottery tickets.

Omar wore a date seed tasbih around his wrist, but she did not have the courage to look at his face. The air drew tight around them, and Zeinah cracked the window, exhaled into the afternoon. Omar pressed a button, and she watched the glass slide up beside her, and then close. His power was unapologetic. He drove one-handed with an easy steer of the wheel and parked in front of a makeshift women's clinic.

She watched as he squinted into the sun.

"I've arranged for you to have an IUD."

A pink plastic bag blew across the street, and she watched as it skimmed the dusty sidewalk away from them. "You don't want to have children?"

"No."

A heavyset woman left the clinic with a young boy, who ran ahead of her. Wind billowed beneath her abaya, and she held it down as she lumbered up the street, trying to keep pace with her son.

"I thought that was the point."

She felt his body stiffen, but his voice was flat: "For some. Not me."

"I don't understand."

He closed his eyes. "It will weaken my will to serve God."

Wind blew through the empty truck bed behind them. Neither said a word. Zeinah thought, This is our first conversation.

The door lock popped open.

"I'll wait here."

———

Zeinah lingered in the entrance of the health clinic. Women sat in chairs lining the walls while others paced with crying children in their arms. The mood was heavy, the facility understaffed, and people were irritable. She approached the receptionist and gave her name.

"We've been expecting you. Please come with me."

Zeinah felt the judgment of the women in the waiting room and disappeared down the hallway, ashamed she'd cut the line.

The receptionist escorted her into an examination room. "The doctor will be right in. You can sit on the table." Zeinah stood in the barren room, noting the rectangles of pale paint where medical posters of female anatomy must have hung.

The door opened and the female doctor entered. "Zeinah?"

Zeinah nodded.

"You're here for an IUD. Do you know what that is?"

"Birth control."

"You're lucky. Have you ever had a gynecological exam?"

"No." Zeinah regretted the lace underwear her mother had given her that morning.

"Why don't you scoot down and put your feet in these metal stirrups."

Zeinah slid down the table, unable to meet the doctor's gaze.

"Okay, I need you to open your legs."

Zeinah spread her legs, and the doctor folded her dress and abaya above her knees.

The doctor sighed. "I need you to remove your underwear."

Zeinah rolled down her underwear and held the crumpled lace in her palm.

"I'm going to insert this metal device to open your vagina, and then I'm going to insert this small string. It may hurt, but it'll be quick. Are you ready?"

She nodded.

"I'm sorry, but I can't . . . I need you to open your legs."

Zeinah's body trembled as she willed her knees apart.

"I'm going to insert my fingers into your vagina with some gel."

The cold metal of the speculum startled her, and tears rolled down her cheeks. The icy instrument slid deep into her vagina, where no one had gone before, and spread her insides open. Zeinah felt a pinch followed by cramps, and she wondered if the IUD was an act of kindness or preparation for abuse. She knew nothing about Omar, the man she'd married, but she was not going to eat rat poison; she was determined to survive.

ESKEDARE

The baby unfurls in the needled grass and blinks into the bowl of sky above her. It's March in Ethiopia, before the rainy season, when the dirt smells like cattle and the air is full of jasmine. Her mother traces the stem of a blue birthmark arcing across the tiny hand and presses against the bloom beneath her pinky. She gathers the infant to her breast, and her mouth stretches into a painful yawn as milk releases into the eager jaw. For hours (it might've been days), the mother and daughter lie together, ears to the ground, listening to the earth breathe and sigh beneath them.

The infant points to a peak burning orange against the sky, a flame of promise.

"Eskedare," whispers the mother.

Eskedare, the furthest and farthest point.

Eskedare.

∾

DOUNIA

Duty tugged Dounia out of bed like a marionette, belly first, then limbs. The chandelier caught the morning light, tossed red marbles across the tiles, and illuminated a path to the kitchen, where she waited for the water to boil at the soapstone sink. This part of her day was routine. She poured steaming water over the tea and set the timer to three minutes.

Outside, in the Saudi Dream Development, a gardener worked beneath a green mesh tarp. Rows of tomatoes and clementines slouched against wooden stakes and received a daily soaking of desalinated water from a Dutch sprinkler system. Despite these efforts, the plants wilted and lost their leaves. Today, the gardener arrived with a fresh pallet of plants, a different breed of tomato. The gardener's efforts were futile, and Dounia found Basma's insistence on harvesting fruit and vegetables from sand an indulgent form of torture on the plants. But the tomatoes reminded Basma of childhood, a time when she ran free from house to house and ate lunch from the neighbors' gardens. Yes, it's painful to accept the past is over, thought Dounia.

The timer rang. Dounia poured condensed milk into the tea until it turned caramel, added two heaping teaspoons of sugar, and set the silver tray with a white lace napkin. Once she considered adding her own teacup, but this ritual was about service, not camaraderie. She balanced the tray in one hand and pushed the elevator button, stepped inside the steel room, and watched the doors close.

There was the familiar lilt of loneliness as she ascended the two floors before the doors opened.

"Dounia, is that you?"

She hesitated outside Basma's room before entering. Minutes late, already a failure. She situated the tray on Basma's lap.

"I didn't know where you were."

"The water took longer to boil today."

Dounia took the tub of Vaseline from the nightstand and struggled to lower her pregnant body—legs spread, almost squatting—onto the stool at the end of the bed. She scraped beneath Basma's toenails with an orange stick, washed her feet and legs with a warm towel and sandalwood soap, and then buffed her toenails with a pink felt board. For thirty minutes, she scooped tablespoons of Vaseline into her hands and spread the milky grease around Basma's swollen ankles, across her arches, and between her toes. She traced the woman's blue roped veins with her palms and circled her walnut ankle bones with her thumbs as Basma closed her eyes for quiet time, a time for Ibrahim and mourning. And in the silence, Dounia entered her own sorrow.

Mid-May. Paris. The Tuileries Garden. Months before the wedding. A dress fitting. Her sister had come along, and in retrospect, the entire trip was planned around that afternoon: the intervention. They'd gone to the Cy Twombly show at the Louvre. Dounia bought a postcard from the exhibition of a sand dune with the words "Wilder Shores of Love" scrawled in red across the sky. Twombly was an artist "who straddled the raw and the cooked," and she wrote to Hamed how this could be their anthem. She was on the precipice of things and felt the adrenaline of an uninhabited future ready to take form, but she also was aware of trying to conjure something that still felt precarious and remote.

They ambled along the gravel paths of the garden, stopped at a cluster of green metal chairs beside a bed of hollyhocks, took off their shoes, stretched across the slats, and raised their chins to the spring sun. Not far away, men played bocce in the sand, and Dounia listened to the thud and tap of wooden balls.

Her mother had grown up in Paris, in Barbès, an Algerian neighborhood near Montmartre, a place she refused to show her daughters, because in October 1961, five months after she was born, her parents had marched in protest of the Algerian curfew and her mother, Dounia's grandmother, had been killed. Her mother grew up with a single Algerian father who worked hard and was fearful of public transportation, a man who installed extra locks on doors. When her mother was twenty-seven, she met a Saudi man at the café where she waitressed near the Sacré Coeur and agreed to marry him and move to the Kingdom. When Dounia pressed for more details, her mother would shut down and say, "The story's simple. France was never home." And yet Paris was the location her mother chose for the conversation.

A plane flew overhead, and the three women looked upward toward the white trails blooming across the cloudless sky. In the silence that followed, her mother and sister regarded her.

"What?"

"I want you to know . . . I love you very much, and no matter what you decide, my devotion to you will never waver," said her mother.

Dounia shaded her brow with her hand and looked at her sister, who now sat upright beside their mother. "Okay . . . ?"

"You've always been so . . . spirited," offered her sister.

"Weddings feel exciting, but times are different now," said her mother.

"And picking the flowers, food, and gifts for the registry feels festive," added her sister. "I've been to dozens of weddings and seen what awaits you on the other side. I know you don't want to end up like me, thirty and living with our parents, but I have more freedom than all my friends. Don't think you'll be the exception."

But I am the exception, thought Dounia. I am different.

"After all this planning and stimulation is a life, your life," continued her mother. "I want you to understand what you're choosing. More and more young women are deciding not to get married. You can run the date farm, a very successful business you'll both inherit. You'll have your freedom. There are different ways for women to form a life."

"So many of my married friends are unhappy," said her sister.

"People get divorced now. Women can leave," said Dounia.

"It's a legal commitment, not easy to undo," said her mother.

Dounia and her sister met each other's gaze. "You want me to call off the wedding?"

"No. I'm asking you to think seriously about getting married."

"Do you think there's something wrong with Hamed?"

Her mother shook her head and seemed pained by her inability to adequately express her concerns. "Marriage is a relationship with the entire family. Your mother-in-law has tremendous power. Marriage is not for everyone. Motherhood is not for everyone. I did not understand how lucky I was. Nana taught me to manage the date farm, but now there are many opportunities for women to work in Saudi. You don't need to get married. Not every woman should follow in the traditions of marriage and motherhood. You could start your own business."

Dounia watched the men play bocce and envied the loose throw, the flight of balls hurled into the air, the thuds in sand, the huddle around landing. Her mother's concern for her freedom was ill-timed and dubious. When she'd surprised her parents with her acceptance to Berkeley and Yale, her mother forbade the opportu-

nity. True, she'd applied in secret and had not shared her passion
for conservation and political science, but that was to avoid the
public humiliation of rejection. Her months of research—taking
virtual tours, following students on Instagram, and imagining afternoons on green quads, in large lecture halls, and all-nighters
with black coffee—had ended in success. And she wanted to bring
everything she learned back home, to contribute to the conservation and governance of the country she loved. She was nervous
to tell her parents, and when she finally did, she was devastated
by their response. Her father was proud but guarded in his congratulations. Her mother was furious and didn't speak to her for
days. There was no brother to be her guardian in the States, and
her mother wasn't about to move to California, much less New
Haven. A week later, her mother hosted a celebratory dinner for
Dounia's acceptance to the women's campus at King Saud University in Riyadh. She would never attend college in the States, and
when Dounia was sullen, she was called ungrateful. Her mother
determined the boundaries of her freedom, and this conversation
in the Tuileries Garden was no different.

True, Dounia could stay at home, take trips with her family to
London, Paris, and Japan, care for her parents as they aged. She'd
inherit the date farm and beehives that had been in the family for
generations. She'd become a steward, alongside her sister, of their
history. But who wants to inherit a life?

Dounia fingered the edge of the postcard she'd written to
Hamed. She knew she was trying to conjure love, but the desire
to leave, to catapult into something new, was better than rooting
into the familiar. Ibrahim, her father-in-law, was an impressive
man who saw her potential. She'd thrive under his care. Her sister,
whom she loved, would not, could not, become her life partner.
She thought of Cy Twombly's sculptures. House paint, wax on

fabric, twine, wire, and nails. Marriage offered the same materials as her old life, but with the opportunity to reimagine something new. Twombly expressed ambition with household items. I can do that, she thought. I can change how I see. Create strange things from the familiar. She wanted to talk about the white sculptures, the crayon and colored pencil drawings, the still life series created from jars, but it seemed impossible to explain any of this to her mother and sister, who sat across from her, waiting for a response.

The next morning, they returned to Riyadh. Under June suns, wedding plans commenced: fonts, the weight of paper, shades of cream. A guest list of hundreds. No expense was spared, the invitations alone were $30,000, and when they toured the hotel on the Arabian Gulf, her father mistook Dounia's longing and believed it could be sated with a view.

Basma's sighs summoned Dounia back to the room, to her mother-in-law marooned in bed. A woman who described her feet as cushions of pins and needles. Neuropathy stunted her mobility, but her mind was still alive. Petite, like Hamed, her face maintained a dignity that failed to respond to any kind of touch. A woman who, despite her formality, insisted on the importance of human care and duty among family members. Dounia searched the woman's features for signs of pleasure, to mark a path for her to follow, but nothing seemed to matter. Whether Dounia rubbed, pounded, or stroked across the woman's skin, Basma's eyes remained closed, her face indifferent, and Dounia dreaded the day when she'd drain and bandage Basma's bedsore wounds.

JUSTINE

They'd started collecting boxes from their local grocery store. Sean assured her they'd get a sublet from someone going on sabbatical, but she'd begun to research apartment listings on her own.

Justine and Wren ducked beneath an umbrella of a fruit vendor on Broadway and passed melons back and forth, searching for the ripest one. Wren cradled a watermelon in her arms and gazed up at Justine: "Are we going to be okay?"

Justine took the melon from Wren, slapped the rind, listening to the pitch of the hollow thud, and handed it back to her. "That's a good one."

When they got home, Justine wrote to Callum and Khadijah and accepted the job offer.

Sean slept beside her. She wanted to fling her arm across his chest and wake him, curl into his body and tell him what she'd done, stock the room with whispers and plans for the future, but she sensed caution was called for. Outside, rain fell against the locusts in the courtyard. The thorned branches fanned into leaves against the grey-lavender sky. She'd miss this bedroom, the steam radiator, the curved window seat beneath the generous panes. The kind of room that promises a bright future. She'd tell him tonight after Wren had gone to bed.

———

Justine paced the apartment in a heightened state of elation and terror. She opened and closed refrigerator and closet doors. She couldn't tell whether she was being reckless or heroic. She got out the cleaning supplies and poured Comet in the bathtub, imagining their future as she scrubbed the porcelain and grout. They'd save money. See the world. Things they'd always talked about.

And it could not come as a surprise. Sean had seen her these last few weeks, in the throes of intellectual adrenaline, sleepless nights of cutting and pasting links into research folders, printing out historic images across cultures and mediums. She had a photographic memory and would repeat details to anyone who would listen. Falcons were sexually bimorphic, portraying traits of the opposite sex; the female was heavier and fiercer than her male counterpart.

There were eggs, bacon, and fresh pasta in the fridge. She could make a carbonara. And in the cupboard was that bottle of expensive wine from one of her colleagues.

For Justine, a new research project was like falling in love: a time of endless possibility and discovery. Her appetite for knowledge was voracious, unrelenting, and exhausting for those around her. Clocking 242 miles per hour on the downward stoop, falcons were the fastest animals on the planet and had the capacity to hunt midflight because of a third eyelid that was activated on the steep descent. Once on the ground, they ravaged their kill. Mating videos revealed the male spinning in midair and the female responding, belly-up, backstroking into the wind. Once coupled, the birds mated for life, a span of approximately fifteen years.

They would eat in the courtyard. Sean might complain about the cold and wobbly table, but the day had cleared. She brought out the broom to sweep and found herself removing dead leaves from the beds of fading daffodils and budding tulips.

And Sean knew how much she loved birds. When Justine was pregnant, house wrens had nested in the linden tree outside their window. She loved their upturned tails, plump stomachs, and loud birdsong. In Europe, the wren was considered the king of birds, hiding in the eagle's feathers and departing high into the sky when the eagle tired, and in Japan, the wren was considered a hawk, hunting boars by flying into their ears and driving them mad. Their feathers were protective talismans. Wren, the perfect name for a child.

———

They pushed their plates aside, and Sean searched for constellations in the light-polluted sky.

"And the tradition's global, spanning continents, cutting across race and class. Even women." She'd been stalling, going on about the falcon for some time now. "And today, I found a Syrian stone carving of a hunter with a falcon on his arm, prey in hand. And paintings from China and Korea with similar scenes from five thousand years ago." She sensed Sean's wariness and picked at the bread between them.

"I don't want you to immediately dismiss what I'm about to say." He was weighing his thoughts, choosing his words with care.

"Just say it."

"Is it possible you think it's exotic?"

She noticed Sean's untouched glass and poured herself more wine. "Go on . . ."

"The travel, the subject matter, a museum built in the middle of the desert. It's just . . . what do you even know about the falcon? How can you, as an American, curate an exhibit about Emirati national identity?"

"What did I know about the opossum?"

"That was an American exhibit."

"Too much time with students."

"Who?"

"You. Besides, I don't question your obsession with concrete."

"I think you just did."

They were swerving into precarious territory, and Justine was desperate to veer out of their bitterness. She clasped his hands. "Look, there's something I want to tell you. Something exciting."

There was apprehension in his eyes, but she pressed on.

"I received the offer. Private school for Wren. A travel stipend. I was looking at the map. We could go to India, Lebanon, Ethiopia, Nepal ..." Barely able to contain her excitement, she leaned in and whispered, "Two hundred and fifty thousand dollars."

She desperately wanted him to embrace her, but something unfamiliar flashed across Sean's face and then disappeared.

"And there's more ... I don't want you to be angry."

His expression lacked reassurance.

"I said yes."

He regarded her, stunned. An awful silence enveloped the courtyard.

She reached for his hand. "I did the calculations. We'll make enough money for a down payment on a house."

"Do you know how many people go to the Gulf to make enough money for a house? It doesn't end well."

"You're going to dismiss eighteen million people sending money home? For most it does."

Sean withdrew his hand. He didn't seem at all grateful. Nowhere in his tone or demeanor did he register any relief or acknowledge that she'd found a solution to their problem.

"I'm sorry. It's amazing news. It's just ... I'm not some trailing spouse."

"Like when I came here for your PhD."

"I'd say that worked out pretty well."

"I didn't know anyone. I didn't have a job."

"Christ, Justine. I can't just escape my life. I need to be here for interviews. Once my article comes out and the book is published..."

"You don't have a publisher."

"University of Chicago has expressed interest. It's out on peer review. And I have a class at Brooklyn College."

"As an adjunct. That's seventy-five hundred dollars. Where are we going to live?"

He grimaced, and she watched as he tried to gather his strength. "I'm happy for you, I am. You should go."

Like the headlights of a daytime funeral, his response sobered her mind, and she was suddenly aware of the bigger picture.

"You want me and Wren to go to the UAE without you?"

"Or Wren can stay with me."

"What?! I'm not leaving Wren. It's her last year of middle school. Besides, it will be good for her."

"We agree on that."

"Where would you even live?"

"David's going on sabbatical."

David lived in a studio in Washington Square Village, and it dawned on Justine that this was not the first time Sean had thought of living apart. He rubbed his face, aware of the pain he was causing.

"A separation?"

"Not a separation. Just... time." His eyes pooled with tears. "I need to get myself sorted. This won't go on forever."

She wanted to believe him, but she feared his depression, his vulnerability, had no limits, no edges; that it would consume her, consume all of them, and she needed to contain it.

He regarded her, his eyes pleading. "Have you never felt this way?"

She thought about her life, how from an early age, she'd created a home in the darkness, angled toward it, and found comfort there. Her years of creating and restoring dioramas, conjuring the illusion of life, were her small retaliations against death. Her anxiety catapulted her into action, energy, a violence that refused the void.

"It's different for me," she said.

They sat in the courtyard and nighttime gathered around them. Sean's posture of control dissolved, and he began to weep. Justine felt his shame and aloneness, but despite her love, she could not bring herself to hold him.

FLORA

It was the Friday before Flora's departure; by Sunday she'd be at the domestic training center in Manila. She'd gotten Pia settled in at her great-aunt's, and they'd all gone to bed, but Flora lay sleepless in a cot on the porch, haunted by her betrayals of Datu, Pia, and herself. When her mother left, everyone consoled Flora, told her the missing would get easier, that her mother was giving her a better life. And in the beginning, the care packages and recorded messages on cassette tapes were exciting. Her mother's remittances sent her to a good school with a uniform, and after twelve years, her mother returned home for medical reasons and died soon after—a stranger. Self-loathing soured her gut. Flora had promised herself and the Virgin Mary she'd never leave her children. Maybe one day Pia would forgive her. Maybe because Pia was older, her absence would be excused.

Flora wanted a cigarette, but she did not want to leave Pia with the smell of tobacco when she said goodbye in the morning. Still, she slipped through the screen door and out onto the splintered stairs. Bare beneath her thin cotton nightgown, the yellow bulb flickered above her, the buzzing and bumping of black flies and their blue wings in the night. The dirt was damp beneath her feet, and she felt empty and alone beneath the vast sky.

Puffs of smoke hung in the humid air, her elbow a triangle and then a line as she pulled on the tobacco and then exhaled. Flora heard the slap-spring of the screen door, flicked her cigarette to the dirt, and watched her daughter coming toward her: a long t-shirt tight across her expanding hips, brushing the hair out of her eyes, long brown calves sauntering forward, a glimpse of her future daughter.

"It's okay. You can smoke."

Flora's heart fell between her legs, and she began to tremble. Pia stepped forward and wrapped her arms around her mother.

"Mom. I'm going to be okay."

From the perch of her daughter's shoulder, Flora watched the cherry from her cigarette fade.

This was not how she wanted to say goodbye.

In the morning, Flora caught a ferry to Manila by way of Cebu. The trip was forty-two hours up through the Palawan waters of the Philippines. She ate salted pistachios from a plastic bag on deck, created designs with the shells: snails, spirals, homes. But she spent most of her time with her eyes closed, sun and salt curing her wounds, soaking her dry—the destruction on shore suspended in a haze of flaring light. And she wondered if this was how her mother felt, if on some level it had been a relief to leave.

ZEINAH

A weeping willow shaded the building. Yellow leaves stuck between the cracks of the broken terrace. Omar led Zeinah up the dim and slanted stairwell to an apartment he said once belonged to an Assad official. He halted on the second landing and fumbled with the locks. The metal barrels resisted and finally clicked open.

Omar handed her the keys. "I hope you like it. They offered me an apartment on a higher floor, but the elevator's always broken with the power outages."

Orange curtains hung over the windows. The floors were bare, and a brown couch and matching chairs clustered around a glass coffee table with a twisted silver base. The kitchen was small and clean. Zeinah spread her palm across the glass of the microwave. "I've never had one of these."

Omar opened the cabinets to reveal a fully stocked pantry: canned vegetables, fruit, and an entire shelf of beans. They laughed. A five-gallon blue water jug sat in a dispenser. She poured herself a glass, and he watched her throat open and close as she gulped and swallowed.

"Good?"

"Very."

"I want to show you something."

He led her into the bedroom. At the foot of a simple double bed, a Qur'an rested on a kursi stand. Omar unfolded a piece of paper from his pocket and awkwardly reached for her fingers.

"It's from a book I had as a child. A book from my mother. Sorry, it's torn. I ripped out the page."

Omar's hands trembled as he flattened the paper so she could see.

"She would read me this story. A love story. Between a boy and girl who meet when they're ten. There are three plates. See? Here on the right, the girl carries the Qur'anic script, and on the left, the boy holds the tablet. In the middle, the couple bends over the Qur'an— bonded in their love for Allah—their teacher behind them."

This was not what Zeinah expected.

"Please."

He invited her to kneel at the kursi displaying the Qur'an bound in engraved leather. She ran her fingers along the indentations.

"It's from Sudan. I took it from my family in Iraq before coming here."

She unwound the leather cord and opened the onionskin pages. "It's so old. So beautiful."

"I was told you like to read. There are no books in the apartment. I hope it will sustain you."

He stood behind her. She could feel that he was moved, and she turned to one of her favorite suras: "God is the light of the heavens and the earth."

He responded. "We indeed created man; and We know what his soul whispers within him, and We are nearer to him than the jugular vein."

"The jugular vein . . . That is so close," said Zeinah.

Long shadows cast across the floor.

"I'm sorry, but I must go."

"Now?"

"Your old phone and social media have been disabled. I've left you a new one on the dresser and inputted my number and your family contacts."

She felt flustered by the news of his sudden departure, and the sparsely furnished apartment and bare tile floors began to spark a wariness in her. "What am I supposed to do all week?"

"I've arranged for people to bring what you need. Don't go out. I'll be back Friday."

But Zeinah had never been alone.

ESKEDARE

The child is wild and fierce, and there's no taming the twitch in-side her.

"That girl makes elders feel small," says her father.

Eskedare kicks off her mother's back and runs ahead, scram-bles down twisted paths with a water bucket. Her bare feet hold the seasons: soft in summer moss, itchy from dead daisy heads in fall, bruised from field stones in winter. She stacks rocks on trails to point the way home. By age six, she herds cattle, thwacks fur and muscle into line with a stick balanced between her wing blades. From dawn until dusk, she ventures further and farther away. Eskedare.

From the top of a hill, she watches men unroll a new image across a billboard: a golden cage, surrounded by palm trees, im-prisons a woman with her mop and bucket. It's an illustration, like in some kind of fairy tale, like some kind of warning. A lone woman locked away, but the cage is so beautiful.

The sun brings out the specks of green in her brown eyes, and as the sun sets, her shadow slips between the rocks, a tent of sky tears open above her and reveals the vastness of forever. Later, she swims through the dampness of night, drops her day on the floor, and wraps the stench of sweat, dried grass, and dung around her mother.

Angered by his daughter's passions, jealous of her love for

the mother, her gifts of wildflowers, seeds, and sketches in the dirt, he drags his lame foot across her offerings just to watch her blaze.

"You're like wildfire in wind," he says.

⨭

DOUNIA

Today, after the foot ritual, Basma asked Dounia to lie beside her on the bed. Dounia sat immobile as her mother-in-law moved her palm across her womb like a dowser divining for water. Every kick produced an unexpected hum of joy. Dounia closed her eyes and endured Basma's incantation of possible names:

> "Yaser.
> "Mohammed.
> "Omar.
> "Ahmed. Oh, he kicked."

Dounia evaded Basma's beaming gaze.

> "Saif.
> "Abdullah.
> "Karim.
> "Rashid. That's a foot."

Dounia closed her eyes. She'd already decided her daughter's name: Qadira Ibrahim. Qadira, who was powerful and able.

> "Ali.
> "Youssof.
> "Abdullah—I keep going back to that.

"Shahid.
"Ibrahim."

Ibrahim, thought Dounia. Ibrahim, who surrendered to God when the world was whole. Ibrahim, who purified spaces. Ibrahim, whose absence pervaded their lives. Qadira Ibrahim, a child who would animate and heal this home.

"Haafiz.
"Nasser.
"Bassam.
"Majid.
"Wasim. I always liked that name.
"Waleed. Not so much."

Outside, Dounia heard trucks pouring gravel, the singsong alerts of vehicles in reverse. She imagined sending up a flare, hammering through the polished cement, but she was pinned beneath Basma's hand on her tightening belly while her daughter punched through her womb like rising bread.

———

Hamed was rarely home. This week in London. Last week in Riyadh. The Dream Development rendered a promising life in 3D drawings: a boardwalk on the beach, a pool with cabanas and a café with papayas and smoothies, a grocery store, and a gym. Women walked their children to a day care with climbing rope structures based on designs from Japan. If Ibrahim were alive, she'd believe it, but without him, it seemed impossible. He'd energized her life with prospects, and now she felt useless and rotten. Like the tomatoes beneath her bedroom window, she'd never thrive.

The nights were particularly lonely, and sometimes, after
Basma had gone to sleep and Raj had switched off the light in his
room above the garage, Dounia took the car and drove to the beach,
where she could watch the lighthouse. If Basma or Raj knew what
she was doing, neither of them said anything. Her grandmother
had taught her how to drive at the date farm. It was common in
the rural areas for women to transport produce and livestock to
the market. Her mother and sister had been right: beyond the
wedding was a life, her life. She rarely saw another car on the dark
roads. Hers was an immense country, and outside the major cities,
different rules and ways of life persisted. One of her best days of
courtship was when Hamed and Ibrahim visited the date farm.
She'd driven them beneath the kaleidoscopic branches, explained
the stages of growth and harvest, the differences between ajwa, sa-
fawi, and mabroom; the car had been a gift for her, a testament to
that afternoon of dirt roads and brown fruit hanging in dark trees.

She rolled out of the compound and through the security
gate. Once outside of the Dream Development she lowered the
windows and switched the high beams on. She followed the
empty highway toward Road 7, curving along the coast. She'd
discovered the lighthouse online: a tower of red and white
stripes anchored not far from shore, a signal for boats docking
and departing from the largest port in the world. It was something she imagined talking about with her father-in-law. The
largest port in the world should have a significant lighthouse.
Jeddah has the tallest lighthouse in the world; Spain, the Tower
of Hercules. Ras al-Khair deserved something noteworthy. He
would've agreed, maybe even encouraged her to research light-
houses and speak with architects, maybe even put her in charge
of the project. The family had lost its warmth without him. One
person can make all the difference. Perhaps that's what they

needed, another person in the house. Someone warm. Someone who could change the dynamic, take care of Basma, the baby— all of them, really. If she insisted, Hamed could get his mother to agree.

She signaled off the highway and merged onto the connector road, a dirt strip following the shore along Jubail Conservation, a preserve created after the oil spills of the Gulf War, when Iraq released millions of barrels of oil into the sea to prevent U.S. forces from landing on the beaches of Kuwait. Dounia had watched video footage of the oil fields burning on YouTube: towering flames, black clouds, and oil-slicked beaches set to harrowing orchestral music. Currents and wind had brought environmental devastation down the coast of Saudi Arabia, and the Kingdom had forged preservation initiatives. Now, more than two decades later, meandering tidal channels, mangroves, and turtles nesting in dunes had returned. Tucked between the two industrial cities of Jubail and Ras al-Khair were unexpected pockets of shoreline where red foxes, golden jackals, and flamingos lived. The orange moon hung low in the sky, and she switched off her headlights as she drove along the Gulf toward the lighthouse in the distance.

Dounia took off her shoes and walked down to the beach. The water and wind were the same temperature, and she hiked up her dress and sat on the sand—feet in foam, swollen belly between her bent legs.

Weeks away from birth, the baby was restless, impatient, and woke Dounia with kicks in the middle of the night, yanking on the cord of their connection, ready to hatch, insistent on being born. I was like that, thought Dounia. But it seemed the baby no longer listened, and tonight, with her ankles buried in dark waters, Dounia began to fear the infant's departure. Misgivings clenched her chest as she considered her miscalculation: the pregnancy and looming birth. Had she incubated a stranger who'd leave her ransacked? Were the knocks on her belly, once signals of companionship, now bangs of mutiny? But worst of all, she resented her daughter's strikes toward freedom.

JUSTINE

i.

They all embraced on the airport curb as the bellhop loaded their luggage onto a cart. Justine was the first to break away, and she watched the place she'd occupied disappear as Sean and Wren held on to each other.

"Before you know it, we'll see each other in Nepal for the school trip. Honey, do you have that letter?"

Sean pulled away from Wren and extracted an envelope from his pocket. "I was gonna give it to you."

He'd procrastinated on the form, a No Objection Certificate granting Justine permission to sponsor Wren on her work visa. He'd waited until the last minute to get it translated into Arabic. It was on Columbia University letterhead, but Justine let it go. No one was going to check his employment status.

To: Khadijah al-Daheiri
Date: August 24, 2014
Subject: No Objection Certificate: Wife & Daughter

Dear Madam,

This is to certify that I, Sean Barron, holder of passport no. 8412694, have no objection to my wife, Justine Willard,

holder of passport no. 234690, undertaking full-time
employment at Saadiyat Cultural District as a curator
for the Sheik Zayed National Museum in Abu Dhabi,
United Arab Emirates, to sponsoring our daughter, Wren
Willard, holder of passport no. 261774, on her work visa.

Regards,
Sean Barron
Columbia University
New York, New York 10027

ii.

They arrived in Abu Dhabi at sundown, seven thousand miles
and thirteen hours later. Before customs, Justine passed a liquor
store where expats stocked up on wine and liquor, but she was
too exhausted to shop, and in a jet-lagged haze, they waited outside in the pickup area beside large portable air conditioners
struggling to conjure a breeze. An Etihad driver greeted them
and opened the back door of his limo, where a console of bottled
water waited, and as they pulled out of the airport, Justine and
Wren gazed out their respective windows onto a highway lined
thick with palm trees and sprinklers arcing across green-grass
meridians.

"I read somewhere that the UAE has more than forty million
date palms. Those netted bundles up there weigh more than three
hundred pounds."

Wren did not say a word. Justine watched the red taillights of
the cars and wondered what was really happening. For seventeen
years, she and Sean had known the details of each other's days, familiar with the books on their office shelves, the mugs they drank

from, the socks they wore. Now she lived in a country Sean had never seen, in a time zone eight hours ahead of Manhattan.

iii.

Thirty-five floors above the city. Never had she lived in rooms like these: air-conditioned, cold tile floors, views overlooking the city. The corner apartment faced north, with views of the Gulf. Directly below them was Qasr al-Hosn, the first fort built in 1761 and home to the first national archives. Beside it was a roundabout, and in the center was a fountain in the shape of a lotus flower, no longer in use. On a clear day, she could see the bridge to Saadiyat Island—the future site of the Louvre, the Guggenheim, and Sheik Zayed National Museum.

Justine let Wren take the master bedroom with the terrace and said she could do whatever she wanted with the walls. In the windowless kitchen, they hung a world map on a bulletin board and pressed a red pin into the UAE. On the cabinets they taped images of places they wanted to see: the bamboo forests of Japan, the sunken churches of Lalibela in Ethiopia, the wildebeest migration in Masai Mara, and the lazy river at Yas Waterworld in Dubai.

iv.

Cornelius arrived in a carrier from his transatlantic journey and kept Justine company as she did research at her desk, thirty-five floors above the ground. No bugs or beetles or birds, but last week, a man in a blue jumpsuit and harness arced across her windows with a squeegee. She did not know whether to wave or pull the blinds, and she'd retreated into the kitchen and waited for him to leave.

v.

Three mornings a week, Justine passed women walking beneath colorful umbrellas as she jogged around the abandoned Al-Manhal Palace, once home to Sheik Zayed. Through the cracked walls of the back perimeter, she saw remnants of formal gardens, sheds with broken windows, and shirtless men brushing their teeth at an outdoor spigot.

vi.

The top bunk in Wren's room remained empty. Despite having friends, it was not a sleepover culture; weekends were reserved for family. Justine planned excursions: kayaking in the mangroves, bicycling along the corniche, jumping on the trampoline at Mina Port, skiing at the mall in Dubai, an outdoor concert at the Sharjah Art Foundation, but there was a loneliness to their lives, the empty air-conditioned malls, the city built on top of a desert. The fantasy of her and Wren taking on the world dwindled, and she felt her daughter withdrawing and assessing her.

The penthouse had a gym, sauna, and pool, and on Saturdays there was a snack bar that served ice cream and hamburgers. They'd swim and lie on deck chairs, Justine tucked beneath an umbrella with a book. Wren spread out beneath the milky sky lost in the world of headphones.

At home, Wren spent her time on the terrace knotting bracelets and belts for new friends. She'd sit with her back against the wall, tie colored strings around the neck of a large blue water jug between her legs, and watch the sun go down. Justine yearned to sit beside her and make macramé belts, but she sensed she wasn't

welcome. She considered her life after Wren departed for college
and began to fear the future.

vii.

While Wren was at school, Justine worked alone at her desk on
the falcon. Sean had instructed Wren not to tell people her father
was Jewish, that kids have their own code and will find each other
through apples and honey at lunch.

In the afternoons, the neighbor practiced his clarinet, the same
notes, up and down the scales, day after day, invoking an atmosphere of lonesomeness and dread that she tried to amend with
honey cake and sugared cookies with coffee.

viii.

She visited the falcon hospital, where a fifteen-foot sculpture of a
peregrine greeted her in the roundabout of the parking lot. Like
so many things in the UAE, the falcon hospital was the best in the
world, taking in more than eleven thousand birds annually. Since
the capture and training of wild falcons had been outlawed, breed-
ing had become one of its specialties. Inside, pale leather couches
lined the beige walls, and falcons waited on Astroturf benches in
leather hoods and jesses to calm their nerves. Low-angle portraits
of sheiks and their prized birds were displayed prominently on the
walls and above the reception desk.

On her way to the bathroom, Justine discovered a small falcon exhibit tucked into a dark room. Wall text accompanied jars
displaying the stages of development in formaldehyde. Cracked-
open eggs revealed blue-headed babies with resin beaks and three-
pronged talons. Farther along, a striped falcon folded in upon

itself, its claws like swollen fingers. Another specimen bent forward as if preparing for a somersault; a purple bruise extended from eyelid to scalp, red feathers frayed across its pimpled skin, and tiny teeth pointed outward from its gums. Justine recorded reference photos on her phone.

Inside the hospital at least twenty falcons donned headdresses like old women perched on park benches: black leather with beads and fringe, brown with beige stitching, some with feathers like those on a tomahawk. The birds were different sizes with various striped markings. Some were solid black or brown, and most of them were there for annual checkups, infections, or broken wings.

A vet in scrubs examined falcons on a stainless-steel table. He held a bird down and removed the hood as an assistant slid a cone over the bird's head.

"Calms the nerves," he said.

The falcon was weighed, claws clipped, beak cleaned, and blood taken. In Justine's conversations with the doctor, she discovered that most of the falcons slept in the same room as their owner and had their own perches throughout the house. "Nothing like dogs. Trained but never domesticated. They're not pets, their wildness is respected."

Justine wandered outside to a vast green tent with a vaulted ceiling and mesh windows that housed the birds overnight. Inside, her feet sank into the sand, and the air was cool. The sun cast green-and-turquoise shadows through the tarp, and she felt relieved to be in this makeshift oceanic atmosphere with falcons flying overhead and landing on perches. So much of what she'd seen in the UAE was the built environment; the heat kept people inside. The birds called to one another, swooped from perch to perch, tiptoed and took flight. When they stopped to listen, Justine listened too. Birds had always existed for her at a distance, however slight—at a bird feeder, in the woods, on the marsh or seashore—but that afternoon, as she lingered in the dim green light, she ventured into a different kind of closeness, an intimacy that reminded her of the visit to the Grand Mosque.

At the Grand Mosque they'd put on abayas and taken selfies in the bright marble courtyard lined with pillars. Inside, they'd walked on the largest carpet in the world. She'd never been inside a mosque before coming to the UAE and knew little about Islam, but the central conceit of submission, of the public call to prayer inviting people five times a day into a relationship with the divine, was different from anything she'd encountered in Judaism or Christianity. Each day, Justine was becoming more aware of the differences between her American stance of manifest destiny, bending the world to comply to her will, and a more open and reciprocal relationship to the world offered in Islam, and this fundamental difference was evident in each country's national symbol: the eagle and the falcon.

On the face of things, the birds appeared similar, living on currency, aviation, podiums, and state buildings. But the eagle and falcon were fundamentally opposed; the eagle was a loner, while the falcon was cherished, in a profound and bonded relationship with humans that had persisted for centuries. But Justine feared these insights were the thoughts of a foreigner and perhaps Sean was right: it was impossible for an American to curate a show on the falcon, the national symbol of a country she had no part in.

ix.

The adrenaline of curating a high-profile exhibit halfway around the world, the money, the buildup of goodbyes, the private school for Wren, and a spacious apartment with in-unit laundry had been heady and exciting, but now Justine felt unsure of how to proceed. She'd been excited to leave the safety of archives, her solitary years of conjuring the illusion of life through painted backdrops and skeletons wrapped in wire and fur, her perfect dioramas. She'd felt ready to get outside, to join the living, but the landscape felt impenetrable, and she'd failed to make a single friend.

FLORA

Women from all over the country checked in and received their welcome packs. Flora sat in a metal folding chair beside rows of potted plants used for class demonstrations and flipped through the pages of her training handbook:

WHAT YOU SHOULD NOT DO:

1. Do not steal.
2. Do not run away.
3. Do not lie.
4. Do not be rude.
5. Do not show "long face."
6. Do not be homesicked.
7. Do not be stressed.
8. Do not look for a boyfriend.
9. Do not abuse the kindness of your employers.
10. Do not use employer's telephone.
11. Do not stay overnight outside employer's house during day off.
12. Do not bring any friends or visitors if you are left alone in the house.
13. Do not sit in the sofa or in the dining area in relaxed manner. Do not sit on employer's bed.

14. Do not wear tight-fitting clothes, thin blouses, shorts, sexy underwear.
15. Do not wait for the employer to push you and remind you again about your tasks.
16. Do not eat at the employer's table unless permitted to do so.
17. Do not request for a Saturday or Sunday holiday.
18. Do not use radio or stereo.
19. Do not drink alcohol or smoke cigarettes.
20. Do not mingle with maids who are a bad influence. Do not gossip.
21. Do not resign.
22. Do not open employer's personal email.
23. Do not open drawers in the house without employer's permission.
24. Do not join organizations or groups because they might put you in trouble.
25. Do not use employer's belongings without permission. Better, do not even attempt to borrow.

She was thinking about Joenard, how she'd left without saying goodbye. She was still angry. The store they'd created before the typhoon had been so much effort, mostly hers, and her money too. Sure, he was the one who sledgehammered through the living room wall and got the project started. He'd built shelves and done some good negotiating along the supply chain, but once the sari-sari was open, Joenard saw his role as welcomer, the customers' companion. He'd fashioned a seating area from milk crates and cushions on a patch of dirt outside their home.

No one's ever gonna want to sit there, she thought.

But she was wrong.

People arrived to buy toilet paper, and Joenard invited them to sit down: "Buy a drink. Soda, water, beer . . ." And they'd fork over the money and join him on a milk crate. Eventually, he "built" a low table from driftwood on buckets and persuaded her to stock nuts and snacks. Joenard bought an extension cord and hauled the TV outside. The neighborhood gathered for sporting events, kids on the ground with grown-ups cheering all around them. And in this haphazard way they'd created a community, a store, a bar, a café.

But she was the one stocking shelves, ordering supplies, and taking care of Datu. Yes, Joenard brought in money with his affable and entertaining spirit, but she was resentful of how hard she worked while he sat on a milk crate and talked to the neighborhood. And he drank too much beer. And he was getting fat.

During one of their fights, he said, "Okay, fine. Let's trade. You sit outside and bring in the business, and I'll take care of Datu and the store." Even in the heat of the moment, she knew the deal was rigged, but she took him up on the proposition, and for one week she sat outside with her friends. The women talked, had an occasional beer, but they needed to get back to work, their homes, their children, their chores. Joenard said nothing, but at the end of the week when they reviewed the takings, he'd smiled.

"See? I contribute. More than you think."

The ledger didn't lie. Still, a part of her missed the store, and Joenard. Though she still felt bitter about the men spending hours on the blue milk crates while she stayed inside and worked. But it was pointless to think of these things: she'd borrowed money from the agency, money that would come out of her first earnings, money that covered her flight to the Gulf. She'd signed a contract.

ZEINAH

Sunday

Her first day alone. The call to prayer was a relief, a way of ordering her day. Never had God been her only companion. She thought about the sura Omar quoted, the one about Allah being closer than the jugular vein. The jugular vein connected the head to the heart and was the most vulnerable to attack; she remembered that from school. No mirrors. The only glimpse of herself was in a window at night or in the low-resolution screen of her flip phone. Selfies were pointless. Since the schools and universities had closed, she'd spent her days at home with her mother, in hibernation—molting, praying that she would not die a virgin, that she would have some kind of love, some kind of life. Never this. But against the backdrop of uprisings and instability, a will to survive, to live, had taken hold, and she wondered if she could love this man.

Monday

She was surprised by her openness to face east, to slip into a role. Stand. Kneel. Touch her forehead to the ground. Submit. She felt afraid, and the scaffolding of prayer, the role of wife, was all she had. He had seemed kind. She struggled to conjure an image of

Omar at the "front," wherever that was. All she could see were recycled news images of ISIS, and she needed to channel beyond, into . . . what? They had not had sex before he left. She imagined she would lose her virginity upon his return, and she used prayer time to prepare herself, to imagine and dream. It was all so unreal. She'd barely spent time with him before he left. Their bodies were in separate places, but the call to prayer created a connection. Five times a day, they were both falling to their knees in unison.

She stored the torn illustration inside the bedside table and committed every detail to memory. She tried to imagine Omar in Iraq as a young boy, but she could hardly remember what he looked like now. She conjured a version of him gazing at the picture and thinking of his future wife—her, and she wondered how long she'd occupied a place in Omar's mind. He struck her as a serious person, and she sensed trauma behind his stoicism. She'd never really thought about her future husband in any real way. Her life had been about friends. Friends who were now gone.

Tuesday

A yellow sponge. She scrubbed the white tiles, the water in the bucket turned grey with dirt, and she wondered about the other people who'd lived in the apartment, hoping she'd find an artifact, a clue, but the only evidence of previous habitation was the green mosaic paper lining the drawers of the bureau and a water stain on the wooden bedside table. Perhaps the wife of Assad's governor. This used to be that kind of neighborhood.

Wednesday

She opened the windows and noticed the different sounds through-out the day. In the morning, the bang of water pipes as her upstairs neighbor drew a bath. Squeals of delight from a child, followed by footsteps scampering across her ceiling. Midday, sirens chang-ing octaves, climbing up and down the scales. The loud revving of motorcycle engines. Around five p.m., the shuffle of the old man ascending the stairs. He caught his breath outside her door and rested a shoulder against the wall. At night, nothing moved. Zei-nah strained into the absence and tried to learn its language.

Thursday

A black fly with blue wings kept her company. It entered when she opened the windows and followed her from room to room. It glided from the windowsill to the table, always returning to her and then leaving again. Out her kitchen window, she saw long-legged weeds bang their heads against the curb. A flattened Coca-Cola can skidded across the rubble and lodged in a wall of sandbags. Down the street, a car lay upended like a dead crab on its back. She longed to go outside, roam her neighborhood streets, jump off the bridge into the Euphrates, and drink coffee in the central square. Instead, she ventured out onto the apart-ment landing and gazed up into a blue stairwell stained with dust.

So much time alone was beginning to make her strange. She bumped into her thoughts—bruised her mind. On the windows, splotches of dirt opened their eyes and watched. And the power outage brought a different kind of darkness. The couch breathed, threatened to move, and she locked herself inside the bedroom.

Friday

The smell of mildew. She detected black mold beneath the freshly painted walls and dragged a chair from corner to corner, mapping the journey of purple blossoms. A fresh coat of paint cannot hide the blight held in these walls, in this city. I am weak, she thought. What kind of person can be swayed by appliances, water, and a Qur'an a man stole from his family? She felt homesick and afraid of the lonely days unspooling out before her in this apartment.

That afternoon, Omar would return, and she endured the hours with dread and anticipation, fearful of his return and anxious for his touch.

ESKEDARE

A clear day in December. Alone with the cows in a garden of blue stones and blue stars: blue thistles, blue wings of flies. The cows chomp on tough stalks, and Eskedare chews along with them. She breaks off blue flowers blooming in the dawn and sucks on their bitter seeds. She lies in the cool shade and feels the petals dissolve around her tongue. Her fingers tingle, her lips swell, and inside her mouth, berries bloom and grow. A current surges through her limbs, and she dances on the backs of cows, twirls between stones, and hollers to the herd. She circles through the garden of blue stones and blue stars, giddy with a powerful might, until she collapses on the ground and sweeps her limbs across a fresh mound of soil, engraving an angel in the dirt while daydreaming into the blue above her.

Her arms and legs arc and swoosh across the dirt. Black flies with blue wings buzz, tickle her face with their black threaded legs, urging her toward recognition. She swats them away, but they return and will not let her go until a knowing stuns her mute.

Her mind opens.

Those blue stones and blue stars. Those black flies with blue wings. The dead all around her. But she's not scared; she welcomes the company and engraves angels in the dirt. The cows watch as she tiptoes from blue stone to blue star, listen as she whispers into the ears of the unliving. To think, she's been ignoring them. Those blue stones and blue stars. Those blue flowers and blue seeds. That milky stalk of pulp. And when she leaves, she promises to come back and live beside them one day.

∾

DOUNIA

Dounia pressed her spine against the back of the orange plastic chair. The receptionist looked middle-aged, maybe younger, hard to say with her red-tinted hair and casual manner. The scuffed linoleum tiles and smudged walls reminded her of childhood classrooms.

"There's water if you want."

Dounia's eyes shifted to the watercooler and a stack of plastic cups.

"She's always late. You can read." She pointed to a haphazard pile of magazines on the table.

Dounia listened to the buzz of the overhead lights and the woman's sequined nails tapping against her phone. She closed her eyes and recited a mantra that helped stabilize her in these last weeks of pregnancy: *And it was so.* She felt anxious about the child being born, the consequences of her lie, and feared a madness waiting to take root in her barren womb. *And it was so.* She'd cede to whatever lay ahead; submission would be her strength.

———

Miss Adya entered wearing a half-open abaya and carrying what looked like an empty briefcase. Her black hair stuck to her forehead in clumps, and she wiped sweat from her brow with a wrinkled tissue. A green dress with white polka dots pulled across her midsection and fell to her ankles, exposing cheap rubber sandals.

"Please, come in."

She disappeared into the adjoining room, switched on the light, and sank into her chair, already exhausted by the day. Dounia sat across from her at the desk.

Miss Adya, still catching her breath, smiled. "Congratulations. Do you know what you're having?"

Dounia smoothed her hands across her womb with pride and exchanged a knowing glance with the woman.

"Ah, blessings upon you. A boy. You must be proud."

Dounia's arms fell to her sides, and she basked in the energy of good tidings.

"I imagine you're wanting a Filipina, educated, experience with children. Does religion matter? It's more difficult to get a Muslim, but it can be arranged." Dounia watched as Miss Adya leafed through a stack of manilla folders covering her desk. Gold rings with semiprecious stones adorned her swollen fingers. Unmarried.

"Christian is fine," said Dounia.

"Age? Some people don't want a younger woman in the house."

"She needs to speak English."

"High school diploma? Two-year preprofessional program?"

Dounia hadn't thought about that. "Fine."

"Married?"

Dounia heard voices in the reception room. Someone else had arrived.

"I'd recommend that. You want the experience with infants, and it's better if they're here solely to make money for their family. You don't want them going out. I've seen everything: boyfriends, prostitution, pregnancy. You're her sponsor. Under the kafala system, employers have control over hours, days off, pay, and legal status. If anything goes wrong, you're responsible. My advice: keep it simple. Take her passport until the contract is up. If she's Christian, don't let her go to private homes for services. That really becomes a problem—the gossip. Cell phone on Fridays. That's it. Some gather in the public park on Saturdays. I wouldn't encourage that, but it's up to you."

Dounia knew all about Catholicism. Dali, her Filipina nanny, prayed throughout the day to the Virgin Mary. These prayers and hymns were the soundtrack of her childhood. After school, Dounia would drape Dali's prayer beads around her neck and create homes and mangers for baby Jesus. Around age nine the comfort of these prayers led to terror when Dounia realized that her nanny was going to Hell; she did everything in her power to convert her to Islam. Night terrors of Dali burning in flames haunted her sleep, and it was Dali who comforted Dounia as she recounted her dreams. Eventually, Dali relented. She wrapped her crosses, Jesus sculptures, and portraits of Mary in tissue paper and converted to Islam; the nightmares never returned.

Miss Adya held up a picture from one of the folders. She'd already gone through a few folders, and Dounia's lack of response compelled her to continue. "It'd be good to get an age range. There are so many, and I have other people waiting."

"If it's all right, I'd prefer to review them myself. I'll sit outside."

———

It was almost three p.m. Miss Adya stood in the doorway of her office. "You'd think she was picking a bride," joked the receptionist as she powered down her computer.

"You're welcome to come back tomorrow," said Miss Adya.

Dounia gripped a folder in her hand. Unlike all the other passport or formal school photos, Flora's image was casual, slightly out of focus. She stood in the shade of a palm tree on a beach covered in brown leaves, wearing cutoff jeans and a t-shirt, her arms spread wide toward the person behind the camera. Later, when she'd think of Flora, she'd recall this image. Someone older than me would be good, she thought. Someone kind who can take care of us.

Dounia stood up and brought the folder to Miss Adya, who confirmed the name: "Flora Santos?"

"Yes."

Miss Adya glanced at the photo and flipped through the pages. "Sometimes these women have trauma from the typhoons. I can go through other—"

"No. Thank you."

"Any special requests for her training—food preparation or otherwise?"

"Machboos. Please make sure that she knows how to make machboos."

JUSTINE

Justine and Wren ate soft-boiled eggs in silence.

At assembly on Friday, the principal had reviewed the rules of the UAE. Wren had come home eager to express her outrage, stomping across the tiles in her clogs. "Respect Islam. Respect the government. No public displays of affection. Homosexuality and abortion are illegal." None of this was news. They'd reviewed it all before deciding to move and agreed: Their country. Their rules. But then, over the weekend, they'd gone to the movies, and Wren was offended by a deleted kiss from the animated film. Justine had tried to pivot and said she was moved by the public service announcement shaming people for placing the elderly in nursing homes, that she admired the Emiratis for protecting their traditions and faith and felt envious of their compounds and devotion to family. But Wren wouldn't listen. She wanted to go home and had tunneled into her burrow behind closed doors and screens. Communication was polite and ceremonious: "I need you to sign this permission slip." "Would you drive me to get art supplies at Marina Mall?"

Wren had spoken with Sean, and Justine felt an alliance brewing; he had not come to Justine's defense. She'd bowed out of the school trek in Nepal to meet with a preeminent falconer and work on her presentation for Khadijah and the museum. Sean had offered to go in her place, and, after the trek, they'd agreed to spend time together as a family in Abu Dhabi.

Justine watched egg yolk drip from Wren's toast onto her uniform, a white top and navy skirt. Wren chewed on, daring her to comment, her eyes alert, ready to flash at any perceived infraction. She cleared her plate and disappeared into the kitchen. Justine heard the water running, the zip of a backpack, the front door close.

————

To be alone was a great relief. Wren didn't know, but Justine had taken up smoking. Newports, no less. Never smoked a Newport in her life, but the name and the green packaging compelled her, and as she exhaled into the muggy air, she watched a woman wait with her daughter at the bus stop in front of the hospital across the way. Justine would walk to the bus station and buy flowers from her favorite florist for Wren, a peace offering.

As she navigated the 120-degree heat and broken sidewalk, sweat formed between her breasts and seeped into her undergarments. Her glasses fogged and threw the world out of focus. The truth was she was beginning to like it here. Despite the politics— artists boycotting the Guggenheim and professors outraged about academic freedom—she found an uncanny comfort in the superblocks and sand; the smell of the sea; the green glow of the pharmacy at night in the fog-filled air; the burlap bags of cardamom, pistachios, and red onions at the corner store; the rusty bikes in the shade of buildings; the men in tunics gathered beneath spare-limbed trees on the median. Initially, she'd been put off by Khadijah saying "Our Father Sheik Zayed." So paternalistic, but with more research and reflection, she admired this man who'd created a unity among the trucial states and led them into a future as a thriving nation. Fifty years ago, there were no schools, hospitals, highways, or airports in this desert landscape.

The bus station was designed by a Romanian couple in the late '80s against the backdrop of the Cold War and possessed a modernist sensibility with space-age flourishes. The sweeping lines reminded her of the Guggenheim, and while most buildings moved upward in Abu Dhabi, this one hugged the ground and spread across the superblock. People either loved it or hated it, and she was one of its biggest fans.

The triangular interior had a wall of windows facing north. She paused in the open hall and scanned the location names displayed on the board: MARINA MALL, FISH MARKET, ADNOC, AL-RAHBA HOSPITAL, AL-AIN. She liked to test herself and see what new places she recognized. AL-WATHBA WORKER CITY. She'd seen the labor camps, clusters of sandstone buildings set back from the highway, but she knew little about them.

She ordered Lipton tea with condensed milk from a café counter and wandered with her Styrofoam cup into the magazine shop, where she perused the colorful books on display, weekly romances in Urdu, Tamil, and Tagalog. Dictionaries in dozens of languages stuffed the back shelves amid English primers. This small shop captured the international landscape of the country more than any other place she'd been. Everything about it, including the round mirror hung high in the corner with a cutout of Sheik Zayed and his falcon watching over the customers, epitomized what she was starting to appreciate about the UAE.

The icon of the veiled woman signified the ladies' room. In almost every gas station, mall, restaurant, and bus terminal, bathrooms were often located beside a prayer room, denoted by a swoosh of a woman kneeling or a crescent moon above a mosque. She found the pairing of these human impulses, prayer and defecation, grounding amid all the commerce and economic growth. When she entered, an attendant stopped mopping the floor and let her pass.

"I'll be quick."

The girl nodded.

Justine peed and, when she went to wipe herself, saw she had no toilet paper. She knocked on the stall door. "Excuse me. Could you hand me some toilet paper?"

"One moment, ma'am."

The girl's arm appeared beneath the stall with a roll of toilet paper, and Justine noticed a birthmark inked in blue: a delicate stem traveling across the attendant's hand, blooming like a cluster of baby's breath beneath her pinky.

"Thank you."

At the sink, Justine watched the reflection of the young woman in the mirror. She was older than Wren but not by much. She returned Justine's gaze with a broad, open expression, then returned to mopping the floor in robust, generous arcs. Justine reached into her wallet and left ten dirhams beside the soap dispenser.

Justine bought blue irises for Wren at the florist in the atrium. None of the flowers in the black buckets—the roses, carnations, freesia, or lilies—had a chance of growing in the desert, but Justine learned from her mother years ago: cut flowers make a home.

In the Berkshires, her mother had a garden of peonies more than sixty years old. Peonies dated back to 1000 BC in Chinese gardens, known for their medicinal properties and ability to relieve pain in childbirth. They bloomed in June, and her mother would cut the stems at the white porcelain sink in the kitchen, drop them into vases of cold water, and then meticulously place them on tables, toilets, and dressers. When they sold the house, her mother dug up the plants and drove through the town giv-

ing away the precious perennials. "Beauty can't go to waste," said
her mother. "The new owners will plow the whole garden under."
And she was right.

In the atrium, Justine watched the man pull the tight buds from
water. She thought of the bathroom attendant, her own job when
she was fifteen at the Village Florist. On summer mornings, she
rode her bike three miles beneath the shade of oak trees into town.
The road followed the turns of the Green River, whose smells and
sounds had been her companions since she was a child. Beyond
the old cemetery, she jumped from rock to rock up the river, built
stone dams on August afternoons, and spied on the bare-chested
boys in cutoffs, sunbathing on boulders. At night, she'd pull her
mattress across the floor to the low window so she could listen to
the sound of the river while the occasional headlights doused her
room in white.

The flower shop had broken steps, a pipe railing, and a war-
ren of small rooms. The entryway had a skylight and, beneath it,
a huge ficus tree surrounded by ferns and spider plants bound in
macramé. A small fountain dripped, and dusty wooden chimes
hung in the window.

The refrigerators stored cut flowers, bouquets, and corsages.
Along the wall, the owner arranged high counters covered with
ferns, clippers, and tape. A brown phone clung to the wall like
a squirrel and was surrounded by phone numbers and notes jot-
ted down directly with markers and pens onto the paint. "My
Rolodex," said Dell, a wide-hipped woman who wore purple bell-
bottoms and halter tops, who parked her old blue Volvo station
wagon outside, smoked pot up in her office, and ordered pizza for
her employees at night. Justine's first task was dusting the ficus.
Fill a bowl with warm, sudsy water. Use a sponge. Clean the leaves.
The eight-foot tree below the skylight had hundreds of leaves. She

stood on a stepstool and worked her way down, holding each leaf, cleaning the front and back, checking for spores.

The roses arrived in long white cardboard boxes. Inside, a tangle of stems and leaves to unravel and clean. If she didn't remove most of the leaves, they'd contaminate the water, and the roses would go bad. Her boss's instructions:

1. Five inches below the rose head, run a dish towel along the stem to remove leaves.
2. Cut the stems at an angle with a knife.
3. Pluck the wrinkled petals off the rose.
4. Mix a scoop of rose food with lukewarm water.
5. Refrigerate.

Justine swept up the leaves and thorny stems into a black metal dustpan, aware that the flowers were already dead.

———

In the atrium, the man's hand swept across the grasses.

"I'll have baby's breath today," said Justine.

"I thought madam only likes baby's breath on a Christmas tree."

She shrugged. It was strange, the small things they knew about each other, how they exchanged tender cuttings of themselves. The man told her he was from the land of blue cornflowers and flame trees, from a mother who put petals in her bra.

———

At the Village Florist, Justine learned to make boutonnieres, piercing the base of the flower with a wire and then folding it in half along the stem. She cradled the flower in baby's breath, wrapped the stems in green floral tape, speared the base with a white-pearled needle, and rested the finished piece on a fern sprayed with water and stored in a white cardboard box. Boys entered the florist in rented tuxedos, and Justine was asked to pin her creations to wool, polyester, and rayon. At night, on her low mattress beside the screen, she imagined boys bending down to kiss her, taking her by surprise.

At the end of summer, the owner hired Justine for the day to help her move. She drove the blue Volvo, crammed with boxes and belongings, up the Taconic State Parkway. Her boss sat dazed in the passenger seat. A breakup. The new apartment was above a metal studio in an abandoned brick factory. They unpacked the car. Her boss went into the bathroom and ran the faucet. Justine wandered outside and picked Indian paintbrush from a field across the street. She filled a jelly jar with water and arranged the orange flowers beside her boss's mattress on the floor.

———

The man wrapped the blue irises with care, rolling the buds and baby's breath in tissue paper. A loose bow of raffia around the stems.

———

Justine stood in the terrace doorway with a bouquet of blue irises in her hand. Wren was listening to music on her headphones, knotting a bracelet, when she noticed her.

"I got you flowers."

Wren did not remove her headphones.

Justine stood above her awkwardly. "I'll put them in your room."

FLORA

Forty women wearing matching red t-shirts mingled around the ironing boards positioned against the wall. The instructor split them into small groups and instructed them to bring an ironing board to their respective station, where a spray bottle, iron, and basket of wrinkled clothes awaited them. As each group struggled to set the metal legs free, laughter infused the room. Their teacher, Miss Carmen, stood at the front in a blue pressed dress that hugged her egg-like figure. She wore stockings and black flats that accentuated her bulbous calves, and she'd pulled her hair back into a bun. Her coral lipstick was the color of Datu's baby blanket, and Flora felt the sudden swerve of loss as the iron grew hot.

"How many have used an iron?"

Only a few hands went up. There was an air of girlhood competition.

"Don't worry, I was the same." Miss Carmen waved a wrinkled shirt in the air with one hand and an ironed shirt on a hanger in the other. "You'll see it feels good to turn something wrinkled into something smooth. Ironed clothes lift a household and can win your employer's heart. Give a sense of order." The teacher raised the iron above her head and pointed to the dial. "One dot: cool, synthetics."

Flora's grandmother taught her to iron by hand; the old woman's thumb pressed upon her own, and together they traveled across damp collars, cuffs, and cold cotton skirts.

"Two dots: warm, silk and wool."

She recalled a red shirt on a clothesline, bleached orange by the sun.

"Three dots: hot, cotton and linen."

Summer winds ballooned pillowcases on branches, napkins snapped and swayed. During the rainy season, clothes hung from rafters, moist underwear stuck to her bottom, and sheets smelled like woodsmoke and ash.

"If you have the right attitude, you can free your mind," said Miss Carmen as she ironed a dress, back and forth, back and forth.

Flora had the right attitude, but she was also clumsy and broke things. A pile of splintered tools and broken handles had littered her garden at home. But freeing your mind sounded good to Flora, and she swept across the ironing board with abandon. The teacher paused at her station and addressed the class: "Enthusiasm is good, but you need to slow down. Be mindful of the equipment. Some employers will deduct broken appliances from your pay."

Flora presented the plate of soft scrambled eggs. Miss Carmen inspected the hard yolks and white jowls, made a mark in her binder, and then dumped the scramble into the bucket beside her desk.

"Again," she said. "Beat. Butter. Burner: low and slow."

Flora slumped by the women who had already aced the egg test and were waiting for the rest of them to finish. Large menus hung above them like marquees, red letters in Cantonese and Arabic announcing the day's culinary challenge. Flora felt humiliated and competitive. She wanted to make amazing eggs, the best eggs in the class, the best eggs ever made in this kitchen. She wanted her eggs to be the picture of perfect eggs, featured in the training handbook with her name beside them. And yet, she hated eggs, the taste, the consistency, everything about them.

She returned to her station: a two-burner hot plate, a cardboard tray of eggs (now almost empty from failed attempts), and cooking utensils. She cracked two yolks into the brown bowl and banged the whisk against the sides. The eggs paled, bubbled, and frothed amid the swirl. The butter burned, and she turned down the flame, poured the brown liquid out, and started again. The eggs spread across the pan, the sides flattened to paper as she stirred, and she watched as low hills began to form. Flora took them off early. They were wet, perfect. Better than the best.

She waited in line behind the other women, watching her eggs stiffen. Again, she presented her work. The teacher put a check beside her name and gave her a spatula badge without even looking up.

"Flora?"

"Yes?"

Miss Carmen read from her file. "You'll need to cook through lunch. It says here that your employer wants you to learn how to make machboos."

"Mocbooz?"

"Machboos."

Oil spit in the pot, and Flora cried over onions. Miss Carmen explained the recipe and promised to return, leaving Flora alone on the fifth floor while her classmates ate lunch in the courtyard below. At first, she felt sorry for herself, isolated in her cooking station, but the smell of browning meat revived her, and she noticed the plastic bins of purple eggplants, pineapples, and ripening mangoes. Sun angled through the dirty windows, and the sounds of children playing and music from the repair shop across the street kept her company.

As the lamb browned, Flora squeezed the black lime known

as loomi—hard and barely green, a collapsed version of cala-
mansi. At home, this would have ended up with the pigs. She
cut the fruit in half and found stiff trails of white encircling the
yellow-orange pulp. It smelled sour, tart to the taste, but also
muddy like dirt. She squeezed the juice over the meat, dropping
the rinds in the pan as instructed. She pounded the cardamom
seeds with the back of a wooden spoon and added sweet cinnamon and bitter cloves to the pot. Next, she assembled a sauce
of tomato paste, onions, lemons, and more cloves. She'd have to
write Pia about this.

And as she stirred the lamb, she began to think about the
woman who'd ordered machboos. It would be like Flora asking
a stranger to learn how to make sisig. Hard to believe that anyone would be able to marinate the pig head and liver the way she
liked, but the request was also an invitation from a woman who
wanted to include her, who cared about tradition and home, and
this made Flora feel better as she poured in the rice. She wondered
about the extended family, how many children, what kind of car
would pick her up at the airport (she'd heard all about the cars),
her new room. She'd improve their lives, they'd appreciate her,
and the time would go fast.

The rice, no pandan—how could it be? She did not know what
to make of this lamb and rice dish. Not bad. Heavy, like it came
from the ground. Next time, something different with the sauce,
and she didn't like the tomatoes with the lamb. Maybe keep the
tomatoes and add some chilies. It needed something. She'd figure
it out. She had the capacity for devotion.

Flora volunteered to model the black cloak for the class. At the
front of the room, she traveled through the tent of polyester,

touching the skin of her future life. The abaya twisted around her torso; laughter seeped through the seams. She wrapped the headscarf around her hair according to the illustrations in the handbook and then walked, and stumbled, back and forth in front of the chalkboard, struggling to pick up the hem of her cloak.

"Who can work in this?"

"You'll be given a uniform. The abaya is for going out in public." The teacher got quiet. "They're different from us. We don't wear the cape and cloak, but over there we wear special clothes for when we go outside the home."

Miss Carmen sat at her desk and assessed all forty of them: "This time tomorrow, you'll be gone."

An unfamiliar quiet settled in around them, and the women began to cry.

"You need to understand that it will be different. Hard. You need to get the proper thinking. You're there to work. For some of you, the phone is not possible. When I arrived, I thought, What would I do? What will I see? It's scary! But you are also happy. Happy because this is a step forward, toward your dreams. Two years. Save money. Make a better future. Some will stay longer. Five, six years and then go home. You'll build a house. Send your kids to school. Feed your families."

The teacher drew a car on the whiteboard with black marker. "Take a picture."

All the women got out their phones and pointed them at the board.

"This is a car with a driver, and this is the tank." She pointed to the class. "You are the driver." She drew an arrow toward the tank. "Your employer is the gas. Remember that."

Months later, when Flora was unable to sleep, she recalled this picture, but it always felt like a riddle: Was it better to be the driver or the gas?

"If you really want to do yourselves a favor, delete the photos on your phone." The women resisted the idea, but Miss Carmen pressed on. "Especially the pictures of your family." The women shared Kleenex and gathered their things. Miss Carmen watched them file out of the room. She called out to them one last time: "Trust me, those pictures will be your torture. Carry them in your heart, not on your phone."

ZEINAH

She heard his boots, heavy on the stairs, shuffling on the landing. Zeinah gathered herself on the couch, determined to stand up straight in her mind. The door swung open, and Omar emerged with bags hanging from his body and something hidden behind his back. His energy was contagious, and he planted a kiss on her forehead, leaving a ring of sweat. The relief of companionship flooded her body. His lips contained a smile and her mind loosened. Man as boy.

"What?"

"Guess."

Infected by his levity, Zeinah sifted through possibilities.

"Ghraybeh? Harisi? Baklava!"

He laughed easily. "No, but you're hungry."

He presented a black creature—a frightful mess of knotted hair with a wrinkled face and a front tooth protruding from its jaw. He raised it toward her, and she recoiled.

"C'mon. Look at that fang. She's a beauty, this one. A warrior." He brought the kitten up to his cheek and brushed his chin across the top of her head. A purr. "See? Huh?"

"It's ugly."

"Well, you just learned something about me. I love ugly."

He strode into the bathroom with the kitten and left Zeinah on the couch, blushing. In seconds, he'd disarmed her. She heard him unzip his duffel bag.

"C'mere."

He knelt in front of the bathtub on his military jacket. The kitten meowed. Zeinah noticed his tailored shirt, trimmed beard, clean nails.

"Hold here."

She joined him on the cold floor and gripped the kitten's head and hind legs while Omar meticulously shaved the matted fur with his electric razor. The kitten mewed and pawed against the slippery tub.

"Shhh, it's okay," said Omar as the razor reached her tail.

"No, leave her tail. She's not going to the grave." She brought the kitten into her arms, rubbed its head, and rotated her belly upward so Omar could finish the job.

"You're covered in hair."

Zeinah shrugged, caught his eye, and her chest lurched because she liked this man, and she knew she'd succumb to these feelings. She willed her mind to harden, to leave his side, to utter all the words she'd prepared, but instead, she remained on the bathroom floor and rubbed the cheek of the small creature in her arms.

He shaved the cat's stomach, between its legs, and under its chin, all the while brushing the cat hair off Zeinah's chest. When he was finished, he placed the razor on the sink, retrieved the naked cat from Zeinah's arms, and raised it toward the ceiling.

"Mewww," he said.

Zeinah pulled on his arm. "Don't do that. You're scaring her."

He handed her the cat, and she cuddled it willingly.

He scratched the cat's belly. "My little monster."

That night, Zeinah and Omar lay together for the first time. She opened her thighs. His chest smelled of soap, and she felt shy.

She forced herself to open her eyes and noticed the shadow of the streetlight etched on the ceiling. This man I don't know is now part of my story, she thought. He touched her in places she'd never been touched before. He explored the deep thicket between her legs. Before closing her eyes, she noticed the teacup on the bedside table, and then she felt a swelling, an inlet open.

He slept with his arm slung over her torso, and she lay awake, holding still, fearing he might move. This stranger was her husband. His black hair, cut to the root, circling across his skull in cowlicks. She observed him as a specimen: bones wrapped in muscle, forearms of twisted tendons. Even in sleep—a resolute mass. Since her brother died, she'd not been in such close proximity to a young man. Her brother's body so different—lithe, long, soft. Spirit inflecting form. Adrenaline kept her awake, and for the first time in many months, she found herself thinking she might have a future. Perhaps she could make a life with this man. Already the apartment was becoming a home. A cat, a shared bed, a bathtub.

ESKEDARE

Her mother had been fifteen and her father decades older when they married.

And when the husband, the father, dies: he's just dead.

Neither wife nor daughter miss him.

After the funeral, the father's brother escorts them home and instructs Eskedare to wait outside. She crouches beneath a window, arranges rocks around her feet, and strains toward the murmurs. Whispers and negotiations. Something about Eskedare. Not now, but later. When her uncle leaves, he backs out of the door with his hands in his pockets, and she watches as he strides to the cattle pen, ropes her cows and ox together, and leads them out of the shadows. They stall in front of her; the eyes of the cows and the eyes of Eskedare go cloudy. The uncle steps between them, yanks the rope, forbidding a goodbye. Eskedare presses stones into the dirt and listens to the hollow clang of cow bells moving further and farther away.

Her mother comes outside and crouches beside her.

"He said we can stay. He's taking the fields, livestock, and gardens, but we can keep the house, the chickens, and kitchen tools. He promises to give thirty percent of what they sell."

Eskedare senses her mother's wariness, the silence of anger and defeat.

———

Her mother brings the father's plate, cup, and clothes to the church. After hymns, the mother hauls her husband's bed outside and shatters the frame into firewood. Women in white dresses and headscarves hold hands and avert their gaze as they pass. Later, as the wood burns, smoke kills the mildew and termites in the thatched roof above them. Later still, the mother nails eucalyptus limbs while Eskedare covers foam with cloth for their new bed. And later still, when the moon casts wide shadows across the floor, the mother presents Eskedare with a misshapen package wrapped in tape and twine that had been hiding in the corner where the bed had been. Eskedare tears the package open with her teeth.

"Gentle."

A clay pitcher—handmade. Eskedare holds the thick handle and pretends to pour liquid into cups.

"Not for now. Just to look at."

Eskedare considers the jug, the red clay and diagonal lines glazed in white.

"My mother made that when she was a young woman in Yemen. She gave it to me on my wedding day."

Eskedare presses her small fingers into the indentation on the handle and imagines her grandmother's thumb.

Her mother displays the pitcher on a high shelf. "One day it will be yours."

The empty pitcher sits and waits.

At night Eskedare eyes the jug, its white triangles, curved handle, and puckered rim. A timekeeper. Eskedare wraps around her mother's limbs like rope and feels afraid. Afraid of her mother's unspoken words. Afraid of the seasons tossing her forward. Afraid of the day when the pitcher will live in the palm of her hand.

ೂ

DOUNIA

The early ultrasounds had been sublime; milky galaxies rimmed the baby's skull, abstract blobs feathered into fingers, slits grew into ears, and in her sixth month, an earthquake of hiccups was followed by jabs and a somersault. But now, the child refused to move.

The ultrasound wand spread cold jelly across Dounia's stomach as the monitor revealed the shadowed pyramid of her womb. Her daughter, very much alive, sat upright, eyes closed, arms crossed, her feet tucked beneath her in protest: a sit-in. She would not leave. Finally, she understands, thought Dounia. I don't want to be here either.

The only way to get her out was a C-section.

The hospital bag lurked in the corner of the bedroom, a reminder of the impending violence, the hijacking of her womb, her lie soon to be exposed. Hamed sat on the edge of the bed and cut his fingernails as Dounia watched the clippings drop to the floor. He was particular about trimming hangnails, cuticles, and calluses, unaware of the detritus he left behind, oblivious to her and the suitcase in the corner. She was a box on his to-do list, now marked done.

Ibrahim Qadira. Qadira Ibrahim.

Like a lover on the precipice of abandonment, Dounia squandered the last week of her pregnancy weeping. Other mothers might've distracted themselves with decorating a nursery, buying

onesies, blankets, and mobiles, but Dounia did only the bare minimum—a crib and a bureau with a changing pad on top. Basma
had reserved a VIP luxury suite at Almana General Hospital in
Khobar, and a steady stream of packages arrived for the occasion: lavish nightgowns, colored sheets, platters for the confections
and dates, an electric incense burner, a traditional coffeepot and
matching cups. One day, a breastfeeding rocker appeared, but
when Dounia looked in the nursery she was overcome with grief;
all she could see was a chair beside a hollow grave. And she knew
Basma found her insatiable; a girl never satisfied. Her mother-in-
law's gossip, whispers, and complaints echoed through the house.
On and on about Dounia's desire to live apart from the family,
how it was Ibrahim who'd insisted on the marriage, never Basma.
Dounia felt on the brink of catastrophe; the pregnancy had been
her mooring, her anchor in the Dream house, and without it she
feared she'd disassemble, unspool into something unknowable but
dire.

Flora would rescue her from this misery. Dounia composed a
list of items for Hamed to purchase: twin bed, mattress, dresser,
sheets, towels, shower curtain, toothbrush, toothpaste, soap, shampoo, conditioner, uniforms. She wanted the woman to feel welcome. Every family needs a witness, she thought. They'll all be on
their best behavior, and the woman will bring routine and warmth
into the home. I'll be able to rest after the surgery, and we can start
over again.

On a Tuesday, Hamed returned with a small television for the
maid's room. It dawned on Dounia he was also anticipating Flora's
arrival, and he might have his own notions about the places she
could occupy.

JUSTINE

Wren departed for the school trip, and Justine's longed-for time of working without interruption now left her feeling burdened and alone in the empty apartment. Threats of a sandstorm glued Justine to Al Jazeera for hours. Newscasters referenced the Egyptian sandstorm of 1997 when high winds uprooted trees and felled buildings, suffocated people and their pets. NASA images—beige-and-white swirling brushstrokes—coiled over Iraq and Saudi Arabia with the promise to unleash gusting winds and sand on the United Arab Emirates. A 2005 video from the Al-Asad Air Base in Iraq played on a loop. Justine watched again as a lone woman in a red sweater ran for shelter between shipping containers. Justine muttered along with the cameraman on screen: "Oh, shit." She had to stop watching, but the silence of the apartment and the wind against the panes felt ominous.

She drove to the grocery store, expecting to find a line, but the aisles were quiet. She hoisted gallons of water and canned food on the conveyor belt, and as the cashier rang her up, she watched storm coverage on a TV in the corner. An Emirati woman waited behind her with a *Time Out Abu Dhabi* and a six-pack of Diet Coke. She eyed Justine's items and smirked. In the parking lot, Justine watched the woman disappear into the pale-leathered seat of a Mercedes. The license plate was 27, the lowest number she'd seen. She must be one of the royals. If a princess was out buying diet soda, how bad could it be?

At home, Justine covered the furniture on the terrace with tarps and tried to laugh off her grim scenarios as she wrapped gaffer's tape around chair legs and attached them to railings with her eyes half shut. She wedged the empty blue water jugs between suitcases against the wall. Vertigo sent her stomach falling through the floors, stepping back from ledges. She taped large Xs across windows, inserted fresh DD batteries into a flashlight, and confirmed once again that her phone was fully charged.

Skype rang on her computer in the living room, and she hurried down the hall with her mug of mint tea, spilling bits along the way.

Justine pressed the green icon—"Hi, hi, hi"—and arranged her hair in the small window as she waited for the image of Sean and Wren to load. They crowded into the frame, talking over each other in excitement.

"Hi, Mom." "Hi, honey."

Justine was relieved to see Wren in high spirits. "How's it going?"

Sean put his arm around Wren. "We're about to head off in an hour, and we wanted to call before we lost Wi-Fi."

She yearned to be with them and felt fragile, on the edge of tears.

"Everyone's on the riverbanks offering flowers and sugarcane to the Sun God," said Wren. "All the houses are decorated with these beautiful colored lights."

"Remember when Wren studied the Chhath Festival with Teddy in second grade?"

Justine was reassured by the reference to their shared history and knew it would be a mistake to cry. She imagined her show of emotion becoming a topic of conversation on the trail, a source of worry and even derision.

"Mom, this morning we got up before sunrise and waded into the water with hundreds of people to greet Surya Dev."

"Tell Mom about the swings."

Sean seemed good, confident, and she wondered if he'd started sleeping with someone.

"They're made from bamboo. Almost twenty feet high."

"I hate not being there with you guys. Ready for the big trek?"

Wren rolled her eyes. "Yeah, yoga . . ."

"Well, do some downward dogs for me."

Sean interrupted. "What's that?"

"Honey, you know what downward—"

"No. Behind you."

Justine looked behind her at the Xs she'd taped across the windows. "Oh, nothing. It's just—the sandstorm."

"Honey."

"What? It's good to be prepared."

Sean leaned forward. "Turn. Off. The. News."

He knew her too well. She felt relieved by his concern and affection.

"Seriously. Enjoy your time alone."

He was right. She'd not had a week to herself since Wren was born.

"Prepared for what?" asked Wren.

"Mom is just worried about a possible sandstorm. I mean, don't drive to Dubai. If it's dusty, don't go outside. We'll see you next week."

Justine slumped down in her chair. He was right.

"Okay. Okay." She smiled and leaned toward them. "Have fun. I love you and I'm sorry I'm not there. Big kiss."

They all craned forward; a mess of mouths and chins filled the frame. And then they were gone, leaving Justine alone in silence.

Since coming here, her life had revolved around Wren and her research, and now she was confronted with her stark isolation. Unable to settle down and concentrate, she was gripped by paranoia. Thoughts of impending disaster and premonitions of an accident on the trek seized her mind. She needed to take Sean's advice, exert some independence, and get out into the city.

FLORA

The yellow-brown light of Manila, so different from the dark skies of Palawan. The inhales and exhales of sorrowful sleep—bagpipe breath. Soft bellies downward, mouths hanging open against damp pillows. Two hundred women bound for Hong Kong or the Arabian Gulf. The first forty deployed to Saudi Arabia by morning. A hollowness surrounded the metal bunks, and digital ghosts haunted the hall. Just hours ago, alcohol-inspired jubilation led to bravado and then a dare—the mass destruction of images.

A belt of bills cinched around her waist. A ruffle of pesos around her neck. They danced on grass mats covering the dirt floor of the village, her white veil twirling, her hair piled high. He wore a royal-blue satin bow tie. Pia's father. Her mother sat in a white plastic chair, and most of the kids wore t-shirts and flip-flops. She'd wanted this picture of the two of them in front of the blooming Bani tree.

Delete Photo

The children made wreaths of seaweed and grass. Smells of fish and low tide. Lights in the trees. Handmade signs on the chairs: BRIDE and GROOM.

Delete Photo

The best men wore khakis and white shirts. The bridesmaids wore pink nylon dresses, sweat stains under their arms.

Delete Photo

A bouquet of night-blooming jasmine crowned the blue jeepney, and a trail of coconuts rattled behind them as they left town.

Delete Photo

They traveled to his parents' house and stayed for five days. A balot sa kumot waited for them in the living room. They sat in the middle of a white bedsheet as the four corners were tied up around them, bundling the new couple into a package that the family pushed back and forth. Inside the egg, they tumbled against each other. He belched in her ear and then kissed her, the taste of beer in her throat.

Delete Photo

Her friend wearing a worn *Parks and Recreation* t-shirt, a dirty dish towel thrown over her shoulder.

Delete Photo

Her grandmother in a dirt-stained tank top, eyes smiling but mouth closed, always hiding her missing teeth.

Delete Photo

Flora and Joenard and Datu, smiling in the window of their sari-sari store on opening day.

Delete Photo

Pia at the gate, pigs at her feet. Sun flares and long lashes.

Delete. Delete. Delete.

Flora thought of her mother, her aunt, and the women who'd gone before and the women who'd come after. Yes, there was risk and even death in this plan, but there was also money in those pots of boiling water, toilet bowls, and children. She'd give her body, her work, her time. She wanted to believe there was more to life than those deleted pictures, but she couldn't say. She didn't know.

ZEINAH

"Come. Look at this." Omar was on the couch on his computer. "Do you know this group, Raqqa Is Being Slaughtered Silently?"

She vaguely knew one of the members.

"They cut a 'Happy Birthday Isis' video to mark our arrival in Raqqa. They think this makes us look bad . . . It's great."

He pressed the space bar, and a childish version of "Happy Birthday" played over images of beheadings, lashings, and forced prayers. ISIS trucks and soldiers paraded through the streets waving black flags. Zeinah drank her coffee, looking past the screen.

"The violence is just the first phase of creating the Islamic State. It will not be forever. It will get easier."

"Omar, our whole life we paid off Assad. Now we pay off ISIS. It's the same."

Omar stopped the video. "You can't compare Assad to ISIS. Assad has killed over two hundred thousand people, raped children, used chemical weapons. The West stood by and allowed Assad to kill innocent Muslims. Designed it. ISIS fights against that. We're carrying out the will of Allah as communicated through the Prophet. This is not about what individual soldiers or even religious leaders like Baghdadi want. This is about serving Allah as He ordained. The Qur'an says that the laws do not change according to the times. I am a Muslim, and at the core of that faith is the will—the choice—to submit. Either you do this one hundred percent or not at all. I don't believe in à la carte religion. Let fools take what they like and leave the rest."

Zeinah watched Little Monster swat a fly across the floor with her paw. Dounia's companion from last week, now dead. She searched Omar's face. "I'd like your permission to live at home when you're not here."

"This is your home."

"I'm alone. What do you expect me to do all day? Two years ago, I was going to university. I was studying all sorts of things. Chemistry, literature. I didn't know what I wanted to be, but I was figuring it out."

Omar looked as though he might say something, but he stopped himself, and then his mood softened. "How do you think that will look? Living with your parents?"

Out the window, she saw a new pile of cinder blocks covered with blue tarp, tied down with rope, one of the corners flapping in the wind. Her eyes landed on the blue iridescent wings of the fly, and she swept the carcass into her hand and wrapped a white napkin around it as if it were a shroud. Omar looked at her strangely as she held the dead fly in her palm. She noticed his lip quivering, and an unexpected moment of tenderness passed between them.

"You're a good woman."

"I don't know what to do with myself," she confessed.

"You want to do something useful? Join the Al-Khansaa Brigade."

The connection between them, his tenderness, had vanished, and a gruffness returned. She wanted to weep, to call the other man back.

"Fifteen days of religious and military training and you can walk the streets alone, go to internet cafés, earn three hundred

U.S. dollars a month. You can even get free medicine for your mother."

Zeinah spilled coffee on her shirt, she was trembling so, but Omar's attention had returned to the screen.

She blotted the stain with her saliva. "I'm no policewoman."

"Well, that's your choice."

ESKEDARE

The skirt of her uniform feels scratchy against her thighs. Her mother walks in front of her and does not hold her hand.

"Remember the way. Those trees. That fence."

Eskedare remains silent and follows. She does not tell her mother about the shortcut through the field of blue stones and blue stars. Blue flowers and black seeds. Her favorite day.

The schoolhouse: a tin roof with walls of grass and mud. Orange trims the open door and windows. Her mother watches as she enters the room of children crowding into long benches and desks. She's one of a handful of girls. The boys gape and laugh. The teacher beckons her up front, but Eskedare slides into the back row with the rowdy boys. She's given an English primer with pictures of rain clouds, the sun, and people working: pilots, dentists, marathoners, and shopkeepers. Numbers keep her company as she adds, subtracts, and multiplies stars, eggs, chickens, and teff.

Salim, a skinny boy, stares at her throughout the day. She pretends not to notice. A cousin she's hated since childhood, from her uncle's wife's family who run the tuk-tuk stand, overcharge on fares, and cheat people of their money. A boy who years ago stole a doll she'd assembled from grass and string. A doll he insisted on sleeping with every night. Everyone laughed. No one insisted he give it back. She moves to the front of the class, feels his gaze on the back of her ears, her neck, the top of her spine. He stares without apology, like he has a secret, like he owns her. She won't look at him, not now, not ever.

She arrives early to school, often before the teacher. During the day, her eyes wander to the map taped to the wall and the tilted globe on the high bookshelf behind the teacher's desk. One day, the teacher asks Eskedare to stay after school, and when the scuffling and laughter disappear, the teacher steps on a chair and retrieves the globe. Eskedare joins Miss Eshe at her desk and watches as the wrinkled ball rotates and squeaks. Her fingers pause on a patch of yellow.

"That's us, near Gondar, once the capital of Ethiopia."

Eskedare reaches for the globe and traces the continents, feels the seams of paper and the grooves of glue below her fingertips, and as she spreads her palms across the oceans, the frayed world spins beneath her. But she could never leave her mother. Eskedare is all she has.

Sometimes Miss Eshe brings Eskedare meals in a tin pail.

Whenever Eskedare arrives home her mother calls out, "Is that you?"

"Yes, it's me."

But no one else ever comes to call; her mother no longer seeks the company of others.

She heats the tin pail on the fire, wraps the bottom with a towel, tucks the warmth between her mother's legs, and they use injera to scoop up the lentils and cinnamon clinging to soft onion skins. Sometimes they share mango from a tin plate, picking the orange-yellow slices like a garden between them. And afterward, in the dark, Eskedare will press a glass against her lips and tilt water down her throat until she feels a coldness in her stomach and can consider things.

❧

DOUNIA

The day of the scheduled C-section arrived. Masked nurses and a doctor hovered over her in the operating room, and Dounia watched as they erected a blue tent above her stomach. Hamed was supposed to be there, but she didn't see him. And it didn't matter; she'd requested general anesthesia. She wanted to wake with the child born, the moment of revelation past, the secret told.

But the doctor dismissed Dounia's request. "Really? You need to be conscious for the birth. We're not living in the fifties."

She was given local anesthesia with an opiate for anxiety and pain. Her mind lagged, and she backstroked away from the scene. The lights above her abdomen bloomed into white dandelion threads, and when someone spoke, the seeds departed and floated upward toward the ceiling. She couldn't understand what they were saying, but there was a calm murmur and the steady metronome of her heart monitor beeping. She closed her eyes and smelled disinfectant, plastic gloves, and powder. Rubber-gloved hands reached inside her, dug into the slime and stones of her womb, transplanting the root ball of her child. They'd get all of her and leave nothing behind. Fingers scraped along Dounia's vertebrae and dislodged the mass. She felt a suction, a hollow hole, and then a landslide of organs seeping into the cavity where the baby once lived. The doctor raised a red form of outstretched limbs above the tent. The infant was crying, but Dounia was far away. Nothing moved inside her now.

"What a healthy girl."

Hamed's wire-framed glasses came into view at the foot of the bed. "Girl?"

"You didn't know?" said the doctor.

Hamed took his newborn child from the doctor, recited the adhān lovingly in her ear, and then left without saying a word. Dounia had betrayed and humiliated her husband and mother-in-law, led many to believe she was having a boy through the manipulation and silence of sidelong glances. She knew it was wrong, but she wanted to hoard those blessings, the sense of possibility; to create expansiveness for her daughter and for herself. She'd lied to protect the girl from assumptions and stereotypes in utero, to stake a boundary around the infant, but it seemed so naive now, a Pyrrhic victory. She imagined Basma and Hamed listening to her tangled explanation with vacant expressions and shared glances. They'd express their delight in having a girl and cite all the ways Saudi was changing for women, but they all knew it was not the same; even in the most progressive countries, women and men were not equal.

A nurse spread the baby across her chest.

"Let's get the baby to latch on. We want to activate the colostrum."

The baby's lips opened and closed, searching for her mother's nipple, but Dounia recoiled, covered her breasts, and began to sob. One of the nurses removed the baby and proceeded with weight and measurements.

"Ten pounds, six ounces. Big, like her mother."

JUSTINE

The translucent blue of chlorinated pools illuminated the dark corners of the Hakkasan bar in the Emirates Palace. Glass shelves, lit from below, displayed a wall of curated alcohol, and an innocuous dance beat welcomed the international clientele in kanduras, miniskirts, and designer watches. Having taken Sean's advice, Justine "braved" the storm and now sat alone at the bar studying the exotic cocktail menu, sweet drinks mixed with lychee and passion fruit. She'd heard it was the only place in town for a decent martini. A friend at the Guggenheim fantasized about opening a high-end incognito martini bar for expats and Emiratis—a place where secrecy and exclusivity could thrive. Many of the expats she'd met complained about the hypocrisy of the culture, but it was one of the things she most admired: the ability to hold two contradictory ideas at the same time. Fitzgerald was famous for saying it was a test of a first-rate intelligence. He'd have liked it here.

A bartender wiped a water glass and placed it in front of her. "What can I get you?"

"Grey Goose martini with a twist. Extra olives on the side."

She could hear Sean chastising her for the extra olives: *It's not an appetizer*.

A tall man in a wrinkled linen shirt sat down beside her. Behind him was a man in sweatpants lighting the cigarette of a woman in a pleather vest zipped over her breasts, no shirt. They were an unlikely threesome. The man in linen leaned over and offered Justine a cigarette from his pack of Dunhills.

"Oh, no thanks. I don't smoke."

His shirt was open, and she registered a delicate gold cross dangling amid a tuft of hair. Distracted by his low-buttoned shirt, she imagined herself reaching over and fastening it for him. She hadn't been to a bar by herself in years.

Her drink arrived. "Grey Goose with a twist." The bartender turned to the man. "What can I get you?"

"Seltzer with lime."

Not what she expected. He was either Muslim (unlikely with the cross), an alcoholic, or drunk. Justine took a sip of her drink. Too much vermouth.

He leaned forward. "Australia."

"Nope."

He leaned back, scrutinized her. She wondered how she appeared to him, if the makeup she'd applied appeared false or appealing.

"It's either New York or Canada."

"New York." Justine raised her glass and nodded.

"Iraq."

"Shit."

"Yeah, my family won't leave."

"Are they okay?"

He scoffed. "You watch the news." He looked down the crowded bar, distracted. "I got my parents an apartment in Beirut, but my father refused to be treated like a refugee. The Lebanese hate the Iraqis. Then I brought them here, but they hated that too. No history. No culture."

"Well, they're from Iraq. The beginning of civilization."

His body eased, relieved to have found someone who might understand. "My family traces back to Eridu. Oldest city in the world. *The world*. Then I bring them to this shithole. They went home."

"I'm sorry."

He shrugged, his pride defeated. "Don't kid yourself about this place. It may feel familiar, but it has a different operating system."

She felt him looking at her, and she took a generous sip of her martini before returning his gaze. "But you stayed . . ."

"I'm looking for a wife."

Justine laughed.

"You think that's funny? I'm thirty-eight. It would make my mother happy."

"Your mother? What is it with Arab men and their mothers? You're like the Jews." His eyes became alert, and she did a quick pivot. "Well, not like the Jews. Not like the Jews at all!"

They shrugged it off and moved on. She knew these were stereotypes, but everyone was completely open about their prejudices here, and it all felt innocent and innocuous. Until it wasn't. She was still figuring out the balance of this walk.

"Well, I'm married."

"I see that. Happy?"

"Very." Justine finished her drink. Time to wrap things up.

He extended his hand. "Wasim. Wasim Naji."

"Justine." She looked for the bartender, who was at the other end of the bar. She caught the bartender's eye, signaled for the check, and regarded Wasim. His cynicism and ease were appealing.

"Let me ask you, what should I be looking for in a wife? I got this." He took the check. "You keep thinking."

"Hmmm."

"Not some bullshit. What really sustains love?"

"The need to grow. Curiosity about the world. A relationship to the body, to the mind. The psychosexual . . ."

Wasim looked up from the bill. "Say more about that . . ."

The martini had gone to her head. She was saying things she'd regret.

He smiled and there was a kindness in his eyes. "You're not happily married."

Wasim turned off the air conditioner and opened the doors to the terrace overlooking the sea. The fervid air of the Gulf blew into the room, bringing the smell of salt, car exhaust, and storm. He collapsed on the bed. She stood in the middle of the dim room holding her handbag. The room was tidy. No clothes flung over the chair. No books on the bed. She'd heard butlers were assigned to each suite, but he'd surely knock. He was perhaps the most handsome man she'd ever been with. The last time she had sex was almost a year ago. Christmas Eve. She and Sean had shared a bottle of prosecco while wrapping Wren's presents in the bedroom. He'd tied her wrists in ribbons. Justine had not been with another man in seventeen years.

She sat on the edge of the mattress and slipped off her shoes. The mirror was framed in gold, and there were white lilies in a vase on the dresser. He gathered his arms around her, and they toppled against the cold sheets pulled taut across the bed. Thick lips. Eyes the color of her mother's favorite blue cardigan, the one she wore over her hospital gown. The sweater she died in.

"You're trembling."

She wondered where Sean was now. Sleeping on the floor of a teahouse. It didn't matter. She needed to be in this room, with this man. Why he was staying at the Emirates Palace or if he was telling the truth about where he was from had no consequence. He smelled of jasmine and cigarettes. She wanted to surrender, to give herself over, to release into his body, and discover a new kind of desire. Her fingers found his necklace, and she put the cross between her lips. She would not rush. The metal tasted of salt. I will not pretend, she thought. I will not attend to his pleasure as a way of avoiding my own, and she rested her cheek against his chest, curious to see what would happen. They lay in each other's arms, unmoving in the dark, and she wondered if perhaps he'd made a similar kind of pact. Someone must make a little effort, she thought, but neither of them stirred until Wasim withdrew, away from her.

The white lights of construction cranes bled through the fog and illuminated the outlines of their bodies, separate and alone, spread across the bed.

"I don't even know why I'm in this shit hotel. My friend comped me. Like it makes any kind of difference."

She felt a great sorrow and bitterness in him. "How long will you stay here?"

"Someone needs to support the family. Omar, my cousin, who'd been helping in Iraq, disappeared. Just left. We haven't heard from him since."

"Where'd he go?"

"Maybe Kuwait. Probably Syria. Fighting. Who knows."

The reality of ISIS settled between them. Justine felt uncertain, but Wasim proceeded, emboldened.

"Yeah, well . . . that's what happens when your country is air bombed. We have the beautiful U.S. of A. to thank for that." His tone was confrontational. "Imagine a barrel bomb. Out of nowhere, a fireball drops from the sky. Your home destroyed. Complete rubble. I think about Omar. Finding pieces of his family, his wife's arm, a child's leg. Gathering what he could find of them, wrapping their remains in a rug from their bedroom. He left them at our house to bury. And who do you think unrolled that rug?"

Justine, chastened, felt herself recoil.

"He took one thing: my Qur'an. The one that's been passed down in our family for generations. It was supposed to be mine. What does he know of God."

Below them, Justine heard the whoosh of brown foam expanding and receding against the shore.

"In twenty years, maybe our country will be suitable for your tourism." Mockery had entered his voice, and she felt she should leave. "Maybe I'll pass you on the street or in a café in Baghdad. You won't recognize me, but I'll remember you. In your arms will be souvenirs, maybe a mabkhara or leather purse, and you'll think from those five or ten days that you know something about my country, but you'll know nothing. Nothing of war, of people randomly creating new names and borders with crayons on maps. Imagine air strikes over New York, Washington Square—a staging ground for rebels. The infrastructure of your life destroyed as the world watches. These are just images for you. Horror and entertainment. But I'm here . . ." He gripped her arm and hit it against his chest. "I'm real. This is happening."

She saw herself through his eyes, his disgust, but also felt the urgency in his grasp and felt afraid. The night had been a painful embarrassment for both of them; the proximity of their bodies on the cold starched sheets, the inability to take root in each

other, even for an hour, for a minute, filled her with despair. And
the way they'd lain there in the dark, immobile in their respective
brokenness, knowing she had no salve for his wounds. The night
had brought no relief, only a deeper aloneness, and she left with
barely a goodbye.

FLORA

> do you know where my green shirt is?

It was Flora's first time on a plane, and she was afraid to text Pia back from the tarmac.

The Airbus to Saudi was packed with women. While others watched movies and slept, she took pictures on her flip phone of the world outside. Flora gazed at the little pinpricks of light in the cabin ceiling, suspended in a canister of stars. She read the names of the countries passing below her on the map, tasted the sounds of the cities on her tongue.

Bangkok, Dhaka, Karachi, Bahrain, Riyadh.

Upon landing in Riyadh, shuttles transported the Filipina women to a makeshift medical facility on the outskirts of the airport. Flora was escorted into a barren room, where she was instructed to change into a paper nightgown and wait in the hallway. The women were cautious, and there were rumors of bad bloodwork sending you home. Flora heard her name and followed a nurse into a large room with medical stations. She stood on the standing scale and watched the metal arm float up and down until it found its resting place. She'd always loved getting weighed; the sound of the metal weight traveling across the calibrated bar reminded her of an abacus, colored beads, the comfort of counting. Afterward, as her vial filled with blood, she observed the nurse's puffy face and thick eyeliner, wondering where she was from, wanting to ask questions, but the room was quiet, and it was best to be cautious. A bus returned Flora to a windowless room at the airport, where her paperwork was processed, pictures taken, her passport stamped. Once she was released through customs, Flora searched for her name on the placards and forgot to say goodbye, already slipping into a world of her own.

ZEINAH

The Armenian Catholic church at the city roundabout now served as ISIS headquarters. The women formed a circle on metal chairs in the dim basement. One seat remained empty, and they waited and listened to the *tick-tick-tick* of the fan blade circling above them. Zeinah wanted to get up and turn it off but thought better of it. An imposing woman entered, almost six feet tall with an AK-47 slung across her chest. Without a word, she sat down, placed her weapon beside her chair, removed her veils, and opened her cloak. Zeinah noticed a dagger in her belt. Rumor had it that she'd been a prison guard in Pakistan or Iraq, before leading the Al-Khansaa Brigade in Raqqa.

She leaned forward and looked each woman in the eye. "I'm known as Umm Humra. This is not my real name. I'm the leader of the Al-Khansaa Brigade and your teacher for the military and religious training: cleaning and using weapons, studying the important role of women under Sharia law, how to patrol the streets and borders."

Her strictness captured their attention and drew the women close.

"Pass me your identity cards." Her fingers beckoned, and the cards passed from one woman to the next. The leader shuffled through them, reading their countries of origin aloud: "Britain, Britain, Tunisia, Canada, France, Saudi Arabia, Syria, Kuwait, Yemen, Sweden."

Zeinah had never been to any of these countries, and she scanned the women's faces to guess where they were from. She was skeptical of these visitors and their reasons for traveling to Raqqa, a city she could no longer recognize.

"So, tell me, why are we called the Al-Khansaa Brigade?"

The tick of the fan returned.

"You've traveled all this way, and not one of you knows?"

A girl raised her hand. She was maybe eighteen.

"Stand up. Give us your name."

"Ghada Romdhani. I'm from Tunisia. Al-Khansaa is one of my favorite poets. She wrote in the seventh century, met the prophet Muhammad, and converted to Islam. Her two brothers and sons were killed in war. She is most famous for her poems praising these martyrs. She wrote lines like 'al-Khansaa weeps in the dark grief, calls her brother unresponding in dust.'"

"Excellent. You make me proud. Except . . . except what? What is wrong with Ghada?"

The leader looked at all of them. Zeinah noticed right away, but she suspected the others, being foreigners, would not guess. Her eyes met Umm Humra's.

"Yes, my local sister, stand up."

Omar must have told her that she was coming. "She is wearing lipstick."

"Yes! Twenty lashes."

Ghada's eyes filled with tears. The women exchanged fearful glances.

Umm Humra laughed. "We are harsh with the infidels, but today, my Islamic sisters, we have mercy." She took a Kleenex from her pocket and passed it to the woman beside her. One by one the women passed the tissue, removing the stain from their lips. Zeinah was last in the circle, and she held the tissue stained with different shades of crimson. It felt worn and soft between her fingers, reminding her of the lipstick-stained tissues she found in her mother's bag while searching for candy as a child.

"Tell us, Zeinah, why are you here?"

She stumbled over her response. She couldn't say it was the only way to escape her isolation, that she was on a fact-finding mission, wanting to know if it was possible to gain freedom for herself without betraying her community. These women had chosen to marry ISIS fighters, had snuck away from their families to participate in what they saw as a revolution. She'd agreed to marry Omar for protection, for herself and her family. Her aunt, people in the neighborhood, even her own parents, would never approve of Zeinah enforcing the doctrines. But what did they expect? Had they thought about children? How did they imagine she'd navigate this life? Did they want her to live in solitary confinement, in hiding? They must've considered what the marriage would mean, and as Zeinah sat in the meeting, she began to resent her family's hypocrisy and the position they'd put her in. Who were her allies? How was she supposed to survive this life?

But these thoughts were impossible to share. "I've recently married a Jihadi, and I believe this will make us closer," she said.

"Very good. Sit down. Let's hear from more of you."

A woman with a British accent spoke up. "As a Muslim woman, I feel like an outsider in my community in London."

"That's how I felt, like there were no real options for me," said the woman beside her.

A woman with expressive hands chimed in. "I feel like the whole Western experiment of feminism is its own tyranny. Whether it's Victoria's Secret, Calvin Klein, or Tinder, it all just feels like freedom to be oversexualized. I want to be part of a group that respects women."

The leader interjected. "See, that's what the West does not understand. Did you see the meme I made that went viral?"

Many of the women clapped and seemed familiar with the campaign. Zeinah recalled the image: a profile of a veiled woman that said "COVERed GIRL . . . because I'm worth it." At the time, she'd found the meme infuriating and was shocked by its traction, but Zeinah saw how these women felt empowered by the image.

"Here, all the faces of women are covered on the hair dye boxes. I love that!" said the woman raising her hands in the air.

"Let me ask you, who did we free in our negotiation with Jordan? Sajida al-Risham. ISIS protects and values our sisters. Women are praised and valued for their divine role as wives, mothers, and nation builders. You are not objects," said Umm Humra. "Women should remain hidden, like a film director. They have the most important role, off-screen, behind the camera."

"I fell in love with a man online. I want to have a family here and have a community of women who share my beliefs," said a woman maybe five months pregnant.

"Me too. I just got married. If the Jews have their own nation, so should we."

"For me, life was kind of meaningless and boring in France. I mean yes, there are nice things that I gave up, but I wanted to be part of something bigger. Something more meaningful than shopping and television," said an eager woman with bright eyes.

"That's what my parents do not understand. They emigrated from Iraq to Brussels. How could I want to come back to this part of the world? For them—"

The leader interrupted. "We don't need your whole life story."

"The dream of marrying a man who has dedicated his life to jihad. When he sacrifices himself, he'll also secure my own place in Paradise."

Zeinah was skeptical of how these women were defining freedom, but she also found herself leaning forward, wanting to hear
everything they had to say. The experiences in their home countries were so different from her own in Raqqa, where she had a
strong Muslim community, was enrolled in university, and did
not face discrimination. Now, there were so many different languages spoken in Raqqa, it felt like a foreign city, a place she did
not recognize. The teachings felt like propaganda, slogans easy to
dismiss, but the afternoon spent with women from all over the
world also brought her out of her seclusion and into a larger conversation with women who saw things differently. People were
quick to say how war destroyed decency, but these women came
to Raqqa seeking dignity. There was the charge of activism, ideas,
and solidarity.

That night, Zeinah lay in bed trying to recall the face of each
woman on the folding chairs, the places they were from, women
who'd left their families and traveled alone to marry strangers.
Some had left notes and run away. All had chosen to inhabit this
city, a gasp of itself, a forsaken place disparaged by locals, but for
these women, it was a destination, a place of hope and possibility,
and she felt herself tilting toward them. Perhaps monitoring dress
codes and ensuring shops were closed for prayers were small prices
to pay for returning to the streets she once considered home.

ESKEDARE

A Monday in May. Amara arrives. Amara, the girl with hair tied up in black knots. Amara, the girl from Addis Ababa, whose mother died and who now lives with her uncle. Amara, the girl who sits beside her on the bench in class.

———

"You must promise. You must swear."

Amara follows Eskedare beneath the electrical lines, away from town.

"Say it," demands Eskedare.

"I swear."

Eskedare leads Amara down a dirt path that was once a stream. They trip over rocks and stumble downhill until the path opens into a clearing surrounded by barbed wire. Eskedare spreads the wires, and Amara squeezes through the thorny fence. They walk through a field littered with broken beer bottles, cigarette butts, and charred dung and feel on the edge of something strange.

Eskedare aims for a rusted-out truck decomposing in the shade of a warka tree, sitting in the dirt, tires stripped, bamboo growing through the holes of the flatbed.

"The passenger door opens, but I'll climb in."

Amara shimmies her hip against the heavy door and squeezes inside. Dust and dirt cover the seat. Eskedare dives headfirst through the open window, her face landing in Amara's lap, and they laugh as she twists her legs beneath the wheel.

Eskedare gazes through the broken windshield and tosses Amara a map. Her lips vibrate like an engine roar, and Amara laughs. Eskedare's eyes shine bright and playful. "Where to?"

Amara unfolds the torn map across her legs and runs her palm along the creases with care.

"We're here." Eskedare points at the map. "And we've got a full tank of gas."

Eskedare's eyes search Amara's face for an opening, a crevice, a place to take hold of her imagination, to move beyond the broken truck and rusting metal into a place of movement and possibility. All they must do is squint their eyes, unhinge their thoughts, and unfold for the adventure to begin. And there it is. A smirk, followed by a laugh, a whoop even. Amara returns to the map, her eyes searching the swaths of green forest. Eskedare inhales something she cannot name. Amara points to a location in the north: "The Simien Mountains. That's where Miss Eshe is from. Let's go there."

Eskedare yanks the stick shift into reverse, then into drive, and soon they're howling as they imagine crashing through the fence and onto the open road. The scent of eucalyptus and mango blows through the windows. They stop at a lookout on the shoulder and hold hands as they approach the rim. Eskedare pulls Amara off the ledge, and they dive together into the deep valleys and roll into the mountains. Afterward, Eskedare bestows gifts from the glove compartment on Amara's lap: a picnic of stale biscuits and flat cola.

On the way back, they drive into the sun and pull their visors down. The truck lurches through tall feather-headed grass, and when they park, a bird lands on the hood and pecks at fallen seeds.

"Next time, you drive."

Before leaving, Eskedare writes their initials in the dust of the dashboard.

That night, an engine turns over in Eskedare's dreams. Clouds of exhaust surround the bed and infect her sleep. She trips over shadows, runs past sleeping dogs, closed storefronts, and the broken bank machine. She tumbles into the smell of gasoline, breaks through the barbed-wire fence, slinks by men smashing bottles on rocks, until she sees Amara by the truck, waiting. Eskedare charges toward her at full speed and awakes to the engine booming in her ears.

ॐ

JUSTINE

Driving home from the Emirates Palace, sand gusted across the highway and a mattress blew off a truck and landed in the middle of the road. The corniche was dense with fog, and Justine was anxious to get home and put the night behind her. Her head angled forward as she gripped the steering wheel and peered into the limbs of palm trees sweeping across the orange charcoaled sky.

Without warning, a figure sprang from the meridian in front of her—arms pumping, legs sprinting, a dress billowing across the highway. Justine swerved, pressed on the horn. The woman catapulted forward, avoiding a collision, but in the rearview mirror Justine watched the woman lose her balance, stumble, and fall into a concrete barrier along the shoulder. Justine fumbled for the hazards, terrified but also furious. She pulled over and got out of the car, her jellied legs trembling, and as she approached the figure face down on the tarmac, she berated herself for her night at the Emirates Palace, the martini, the hours spent in a stranger's hotel room. Please, don't let it be a horror that cannot be undone, and as she neared, she saw the tangled legs move. Oh, thank God. But then the figure froze, aware of her presence.

Justine bent over the woman, only it was a girl, not much older than Wren. She needed to call an ambulance. 911. But that was not the number, and her mind raced in front of her searching for emergency numbers memorized like mantras since childhood.

What if this were Wren? She must bring the girl to a hospital, the one across the street from her building.

"Are you alright? You didn't even look!" She was trying to speak calmly, but there was frenzy and blame in her voice. "We need to go to the emergency room. It's not far."

"No . . . no hospitals. No doctors." The girl slid away from her, got up, and then faltered.

Justine followed the girl's gaze to a blue bench at a bus stop. "Look, I don't think the buses are running."

The girl shrunk from Justine's stare, frightened. Justine was aware of them both being alone on the highway, together in a country that belonged to neither of them. The hazard lights cut through the fog and strobed across their bodies.

And a part of Justine wanted to leave, to let this girl go into the mysterious atmosphere of the storm, to wait all night on that bus stop bench, but then she thought of Wren and her mind softened. "I don't think the bus will come until morning, and I can't just leave you here. My daughter's away. You can sleep in her room." Justine stood up and extended her hand; an offer, an order impossible to refuse.

On the drive home, neither of them said a word, but she could hear the girl breathing. Her presence had a weight and volume that filled the cabin of the car, and Justine felt her desire to escape and was tempted to pull over and let her go, but what kind of person turns a young girl out into the night after almost killing her on the highway? No, she must give her a place to sleep for the night, and tomorrow she'd bring her to the doctor.

In the parking garage, the yellow lights flickered against the low ceilings of the sub-basement, and the smell of leaking oil lingered in the damp air. Justine illuminated the basement with her phone and headed toward the elevator banks. The beam swept across an abandoned BMW in the corner covered in dust. Before she'd arrived, people had recounted the parking lots of orphaned cars signaling the sudden firing and expulsion of expats. The girl lingered and stalled behind her, but Justine waved her along, shepherding her into the elevator.

In the dark kitchen, Justine filled a glass with ice water as the girl stood motionless, waiting. The light of the refrigerator spilled into the room and illuminated the stranger. She was younger than Justine imagined. And tall. She wore a blue dress with yellow flowers and a small purse strapped across her chest. Cornelius jumped onto the kitchen table and meowed. Justine watched as the girl ran her fingers along his back, and his spine arched in pleasure beneath her touch. A birthmark, like baby's breath, marked the girl's hand, and without thinking, Justine reached out to touch it.

"I know you. You're the girl from the bus station. The bathroom."

The girl froze, and she assessed Justine in the dim light, calculating if she was a woman she could trust.

"It's okay. I can help. I know someone at the embassy. I'll call in the morning."

The girl's eyes turned glassy, and Justine thought she might cry.

"Let's get you to bed."

Justine walked down the hall with the ice water, and the girl followed. She flipped on the light in Wren's room. An oversized, stuffed lion looked down from a top bunk, and across an entire wall Wren had painted a mural of a girl. Stenciled above her head:

NOT ALL WHO WANDER ARE LOST, and in cursive across her blue tulle skirt: WILD & FREE.

A mess of watercolors, markers, paper, and glue covered her desk. The girl approached the table and ran her fingers over the brushes and paper.

"She likes to paint."

Justine smoothed the covers on the bottom bunk. "The sheets are clean, and I think there are some fresh toothbrushes in the bathroom drawer." Justine rummaged through Wren's closet and found some large pajamas, which she folded and left at the end of the bed. It was awkward to see each other in the light, and the girl shifted her weight beside the bed, eyes watchful, as Justine dragged the curtains across the terrace door.

"Tomorrow, we'll have a big breakfast. Everything will be better with sleep."

Justine pulled down the blackout shades, undressed in the dark, and slipped beneath the covers. Seeing Sean and Wren happy without her, combined with the atmosphere of the storm, had put Justine on edge. The night left her feeling complicit and responsible for the misery of others; she'd done reckless things.

Work. It was the only thing that could reliably rescue her and get her back on track. An open Sunday where she could devote hours to research and preparing her presentation. Before drifting off to sleep, Justine found herself hoping the girl would disappear, slip out of her apartment before daybreak, and be gone.

DOUNIA

Guests gathered in the living room suite to bless the newborn, repeating the hadith "Paradise is under the feet of the mothers." The girl was welcomed with fanfare and celebration, gifts of gold coins, toys, and clothes were presented, and the lace-shorn cradle was displayed proudly in the middle of the majlis, a rebuke of Dounia's lie.

Meanwhile, Dounia slept in fancy bedclothes between purple silk sheets in the adjoining room. Her mother, who had come from Riyadh, slept beside her and served her chicken broth from her grandmother's family recipe, a soup cooked and passed between women for generations. Her mother held her hand, and together they watched daily life unfold outside their window: a laundry truck arrived, men in green uniforms stacked white sheets wrapped in plastic onto hand dollies, a small woman dashed across the empty parking lot. Beneath her cloak, high heels.

"Look at those red shoes," said her mother.

Occasionally, a nurse entered with Qadira, but already the mother and infant shared a mutual dislike. Qadira Ibrahim rejected her nipple, pounded her breasts with tiny fists, and stomped her feet against her stomach. Dounia winced in pain, her breasts tender and the incision sore. Dounia observed the glances between the nurses and her mother, but instead of practicing patience, she rebuttoned her nightgown and instructed the nurse to give the baby a bottle. She heard the hush in the other room when the baby was returned unfed, the whispers and concerns for her wellness, how the baby had Basma's nose.

Dounia's incision oozed, and when she looked beneath the sheets, she saw a loose stomach stuffed into a diaper, a yellow-stained bandage where her hip might've been. Sitting up was an ordeal, and she refused to look in a mirror. But her mother got her out of bed, supported Dounia's arm, and they meandered the hall-ways, past the rooms brimming with confections, balloons, and vases of long-stemmed roses, past the green industrial couches in the waiting room, beyond the central clock with roman numerals. Dounia drank sugary tea and ate salted popcorn from the café.

Her mother never mentioned Dounia's lie. Never asked why her daughter would do such a thing. Never questioned naming the baby Qadira Ibrahim. But the silence of their private room held the bocce balls of that Paris afternoon, her mother's warning, Dounia's imperious response, her mistake. Dounia wanted her mother's love to return, to dock inside her as it had when she was a child, but Hamed, Basma, and her newborn daughter were her family now, and never had she felt so lonesome.

FLORA

Flora found her name in the rows of cardboard signs held up by drivers. Raj, a young South Asian man in a pressed shirt, took her suitcase, and together they walked across the parking lot. Wet heat, the sun hidden behind a dirty sky. Wind carrying dirt and sand blew across the pavement and stung their faces.

"A dust storm. Not too bad."

Raj pressed the key, and an electric beep identified the boxy maroon Range Rover. He opened the hatch and wiped down her suitcase with a damp cloth before tucking it in the back. She felt self-conscious, aware of the dirt stains and scuffed wheels against the car's immaculate interior. She headed to the passenger seat.

"Miss, you sit in the back. There's water for you in the console."

Flora saw the judgment behind his smile. She should've worn the purple dress. As they pulled out onto the highway, he played Indian music from his iPhone over the speakers. She took in the glistening asphalt, roads with red taillights, fast cars with dim interiors. No potholes, no open windows, no mouthfuls of dust. Palm trees and sand. Sprinklers swayed across the grass meridians.

"It'll take a little over five hours," said Raj. "We drive northeast and then west along the Gulf. You should sleep. I'm a good driver, don't worry."

———

Flora awoke to Raj singing along to his music. They were traveling along the water, which appeared turquoise and grey beneath thick storm clouds. A scruff of purple wildflowers lined the shore. Occasionally, Raj shouted out the name of something, but she couldn't understand what he was saying. The shoreline, once a comfort, was now a source of agony. The storm. Datu. Her inability to hold on. She could feel his wet body slipping against her torso, her arms thrashing through the chaos in search of his foot, hand, or ankle. Remorse sickened her, and she was thankful for the brutal desert out the other side.

They turned off the highway and onto a sand road leading to a makeshift guard station. Raj waved, and they entered the residential area, pink-and-white mansions under construction on desert lots. At the far end of a row of houses they took a right and then another right. A compound wall surrounded the house, and Raj opened the gate with a remote, pulling into a circular parking area beside several other cars. Raj called someone on his phone, speaking in Hindi, and turned to her. "We are here. Welcome. I'm picking up Miss Dounia in the morning. She's coming home with the baby. Your room is ready."

Raj led Flora into the house. Light spilled into the cavernous foyer and refracted through a red chandelier infusing the hall with a rosy glow. She followed Raj down a marble staircase into the basement, where he deposited her things outside a door and left her.

The room was clammy from the air-conditioning, and she fumbled for the light. A windowless room, narrow and small. An adjoining bathroom with a shower stall, toilet, and a single glass pane at dirt level above the sink. Everything was new: the twin mattress wrapped in plastic, a set of sheets with cardboard still intact. A stack of pale yellow uniforms wrapped in cellophane waited on the chair like gifts. There was even a small television at the end of her bed, its electrical cord hanging loose—no socket in sight. She stretched the crisp sheets over the mattress. A stray feather floated from the pillow. She tried on her uniform and admired the rounded white collar before taking a selfie to send to Pia, but once she looked at the picture, she knew there was no way she could send it. Pia lived in a home in Mindanao with only a hot plate to cook on, no TV. Instead, she took a picture of herself in her nightgown against the white wall and texted it with prayer and heart emojis.

——

That night Flora couldn't sleep. She located the postcard—an image of a secluded beach flanked by rock cliffs and turquoise green water in El Nido—a last-minute purchase from the Manila airport. She peeled adhesive from the plastic sleeve encasing one of her uniforms and used it to tape the image above her bed. On the back she wrote a note to herself: "Forgive and you will be forgiven. Soon you'll have a new life waiting."

ZEINAH

Fifteen women sat on grass mats in the dirt as Umm Humra reviewed the rules the female morality police were to enforce. Infractions punishable by fines, lashes, the biter, or worse. Outside, every woman was required to wear a thick "shield" to camouflage her female form. The garment covered the chest and stomach and fell below the knees. On top of the "shield," women needed to wear a two-layer niqab: the first translucent and the second black to cover all facial features. Women could not reveal their eyes or wear lipstick, blush, eyeliner, or makeup of any kind. And shoes: no heel, no colors, no straps.

ISIS was building an Islamic utopia, and there was no smoking, no music, no social media. They should stop people on the street and test their knowledge of prayers, fasting, and the hijab. If they were met with resistance, there was one simple question: "Will you obey or disobey?"

As they learned to dismantle and clean their guns, the emira walked among them conjuring a dream of sisterhood, identity, and meaning: "You are serving Allah through your duty as a wife and mother." Zeinah wanted to ask her about Omar's request for birth control, but she worried this might get him in trouble and decided to wait. At the end of the day, the emira gave the Arab-speaking trainees a pamphlet in Arabic to read: *Women of the Islamic State: Manifesto and Case Study*.

It was a Wednesday evening, not too hot, when Zeinah leafed through the stapled pages of the manifesto, apparently authored by women, promising liberation through the proper practice of Islam. The pamphlet promoted oneness of Allah on earth and in heaven and targeted IS jihadist women already living in the region and female recruits from the Gulf. Women should serve as wives and mothers, lead a "sedentary" lifestyle to anchor the family. Zeinah was skeptical.

But the Al-Khansaa Brigade promised something else—liberty, even if it meant the surveillance of others. The organization seemed to be a loophole in a sexist system, granting women agency, freedom, and status in the resistance. The women in the brigade were political, learning to use guns and patrolling the streets in partnership with their husbands in manifesting the vision of the caliphate. And in some cases, the women seemed more radical than the men, aspiring to embody a mujahedeen family and insisting their husband be frontline fighters. The emira had circulated ISIS pamphlets featuring women wielding AK-47s with captions praising their sisters for avenging their religion.

She felt a strange sense of sisterhood and camaraderie with these women, but she questioned the nature of this connection. It could be so many things: her loneliness; the trauma and violence that had befallen her brother, her family, her city, and everyone she knew; meeting women from places she'd seen only in movies or read about in books; a feeling that her life was expanding after so many months of contraction. But it was more than that. She felt united with these women based on their shared faith and Islamic heritage—something she hadn't really considered much before.

Then there was Omar. For her entire life, religion had been about holidays, family, and food. She'd dismissed God as a superstition from the past, a belief that comforted fearful people unwilling to face the void revealed by science. But Omar's faith moved her. His commitment to Ummah, to building a community around faith, to a cause greater than himself, seemed to anchor his life in meaning. She'd never considered God as something alive, something to be in communion with. Prayer was not a duty but an encounter. It was a simple and profound idea, but something she'd somehow missed and now found herself tilting toward.

The caliphate was a pledge to reclaim what was theirs, but Zeinah found the details antiquated and nonsensical. Beyond the role of women, there were many contradictions. ISIS called for the destruction of heritage sites, denounced scholarship and culture that their Muslim ancestors in Iraq and Syria had birthed. And since when was knowledge a product of "the West"? This region laid the intellectual foundation for modern humanity. The manifesto seemed to argue that "knowledge" distracted people from their relationship with God. How could that be? The notion that knowledge and faith were contradictory was outdated, and she began to wonder who wrote these pages. But she was grateful to be thinking about these things and loved her days outside with the women, feeling part of something larger than herself.

And yet. She allowed the pages to fall into her lap and took in her bedroom, the abandoned apartment of an Assad official, a person who had the sense and the means to leave. Was embracing the brigade, Omar, and God desperate attempts at survival? And if so, was that such a crime? Beneath all her swirling thoughts and confusion lay Sultan. Her brother, who'd been an early revolutionary against Assad. Before the Arab Spring. Before the Islamic State. Murdered. How much of her motivation was buried in the silence around that loss, in a desire to finally be free of her family's heartbreak, to believe in something, to do anything other than hide. And she didn't know whether to feel pleased or disgusted with herself.

On Thursday, the women were escorted to an arbutus grove and squared off in front of trees, their branches maimed and trunks stripped bare. The emira stood with her legs apart, cane in hand, and hollered for the lashings to commence. Zeinah's first swat landed on the tree with a half-hearted thud. The emira's commands grew more insistent, but Zeinah could not focus and instead imagined the possible and absurd infractions of trees: fruit on their boughs, naked roots exposed, their shameful trunks knotted and swollen. She imagined the trees muttering to one another, and Zeinah lost her nerve, her cane went slack. The commander approached Zeinah, snatched the switch from her palm, and beat the trunk hard and fast. They all heard the swish and crack, the sound of a whip beating the tree over and over again.

"That's how it's done."

Zeinah saw the trees as feeble, their dead foliage left a shabby blanket in the dirt. She handed the cane to the next woman in line. Her imagination had put her in peril; she needed to focus her anger into the training. She respected the women who'd traveled from all over the world to express their faith in Islam. There was a revolutionary spirit and sense of community that was preferable to fear.

During her training at the Raqqa border, Zeinah took a selfie with her AK-47 and sent it to Omar. He responded immediately.

Now I have two little monsters 😻

ESKEDARE

The uncle stops paying money for the fields, and her mother joins a group of women making traditional crafts to sell at tourist stalls along the road. Eskedare keeps her mother company and watches the women sculpt clay figurines of Moses, Solomon, and David. She's told to sit beside the Gulf-return girl, the girl who returned home unwilling to speak. A girl gone mute. A girl, a woman, who now spends her days molding clay into scrolls, beards, and doves. A girl who scares Eskedare, whose silence invites the village to imagine what is unsaid. Eskedare moves further and farther away.

In the neighboring village, a chain-link fence overgrown with vines and blue flowers protects a squat building made of mud and painted with blue stars. Eskedare listens to the guides explain to tourists how this was once a Jewish village where Falashas lived.

The women in the co-op tell Eskedare how their mothers used to make dolls until the 1970s, when Takai Elias, a single woman from Wallaqa, created Jewish mementos to sell to tourists. Her success inspired the local government to celebrate the Black Jews of Ethiopia. That's when the women started sculpting rabbis with Torah scrolls and Wallaqa figurines.

Eskedare sculpts lions with crowns of blue stars, each with different facial expressions and headpieces, but when the head of the co-op discovers Eskedare has signed her name on the bottom of each figurine, he chucks them aside and calls them worthless.

One afternoon, a white woman and her friend emerge from a Jeep searching for the old synagogue in the village. Eskedare watches as the guide urges them back inside the car and insists on driving them, but the white woman in the traditional cotton dress, cowboy boots, and a big purse looks at Eskedare: "You, Bright Eyes, can you take us to the synagogue? I want to see your village."

Eskedare knows the way and leads the two ladies and their guide up the dirt road, through a maze of houses. Women and children stand in the open doorways and watch them pass, the children from the roadside follow not far behind, begging.

"You need to pick up this trash," says the white lady. "Why is this so dirty?!"

They walk through a half-built home, and Eskedare points to the limbs in the dirt: "Eucalyptus."

"Your English is very good," says the lady.

"She just wants money," complains the guide.

"I don't care," says the lady as she winks at Eskedare.

The guide yells at Eskedare in Amharic and says she better know where she's going.

Eskedare ushers them along the chain-link fence overgrown with tangled blue flowers and vines, opens the gate, and reveals a round and squat building made of mud. The women admire the blue stars painted on the wall and ask Eskedare to take their picture. Eskedare listens to the words of the guide. "This is an abandoned Jewish village. Three hundred Falashas used to live here until they walked to Sudan or were airlifted out to Israel as part of Operation Moses. 'Falasha' means 'wanderer.' They were not allowed to own land, so they produced textiles, ironwork, and crafts. Those who stayed converted to Christian Orthodoxy, but Jewish stars remain on many of the houses." He shows them old horns and animal skins, and with the flashlight on his phone, he illuminates paintings on the wall made with ash and natural dye. When they go outside, children greet them with baskets, jewelry, and pottery arranged on blankets.

The white lady puts one thousand birr in Eskedare's palm. "You, Bright Eyes, learn this story. Clean this place up. You'll make lots of money." But the white woman doesn't understand the guides own this site and take cuts from the stands they favor on the roadside. Eskedare could never create a route unless she gets permission from the guides and agrees to give them a large portion of her tips. And so that's what she does. She learns the words the guides use, asks her teacher about things she does not understand, and even talks to people about the Jews who left.

Now she has her own version of the story that she tells. But never will she bring the strangers to the field of blue stones and blue stars. Those milky stalks of pulp and angels in the dirt.

৵

JUSTINE

Wind and sand blew against the panes, but inside was an eerie stillness. Justine wrapped herself in a robe, and in the hallway, she felt the coarse wool of the runner beneath her feet. Outside Wren's door, she strained against the silence. She knocked; no one answered. She gripped the metal handle and entered.

The terrace door was open, and the sheer curtains trembled into the room. A dirty fog from the sandstorm hung in the air, misting her arms and legs with grit. Tight sheets. Folded pajamas.

"Hello . . . ?"

The curtains billowed and swelled as she approached the open door. On the terrace, the scent of dead geraniums and salt air filled her nostrils, and a layer of dust had accumulated on the cat cage and water jugs stored in the corner, but there was no sign of the girl. She was gone. Justine approached the terrace edge and grasped the railing. Her legs trembled from vertigo, and it seemed the temperature was dropping, but she forced herself to look down. On the street below, through the muddled fog, she saw the red lights of fire trucks flashing, and she whimpered as she imagined the worst: the girl pinwheeling down thirty-five flights and hitting the pavement.

Cornelius's high-pitched meow called her back from the ledge, and she reached behind the cat carrier for the cobwebbed creature, snuggling him into her chest, relieved to feel his heartbeat in her palm.

She paced from room to room with Cornelius in her arms. The truth was she did not know what happened to the girl, and now that she was gone, she wanted her back again. She threw on some stale workout clothes and grabbed her bag. In the elevator, she avoided her reflection in the mirrored walls and hurried past the security guards and doorman with her head down.

The sky was an eerie orange, and a high wind was blowing. Two women pushed past her, an atmosphere of intrigue in the air, and as she rounded the corner and headed west on Electra Street, she saw police cars and fire trucks blocking the roundabout, yellow tape sectioning off the sidewalk.

Clusters of people stood outside the building, and Alex, a fellow parent from the school who lived on the twenty-seventh floor, called Justine over. Thick blond hair blew across her face, and as Justine approached, she saw people were passing around a phone.

"Did you hear?" said Alex.

A woman Justine had never seen before chimed in: "A girl set herself on fire in the roundabout. The guy from the gas station filmed the whole thing and posted it online."

Justine felt wary and was unable to respond.

"I took a screen shot before the government took it down." Alex held out her phone for Justine to see. The girl stood in the middle of the roundabout, her floral dress aflame, her face stoic. Justine's legs buckled, and Alex steadied her. "Are you okay?"

The buildings swayed, and Justine thought she might be sick. "Is she . . . Did she survive?"

"No. When the fire trucks arrived it was too late. It happened early this morning. Apparently, the gas attendant was arrested.

But he's the only reason we know anything. Poor guy. You can't post stuff like that here. What was he thinking?"

Beyond Alex, Justine noticed a group of men who'd gathered around the police blockade. There were rumors and stories forming on the street. A woman—no, a girl—had burst into flames. A girl who hours before had been in her apartment, drank from her water glass, been in Wren's room. Her mind flashed to the girl's mother, and she wiped tears from her cheeks with the back of her hand.

Alex looked at her strangely but pressed on, "They're not messing around with security. And who can blame them? I don't know what that girl's story was, but she was probably some kind of foreign worker. There are labor issues, for sure, but who wants a revolution? We see how that worked out."

Revolution? Justine was still crouched beside the girl on the dark highway, still noticing her birthmarked hand, still a toothbrush, still Wren's pajamas for her to sleep in.

It was impossible to link the image on Alex's phone with the girl in her apartment. The girl she'd wanted gone. Her gaze traveled to the roundabout. There was the smell of ash and petrol in the air, and on her scalp, along her middle part, Justine could feel the sun burning through the haze.

DOUNIA

Raj had meticulously installed the car seat earlier in the day and now took the child from Dounia on the hospital curb, cradled her in his arms, and covered her face with kisses. Dounia had never seen him so effusive and at ease, and when he strapped the baby into the car seat, he sang to her in a language she did not understand. Dounia felt self-conscious and inept.

"Congratulations, ma'am. She's so healthy, so beautiful."

Dounia sat in the back beside Qadira, whose dark, unblinking eyes observed her. Dounia grew uncomfortable beneath the infant's gaze and smiled weakly. The child stretched out her arms, searching for a finger, a hand, but Dounia could not bring herself to touch the child, much less claim her as her own. She'd been hoping for some complication with the surgery, some reason for the doctor to retain her. She'd grown fond of her hospital room, the view out the window onto the parking lot, the green trays and white napkins, the metal carts rolling down hallways.

"Has Flora arrived?"

"Yes, ma'am."

"How does she seem?"

"Good. She's at home waiting for you both to arrive."

Yes, Flora could take care of Qadira Ibrahim, and Dounia's indifference toward the child would wane. She worried about the consequences of her deceit and wondered if Basma and Hamed would confront her or say nothing now that she was home, and which outcome might be worse. She felt her soft stomach, the pregnancy now impossible to fathom, a ghost. But for Basma and Hamed, the lie would be a scar, an unhinged public humiliation. No explanation would suffice.

"Is Hamed home?"

"Ma'am, he left for Doha yesterday. He'll return tomorrow."

Of course. How could she have thought otherwise? Hamed had already talked to Raj, told him how to respond to the child; his excitement had been rehearsed. She knew now that Basma would greet the baby with open arms, and Flora would never know. They would lockstep in their eagerness for a girl and ignore Dounia's deception. Her transgression, and any reason or rationale for its existence, would never be acknowledged or understood. She saw Raj's glances in the rearview mirror, knew they'd been speaking about her and found her peculiar and strange.

FLORA

All morning, Flora didn't hear a sound. The place seemed deserted. She wanted to explore, but she worried about the mother-in-law and the possibility of surveillance cameras. Later she heard a toilet flush, water running through the pipes. Certainly, it would be okay to find the nursery.

Flora found the baby's room on the second floor. Freshly painted walls, still tacky to the touch. Too plain for a baby, she thought. A rocking chair, a crib, and a dresser huddled in the middle of the room, away from the walls. Like her pillows and uniforms, the crib mattress and changing pad were still wrapped in plastic. No pictures, no toys, no sheets, no blankets. Inside the drawers, no diapers, no creams, no clothes.

The adjoining bathroom was empty. No toilet paper.

She moved the nursing chair to the window with a view of the desert and pushed the dresser to the wall. The plastic wrap stuck to her hands as she crushed it into a tight ball and watched it unfurl on the floor. No trash can.

The house, while grand, was unfinished. Wires stuck out from the ceiling and walls, and Flora imagined a crawling baby grabbing those black tentacles. And they needed more rugs. A child could crack her skull on these tile floors. And dust was everywhere. Earlier she'd felt crumbs and food particles beneath her feet in the kitchen. The house was bigger than she expected, and the driver's spotless car intimidated her. There was the tension

of big plans left unfinished: large machinery parked in the yard,
tubs filled with dried clay, tarps shading dying plants. Flora gazed
across the expanse of sand. Tire treads led to a collection of metal
canisters, rolls of wire, orange fencing. No trees, no grass, no flowers, just dirt and desert. The only shade she saw slid under a roof.

Her phone pinged.

> Got a job making wigs! Kinda fun. All different colors
> and styles. This is my first one . . .

A black bob with bangs sat on a Styrofoam head. There was a
cup of water in the picture, and her heart swerved as she imagined
Pia's lips on the glass, her fingers massaging a scalp, not her own.

ZEINAH

So much skin to cover. Gloves once passed down from grand-mothers and aunts and tucked into drawers were now daily sta-ples—gloves bundled like black eggs and slipped into handbags, stockpiled by the door. Black hems needed to brush across rubble streets while walking, disguise swollen ankles in the heat. Hems washed by hand at night in bathroom sinks. A veil with a hem that needed to fall flat across the shoulders, breasts, and back. The silhouette must be formless, a deflating black balloon skimming the surface, attached like a fishing line to a husband, father, or son. Zeinah, dressed like the women she surveilled, walked the streets with her gun and monitored the lengths of hems, uneasy in her new role and thankful no one recognized her.

———

Despite the dust in the air that morning, the city opened up to Zeinah, and for the first time in months, she strolled the sidewalks and lingered in front of shop windows. Women and children moved out of her way. Her gun, once ominous, provided the relief of safety, and she roamed the streets without a chaperone.

Sour garbage spilled into the roads, and everywhere build-ings crumbled beneath the low sky. She eyeballed bread lines and scouted for infractions: shops open during prayer time, failure to pay utility bills, surfing unapproved sites at internet cafés. Random searches through women's bags yielded lipsticks and phones containing music and inappropriate photographs. She texted Omar throughout the day.

> Confiscating lipsticks. What purpose does this serve?

> All lives have but a single meaning #onenessofAllah

———

Perhaps it was true: all progress contained seeds of violence, but she wondered if she was willing to serve this vision, if she was capable of the sacrifice, the torment.

These were the thoughts she was having as she stood across the street from the pharmacy watching women and their chaperones come and go, dissecting their forms for curves, decorative flourishes on their abayas, or the slightest hint of oval shadows beneath their veils. A woman stepped down from the curb, revealing a pop of pink. Zeinah approached, tugged on the woman's cloak, and revealed her open-toed sandals.

Zeinah grabbed the woman by the arm. "What is the meaning of this?"

The woman tried to pull away.

Zeinah held firm. "You need to cover yourself. You think you can trick God?"

"I'm not trying to trick anyone."

"That's right. Because you can't."

A crowd had gathered around them, and the woman's chaperone stepped forward. He was maybe fifteen, probably her younger brother. "Please. She won't do it again. We live next door. We were in a rush. See?" He held out the woman's gloved hands. "She's covered."

She wanted to let them go, issue only a warning, but people

were watching, and down the street she saw a woman from the brigade.

Zeinah squeezed the woman's arm, surprised by her own strength, and hailed a passing cab. Ignoring the boy's pleas, she opened the cab door and shoved the woman inside.

At the police headquarters, Zeinah and the woman waited in silence in front of a folding desk with an open ledger. The clerk returned to the desk and hung a key with frayed twine on a hook.

"Infraction?"

"Open-toed sandals. Pink," said Zeinah, proud to report the infraction.

"Name?"

The woman hesitated.

"Name!"

"Rima Obani."

Zeinah recognized the name.

"Address?"

As the woman recited her address, Zeinah recalled a childhood classroom, the smell of acrylic paint, rolling across a green rug.

"Am I free to go?" asked Zeinah.

"No. You need to wait for Umm Humra. Twenty lashes," said the clerk.

"I've never been called in for anything."

"If you're not quiet, you'll get ten more," said the clerk.

"But—"

Zeinah grabbed Rima's hand. "Shhh!"

Rima held on to Zeinah and whispered, "Please. I'll pay. Whatever you want."

Umm Humra led Zeinah and Rima into an empty room and closed the door. "Let's see your face."

The woman removed her veils and revealed rouged cheeks and red lips.

Umm Humra grunted. "Lipstick couldn't help that face. Five more lashes."

Rima began to cry.

"Turn around and kneel," commanded Umm Humra. Rima walked around in a circle, dazed from shock.

Zeinah rubbed her gloved palms together in agitation.

"Come on, let's go. We have other things to do," said Umm Humra.

Rima fell to her knees.

"Head bowed. Arms in front."

She complied.

"As a Muslim, you have a responsibility to God to encourage good and prevent the bad. It is up to us women that everything is covered. Curves, flesh—anything exposed of the female body creates lust."

Zeinah wanted to get this over with.

Umm Humra grabbed the cane from the corner and approached Zeinah. "Arms out."

"But I don't . . . I've never."

"Arms out. Palms up."

Zeinah raised her arms and received the cane lengthwise across her hands. She'd held a cane only once before, during practice when she'd flogged the tree trunks. She'd imagined the tree as a delinquent, something absurd, not this.

"Bring the cane back in the air, arm taut. The blows need to be sharp and quick."

Outside a wild dog barked. Zeinah bit her tongue to keep from crying.

The first blow landed on the back of Rima's head and threw her forward.

"Get up," said Umm Humra.

The woman resumed her kneeling position. "Please, stop."

"That was a little high. Aim for the back or buttocks. It should be fast. Four lashes a second. Otherwise, it is cruel." Umm Humra took a step back. "Okay, let's go."

Zeinah extended her arm and came down in quick succession on the body in front of her. She counted to herself, blocking out the moments of impact and Rima's cries. When finished, her arms shook—adrenaline throbbed through her limbs. She brought her feet together and formally presented the cane across her palms to Umm Humra.

"Very good, Zeinah." Umm Humra returned the cane to the corner of the room. "See her out." The door closed, and the two women were now alone.

Zeinah bent down to help, but Rima pushed her away and struggled to her feet. "I know who you are. Bringing shame on yourself and your family. I'll tell everyone what you've done."

Zeinah felt humiliated, and she found herself reciting things she'd learned in the brigade: "Will you obey or disobey?" She continued, feeling strangely emboldened. "It's not that complicated. Follow the rules and you won't have any problems."

ESKEDARE

Meskel, her mother's favorite holiday. Yellow flowers bloom across the hills and meadows, and for days people in towns, villages, and cities drag cactus branches sprinkled with sedge and daisies into central squares and open fields to create demeras, cone totems in honor of Saint Helena, who was inspired by a dream to build a bonfire whose smoke led her to pieces of the true cross.

In the morning, Eskedare and Amara wander the hills collecting armfuls of meskel flowers and bunches of tall grasses to throw on the fire that will be lit that evening. In the afternoon, they put on white dresses and headscarves with bright green borders and walk together beneath a bright umbrella to join the procession to the field, where they spend the afternoon singing hymns, dancing, drumming, and praying in preparation for their renewal and delivery from sin.

That night, her mother gives Eskedare a flaming eucalyptus torch to light the fire. White smoke billows and swells toward the sky as the cactus wood sparks and flames. Young children run round and round the fire, howling and laughing, but Eskedare and Amara stand silently beside the demera holding hands, feeling the heat flush and sting their faces until they must step back, and back, and back, until the fire is as tall as a fir tree rising high above them. And when the fire rages, her mother leads Eskedare and Amara up the hill to watch, saying, "The fire greets our eyes just as it must have met Helena's."

It's the time of year when her mother feels part of something bigger, something grand, and she uses that word, "eternal." Eskedare is not sure what it means, but she loves her mother when she drinks honey wine, when she seems almost like a child, singing freely, inhaling prayers, lighting sticks and planting them around their feet.

For hours, the three of them lie on the hillside watching the demera glow and spark against the sky. They inhale the smell of burning wood and find the many colors in the flames—oranges, pinks, reds, yellows, and blues. And when the fire goes out, they search for their names in the stars, and Eskedare asks her mother to tell Amara the story of her birth in these hills, the distant patch of orange on the mountain peak, further and farther away.

Eskedare falls asleep on the hill in Amara's lap, to the sound of her mother's voice singing old folk songs. In the pale chalk light of dawn, her mother wakes them, and together, they return to what remains of the demera in the field, gather warm ash from the fire, and mark each other's forehead with a cross.

JUSTINE

There was the silence of aftermath. Justine lingered absently in front of storefronts on Electra Street, her mind reeling, as she stared into shop windows selling cell phones and calling cards, light fixtures and bulbs. Men lined up outside a Western Union to send money home. The image on Alex's phone, the girl on fire, the girl who just hours ago she'd put to bed in Wren's room; the girl now dead. There was a heightened atmosphere of fragility on the streets; the roads were deserted, and people on the sidewalk spoke in hushed tones. Everyone stood at attention, waiting to see what would happen.

The call to prayer rang out across the city, not like a church bell marking down the hours, measuring productivity and reminding Justine of her brief time on earth, but a spiritual toll calling them to something greater within themselves. And as the words of the prayer echoed across the city, Justine tried to imagine what it would feel like to surrender, to submit, to accept the treachery of being human.

She wandered through the superblocks, the image of the girl on fire arising and receding in a perpetual loop as her mind tried to sort through the details, the horror, to make sense of what had happened. She tried to ground herself in the details of the neighborhood. There was the electric door of the emergency room and the row of blue wheelchairs. There was a woman sweeping up flour in the dukkan. There was a floral quilt hung over a line on a terrace. There were men's shoes displayed on the sidewalk outside the cobbler's store. And there was her phone, like a rock from a river, in her bag. She could not bear to look. There was the sound of another fire truck. A police car passed.

Cartons of chisels and pipes stood outside a junk shop, and Justine wandered inside. Her hands skimmed over objects: a telephone cord, a brass bell, a Bible. She randomly opened to a page. She could not bring herself to read the words, but the small typeface, the thin vellum, the large capital letters that began paragraphs, even the frayed silk ribbon brought a kind of comfort. Everything inside her wanted to scream, *A girl has set herself on fire*.

She thought about her mother, dead three years, but still the person she reached for. Like everyone she knew, she'd punished her mother for her own disappointments, blamed her for the inevitable pain of living, but she was the person she wanted to talk to now, and she imagined the toll of the long-distance call traveling across oceans and phone lines, ringing and ringing.

Justine walked beside the broken walls of the local mosque, now a hedge of shadows, and crossed the vacant lot of bus bays outside the bus station. She should've checked on the girl in the middle of the night. She would've checked on Wren. Passing through the sliding doors and plastic curtains, she entered the main hall. Inside, storefronts rolled open, hot oil popped corn in a red carnival cart, and thick blue dresses with rhinestones hung beside abayas in a dress shop window.

Justine stood at the Cinnabon counter and ordered a pastry. Sitting at a table in the empty food court, she traced the frosting surrounding the Cinnabon on her plate and wondered what she was doing here in this bus station, in this country. The smell of fried dough, sugar, and oil turned her stomach, and when she licked the icing from her finger, she tasted nothing. She wanted to go into the restroom and see if there was an attendant she could talk to, if there was any information about the girl, where she was from, or something about her mother.

A security guard approached the table. "I'm sorry, ma'am, but you need to leave. All offices and establishments are closing due to government orders."

Yes, this is a big deal, she thought, and she picked up her orange tray and tossed the Cinnabon in the trash. On her way out, she passed the florist and nodded to the man returning his black buckets of tulips, roses, and peonies to the cooler.

FLORA

Flora awoke to a crying infant.

"I think it's hungry." Raj deposited the wrapped bundle, the weight of a melon, into Flora's arms. "Madam's tired and said she'll meet you in the morning. There are bottles and formula in the bag. I'll bring in everything from the car. So many gifts and clothes."

Flora called after him, his footsteps already on the stairs: "Excuse me, but there are no diapers, wipes, or creams."

The child had a square face and red cheeks damp from screaming. Its body stretched and tensed across Flora's torso, lips searching for sustenance. Flora's breasts swelled and tightened, and without thinking, she fumbled with the buttons on her shirt. She released her bra and guided her breast to the baby's lips. She'd heard of other women whose breasts had not gone dry. It seemed impossible, but the mouth latched on, the jaw sucked, and Flora felt her milk let down, not like a summer downpour, but like a light rain. Tears flowed down Flora's cheeks and pooled into her ears; her other breast leaked a small moon. She hugged the child to her chest and closed her eyes, transported to a time before. The time of Datu. Hot afternoons and black shade beneath trees. The crack of dried seaweed and leaves underfoot. Flora opened her eyes; the world had shifted. Sacks of concrete, buckets of loose stones, and the sun setting behind the distant mosque were now part of slow-motion days. It all came back to her now. The marrow of connection a child brings into the world, the sweet meat.

She checked the diaper and discovered she was holding a girl. Flora hummed and watched the sturdy jaw go slack to reveal her swollen nipple. The infant was relaxed and calm, in a post-feed haze. I must never do that again, she thought. She removed the pink mitts from the hospital, and the child reached out and gripped the branch of Flora's finger before drifting off to sleep.

Two years. I can do this.

ZEINAH

That night, Zeinah couldn't sleep. The flogging was not her fault. It was the rules; they needed to be communicated more clearly to the public. If a woman committed an infraction, the consequences were her choice, her responsibility. Guilt did not reside with the person enforcing the regulations. Zeinah worked through the night making flyers.

> Infidelity/adultery—public stoning
> Running away when caught—60 lashes
> Breastfeeding in public—biter or 60 lashes
> Form-fitting abaya—20 lashes
> Colored/heeled shoes—20 lashes
> Lipstick—5 lashes
> Noncompliance when caught—5 lashes

DOUNIA

For the first time in nine months, Dounia was alone. Unable to sleep, she paced the cold marble floors, climbed up and down the staircase, and circled the steel island in the kitchen. During the day, she sank into the sofa and stared into the flat-screen TV playing soap operas on mute. Lavender air freshener pumped into the living room and settled on the furniture. A life gone numb from air-conditioning—closed windows, locked doors. Let them bury me, she thought.

Raj appeared with a glass of water. "Hamed said you need to drink more water to breastfeed."

Hamed had left instructions; her body was a public space. The water would remain untouched. Upstairs, she heard Raj's footsteps and whispers with Basma. A silver platter on the coffee table displayed a pyramid of dark chocolates wrapped in purple foil left over from the wedding. They sat untouched, perfectly stacked, taunting Dounia for her foolish hopes and plans. Never would she eat dark chocolate again.

The wedding: five hundred women, most of them strangers. A banquet hall transformed into a Zen garden. Cherry blossoms flown in by the armful, $100,000 of petaled stems dropped into cut glass vases. An arbor of twined bark and rosebuds welcomed guests, and rocks inscribed with HARMONY, PEACE, and LOVE were given as parting gifts. When Dounia arrived at the Dream house, Basma had welcomed her with the rocks and their hopeful messages displayed on tables, counters, and windowsills.

And the juices. Lychee, lemon mint, grass, blood orange.

And the seeds of licorice encased in sugar.

And the monogrammed chocolates flown in from London.

And the qahwa made with cardamom from India.

And the milk from camels delivered from her uncle's farm.

The night of the wedding, she'd waited in a room with her mother and sister offstage. The discussion in the Tuileries Garden was a distant memory, and her decision to proceed felt like watching a ball roll into traffic. The muted lyrics from the Lebanese singer seeped through the walls. Guests, once names written in cursive on gold envelopes, were now women murmuring in the banquet hall, waiting for her appearance. Dounia heard her name announced over the loudspeaker and began to cry. Her sister wiped away the tears with the bottom of her dress; her mother remained silent. She did not say that it would be okay or that all brides are nervous. She did not whisper that her daughter could still change her mind.

Alone, Dounia walked out of the room and onto the stage. The spotlights blinded her, and she was unable to recognize her friends in the crowd. The runway stretched like a pier into unknown waters, into her future, and she stepped forward, finding her footing in her high heels, and strolled back and forth in her wedding dress, parading all the money, effort, and time the two families had invested in the union, while the older women trilled in their burqas and her friends snapped pictures on their phones. She walked the runway three times and then took a seat on the white couch on the stage, where she sat for two hours as young eligible women danced on the platform, signaling their availability to matchmakers. Extended family, friends of her aunts and cousins, and people she'd never met waited in line to greet her. Amid the kisses, squeezes, and clasped hands, she couldn't recall anything whispered into her ears that night, and she sometimes wondered if even one person had said anything that mattered and, if so, what it might have been.

Her mother and Basma joined her on the couch, and they waited for the men to arrive. The anticipation was tiresome, and she found herself impatient for their arrival so the evening could end. Finally, the doors opened, and the ardah commenced. Fifty men with swords and drums entered in colorful embroidered coats, leather ammunition belts strapped across their chests. Ibrahim emerged carrying the Saudi flag, and beside him was Hamed. The men recited poetry to the beat of drums and danced for her. She'd never forget that moment; all tedium was erased, and she was flooded with a sense of belonging, possibility, and pride. She'd not been wrong. Hamed joined her on the stage, and the mothers disappeared. He held her hand, and she believed they would forge something private, a powerful love they could call their own once the spectacle was over.

Dounia wanted to ravage the girl she'd been, the naive child who led her into this life with false optimism. And that girl was everywhere in the world, in every country, city, and town, not just in Saudi——in malls, on farms, in uniforms, on podiums, and in courtrooms. This girl, this jinn, could distance even the strongest woman from herself.

ESKEDARE

"Seed." That's what Amara calls Eskedare.

Tall Amara with limbs like bent metal. She doesn't eat much, prefers things that live inside other things, things that need to be peeled or cracked, like eggs, oranges, and bananas. She eats nuts and walks around with pockets full of shells, littering the seats and floor of their truck with the casings of things.

"I like to get inside a thing." And Amara smiles until Eskedare blushes and looks away.

Amara has a way of saying things that fall like boulders on her mind. She stirs feelings backward and forward like batter on a hot pan. After years of being alone, here's another girl who wants to explore, where every day is a little life.

———

Eskedare loves the old bodies of rivers, the way she loves cows, the way she might love someone else one day. They hike to the site of sunken streams and map what was. They walk dry river-beds and recline in hollow basins. Silence floods the stones below them; they watch the departure of birds and the puffs of dust they leave behind, their calves barely touching. Spread out on dry boulders, they float downriver, sometimes hear a splash and feel the ripple of an imagined fish beneath their spines. Sometimes Amara drifts ahead and then returns to Eskedare bending over a carcass or half-formed thing in the sand. They linger and observe. Sometimes they chew stalks of grass, sometimes the trees shake their leaves like tambourines, and sometimes the sun sends up a flare and liquidates the sky. And sometimes on cold mornings they watch planes plow through the blue sky, carving trails for them to follow, until the paths break apart and fade away. And afterward, Amara heaves with the weight of something heavy on her mind and wanders off, alone.

———

It's Amara's seventeenth birthday, a Friday evening when people walk along dirt roads holding hands. Eskedare sweeps her hair back into a bun, the way Amara likes it—big eyes gleaming.

She wraps Amara's present in paper and tucks it into the waistband of her skirt. She's gathered thorns, stones, and seeds from the places they've been and strung them into a necklace. They meet at their favorite bend in the river, a curve whose muscle has begun to strengthen with spring rains.

When she gets down to the river, Amara seems different: her hair is wet and newly parted, her face has shifted as if to make room for something new. Soft currents circle their legs as they wade in the stream. Eskedare walks ahead in search of an arc in the riverbank to soothe herself down. Behind her, Amara sifts through rocks the size of mangoes and tosses the rotten ones aside. This is their favorite creek. Amara's birthday. The reason they are here. Eskedare glances back and swears she sees Amara's lips moving, talking to herself, but she cannot hear what she has to say.

Amara abandons the rock pile and wanders upstream, but her thoughts are elsewhere, and she does not see Eskedare waiting on the shore.

"Find any good ones?"

Amara drifts out of her trance and shrugs. "What about you?"

Eskedare points to a stack of small stones she's gathered. Amara sits beside her, but her eyes continue to drift away. Eskedare feels unsure about the necklace, and she fidgets with the remaining pebbles in her palms. But she wants to keep Amara close, so she retrieves the present from her skirt.

"Happy birthday."

Amara unrolls the slender package and regards the woven necklace in her palm.

"From all our favorite places."

Amara's chin points downriver, away from her. Eskedare sifts the riverbank between her fingers and waits for a word, anything. A flock of blue-winged geese flies overhead, and afterward, nothing moves.

"Don't you like it?"

Amara looks at Eskedare and threads her fingers through her hair. The part she drew disappears, and Amara becomes herself again. At last, her lips move, and her voice begins to sound: "My uncle says they're building soccer stadiums in Qatar. I'll work in a hotel. I leave next week."

Eskedare cries into the hollow between her mother's hips and enters a stalled time between now and Amara gone. Her fingers count down the days until her hands are stubs, paws unable to hold time, hold the girl.

Then, that day, that hour, that minute. Amara on the bus, her luggage roped to the roof; the jaws of two girls trembling.

❧

FLORA

Flora heard a brass bell and realized she was being summoned. She followed the sound up the stairs and paused outside Dounia's bedroom door.

"Flora!" Dounia waved her inside. "Welcome."

The young woman spread the covers flat around her and was propped up by pillows. She was big-boned and her features striking. Flora stopped at the end of the bed and, feeling awkward, folded her hands in front of her. "Thank you, ma'am."

"Call me Dounia."

"Yes, ma—Dounia." They both smiled.

"Yellow's a nice color on you, but that uniform—a little tight. Let me see. Turn around."

Flora moved slowly, self-conscious of the places where the uniform hugged her curves. On the back wall, Flora was confronted a flat-screen television on mute. Shaky cell phone video of a girl on fire in a roundabout played on repeat. Flora froze, shocked by the scene unfolding on the screen. The girl was Pia's age. She sensed Dounia watching behind her, and they were both silent, stunned in a liminal space of horror as they watched the girl burn. Neither of them moved, and then an anchor appeared on screen.

"Keep going," said Dounia.

Flora's eyes stung and her legs trembled as she returned to Dounia's gaze and was relieved to find comfort there. Yes, she saw it too, thought Flora. But Dounia reached for the remote, the screen powered off, and the moment between them vanished.

"I can see the lines of your underwear, beneath your buttocks, and the top button pulls across your chest."

Had the woman not seen what was on the screen?

"I left you three sizes. A larger one would be best."

"Yes, ma'am. I thought they were all the same."

"It's okay, give the others to Raj. He'll exchange them. And your hair . . ."

Flora's thick black hair fell below her shoulders.

"You'll need to always keep it back. I hate hair on furniture, left in sinks, and I don't want it in the food."

"Yes, ma'am."

Dounia patted the end of the bed, inviting Flora to sit down. "I hope you're happy here. You have what you need?"

"Yes, thank you."

"I don't know if . . ." She started again. "In the Gulf States, your employer is your sponsor. I'm responsible for you. Your job is to take care of the house and the baby. My job is to take care of you, make sure you're safe and that nothing happens."

Flora nodded. She'd heard all about the kafala system in her training.

"It's common practice for your employer to keep your passport safe. You can keep your phone for now unless there's a problem. I'd like lights out at nine thirty p.m. No gossiping with the other domestics or drivers in the neighborhood. No sneaking out at night or going to other people's homes. You understand, if anything happens to you, it would be my fault."

Flora shifted her weight on the bed and smiled. I think she's telling me what time to go to sleep, she thought. This woman who could almost be my child is telling me not to sneak out at night.

The neighborhood is a construction site. She's worried that I'm going to do something that will get her into trouble. Flora stopped herself. This line of bad thinking would only lead to problems. Perhaps these early-to-bed nights were just what she needed.

"Would you like to see the baby?" asked Flora. "She'll need to be put on a feeding schedule."

"I don't know if you saw all the formula I ordered. It's in the kitchen. I won't be breastfeeding. I'm not feeling well, and I need to rest. I don't want to manage anything. You're in charge."

Flora got up from the bed feeling both empowered and infantilized.

"Of course, ma'am. Just one thing, the baby. What's her name?"

Dounia slid beneath the covers. "Qadira. Ibrahim. Call her one or both. Call her what you like."

JUSTINE

Justine opened her laptop. The British Museum had granted Justine a VPN to circumvent the government blocks on the internet. An article about Daesh and the al-Khansaa Brigade cracking down on local women in Raqqa appeared in her feed. She opened a new tab and typed into the search bar: Abu Dhabi Foreign Worker Woman Self-Immolation. Images of domestic workers standing on balconies in pastel uniforms, huddled atop air conditioner units on the outside of buildings, and in body bags appeared on the screen. She scrolled through pages of X-rays: broken ankles, shins, and thigh bones of women trying to escape. Headlines announced employer violence toward domestic workers, the broken kafala system, a Filipina worker found guilty of murdering a child in her care. A woman later executed by the state. Pages and pages of news stories and reports of domestic work and modern-day slave labor.

New search: Ethiopian girl fire abu dhabi.

In Ethiopia, a teacher in 2011 had set himself on fire. She read on: "It was a decision that a life of humiliation, subordination, and betrayal is not worth living . . . a call to humanity, an appeal to the best in us, . . . a call to reject authoritarianism in all its forms." She hesitated and then pressed the images tab—the girl appeared, screen grabs from the gas attendant's video. Her heart pounded as she forced herself to confront the brutal and shocking act. She paused on a wide shot, her fingers trembling above the keys, the girl no longer recognizable in the flames.

She sat paralyzed in front of the screen, her mind and body mute. The low hum of the modem beside her, the air conditioner powering off. Thirty-five flights above the pavement, not one sound from the natural world, insulated and hermetically sealed. Sometimes she literally woke up inside a cloud, moisture condensing on the glass, tall buildings sprouting through the mist. But this morning, the world entered. Like a sudden gust of wind that bangs doors, scatters loose papers, and tips over vases, the girl had entered and was now gone, leaving only traces of her presence behind. On the bottom right of the image, beside the girl, her eye caught a blur of blue, and as she zoomed in, a water jug toppled on its side appeared. The kind everyone had delivered. Justine's mouth went dry. She pushed away from her desk and forced herself across the living room and down the hallway. With trepidation and dread, she entered Wren's room and approached the terrace door. She peered through the glass out to the balcony: one of the jugs was gone. The jug that carried the gasoline. The jug that poured . . .

The doorbell rang, jolting her out of her revelation, then rang again. Justine headed down the hallway. "Coming!"

Sammy, her favorite security guard, and the man in the brown suit stood in the hallway.

"Sorry to bother you, Justine, but we're talking to everyone," said Sammy.

"Come on in." Justine led them to the long wooden table in the living room. "Can I get you anything?"

"No, no," said Sammy.

"I'd love a glass of water. If it's easy," said the man in the brown suit.

* * *

In the kitchen, Justine tried to steady herself. She was just a woman getting a glass of water for the man in the brown suit. Leo, that was his name. Just make him feel comfortable, answer a few questions. She knew this man, Leo. He'd emailed her apartment layouts, paint colors, and schools for Wren. They'd flirted, and he'd pulled some strings and gotten her this coveted corner apartment on a high floor in a building where almost all the residents were working on the cultural district. He worked for the government and was in charge of overseeing expat workers on high-end contracts for the museum district: a fixer, a man who knew how to navigate cultural differences, who could get censored books into the country, a man who had what they called "wasta."

She returned with the glass of water, and she watched as he gulped it down in one go. "I was thirsty."

She laughed. "Would you like some more?"

"Oh, no, no."

Justine slid down into a seat at the table and watched as he reached into his soft briefcase and retrieved a yellow notepad and pen. He flipped to a blank page.

"We've talked to so many people today. Everyone in the building, and we started on two."

"Well, you're almost done."

"I'm sure you're aware of the incident at the roundabout . . ."

"Yes. Awful."

"Horrible, what happens to these girls. Usually it's jumping out of buildings, running into traffic . . . Anyway, we're asking everyone. Do you know anything? Remember seeing a young woman—they suspect Ethiopian—in the building last night? The gas attendant said he saw her leave from this building and cross the street."

"What do you know about her?" said Justine.

"Not much. Here on an illegal passport. Probably terrified of getting picked up by the police . . . turned over to the embassy. Those embassies can be a nightmare."

That's what she'd said to the girl, that she'd call the embassy.

Cornelius jumped into her lap and regarded the two men. He meowed, and she appreciated his protection. She ran her hand along his spine and rubbed his ears, recalling the girl's blue birthmarked hand in his fur . . . Antigovernment sentiment was a serious crime. Inflated rumors of censorship, surveillance, and imprisonment circulated in the expat community, but now she wondered if these stories were true. There was the British woman who'd been imprisoned for posting a photograph on Facebook of a car with Emirati license plates parked across two handicapped spaces.

She heard herself say, "Well, if I hear anything . . ."

"Call me." Leo tapped his card on the table.

"I don't need your card." Justine laughed. "I have your email and phone number." She escorted them out. "And good luck."

"We don't need that. There's surveillance footage throughout the building. From the parking garage on up. Elevators. Hallways . . . If she was here, we'll know where."

Justine's mind froze, and she smiled. "Of course. That's one of the things that makes this country safe."

———

In Wren's room, Justine steered the bristled head of the Dyson across the floor with focus and intensity. She switched off the vacuum cleaner and listened to the motor power down. Terror of her affiliation with the girl, of gossip accusing her of sympathy, perhaps even encouragement, for the act of protest, gripped her mind, and she entered a frenzied state of removing all evidence.

Her gaze landed on the water glass and, beside it, a pile of cash she'd failed to notice before. She didn't care how much it was; she didn't even bother to count it or wonder why the girl might have left it, before stuffing the money into her bra and heading out to the trash room in the hallway. The space reeked of sweet chemicals and rotten food. Her foot depressed the pedal on the wall, the metal bin door opened, and she flung the money down the chute, imagining the dirhams falling between floors and landing on torn trash bags.

DOUNIA

Dounia wanted to be swaddled, wrapped in duvets and held like her daughter. But unlike Qadira, who was pushing outward, becoming more alert and awake, a cocoon grew around Dounia, rough and fibrous. She could only imagine doing nothing. Even going to the bathroom felt impossible, and her urine was dark and smelled of fish. She drew further and farther away from people. Hamed would enter the room, and she would weep, unable to put words to the physical feeling that enveloped her.

When Hamed was gone, Raj lingered around the house and waited for a moment to approach: "Let's take Flora and the baby for a drive. Anywhere you want to go." But the thought of leaving her bed, sitting in the back seat of the car, the windows closed, more air-conditioning, led to fantasies of hurling herself out of the car, tires rolling over her torso, tread marks on her body.

When Flora entered with a tray of food, Dounia wanted to disappear from shame. Flora became her surrogate and made it possible for her to vanish. And what was the nature of her hibernation? What was it she could not bear? Just as she suspected, no one mentioned her lie or the fact that Qadira was a girl. No one showed any interest or curiosity about Dounia and what would cause her to do such a thing. The transgression had been struck from the record.

The thought of breastfeeding repulsed her, turned her stomach sour, and filled her with disgust. The thought of milk coming out of her nipples, those small lips sucking on her areola, induced nausea. Dounia's body was a site of demolition and bad reconstruction. Her stiches oozed, some had come out, and a thick pink scar was forming. Her breasts were hard, red, and engorged. Her stomach sagged from side to side when she moved in the middle of the night; she could not face her reflection in the mirror.

She deleted all her social media and refused to pick up the phone. She no longer checked her email, and like an abandoned buoy, she floated out to sea, losing contact with the world, becoming more and more distant. But some nights while she was out there adrift, she imagined her daughter cooing, and because the calls were faint, Dounia rested her ear against the black surface of the gulf between them and listened. Listened and then hummed—perhaps a lullaby, rocking them both to sleep.

ZEINAH

Umm Humra approved the flyers, and Zeinah spent the day posting them at bread markets, pharmacies, internet cafés, outside of mosques, and now the last one—her old neighborhood supermarket. It was a few minutes past curfew when a woman walked into the market with her husband. She recognized her uncle right away and knew from the woman's gait that he was with her favorite aunt, Miriam, her mother's sister.

He disappeared down the rice aisle, and Zeinah approached her aunt inspecting apples and placing the ripe ones in a basket. She selected a ripe apple before coming closer. "It's past curfew. Tell me what you want, and I'll get it. You need to get home."

Her aunt stopped what she was doing and took stock of her niece. Zeinah could not see her eyes, but she remembered them, remembered the marbles she rolled across her floors, the kitchen tablecloth she'd covered with textbooks while studying for exams.

"I'm not done shopping," said her aunt.

The aunt who had boycotted her wedding.

"I think you are."

Her aunt removed Zeinah's apple. "Everyone knows what you did. What meanness do you have planned for me?"

"Women need to be home by curfew. You know that."

Her aunt studied Zeinah and the AK-47 strapped across her chest. "You're not the same girl I knew."

Zeinah stepped closer. "There'll be nothing I can do. You need to watch yourself."

"You're the one keeping me here."

Her aunt abandoned the basket of apples and searched for her husband. Zeinah followed them out of the store and watched as they ambled up the empty street. Somewhere a loose door banged. At the corner, her aunt looked back. Zeinah had not moved; she remained in the middle of the street, watching.

On her way home, a couple of boys threw rocks at windows, and she waved them inside. Electrical wires sagged against the thick sky heading into darkness. Sandbags lined the streets, and she heard the screech of metal gates rolling over storefronts. Most of these low buildings were abandoned. The air reeked of tobacco, fire and smoke, and she avoided the central square where motorcycles and ISIS flags circled a bonfire of confiscated cigarettes. Rumors of a girl burning in a roundabout in Abu Dhabi flared inside her. Women in Afghanistan were also setting themselves on fire in their homes, at weddings, and on the streets.

More and more people were leaving Raqqa. Cardboard boxes, plastic containers, and crates accumulated beside dumpsters and outside buildings. Zeinah usually brushed past these offerings, but tonight she hesitated beneath the flickering bulb in the lobby of her building. A box marked FRAGILE sat beneath the defunct mailboxes. She opened the flaps and discovered a meticulously packed collection of china. She unwrapped a plate from newspaper and discovered the pattern she'd eaten from as a child. Birds in teals and browns, vines wrapped around the border. Her grandmother. An entire set of bowls, plates, cups, and saucers. She closed the box and carried it upstairs, excited to share the windfall with her mother.

Before going to sleep, Zeinah emptied the lipsticks from her bag onto the bed. She wrote down the colors on a piece of paper and then added them to her collection in the medicine cabinet. They were organized by shade. Initially, she thought she'd cut the head off each lipstick and display them uniformly by tint, like toy soldiers, but when she uncapped the first lipstick and turned the base, she found herself lured into the intimacy of painted lips, each one unique. Some women used both sides of the stick, creating an arrow, others rubbed the stick perfectly flat, and others formed a delicate triangle by using only a single side. Each lipstick signified an encounter with a woman, an homage to the past, and as the collection grew, they became her companions, and she committed the names to memory, reciting them like a prayer throughout the day and before bed.

Tulip,
Cherries in Snow,
Dare to Bare,
Bruised Plum,
Russian Red,
Revival.

Intense Nude,
Violet Femme,
Viva Glam,
Heroine,
999.

Jungle Red,
Lady Danger,
Fire and Ice,
Black

Honey.

II.

II.

JUSTINE

In a dream, Justine wanders from room to room in a New York City apartment. She kneels in front of the dollhouse they'd all painted pink, the red shutters smudged. She sifts through the basket of dollhouse furniture and adds things to rooms: a rocking chair, a metal music stand, a clarinet. She finds tiny tin cans of peaches and peas and stocks the pantry. Shoes paired in closets; beds made. No one's home. No half-finished art projects on the table, no cardboard forts, no stacks of unopened mail. The kitchen sink, clean and dry. No food scraps in the drain basket. No crumbs on the cutting board. She sets the table. A full bowl of sugar. She sits at the kitchen table and waits. No scampering feet in the hallway. No soft knuckles on the door. A sealed and silent home. She picks at the nail polish on her toes and remembers her family is dead. She's been living this way for months.

She surfaced from her dream before sunrise, the lights of construction cranes dotting the dark shore along the Gulf. There was no need to restock the pantry with peaches and peas. Her family was not dead. Soon she'd be heading out to the falconer's farm, driving west on the E11, then south toward Liwa, toward the Empty Quarter and, beyond that, Saudi Arabia, though she would not venture that far today.

* * *

She drove with the radio off, windows open, and pulled cigarettes from a soft pack on the seat beside her, using the embers of one to light the next as the road moved beneath her. The rhythm and glare of the flaring lights expanded in the rearview mirror, passed, and then disappeared into the vast darkness. The girl appeared in flashes, a girl she could barely comprehend but to whom she now felt permanently bound. Taut sheets, folded nightclothes, the open terrace door, curtains swelling into the bedroom. She could not shake the eerie image of the water glass in the refrigerated light, the girl's birthmarked hand reaching out for Cornelius, the smell of fire, ash, and gasoline in the air, her impulse to say, *I know you.*

She signaled off the E15 and reached for a piece of paper with scribbled directions in her bag. First light smudged the darkness, and a barbed-wire fence guided her along a dirt road. These farms had nothing to do with New England horse barns, rocky pastures, or cows sleeping beneath trees, signaling rain. Camels slept beneath open tents, and she wondered what their humps foretold; some said fertility.

Of course there were security cameras throughout the building. Anyone could see Justine bringing the girl up to her apartment. And now she'd blatantly lied. And she was culpable, at least partially. She'd swerved, almost hit the girl, and then forced her to come home with her, threatened her in fact. She'd hesitated before offering Wren's room to the girl. The room with the terrace. She'd heard how distressed foreign workers jumped from windows, and yes, the flash of a fall had crossed her mind, but never this. Not this. She'd scared the girl with talk of the embassy and naively believed that a fresh bed and sleep would solve her problems. Justine flinched as she recalled the girl's look of terror on the roadside; she'd wanted Justine to leave.

A rock scraped along the undercarriage of the car. Justine

shifted into second gear and navigated along a rutted embankment. The road forked. She killed the engine, checked her directions, and realized she'd missed a turn. A gentle wind blew
through the open windows, thumbing her jaw, and in front of her,
a bronze line cinched the dark horizon.

Through the dust-covered windshield, Justine saw a blue tarp
supported by tree limbs: the kind of structure she'd built as a child
in an abandoned orchard amid rotting fruit and yellow jackets.
She got out and noticed a white arrow painted on a rock, pointing to the rising sun. The tarp billowed in the wind, and frayed
twine wrapped around the supporting branches. One of the corners flapped loose, and she tied the grommet in place.

A mosque made of nothing. Sun wedged into the shaded dirt
floor; the air was dry and smelled of gasoline. She said a prayer for
the girl, but really, she was thinking of herself. What did she know
of Islam and its holiness? Of any religious faith and its convictions? There was a sudden rustling in the leaves behind her, and
Justine pivoted toward an olive tree. A goat observed her through
limbs and leaves, scowled, and seemed to say, *Go on, now. Move
along.* Justine returned to the car, embarrassed. She backed away
from the glaring goat who seemed to know who she was—and
didn't like her.

FLORA

Hamed's manicured hands pointed to the overhead mesh and sprinklers. Qadira stirred inside the sling, feet pumping, mouth searching. Flora smiled up at Hamed, but she was distracted with thoughts of lunch, laundry, and the baby's feeding. What had started as an impulse that first day with Qadira had become routine. No one suspected when she went upstairs with the bottle of formula that she was breastfeeding the child. She knew it was wrong, and every day she promised herself she'd stop, but she could not help herself. The release of milk into the child's mouth, Qadira's hands clasped around her breast, her eyes wide and watching: she strung these stolen moments together to get through her day. Oblivious, Hamed led Flora down the rows and gesticulated toward the black leaves and wilting tomato stems. Everything took so much effort here, she thought. At home, seeds sprouted in days, buds opened and drank in the rain, but she knew from the way Hamed looked at her that he wanted her to make this garden grow.

Heat bore down on the concrete house. Never had time passed so slowly. She'd imagined herself memorizing the names of extended family members before bed. Never this: a family, a wound in need of constant care. When Flora was a child, kids brought her dolls, airplanes, and radios to mend, and as she grew older, her sympathies bent toward living things: birds, snakes, chickens, even pigs. She was good with the physical world, like Qadira's gassy stomach or Basma's cramped legs, but injuries of the heart and mind were out of reach, and she avoided them. When Flora's mother returned from Japan, Flora sensed her mother's injured existence and slid out of reach. But here it was again, the same insatiable need, only this time it was tucked between silk flowers and shriveled leaves.

Hamed peeled the orange and offered her a slice. Flora was behind schedule. For him, this was a moment of relaxation. For her, the garden was a new task added to the expanding list of chores. It would be one thing if she could just sweep the floors and breakfast was milk and cereal, but she was ironing sheets, learning how to make poached eggs, and now she was expected to rejuvenate rows of tomatoes planted in sand. She chewed the mealy orange and smiled. "Very good."

Flora noticed Dounia watching from her upstairs bedroom window. She worried about the young woman and her mental state, her lack of interest in the child. Every day Flora offered to bring the baby into the bedroom, and once, just as an experiment, she'd brought the child in unannounced. Upon entering, Qadira began to wail, and Dounia ordered them out of the room: "I don't want to hear it. I've told you that before." She'd seen this kind of behavior back home, women isolating themselves after childbirth, sweating in steam baths, roasting above beds of burning coals and turmeric, scorching themselves clean.

———

"You have to promise," Flora whispered into the darkness of her basement room. She offered her pinky to the small fist. "Can you promise?"

The infant took hold like a squirrel. This was their hush-hush, Flora's secret as she mopped the tiles, dusted windowsills, watered the tomatoes, chopped onions, scrambled eggs, scrubbed bathtubs, ironed napkins, and folded lingerie—the best part of the day, her reward.

In the middle of the night, in her air-conditioned, mildewed basement room, Flora listened to the small breaths of a newborn. Not her baby, but in the cement darkness it was close enough. The child's mouth opened, searched for her nipple, soft lips latching on. The suction and the suck. A milk river flowed into gulping cheeks, and small hands kneaded her breast, sent her home, across the seas, to Datu, Pia, her life before the storm.

It started as a solution to her exhaustion and the nighttime feedings. She pushed the bed against the wall and secured a place for the child to sleep beside her. Sometimes she heard Dounia coming down the stairs, opening and closing cabinets in the kitchen. Dounia wasn't sleeping at night, but she'd never come down these stairs. She'd never know her baby slept with the maid. Not that Dounia would even care, quarantined in her room by day, skulking the house by night.

No one would know. Soon, these midnight feedings would end, and the child would sleep through the night. Still, the house had paths and boundaries. She could sit in the kitchen but not on the sofa and chairs, eat leftovers after cleaning up, wash her underwear in the sink but not in the machine where it would mix with sir's and ma'am's. She was even welcome to sleep on the floor in the baby's bedroom, but to bring the infant underground, into her dank world, was forbidden—a gesture of ownership she didn't need to learn from a handbook. Flora recalled her teacher saying, "Be like the air: essential and invisible." To bring the baby to bed, to cuddle beneath the postcard of El Nido in the furtive hours of the night, was a kind of kidnapping; to walk up the stairs with a bottle of formula was a lie.

DOUNIA

Dounia splayed across her covers and surrendered to the global heat wave. The upper atmosphere bore down on the earth, and in an act of solidarity, she'd switched off the air-conditioning in her bedroom, opened the windows, and invited the heat inside. She spoke to no one. Flora entered and disappeared, replacing water glasses, gathering plates of nibbled toast and strawberries stems— all without acknowledgment. The milk in Dounia's breasts curdled and grew hard. Meanwhile, sweat puddled beneath her body and stained the mattress with her damp silhouette. A steady drip of YouTube "swelter" videos played on her computer where it seemed the world was coming to an end.

In Harlem, a woman rotated a handheld fan across her chest.
In Mumbai, the elderly collapsed on melting streets.
In Ethiopia, riverbeds evaporated into trails of stone.
In Egypt, horses collapsed in fields.
In Manila, bare-chested boys hosed each other down.
In Sharjah, women donned blue face masks beneath umbrellas.
In Syria, refugees hid beneath the shade of canvas tents.
In Saudi, eggs fried on pavement.
In São Paulo, beachgoers risked death from dehydration.
In China, authorities issued a yellow heat warning.

Five times a day, the newly installed speakers in the Dream Development amplified the call to prayer and reverberated across the gravel roads and barren dwellings. Though she did not pray, the recording of the man's voice was a comfort, and as she became acquainted with its lilts, breaths, and passion, she felt in a strange way that she knew him, and he her, and for those moments his voice brought her relief, but then he was gone, and silence filled the air around her where his song had been. She thought of her mother and sister in Riyadh or maybe at the farm. Sometimes she gazed out at the garden and other times at the sand and sky. At night, the walls simmered, and her reflection haunted her from the black panes. Dounia wanted to burn, to char her life clean.

She recalled the palm frond bonfires at her grandmother's date farm when she was a child. Workers and family members would gather dried date limbs, drag the long, jagged leaves across the dirt like brooms toward the open field where they built a brush fire higher than the tallest man. Her grandmother struck the first match before taking a seat on the cane chair she'd requested from the house. She'd lower her stiff hips into the seat and beckon Dounia to sit on the ground beside her. Together, they'd watch the branches catch fire, form caves of ribs and skeletons. The flames ignited the sky in a mood of celebration, but then the kindling and leaves gave way to older limbs burning orange, then black, and finally blue. Dounia would rest her head in her grandmother's lap, and when she tried to speak, her grandmother hushed her: "Shhh. Now's the time to listen." Embers cracked, branches fell, and a dense heat engulfed them. That night, she'd go to bed with ash and woodsmoke in her hair and refuse to bathe for days.

She became large and silent, a watchful mass refusing to move, an embodiment of inertia that provoked unease in others. One day, she noticed Hamed leading Flora between the narrow rows

of the garden. Flora followed a few steps behind with Qadira Ibrahim in a sling across her chest, her index finger slipped inside the
child's mouth. The baby had colic, convulsed in the throes of inces-
sant wailing, sucking, and bouncing, but Flora told Dounia not to
worry, she had the cure. Of course, she'd asked permission first—
presented her clean hands and nails cut down to a stub so she could
safely insert her fingers between the baby's lips and press against
the roof of the infant's mouth. Dounia didn't care what she did
as long as she kept the baby quiet. The way that child screamed,
you'd think she was the only one in agony.

She noticed how Hamed touched Flora's elbow, how together
they bent over an orange tree. Hamed presented a yellow fruit
that Dounia had spotted weeks ago—one of the last secrets she'd
shared with the baby before her birth. She watched the three of
them. Hamed picked and peeled the fruit. Dounia felt infantile
and pouted. Let them have it. Weeks ago, the smell of dirt and
citrus held promise in the air, but today the pulp was dry, and the
stench of salt lingered in the heat.

Dounia had relegated Hamed to the guest bedroom for her re-
covery, and every night she awoke with anger. While her husband
slept beneath books and high school trophies, pain traveled from
her incision down her left leg. The thought of his penis, like a
stem, pushing inside her and then retreating was more than she
could bear. Just that morning, Hamed paused outside their bedroom, testing for an opening. She looked up from her screen, from
the power blackout in Yemen, and regarded him as if he were a
stranger.

———

Dounia was not accepting visitors and refused the knocks and
cajoling at the door: no bedsheets changed, no floors vacuumed.

Crumbs, like sand, accumulated in her bed, encased her skin like a thin glass bulb on the verge of shattering from the fuse inside. Her brain, once a comfort, short-circuited and at times went dark. She recalled a photograph on an artist's Instagram of dirt bulldozed into a living room and a woman gazing out a picture window onto a dark and empty street.

That's me, she thought.

Dounia ruminated and mulled. It seemed the government and marketplace influenced everything in her home. The housing development, architectural designs, appliances, sofas, and textiles, even the maids, were all domestic theater. Hamed's insistence she breastfeed was just another gesture of control. Out there, Flora (the understudy) was now the lead, each morning entering stage right and providing the production of care. A woman she'd come to depend on and hate for inhabiting the role she'd forfeited. Indolence bloomed; she'd learn how to live off the grid.

Dounia was the outcast. Just this week, she heard cooing and laughter from the third floor: a new morning ritual was unfolding. Flora would bring Qadira to Basma's room, and Hamed would breakfast with his daughter and mother on the bed. Dounia swore she heard their whispers in the vents as they spread into her absence and claimed the child as their own.

ZEINAH

The front door was ajar. Zeinah hesitated in the dim light of the landing, motionless and alert. She held her breath and listened: metal scraped against tile, the clink of cutlery, footsteps. She pushed on the door with the end of her rifle and scanned the room. The furniture had been pushed against the walls and a tablecloth spread across the floor set with the blue plates she'd been saving for her mother.

"Hello?"

Omar emerged from the kitchen, swaying slightly. He took her face in his hands and kissed her. His breath smelled of garlic and butter, and today was Tuesday. "You're late."

Zeinah hung up her cloak and gun. The scent of roasted lamb filled the rooms, and the atmosphere felt festive but also unnerving. "How do you know what time I get home?"

"I know." Omar disappeared into the kitchen.

Zeinah joined him and watched as he removed glasses from the cupboard. "Where'd you find lamb?"

"Not just lamb. Prunes and pistachios!"

He poured red liquid into a jelly jar and handed it to her.

"Sharbet zbeeb, my mother's recipe."

"We're celebrating?"

He filled his glass. "Tonight, we feast."

What he'd undergone these last few days, she did not know, did not want to know.

Omar raised his glass to hers. "To you, Zeinah. To you. I am so blessed."

He clinked her glass a little too hard, causing her to spill some on the floor. He didn't seem to notice or care. Instead, his gaze rested upon her as he waited for her to take a sip. She pressed the rim of the jelly jar against her mouth. The burgundy liquid slipped between her lips, rolled across her tongue.

"Hold it. Breathe."

Zeinah inhaled.

Raisins, vinegar, and dirt.

———

Zeinah's mind was soft with lamb and honey. The fan rotated above their entwined limbs on the floor, dirty dishes pushed aside.

"Do you think of me while I'm gone?" asked Omar.

Zeinah attempted to see the individual blades in the twirl above them.

Omar rolled toward her and waited.

"Yes," said Zeinah.

"No, I mean do you pleasure yourself and think of me?"

Zeinah flushed.

His tone was serious. "Do you?"

The lights of an ambulance flickered past, and she suddenly felt sober and sad. "Sometimes I do. Yes."

"Good."

Omar rolled away from her, and they didn't say a word. Not for a long time. She closed her eyes and willed her mind to return to the initial excitement of the evening, to what just hours ago had felt like a celebration. She reached for Omar's hand, threaded her fingers around his chapped knuckles and allowed herself to sink through the bed of soft lamb—prunes, lemons, the humid night moist upon their faces, and above them, she imagined, not the fan, not the murky sky, but stars. She saw them, side by side, appearing and disappearing in a sand-swell offing. She moved closer to Omar and took comfort in his presence, his heartbeat in her ear. Never had she felt so whole.

Omar finally spoke, his voice measured: "I'm going to leave you."

Her throat closed, and she loosened her grip around his knuckles, but he reclaimed her fingers. The ceiling went fuzzy, and the fan blades returned.

"Not now. But sometime very soon. I will leave and not come back."

"If . . ." Zeinah's voice faltered, and her nose began to sting. "If it could be different, would you want that?" She felt that he did not want to hurt her, but that he would tell her the truth—a cruel kind of love.

"This is enough."

Zeinah's chest swayed; her throat contracted. She did not want to cry.

"I'll do what I can to take care of you. I hope you'll still think of me. At least sometimes."

Omar brought Zeinah's fist to his lips.

Her mouth trembled. He's asking me to love him toward death, she thought. And so she burrowed into the musky smell of him: the dried and rough textures of his skin, the warm yeast between his legs, his burned cheeks, his heavy brow. He pressed hard against her, and as his legs shook, he called out her name, and Zeinah tumbled through darkness beneath him.

Afterward, Omar softened inside of her, and she believed he might be crying.

"Thank you," he murmured. "I was wrong about things getting easier, it only gets harder. In the beginning there was a bang, and there will be no end."

She slid out from under him, disappearing like a fish into deeper waters, but when he thought she was asleep, he wound himself around her, squeezed what love remained for him from the pulp and folds of her abdomen and thighs.

The streetlights dimmed and the fan stopped as the city's power grid went black. She smelled the chewed grizzle on the plates. Fury stocked her spine, vertebra by vertebra. First with Omar, but then with herself and her stupidity. Everything she needed to know he'd told her that first afternoon outside the women's clinic. It made sense now. No children made it easier to be a martyr. She hated herself for being so naive, for thinking she (they) would be an exception. And worst of all, the thing that was unforgivable: she'd fallen in love with a man who would leave her and soon kill innocent people. Scorn and despair braided the night, teased and knotted around Omar and herself. Heartache, yes, but much more: a reckoning impossible to square. Omar was traveling to Allah. Leaving her. Where? Did she share Omar's mission? A mission she'd bent toward. For what? To secure her parents' safety. To move past the loss of Sultan. To find love. To save herself. True, she'd found comfort in the doctrine, but only because it deepened their connection, but now she was alone with her choices and she saw herself as weak, a coward. She recalled an interview she'd seen months ago on television. An FSA fighter warned viewers that fighters were going into jail as prisoners and leaving as terrorists. Had this happened to her?

She could not say.

ESKEDARE

She stops going to school and spends her days on the banks of flooded rivers. Amara was here, and here, and here. Eskedare stands on the edge of things and aches. Amara said, and said, and said. Branches tremble and shudder in the rain. Amara did, and did, and did. Truck. Riverbank. Seed. And there's no place to put her aching down. Loss presses her like a flower, folds her in half, and half again. She's a bullet shooting into dirt, a glass bottle crammed with stones.

Her sighs tally down the days, exhales her companions. Trapped in a house of damp limbs and smoke, Eskedare sweeps patterns into the dirt floor—circles, triangles, squares—borders impossible to flee.

Unmoving, the pitcher keeps watch from the shelf.

அ

JUSTINE

Justine drove up the dirt driveway and parked in front of a modest ranch house that overlooked the desert. The scent of dry leaves and cold sand welcomed her as she stepped out of the car into the dim morning light. A compact man wearing a white kandura wandered out to greet her. Sunglasses swept back his black curls like a headband and exposed a high forehead and wide cheekbones, and while so much of his face appeared open, his eyes retreated, refusing connection. He stopped several feet away from Justine and kept his distance. Perhaps they were the same age. From her research, she'd learned that he came from a lineage of falconers, and before his success with the star peregrine Shema, he'd lived a modest life, entertaining tourists with falcon tricks at heritage events beneath the stars.

"Welcome."

His voice was neither warm nor rude, but she knew he didn't want her there, he was acting out of obligation. She'd heard about his negative experiences with the BBC and National Geographic, but the request from the royal family was impossible to refuse. The five a.m. meeting time was meant to dissuade her.

Justine looked out onto the desert surrounding them. "Quite a spot."

"Come." Majid headed behind the house.

As Justine followed, she was aware of how much she wanted him to like her, but his solitary nature was not up to the task. His

one-story home on an expanse of desert suited him, and she imagined that no matter where he was—with his family, at a party or
a soccer match—he'd be in the corner watching. He stopped in
front of a truck and a four-wheeler parked out back.

Justine watched the sun crest the dunes.

He pointed in the opposite direction. "That way."

Justine adjusted her gaze.

"We'll take the truck." Majid got in and revved the engine, the
smell of exhaust charging the air.

———

As Majid sped across the desert trail, the landscape blurred, and the
sky opened above them. She held on to the ceiling strap and braced
her arm against the dash as they ascended the dunes. Plumes of red
dust followed them across fields of sand, and Justine was giddy
with the momentary freedom, suspended in time, outside of real
life, in a place seemingly void of consequences. A place where she
could do things no one would ever know, where if she were alone,
only fleas and scrub would be her witnesses. She reminded herself
she was here for work, for the exhibit, to learn firsthand about
falconry and innovative training techniques.

They headed down a dune and into a basin scattered with shelters constructed of metal poles and fabric faded pink from the sun.
They slowed down, and beneath the tarps, Justine saw the shaded
humps of camels, long legs folded beneath them, necks thick and
full, and nostrils wide in greeting. Majid picked up speed and followed a fireman's hose leading to a footed bathtub in the sand.
Justine wondered how they got the bathtub out here, in the middle of nowhere. A bathtub that perhaps traveled by boat, then by
truck, to serve as a reservoir for the marble-eyed creatures and
their leather lips. Majid accelerated out of the valley and up a steep

swell. Justine held on tight as they rode along the ridge of a dune, dipped down again, and ascended another hill until Majid stopped on a crest and pointed into the valley below, where Justine saw an arish shelter and a couple of tents.

———

Majid disappeared into the shadows of the structure and Justine followed. The air was cold. Orange light filtered through the palm frond walls and fell into darkness. A man got up from a cot and Majid nodded, a greeting that acknowledged a previous discussion regarding today's duty.

"This is Bassam. He guards the falcons, takes care of them when I'm not here. People try to steal them. As you know, they're quite valuable."

A large carpet covered the desert floor. Falcons rested on pedestals in corners. Leather hoods covered their eyes, and around their claws, jesses secured them to their posts. The hooded creatures shifted on their talons, restless.

"They sense a stranger," he said.

Bottles hung from wires and shifted in the breeze, lightly bumped into one another, jangled, and chimed.

"For the birds?"

Majid crossed the room toward one of the falcons. "Birds? Peregrines. The tiercel. Shema. My star. The one you've come to see. Fiercer than her male counterparts. The deer killer. One of the most prized falcons of all time." Majid stroked the falcon's head and whispered in her ear: "Shema, Shema, Shema."

Shema's head and shoulders were grey, her barrel chest brown and white, and her overall height was maybe twenty inches.

"Hard to believe she could kill a deer," said Justine.

For the first time in the semidarkness, Majid regarded Justine.

"It's illegal now, but everyone knows I caught her in the wild. It's always better if they've molted at least once before you train them."

"Is it okay if I take notes on my phone? Some pictures?"

"You can film the falcons. Not me."

He untied Shema from the pedestal, and she hopped onto his gloved arm. "She was impossible at the beginning. Stubborn. She didn't like me, but that was no matter. Sometimes the strongest love is born in conflict. The most important thing is the relationship forged between man and falcon."

Justine sensed the many times he'd told this story, and she watched as Majid stroked Shema's back and her hooded head leaned into his arm.

"You must train her to trust you, and this is not in their nature, but I could see it in her left eye." Majid held her head still and removed her hood. "You see? Her right eye is very fierce, does not acknowledge me, but in her left eye . . ." He held her eye open. "Right there. That is the connection. She sees me. I can feel it. I knew that if I could win her trust, she would be the greatest hunter."

"But how did you know?"

The bottles tapped against one another, and Justine sensed Majid's impatience.

"The more difficult, the more resistant the bird, the better the hunter. This is always true. The art of falconry is gaining her trust without destroying her edge, her wildness. It is a very fine line between training a falcon and breaking her spirit. You must love the wildness, honor it, and know how to make it stronger. I can train her, but she'll always be feral. The best falconers respect and cultivate wildness."

Justine recalled the vet at the falcon hospital, his derision for dogs and their obedience.

"When I first caught Shema, I placed the hood on her head and took it off. Hood on. Hood off. I stroked and petted her for almost three days. She slept in my bedroom. I did not leave her side. Then I got her on my wrist with the glove. I placed meat around her feet and tickled her talons. She started to eat from me. Only then did I start to work with her catching prey. First the pigeon and then the bustard. I let her catch the bustard, and while she was still taking her first few bites, I crawled to her, calling out her name, and then I dragged her toward me while she was still on top of her prey. Only then did I take the kill away from her. She must remain hungry. Hunger is very important. You must imagine yourself as the falcon, hungry but strong. Too much food, she becomes lazy. Not enough, she becomes weak."

Justine thought Majid might be describing himself: a man who could survive on little, who conserved his resources for distance.

"But you'll see for yourself."

———

Justine watched as Bassam prepared the drone. He placed a black bird the size of a pigeon inside a cage attached to the undercarriage.

"We use bustards for training. Most people train for racing and do not use prey, but birds are the best practice to train hunters."

Bassam clicked a black remote, and the drone with the caged bustard ascended into the sky. The small helicopter hovered above them, and Justine watched with her phone ready to record.

Shema waited on Majid's arm. "Their eyes are twice the weight of ours. See here? That's her double lid for steep descents."

Justine watched as the drone departed and climbed higher into the sky.

"Now," said Majid.

The aerial cage released the bustard. Shema became alert.

"I'll let the bustard get some height before releasing her."

Majid untied Shema's jesses, and she lifted off his arm and hovered about fifteen feet above them before she spread her wings and revealed the intricate brown-and-white geometric pattern of feathers and her pale throat.

"Look. She's showing you."

Shema thumped toward the sky, bringing Justine with her. "How fast can she go?"

"She's almost three pounds and has clocked over two hundred twenty-five miles per hour. It's her wings. They're strong, like a feathered fighter jet. She's a falcon of the twenty-first century, trained with traditional methods and drones, ATVs, and Google Maps. Falconry has evolved and so has Shema. Look."

The bustard, sensing danger, headed higher into the sky, Shema in pursuit.

"What makes her such a good hunter?"

"It's how I train. No one else could have trained her, I am sure of it. All my hours building trust, being tough, and then loving her, breaking down her inhibitions. And then I would let her go. It's terrifying. But also, what a thrill: she can leave. The possibility of freedom must always be there, must be on her mind. Every time she comes back, it makes our relationship stronger."

Thump, thump—glide. Shema beat her wings upward and then glided above her prey in a figure eight. *Thump, thump*—glide. Then she somersaulted backward, tied back her wings, and dived, falling like a lead anchor toward the bustard. She attacked her prey in midair, and together, they hurtled to the ground. On the sand, the bustard broke free, puffed out its chest, fanned its wings, and doubled in size. Justine watched as Shema charged the bloated bird, sent it tumbling backward, and the birds rolled into a ball of black and brown feathers, tufts tearing loose on the scraggy desert floor. There was a high screech and squawking, and for a moment it seemed they were mating, followed by the ominous silence of death.

Shema stood on top of the bustard.

The power of Shema's wings knifing the sky, her cartilage and feathers thumping the air, her tumbling kill, left Justine stunned and bewildered. She could not account for her emotional reaction, her reverence for Shema. She needed to capture this feeling in the exhibit, though how she'd conjure this experience was a mystery. Shema had made an impression, and for a moment Majid's countenance loosened.

"Watch. She uses her toe to puncture the internal organs. She'll remove some of the feathers, but not all of them. I won't let her eat too much."

Majid approached Shema as she ate. He let her take a few more bites and then crawled to her on his hands and knees, whispering, "Shema, Shema, Shema." He held her torso and slid both Shema and the prey toward his chest. Then he removed her talons from the bustard and replaced Shema on his arm, praising her as he brought her back to Justine.

Majid held out the dead prey for Justine, boasting about Shema's kill. "See her strong hooked bill? She hammers it like a nail between the neck vertebrae of her prey and then twists, snapping the spinal cord." He stroked her back and smiled.

"How much if I wanted to buy her?"

"She's not for sale."

"But if she were . . ."

"She's the most famous falcon in history. Even the Shebas who crossed the Silk Road with their falcons could never afford her. She excels in competitions, but no other falcon has ever killed large prey, like that deer, in the wild. She's the lion of the skies and has no price."

"She belongs to the Sheik?"

Majid's expression went blank. She'd offended him—no, worse, she'd stumbled into the conflict between his duty to the Sheik and his connection to Shema as if she were his own.

"Yes, but she hunts for me. I am the reason she returns. If I were not here, she would leave. I am sure of it. Shema belongs to no one."

DOUNIA

Dounia paused outside the laundry room and watched Flora's arm travel through the bellows and folds of her wedding dress with a steamer, flattening the wide pleats covered in pearls, seams stitched with silver thread. Pierre Cardin. Dounia had stashed the dress in one of the downstairs coat closets when they'd arrived, but now Basma was asking Flora to perform futile tasks like steaming clothes in storage closets.

Dounia watched Flora's fingers caress the pearls and trace the embroidered flowers, and the tenderness stirred a sadness within her, reigniting a schoolgirl longing for admiration and fawning, a desire which led her into marriage and left her feeling swindled.

Dounia stepped into the doorway, startling Flora. "Try it on."

"Oh, no, ma'am."

Dounia unhooked the hanger from the door and pressed the dress into Flora's arms. "You should take it. I'll never wear it."

"But your daughter, ma'am."

"No. No, I don't want it. Take the dress for . . ." Dounia had already forgotten the name. ". . . your own daughter." Dounia scooped up the train from the floor, rolled it like toilet paper around her arm, and stuffed the dress into Flora's arms. "She'll love it. No one else will have a dress like it in the Philippines."

Flora stood motionless with the tulle in her arms.

"Well, what's wrong?"

"Ma'am. It's just . . . I'm not supposed . . ."

"Stop calling me that. I'm telling you: I want you to have it. Bring it down to your room. I don't want to see it."

———

That night, the dress appeared in Dounia's dream, swelling and inflating like a white egg sac in Flora's basement room. The skirt expanded and pressed against the bed, the bureau, and the walls until it burst, and hundreds of small white spiders crawled out of the pearls and scampered along the floor and walls, looking for escape. The egg sac, empty now, deflated and covered the floor— thin and fibrous, like nothing.

ZEINAH

Zeinah hugged the cardboard box of plates to her chest and walked through the empty streets of her old neighborhood. Omar had not called in several days, and she pushed back thoughts of a perpetual silence. The sand blew on, disguised bloody sidewalks, burying the evidence of lives. Refrigerators and rusted bedsprings. Table legs twisted, appendages in the dust. She could no longer tolerate feeling helpless, like a victim. ISIS gave her a sense of community and purpose, a sense of safety. And yet she took the long way around to avoid the playground, the stage for ISIS cautionary tales. Dead men in orange jumpsuits hung from the chains of swing sets, chains that jumped and creaked when she was a girl pumping toward the sky. Lengthy debates about how to save their city, what groups to join, and who needed food and medical care had long been silenced. Now it was survival that occupied people's days.

Her parents' house was the last on a dead-end street. She pushed on the ground-level door, and the stench of mildew and shuttered rooms greeted her at the bottom of the steps. Stone stairs in the dark—a hideout for Zeinah and her older brother, Sultan, during the heat of summer. A stairwell where they traded sports cards and bounced a pink ball into shadows. Five of them used to live in this house: Zeinah, Sultan, her parents, and her maternal grandmother, Tita. Zeinah stumbled with her box of china and steadied herself against the wall. When she was little, they used to argue. Argue about whose turn it was to lug the crates of tomatoes up to the kitchen. She'd have to take a break halfway up. She'd sit on the stone stairs sucking wind, inhaling bitter stems and dirt. For breakfast, lunch, and dinner, Tita used a blunt bread knife and severed tomatoes into thick slices that she served on blue plates. Sultan would disappear from the table and leave a crumpled, red-stained napkin on his seat, where it would remain after the meal was finished and the long shadows had moved across the room.

Back then everyone used to have crates of tomatoes in their kitchen. Zeinah read somewhere that close to four thousand greenhouses had been destroyed by the violence, the drought, the storms. She'd seen pictures of plastic walls and ceilings depart-ing into the wind. What remained of these makeshift, light-filled rooms? Farmers were killed, livelihoods abandoned, and the to-matoes were left to rot, mildew, and suffocate beneath dismantled tarps.

Sultan, who painted black graffiti on a green wall, who joined fighters to resist Assad before the Arab Spring, before ISIS. Her brother, who believed in a Syria beyond corruption. Sultan, who was kidnapped, who disappeared. Maybe on his way home from work. Her father found the family car abandoned in a back alley, behind a restaurant where dogs ate from dumpsters. And when her father returned home, he carried a black umbrella he'd found in the back seat of the car. Silence for two weeks and then a phone call. A voice demanded two hundred thousand dollars. They put Sultan on the phone. He begged them to pay the money. And they did. They went to everyone they knew, sold jewelry and furniture, borrowed money from the bank against their home. They did as they were told. Left the money exactly how, when, and where. They'd gone over the details hundreds of times. Followed the in-structions perfectly.

That was six years ago.

For weeks, Zeinah went out with the umbrella, rain or shine, hiding her slender frame beneath the black nylon tent and broken metal spines, walking the streets, sending out a signal for her brother to come home. Her mother refused to leave the house, insisted she needed to be home when he called or walked through the door.

But Zeinah knew. Everyone knew.

Still, she bumped into her brother in unexpected places; he bent her mind in certain directions, like agreeing to her father's marriage request and joining the Al-Khansaa Brigade. What would he be fighting for now? The FSA. Raqqa Is Being Slaughtered Silently. Anyway, either way, he'd be dead.

FLORA

Recycling was new to Saudi Arabia, and Flora spent her Thursday mornings going through the trash and separating paper, tin, and plastic: sixty-seven cans of Coca-Cola, six frozen pizza boxes, eleven pints of strawberry ice cream. What Dounia wasn't eating during the day, she packed in at night. Flora flattened Hamed's credit card bills from his time away: meals at al-Sanbok, Spazio, and Mirage for over 3,000 riyals each, receipts from another world, far away from the Dream Development. She stacked and tied a week's worth of Arab and English newspapers: Ebola, US Airstrikes on ISIS in Syria, Al Qaeda Attacks in Yemen. Her life unfolded in the compound with brief glimpses of the world on Thursdays when she lugged the trash out of the house and down the unpaved road to the garbage bins.

First, she carried the clear blue bags to the locked compound door and buzzed to leave. Dounia appeared in the foyer window and watched as Flora heaved the bags across the threshold. Then the door closed, and Flora was free.

She relished the walk. It took ten minutes to carry the trash to the industrial receptacles at the end of the dirt road, past the lots under construction, the smell of sawdust and wet cement, the sound of pounding hammers and whining drills. She never saw anyone, but the evidence of labor comforted her. Sun warmed her scalp where her hair was parted, and the desert reminded her of the shore, the blue, yellow, and red dumpsters—boats on a beach. She took a picture in her mind and promised to share it with Pia.

Today, another person appeared: a woman in a pink uniform. She walked on the road ahead of her, also with bags of trash. Flora watched the woman open the bins; pieces of paper flew away and scattered in the wind. She was not in a hurry, and Flora joined her at the recycling center. Her name was Jessa, also from the Philippines, but from another part, Pampanga. "There's a group of us that get together on Saturdays for prayers and manicures. Ask your employer if you can come with me."

Asking to leave had not occurred to Flora. Who would take care of the baby?

"You're supposed to have a day off," said Jessa. "It's in your contract."

"Maybe . . ."

"I heard about your boss. Something's not right with her."

Flora felt strangely protective of Dounia. "She's fine."

Walking back, Flora wondered where the women met. She wouldn't want nail polish. Maybe clear. Were some of the women from the training center at these gatherings? She hadn't considered a world outside of Dounia, Basma, and the baby. Her existence was ordered. Repetition reassured Flora. The sun would rise, the sky would blacken, the earth would spin. Flora could do anything, and time would still move forward and return her home—to Pia. She just had to endure. If there was no end, no progress, she might feel depressed, but the passage of time was greater than all of them. These Thursday mornings warmed her back, restored her faith, and propelled her into the future.

She rang the bell at the compound gate, but instead of the buzzer, Dounia opened the door, eyes frantic.

"That girl's a gossip." Dounia grabbed Flora and pulled her inside, pinching her upper arm. "What did she say about me?"

Flora broke free, stunned. "No, ma'am. Nothing."

"I know the woman she works for, and she told me that girl's organizing maids, getting people in trouble. You know what will happen to them?" Dounia's eyes brimmed with tears. "They'll end up stranded at the embassy for months, sleeping on the floor, broke, with no passport, no lawyer, and no way home. I don't want you involved with her. Do you understand me?"

"Yes, ma'am. I won't. Don't worry."

"It's just . . . if something happened to you, what would I do?"

Flora took her trembling hand. "It's okay, ma'am. She just told me her name, that's all."

ESKEDARE

A Friday in late June. A package arrives for Eskedare. A flip phone. One contact number. Ringtones skip like stones across the night sky, connecting shores.

Laughter. That's how Amara picks up the phone.

The familiar sound catches her breath, and she grabs hold.

"It's ugly. No green anywhere." She feeds the men building stadiums for the World Cup. "I whisper into the food for an Ethiopian win. I know we've never won before, but that would be something."

Eskedare wants to know everything.

It's hot—almost 50 degrees—and the Nepalese are dropping from heart attacks. "One a day. Not me. They say I'm a camel in the kitchen. Skinny and don't need much water. I'm good on the stoves too. The manager likes me, says I'm doing well. Everyone complains. We rotate beds and share sheets. Our shoes stink, but I'm making money. Already paid off my sponsor. Four months down on my two-year contract."

Eskedare feels herself dislodge from the dirt. She clasps the phone. "Do you miss me?"

"Every minute," says Amara. "Lie about your age and come."

Hope skips a stone into Eskedare's throat and jumps ahead.

Now everything is about Amara. Eskedare grows restless, beside herself, spinning in circles, waiting for the next call, holding on to this thread connecting her to the planes overhead, to the countries once spinning beneath her palm on the globe. She sleeps with her phone, and when it vibrates in the middle of the night, she heads outside and disappears beneath the stars. Amara tells her about the places she's been in Doha. She takes grainy pictures of herself, shadowed outlines, and sends them many miles away. The line goes quiet. She hears Amara breathing, and they go to bed very much alive.

Eskedare understands little of love, but she knows she cannot lose it.

∞

JUSTINE

On the highway heading back to Abu Dhabi, Justine did not re-call stopping for gas or stepping in the flooded floor of the public restroom. The plastic wrapper from an apple turnover fluttered in the passenger seat beside her. Something she'd apparently eaten.

The encounter with Shema lingered. Justine had read Western accounts of falconry: Baker, White, Yeats—men who'd chronicled the falcon and been gripped by a desire to rewild themselves, to leave their humanness behind. Then there was Horus, the divine king of Egypt, a falcon-headed god. She imagined what it might be like to be Shema, to open her mouth and swallow the falcon whole, to feel her taking hold: talons gripped her pelvis, a feath-ered chest expanded inside her lungs, wings spread across her back, a neck stretched upward against her spine. Shema's eyes, one a morning star, the other the moon, looked out behind her own, and Justine felt rooted and expansive, a person who could regard the world with a cold mind, and her thoughts returned to the girl.

It was possible they'd already discovered her with the girl on the surveillance footage: in the car park, the elevator, the hallway entering her apartment. She could talk to Sammy, who worked in building security, but he had no reason to help her. He might even go to the police. He liked Justine okay, but now she realized he was polite. Maybe he didn't like her at all.

Leo, the man in the brown suit. She imagined her predicament might even fall under his job description. She could call him on her

way home. Now even. Meet him at the British Club. He was probably a member. Most Western expats were. Maybe joined when
he first moved to the UAE nine years ago from . . . she couldn't
remember where. Maybe he didn't go to the club anymore, but he
kept his membership active. He'd probably come to the UAE for
money, maybe to find a wife with the plan to move back home,
raise a family. People referred to the Gulf as the new world, the
Wild West. And it was true. Every foreigner she met was here for
money or to stake a claim in something; she was no exception.

Perhaps her terror was irrational. Maybe she wasn't guilty of
anything. And yet a girl had set herself on fire, a girl whom she'd
almost hit and who she'd insisted come to her apartment, a girl
who'd used her blue water jug to carry the gasoline.

FLORA

Qadira Ibrahim's back rose and fell beside Flora on the mattress. A circle of dampness formed beneath the baby's thumb where her lips parted, and her warm foot pressed against Flora's stomach. But tonight, nothing soothed her. Flora needed to get out of the basement, take a walk, leave the compound. The baby's dependence on her, Dounia's hibernation, and Basma's bedridden needs held her captive. She lived in a house where women spent their days in bed, and every interaction led to additional chores. She couldn't tell if anyone was keeping track, but she was. It was an impossible list of tasks.

With no hooks, hangers, or a closet, Dounia's wedding dress hung over the shower stall. Pia would never wear that dress. The gift had nothing to do with her daughter or their lives back home, and she was annoyed with all the space it occupied. An item to be moved when she showered and replaced with a towel wrapped around her torso, water dripping on the floor. But lately she'd been thinking about the sari-sari store washed away in high winds, the pearls and how much they might be worth.

Three floors above, Basma slept—propped up by pillows, hands clasped across her chest, already poised for her morning tray of tea. Two floors above, Dounia tossed and turned, belly to back again. Flora hadn't slept in days. It was just past 3:00 a.m. when she heard a door open and then Hamed's bare feet on the stairs.

The metal latch of her bedroom door released. She faced the

wall, her back toward him, her arm draped around Qadira Ibrahim. Hamed's presence lurked in the doorway; they were two
butterflies, fixed in the dark, wings pinned back, alert. He took
a step forward and then another. He reached for her sloped hips
and slid the covers aside to expose the curve of her thighs. He
pressed his hardness against her bare leg. Her breath caught.
Hamed moaned. He hovered above her and then descended, his
palms landing on the mattress on either side of her. Only not on
the mattress—on Qadira's belly. The air shifted, desire vanished,
traded for confusion, and within moments Hamed understood
the baby to be his child.

Qadira Ibrahim wailed. Her cries echoed through the stairwell. Cries not from the nursery but from the basement. Hamed
scooped the baby into his arms and disappeared, and Flora listened as he scaled the stairs by twos and threes. Dounia's door
opened. Where he'd been and why would never matter. His voice
boomed through the house.

"Our child! Down in the basement. Sleeping beside the maid.
You need to be a mother and breastfeed this child."

Flora imagined Dounia fumbling, barely catching the screaming Qadira in her arms.

"And I'm sleeping in my own bed."

Windows slammed against the desert heat, locks clicked into
place, and the low hum returned. That night, cold air circulated
through the vents, chilled Flora's bedroom, prickled her skin, and
slowed her heartbeat. Flora did not sleep, dreading the trouble
awaiting her come morning, but for the rest of her days, she'd be
grateful to Qadira Ibrahim for saving her from Hamed.

ZEINAH

Out of breath, Zeinah called out to her parents: "Hello?"

They greeted her in the kitchen. Her mother's soft, sagging cheek; her father's beard, his chapped hands taking the box from her. For a frenetic, elated moment it was all about familiar bodies in contact, and all she wanted to do was tuck in at the table, tell them everything, and be forgiven. But when her father took her cloak and the AK-47 came into view, the energy in the room altered. Her mother withdrew into herself. Her father busied himself at the stove with coffee.

The gun hung on the back of the chair, and she removed her abaya and disguised her weapon in the folds of fabric. She slid down into a seat and searched for ways to rekindle the love that, moments ago, had charged the room. She retrieved the medicine from her purse and gave it to her mother.

"You must be low."

Her mother's hands trembled with the white tablets and foil. Her father stood above her with a glass of water and removed a pill. They averted their eyes from Zeinah's gaze, and she felt alone, outside their connection. Her mother thanked her father and returned the cup to his waiting hand. Food stained her mother's housecoat; dirty dishes piled up in the sink.

Zeinah hoisted the box on top of the table in front of her mother. "You won't believe what's inside. What I found."

Her father put the coffeepot on the table. "So long since you've had a present. Right, Ma?"

Two weeks since her last visit, and she'd come home to find her mother afraid and her father skittish.

"I'm going to let you two have some time together."

Zeinah watched as he skulked into the next room, and when he disappeared, she sensed her mother calling him back, her unease with being alone with her daughter. Zeinah pushed the box toward her mother. "Don't you want to see what it is?"

Her mother struggled to open the box, her upper arms dimpled from disuse, her hands trembling, her fingers searching the wrapped objects, and Zeinah could tell she was trying to be cheerful when she looked up and announced, "Plates!"

"Wait till you see."

Zeinah felt herself reaching for an intimacy that was gone and watched as her mother removed the newspaper and revealed the delicate veins of a turquoise plate. In the middle were two blackbirds surrounded by green vines. Her mother ran her thumb along the edge of interlocking hexagons.

"Tita," she murmured.

"Someone left them in the lobby of my building. A full set." Zeinah moved the box closer to her mother. "From our childhoods. Tita's, yours, mine."

Her mother grimaced, and it seemed she might cry as she methodically unwrapped each plate and smoothed each piece of newspaper with her palm. The process was painful to witness, like polishing silver for parties that would never again materialize. In the shadows of the next room, Zeinah noticed laundry hanging from a sagging cord between two walls. Beside the kitchen sink was a bowl of apple cores and onion ends saved for reuse.

Her mother folded her hands across the pile of flattened news-paper and finally met her gaze. "My sister said she saw you. At the market."

Of course her aunt had told them.

"It was past curfew. I offered to get her what she needed. I would've brought it to her house."

"You think you're still welcome there?"

Zeinah's eyes landed on the doorframe that measured the height of family members through the years, the doorframe where just months ago she'd held on to her mother before marriage.

Her mother placed her pills in the bag. "You used to be such a nice person."

"I am a nice person."

Her mother held the medicine in her lap and considered Zeinah as if she were a stranger. "A nice person who does bad things."

"Dad asked me to marry him. You stood by. I'm trying to sur-vive, to have a life."

Tears stood in her mother's eyes, but instead of feeling sym-pathy, Zeinah's mind hardened as she felt the sting of her alone-ness. She refused to collapse into their passivity and decay. The comfort she sought from them moments ago now repelled her. Their morning ritual of stale pastries sogged in coffee soured her thoughts, and she knew there was no respite here, no home in their disappointed and retreating eyes. A plate pattern from childhood could not reclaim what was lost.

"I suppose you think it's better to be a nice person who does nothing," said Zeinah.

Her mother scanned the dark living room for her father.

"That's what you think?" pressed Zeinah.

Zeinah knew it was more than just her aunt who talked about

her. It was probably the neighbors, her cousins, people at the
mosque, and she felt a nip of pleasure. Perhaps there was a certain
gait, a recognizable swing of her arms, that signaled she was coming. And maybe they were right; they should be scared. Perhaps
she wasn't a nice person at all.

DOUNIA

Since dawn, Qadira had slept alone in her crib while Dounia sat perched on the edge of the couch, waiting for Flora to emerge. Without a word, she watched Hamed depart for his trip to London. The chandelier mocked her from the foyer, a cruel reminder of what she'd hoped for in a marriage. Sprinklers swept across the garden, murmured to a hiss, and sank underground. The refrigerator idled. Ice cubes dropped into the freezer tray, and the exhales through open windows were now stifled by glass and locks.

This was Flora's fault. Because of Flora, she now had to breast-feed, to stimulate her milk after weeks of going dry. All because the infant was in her bed. If only the baby hadn't been there, none of this would've happened. Hamed's return to their bed changed everything, and she felt disoriented, even scared.

She spiraled inward toward a remote place. The hot air had calmed her nerves and softened edges. The cold solidified her discontent, and yet she knew survival depended on her surrender. Submission to Hamed, to her baby, to Basma, and, in some strange way, to Flora. Not to Flora exactly, but to the architecture of their relationship, domestic expectations.

———

The door opened in the basement. Slippers shuffled on the stairs. Flora emerged in her yellow uniform, eyes dark, hair pulled back, and when she saw Dounia, she reached for the banister and halted midstep.

"Come."

Flora approached Dounia, her swollen eyes to the ground. Dounia hated Flora's fear, how she never looked at her directly, her supplicant and saintly manner. She reminded Dounia of those dolls with flexible rubber limbs bending in every imaginable direction and then returning to their original form. Flora's kindness incited a schoolgirl meanness.

"I thought you were a responsible woman, someone I could trust. And I'm not talking about Hamed. I don't care about that. You brought Qadira into the basement, into your bed. Because of your self-ishness, your loneliness? Your laziness. You didn't think of me at all."

Flora used the sleeve of her uniform to wipe her cheek.

"That's right. Mop yourself up."

"Ma'am, I'm—"

"I don't want to hear your voice. I don't want to hear a thing."

Qadira began to stir.

"Let her cry."

Flora awkwardly tugged on her sleeves.

"Now that I need to breastfeed . . ."

Dounia scrutinized Flora's hair, perfectly parted, brushed back into a thick bun. Even in her cheap uniform and no makeup, she could see what Hamed found attractive. And it was true, Flora was kind, and her tenderness was infuriating, something she felt compelled to destroy.

"I need your passport and your phone."

Flora removed her phone from the pocket in her uniform and set it on the table.

"You'll receive your wages at the end of the contract. I shouldn't pay you at all."

"Yes, ma'am."

"Go with Raj. You'll make a stop. After that, you'll buy me a breast pump. I don't know anything about them. Ask for help. I'll pump. You'll give Qadira the bottle. And get rid of those slippers. I hate the shuffle."

Qadira's cry came from upstairs.

"Let her be. No one's going to starve."

ESKEDARE

A Sunday, late afternoon. Eskedare's stomach cramps and blood stains her thighs. She cannot let her mother see soiled rags, rags washed in water, rags left on the line to dry, rags announcing her availability to a person passing by.

She goes searching for leaves and stuffs stems inside herself, squats and pulls handfuls of red foliage from her body that she hides at the base of the warka tree behind her home, and at night, as her mother sleeps, she burns the blood-brown leaves into a pile of ash that she scatters along the road.

And when she comes inside to bed, she feels the pitcher breathing, the curve of the handle thickening, the glazed eyes waking. Her body is a traitor.

⤶

JUSTINE

Justine stood beneath the showerhead at the British Club and watched the desert slough away from her. The sand between her toes, in the creases of her skin, and in her hair landed on the tiles and disappeared down the drain. Music piped into the empty locker room—"Happy" played on 101.3 FM, the UAE radio station that played in every mall, health club, and supermarket across the nation. "Happy," American pop culture, still a powerful export. She removed a delicate rim of sand from her ear with a fresh Q-tip and surveyed her reflection in the mirror. She pumped yellow body butter into her palm from a wall dispenser and rubbed it across her fair skin, gargled with green mouthwash that stung her gums, and applied a swipe of lipstick. A pink flush of summer disguised her anxiety, but her hands shook and she needed to eat.

She picked at fried calamari beneath the white sunless sky. The smell of chlorine and coconut mingled with the hot oil from the grill behind her. It was a weekday, so the only men in sight were the busboys and maintenance workers circling the trees with Weedwackers. She vaguely recognized the woman in the yellow bikini. Her kids were younger, maybe four and six. Two pendants hung from a gold chain, the kind stamped with kids' initials. Rumors pegged the couple for bankruptcy back in the States. Now they lived in the St. Regis apartments out on Saadiyat. There were lots of stories like that: ex-cops commanding freelance military units, drunk bond traders needing to sober up. She didn't know what to believe, and after a few failed coffees with various moms, she gave up on the idea of connection and told herself she wasn't here to forge friendships. Most of the women at Wren's school were trailing spouses anyway, and she supposed this was what their lives looked like: school drop-off, an exercise class, lunch, and school pickup, followed by afternoons at the club where the kids would swim, do homework in lounge chairs, and shower before heading home. Days spent in spandex. The women hung out poolside, talking to their friends about God knows what, while their kids cheated during rounds of Marco Polo. She admired the wide-brimmed hat on one of the women and wondered where it was from. Better not to ask. She didn't want to draw attention to herself.

———

"Mind if I join you?"

Surprisingly, Leo wore white. He stood bowlegged, chest forward, above her. Cheeks freshly shaved; hair clipped. She suspected the grooming had been done today, probably since her call.

His chair scraped against the terrace stones, and he took a seat, snapped the back off his phone, and removed the battery. "You should do the same. They can hear everything."

Justine slid her phone across the table, and as he removed the battery, she watched a girl dog-paddle across the pool.

With the task completed, he leaned back in his chair, his arms spread wide. "Justine Willard. I first heard your name through Callum. 'Give her what she wants.' That's what he said."

Justine filled his water glass and offered her plate of calamari.

He dipped the squid in red sauce. "He not only emailed; he called. Insisted you get a corner apartment on a high floor overlooking the Gulf. Not everyone gets that kind of treatment."

A lemon seed floated amid the melting ice of her flat Diet Coke, and she was aware that a kind of loyalty was required. "Were you surprised I called?"

"I had a feeling I might hear from you."

"You've seen the surveillance footage."

"I have. I also talked to Callum."

The woman in the yellow bikini waved to Justine, and she raised her palm in recognition.

"To be honest, I didn't even know this girl," said Justine.

The kids were arguing in the pool. The eldest boy screamed, "Mom." The woman in the yellow bikini told them to work it out themselves.

"What did Callum say?"

"No one needs to know she was in your apartment or see the footage. The last thing the museum district needs is one of their own employees taking on labor issues and human rights."

She'd not considered this response.

"You can come by the control room tomorrow. After business hours. Review the footage and decide what to do. Report it. Delete it. Do nothing. She was in your apartment. It's up to you. These labor issues are real. We respect your convictions, and I understand if you want to talk to the police, but we won't be able to support you in those efforts. If you go down that road, I'd recommend getting a lawyer familiar with sharia law."

Justine's mind recalibrated as she apprehended the larger systems she was serving: institutions, partnerships, and government contracts. They'd encourage her silence while offering the illusion of choice.

FLORA

Raj drove Flora to the outskirts of town and parked at a dingy strip mall. Flora waited in the car while Raj talked to a woman in a salon with a broken sign. She knew Raj was telling her the story by the way they both looked over at the car. She thought of Pia, and even though they could not see Flora's courage behind the tinted glass, she met their gazes with an unblinking stare. Raj waved her inside.

Stuffing poked through the cracked leather barber chairs, and hair cuttings littered the floor. Outdated beauty products and round mirrors lined the walls. The woman, middle-aged in a beige collared shirt and maroon polyester pants, drank coffee from a Styrofoam cup and assessed Flora.

"Perlah! Customer."

A young woman appeared in the back and waved Flora to her station. Flora hung her cloak on a peg and sat in the leather chair in her yellow uniform. The hairdresser, a petite woman with thick black hair tied back into a ponytail, removed the hairpins from Flora's bun and watched it fall below her shoulders. Flora touched her neck, in a hopeful gesture of a bob. The older woman watched from the front, laughed, and barked out orders in Urdu. The hairdresser brushed Flora's hair, scrutinized her face, rotating the chair to a profile, and said nothing. From a jar of blue liquid, she removed scissors and a comb, and Flora felt handfuls of hair snipped down to the roots, millimeters from her scalp.

"Head straight." The stylist lifted her chin and spun the chair away from the old woman watching. The hairdresser gripped her shoulder, bent toward her ear, and, in a low voice, spoke to her in Tagalog: "I've been cutting hair since I was twelve. You have a beautiful head. Don't worry."

She raised a shaver toward her boss, who snorted with approval.

The razor traveled across her scalp. Flora closed her eyes and surrendered, there was nothing she could do. Tears rolled down her cheeks, not for the hair but for the woman she'd become, and when she looked in the mirror, she did not recognize her reflection. The hairdresser wiped her neck and shoulders with a handkerchief and then dropped it into Flora's lap. On the corner, embroidered in red thread, was a narra tree, their country's national symbol.

"Keep it."

DOUNIA

For the first time, Dounia added a cup of tea for herself. Basma, with the help of Flora, would ensure Dounia's obedience to Hamed's request in his absence. The tray rattled, and the steam carried the smell of sweet milk down the hallway. Years ago, Basma was in a similar position when she married Hamed's father and moved in with his parents. A part of her must understand. But Basma did not acknowledge her presence when she entered or the second teacup on the tray.

"Where's Flora?"

"I sent her on some errands."

Dounia offered her arm and helped Basma to the bathroom; the woman closed the door without a word. Dounia sat on the bed and listened to the unsteady flow of urine hit the water bowl. The toilet paper dispenser squeaked, and her soiled diaper dropped into the wastebasket. A picture of Ibrahim sat on the nightstand in an oval frame: his face in close-up, hair blowing in the wind, and a wry smile directed at the person behind the camera—Basma, and Dounia felt envious of her mother-in-law and the life she'd shared with her husband.

Dounia heard the water faucet, the pumping of soap, and then the click of dentures snapping into place. Basma cleared her throat, Dounia's cue to bring Basma back to bed. Once tucked in, Dounia gathered the hand mirror and lipstick on the dresser.

Basma meticulously applied the coral stain to her deflated lips.

Despite the fact she lived in bed, the woman maintained her vanity. Dounia used to think the efforts were for her son, but she now saw the gesture as a cast toward a previous self, a way of maintaining continuity and remain among the living. Basma returned the mirror and lipstick and then smoothed down the sheets in preparation for her tray.

As Basma sipped her tea, Dounia walked around the foot of the bed, fluffed the pillows, and took a place beside Basma. There was the tap of china teacups on saucers before either of them spoke.

"I suppose you want to speak to me about what happened."

She blames me, thought Dounia, and the muscles tightened around her lips.

"Sex is part of the marriage contract. You cannot blame him."

Dounia felt the cup, hot between her palms. "There were other promises."

"I know you had other plans. A home outside the family. You'll see, one day you'll have a daughter-in-law who will take care of you."

Dounia observed the long drapes and closed windows in the room. The walls don't breathe anymore. Growing up, they used to breathe.

"I'm not meant to be a mother." There, I've said it, thought Dounia.

"And you think you're the only woman with these thoughts. All women feel this way at one time or another. It's one thing to think, to feel, but to reject your own child, your husband . . . Does Hamed know?"

"I think it's obvious."

The room went quiet.

"I spoiled Hamed. Ibrahim would chastise me. I can't bear his unhappiness."

Dounia was unsure if this was an admission or a threat, but Basma pressed on. "Motherhood is about many things. Our country. Our culture. Women, including your own grandmother, by the way, are the ones who've kept the Kingdom going. Everything comes from the family, it's the most important unit of society. Everyone knows that. Every man knows that."

Dounia bristled at Basma's convictions; never had she talked this candidly.

"We uphold tradition, guide our husbands and sons in business. It may go unseen, but we're the keepers of heritage and the future. The guardians. Women of your generation can inhabit different worlds—apartments in London, cocktail parties—while also upholding our culture. Things are changing. You must have faith. But what you're doing . . ."

"What am I doing?"

Dounia sensed Basma's reluctance to speak freely, and she allowed the silence to expand between them. Basma's hands clasped the teacup; her stomach rose and fell. Dounia could wait all day.

"You hide in your room, refuse to breastfeed, banish your husband from your bed. You seek attention. You're . . ." Basma stopped herself.

"No, tell me."

"You . . . I don't know."

"What?" She was aware of her cruelty, of forcing Basma to speak her mind, to utter something she'd never be able to retract.

"You've left the herd."

Dounia's mind went numb. It was true; she'd rejected her role as mother, wife, and daughter-in-law, and never had she felt so lost. Basma would never offer refuge, could never understand. Dounia felt herself rise off the bed and gather the tray and teacups. Basma was still talking, but she didn't hear a word, and as she left the bedroom and walked down the hallway, her mind returned to the only woman left: Flora.

ZEINAH

Zeinah headed back to her apartment, inflamed by recriminations, a rage seeded in the home of her parents and their entire rotten generation of nice people who did nothing.

She cut through a soccer game, aware of the sudden silence that trailed behind her, the caution she inspired in others. The sun was low in the sky, sending flares down the block, and she thought she saw a covered woman seated on a doorstep. As she approached, she realized the woman was holding an infant, and the image stoked her longing for a family, for a baby, and the humiliation of the IUD. As she passed, she snuck a view of the child but was instead met by the woman's bare breast, her brown areola, her enlarged nipple like a slug hanging out for all to see.

Zeinah grabbed the woman's arm. Soft flesh squished between her fingers (her mother's dimpled arm). She heard the squeal of a yappy dog (or was that the woman screaming?). A door swung open, and a bearded man with thick thighs grabbed his wife as Zeinah reached for her gun. A toddler appeared in the dark entryway. Coats in the hall. Black umbrellas. Sultan.

Zeinah yanked the baby from the mother's grip, a soft floured weight now in her arms, then gone again, as she shoved the writhing infant into the man's barrel chest. A lunge forward, a fumble, and as he caught the newborn and cradled the screaming child, he pleaded, "Please don't take my wife." Over and over, "Don't take her. No."

The woman's defiance, breastfeeding in public, rattled Zeinah to her core. The flagrant display of creating a life on her own terms, holding a child to her naked breast at dusk outside her door, felt unjust after everything Zeinah had sacrificed. The shame of who she'd become, the respect she'd lost of the people she loved, and the pain of those injuries sent her back on her heels and gathered in a fury.

Sun reflected off dust-covered windshields as Zeinah dragged the woman down the street, beneath a sky cut by broken buildings and sagging black electrical wires. "Sixty lashes!" Her voice was unfamiliar, theatrical with conviction and momentum. "Come see the flogging. Breastfeeding in public."

People gaped, closed their doors, and disappeared into the shadows. Others pointed, while some assembled behind her.

"To the playground," she shouted. With what felt like a wave of power at her back, Zeinah pushed past the swings, toward the middle of her old kickball field. She heard footsteps behind her and murmurs of approval: "Sixty lashes. Sixty lashes! This woman bared her breast in public."

A crowd gathered around them. The woman whimpered, and Zeinah recalled her mother's frightened and downcast eyes at the kitchen table. Cowardice roiled Zeinah's stomach. If only this woman would stand up and fight. Do something. The woman broke free, and the crowd pushed her back into the circle. We are all together now, thought Zeinah. People pushed and shoved. They all wanted to see the terrible something about to unfold, to hide their weakness in a momentary triumph.

A woman's voice yelled out, "Biter. Biter." From the back of the crowd, Umm Humra held up an oversized pair of iron scissors with hooks at the end. A mass of hands passed the metal tool of torture to the front, and it landed on the ground at Zeinah's feet.

Whistles and howls from the crowd urged her forward, and even if she wanted to stop, it was too late.

Zeinah ripped open the woman's cloak and revealed her naked breast. There was a moment of unease as people acknowledged what they saw: nudity, a woman stripped, her shamelessness on display in the public square. Adrenaline pulsed through the playground and needed to be released. They were all vulnerable, and rage promised to burn them clean.

Zeinah reached for the biter. The iron handles were heavy and the blades stiff to open. There was the woman's areola (again), and she could feel the anticipation in the crowd as she approximated the distance between breast and blade and then: contact. The crowd cheered as she squeezed the handles together and felt the metal blades puncture flesh. Blood squirted from the left breast, staining the sleeve of Zeinah's cloak. The woman fell to the dirt in agony as others stood by and took pictures. The woman had not fought, not at all.

Feeling dizzy, Zeinah hurled the biter aside and willed her jellied legs through the crowd, where she believed people were whispering, "Blessings be upon you."

ESKEDARE

August, the nights are getting longer, and her mother mutters beside her in the dark. Uneasiness grows between them, lives in the pop of logs on the fire, the spit of hot oil in pans, the call of night birds. Once, in a half-horror state, her mother bolts upright in bed, grips Eskedare's leg, and appears menacing in the shadows.

One afternoon, before dusk, Eskedare discovers her mother sitting motionless at the table with the pitcher and a tin plate of freshly cut mangoes. Eskedare pauses in the doorway, her mind gone cold. Her mother pours tea, and Eskedare watches the leaves swirl and rise to the surface. Leaves. Her mother has peered through the dung-bark walls and seen her bloodstained leaf piles and nighttime fires.

Eskedare takes a slice of mango. The sweetness slicks down her throat and churns her stomach. The room tightens around them as their female ancestors crowd around the table, flock to the walls, elbow for space, and whisper from the twined ropes in the ceiling. Tears stand in her mother's eyes, and Eskedare does not know what is worse: the pitcher announcing her future or the mango pleading for forgiveness.

For a long time neither of them says a word.

"Who?"

Her mother mutters something she cannot understand. A storm takes hold of Eskedare: limbs sweep and shake wildly inside her chest, her mind churns.

"Who?!"

Eskedare seizes the ceramic jug, the jug that has been watching and taunting her. The room stands at attention. Eskedare holds her arms high, the jug looming over the rocks and stones of the firepit.

"Tell me."

The mother whimpers and then groans.

"I swear, I'll smash it."

The mother's lips part.

"Say it!"

Her mother will not meet her gaze, and her words are barely audible: "Salim. Your uncle chose Salim."

Salim? Salim. The horror of that boy, that family. Losers and cheats. The people everyone spits on in their minds. This is what her mother thinks of her, the best she can do for the daughter she claims to love.

A gale thrashes through Eskedare's heart, raids her body; everything inside her uproots, and all that remains in that moment is an unyielding force and momentum, a hatred for her mother and her betrayal. She smashes the pitcher against the rocks, and shards hurl across the floor. A moan, guttural and full of anguish, moves through her mother's body, and she covers her face in shame. Eskedare regards her mother with a cold distance and sees only weakness. If I stay here, I'll kill her, she thinks.

Her mother calls out to her, but Eskedare is gone. She won't marry. Not Salim. Not anyone. Ever.

❧

DOUNIA/FLORA

Dounia sat, her shirt open, in front of the breast pump that resembled a briefcase. Flora assembled the sterilized tubes and bottles on a paper towel beside her, and Dounia noted her care and efficiency. She preferred Flora stripped of feminine accessories, without the hairpins and elastics, and believed she'd done the woman a favor.

"Maybe I should cut my hair. What do you think?"

"It's fine, ma'am. Very easy."

"Yes, but it suits you."

Flora attached each tube to a suction cup and then a plastic bottle. "Ready, ma'am."

Dounia pulled her breasts out of her bra and felt shy as Flora placed the cups over her nipples. Flora flipped on the switch, and the pump whirred and the suction cups squeezed. Dounia laughed. Flora switched off the machine.

"What is it, ma'am?"

"Nothing. It feels strange. It's okay. Go on."

"You'll get used to it."

The machine resumed, and Dounia watched the empty bottles dangle from her breasts. "Nothing's happening."

"Don't worry, ma'am. It can take a few days for your milk to come in. You can do it on and off again for twenty minutes, a few times a day."

"Sit with me."

Flora hesitated, wiped her hands dry on the towel.

"It's okay. The baby's sleeping."

Flora checked the oven clock. "Ma'am, I need to iron Basma's laundry."

"That can wait. Sit. I want to start again. I'm sorry."

And for the next hour, above the whir of the breast pump, in fits and starts, the two women shared scraps of life: Flora told Dounia how she grew up on a small island without streets or cars, how only footpaths connected their homes. Her father was a fisherman who rode a boat to work, and as a child she'd listened to his small motor disappear across the bay. Salt air and the smell of jasmine hung in the trees. Her store. How she'd cut a window into the living room and made a sari-sari where she sold chips, gum, soap, and phone cards. And about the wild honeybees on her island that sucked nectar from the coconut flowers that bloomed year-round.

Dounia told Flora about a game she played with her sister and cousins at night, how they jumped between two strings staked into the sand, and her father's stamp collection: miniature pictures of palm trees, crossed swords, airplanes, and oil refineries. Her favorite grandmother, whose name was Fahda bint Fasial ibn Hussain. And how to make coconut basbousa with semolina, honey, and rosewater.

Flora did not say how she stepped on a hive of honeybees and was swollen in bed for weeks with blisters on her tongue, or how her father stopped working, or how her mother got her up before dawn to catch crabs with her bare hands, crabs she threw into blue buckets on the shore before she realized it all was pointless and left for Japan. She didn't mention the stench of burning bodies or how she sold Bibles, rosaries, and rum, and not a word about Datu, who was born with a full head of hair and a red birthmark the size of a cherry behind his ear. Nothing about her breast milk, meant for him, now going dry.

And Dounia didn't share how after nighttime games her cousin asked her to watch as his hands roamed beneath his garments, or how her grandmother died of a heart attack during harvest, how Dounia found her face up beneath the trees with a date still in her mouth, how her absence marked her life, or how she'd stupidly felt superior to her mother, the woman she loved most in this world.

The yellow suction cups pumped for milk, activated ducts and dry beds, and by the end of the conversation, drops had formed in the tubes and were traveling to the bottles.

JUSTINE

In the small penthouse gym, Justine went through the nautilus routine while watching Al Jazeera. Alone with the cardio equipment, the Abu Dhabi skyline stretched out before her, and on the TV, a female reporter interviewed Syrian women with pixelated faces and distorted voices, women who spoke out against the West, blamed the United States for invasions in the name of human rights only to leave women and girls more vulnerable to extremist factions. Between her reps of ten, Justine watched footage of cloaked women sitting beneath trees cleaning their weapons as the reporter spoke of the rise of female ISIS fighters. On the other side, up in the north, women from Iran, Iraq, and Turkey were joining Kurdish women in their own liberation army, the YPJ, a female arm of the Kurdish military fighting against ISIS and promoting female equality.

Justine abandoned the leg press, powered down the television, and approached the wall of windows overlooking the roundabout. Below her, the flashing blue lights of police cars guarded the fountain. Since the girl's death, people had been leaving offerings of loose flowers and bouquets wrapped in plastic. At prayer time, men gathered around the fountain, unrolled their carpets, and prayed, but no-one was allowed to linger. She wanted to visit the fountain, acknowledge the girl, but it was late. Tomorrow, she'd bring the lilies from the foyer.

———

From her bed, Justine stared across the city. The lights of empty office spaces illuminated a broth of sky, and she felt trapped inside a room with dirt-covered panes. The glint of Shema's grey-chested swoop, her dives and arcs above the dunes and desert, her kill of the bustard . . . that was today, she thought. Shema was today.

ZEINAH

Zeinah lay on the couch and watched the beams of truck head-lights sweep across the walls. Her breath was shallow. She remem-bered little. Her own ghostly singsong voice echoed in her ears: "Sixty lashes! Come see the flogging." She'd wanted to avoid the playground, but she'd journeyed to the heart of it. She recalled not the adrenaline but the horror in her wake, how the crowd opened to let her leave, perhaps not out of respect but out of fear for what they'd witnessed in her and in themselves. She'd left the woman lying in the dirt.

The red wing lights of planes blinked across the muted sky. Maybe a Russian fighter going to bomb Aleppo, or American supplies traveling to the north, or Kuwaitis headed for London. Omar's parents in Iraq. She wondered if they'd searched for him when he'd disappeared with their Qur'an. She retraced the wounds of the day. That morning, she'd wrapped hope into a box of plates. By evening, she nursed a disfigured conscience, her in-dignation gone. In the city, the call to prayer signaled the pass-ing hours. No one came up or down the stairs, and she wondered about the child who once ran across the floor above her, the water gurgling through the pipes at bath time.

She rolled from the couch onto the floor, barely moving, barely thinking. Her dress tangled around her waist; her legs splayed. The overhead fan blew air across her thighs, and she lay perfectly still, listening to the whirr. Once, she'd removed her underwear and stared at the rotating blades above her, aroused by the breeze against her nakedness, but no thought or puff of air could induce her now. Fantasy was dead. There was no heartbeat between her legs, but still, she wondered if Omar was out there and if he was alive.

ESKEDARE

Eskedare walks alone in the dark toward the men chewing khat, but as she strides past shacks and cattle, her thoughts stumble over Gulf-return girls: eyes-to-the-ground girls, girls gone missing, girls gone dead. But I'm not one of those girls, she thinks. I dance on the backs of cows in downpours and drive a dead truck through valleys of the Simien Mountains.

Loose eyes and swollen cheeks greet her on the stoop. She takes a tip from Amara and keeps her mouth shut. The men chuckle, think it's funny to have a girl standing over them with silence on her tongue and a mark in her eye.

"Get outta here," says one of the men. "Aren't you getting married?"

"My sister's got a dress bleaching in the sun," says the red-gummed man.

They see her as a child, all except the man she's come to see: his crotch swells for everyone. He pinches khat from a pouch and tucks it inside his cheek. She feels the tree limbs keeping watch, hears the leaves begin to gossip.

"Best to wait."

"If you don't help me, someone else will."

Drool gathers in the corner of his lips. He wipes it away with the back of his hand. "Why do you wanna go there?"

"You see the house going up behind my teacher's shack? That woman was four years in Bahrain."

"Don't you know? That woman's gone mute."

Eskedare shrugs and lets them puzzle over her. "I'm going to Qatar."

The fat man's belly shakes until his eyes leak, and he wipes away the tears. "What about your mother?"

Eskedare's throat closes. "Can you get me to Qatar or not? Anywhere near there's good."

The broker spits into a can. "I don't want any trouble. Come back when you're married."

"I'm not getting married."

The motor of a tuk-tuk rumbles in the distance. They listen to it approach, pass, and disappear.

"It will cost you. Fake papers, transport fees, employment placement."

He knows she has nothing.

"With zero down it's gonna be double interest."

"How much?"

"Fifteen thousand birr for fake ID and transport. I'll place you for free."

"How much will I make over there?"

"Around three thousand birr a month."

She does the calculations. After ten months she'd be free.

"My mother . . . You'll check on her?"

He shrugs. "I'll give you eighteen months to pay it back."

That night, she wanders the paths she's hiked with cows and lies in the field of blue stones and blue stars. Her mother can sleep, and sleep, and sleep, and when she awakes, there'll be a house of concrete, a roof of tin. Before her bus departs, Eskedare checks on her mother from the hillside. She tends a fire in the yard, desperate for Eskedare to return, hoping the flames and sparks will call her home.

DOUNIA

Dounia dreamed of honey. Honey poured from her breasts and twisted her hair into mounds of regal braids, and when she woke up, she was euphoric. Her soul had shifted in the night, and she liked herself again. She'd go to the honey festival. She'd seen an advertisement in the paper—an initiative to encourage locals to buy from national beekeepers. She showered, and for the first time in months she put on a yellow dress with shiny yellow sandals. No one would see beneath her abaya, but she'd know. She sprayed honeysuckle perfume on her wrists and neck and put on pink lipstick. Somewhere she had a yellow bag, and after searching through her closet, she found it—a wedding present from her aunt.

Instead of eating breakfast in bed, she ate at the kitchen table. Flora served her toast and a hard-boiled egg. "Flora, do we have any honey?"

"I'm sorry, no, ma'am, we don't."

"Everyone likes honey."

"Oh, I love honey, ma'am. I can eat it with everything. Plantains and honey—that's one of my favorites. I'd love to make you that."

"Flora . . ."

"Yes, ma'am."

"I'm going out today."

"Yes, ma'am. Don't worry."

Dounia left with the secret of bringing back honey. She didn't tell Flora or Basma where she was going or when she'd return. She was excited for the adventure and the vision of bearing gifts for Flora, a woman who would become her ally.

————

The festival was set up as a series of connected tents in the shape of a beehive. More than fifty Saudi honey producers gathered to sell their sweet syrup and advertise their methods. She'd read that Madinah had the best bees, but they were facing extinction because the imported breeds brought disease and attacked the local population.

Exhibitors with wooden ladles stirred large glass bowls of honey and offered testers on wooden sticks. And, of course, there was every iteration of honey: honey candy, honey cream, honey oil, honeycomb, bee textiles and jewelry. Dounia bought Flora a gold pin of a flying bee and tucked it inside her purse. I was much too hard on her, she thought, what happened was not her fault. I will pump and do my best to repair things in the house, and maybe with time I will not be so afraid of my daughter.

The *Apis mellifera jemenitica* was a native bee that had been in Saudi Arabia since 2000 BC and over time adapted to the high temperatures and harsh summers. She'd grown up with these bees feeding on alfalfa, eucalyptus, sunflower, and date palm at her family's farm. After many tastings, Dounia was torn between Asiri and Sidr honey. Sidr was made by Saudis but came from the Sidr trees in Yemen, while Asiri honey came from the Saudi Asir region. Beekeepers transported thousands of hives to the Sarawat mountains so the bees could eat from the different trees, flowers, and shrubs. She liked the taste of the Sidr honey best but felt she should buy the 100 percent KSA brand. She wondered which Flora would enjoy most and decided on Sidr honey because it would also be a good topic of conversation. She'd tell her all about this new local company that was investing in the Saudi honey industry with the aim of becoming the biggest exporter of honey in the region. Besides, Dounia's father had relatives in Yemen who probably ate honey from the Sidr tree, and she liked the idea of thinking about her distant cousins as she ate her Sidr honey.

The honey sat beside her in the car, a three-kilo glass jar, as high as her forearm, with a white lid. The afternoon sun illuminated the golden-brown syrup, and she watched as air bubbles clung to the glass, gathered, dispersed, and disappeared. She unwrapped the wooden honey container and serving spoon and held them in her lap. She'd display them on the kitchen counter. Today had been a good day, but as Raj pulled into the Dream Development, a dull anxiety gnawed at her ribs, and she began to doubt herself.

No one greeted her at the door. She heard Basma's voice and checked the clock: the time of leg and foot massages. She wanted to surprise them both, so she carried the large jar of honey in her skirt and tiptoed up the stairs. On the third floor, she heard Basma telling one of her familiar stories, and she wondered what, if anything, Flora enjoyed in the details of the woman's life. Basma moaned with pleasure. "Such hands."

"Thank you, ma'am. It's nothing."

Dounia paused at the bedroom entrance. Basma stopped mid-sentence, taking in Dounia and her gathered skirt. Flora occupied Dounia's place at the foot of the bed massaging Basma's feet.

"You're interrupting. I'm telling her a story," said Basma.

Dounia watched as Flora circled Basma's ankles with her thumb. Basma groaned in pleasure. "Her hands are magic. Mashallah!"

"Thank you, ma'am."

"Dounia, you're never doing this again."

Dounia's heart stalled. While she was gone, alliances had altered. The chore Dounia despised, Flora had usurped, but instead of feeling liberated, she felt exiled. Dounia stood alone in the doorway.

"And that dress!"

Dounia swore she saw Flora smirk.

"Dounia, either sit down or leave."

Stunned, she backed out of the room, feeling like a fool. She heard sniggering and then Basma—but not only Basma, Flora too (she was sure of it)—laughing, jeering at her awkwardness, her inability to access their shared secrets. Her cheeks flushed and her heart pounded. She'd spent the day selecting honey for two women who had no love for her at all.

She strode down the hallway. At the top of the stairs, she paused and raised the jar of golden honey in the air. Dounia's mind took aim at the tiles, and with a single blow, she smashed the jar against the marble floor. The glass shattered into thick shards. Honey oozed across the white tiles, chunks of glass canted upward like capsized boats, and slivers caught the light, glinting in every direction.

The laughter from the bedroom ceased. The house went quiet.

Flora appeared in the hallway. "Ma'am, are you okay?"

"You'll have to clean it up. None of it can be saved."

"Yes, yes. Of course, ma'am. Be careful."

Flora dropped to her hands and knees trying to contain the mess with her bare hands.

"And don't forget the baby's bottle at five."

ZEINAH

Early morning. The sound of boots on the stairs. After fajr but before breakfast. She was measuring coffee when she heard the scuffing outside the door. Omar had driven through the night once before, but someone was knocking, so it could not be him.

She took her time and covered herself in her cloak and niqab before opening the door. The man, a stranger, took a step back. He had a full beard and was dressed in ISIS military attire.

"Your husband is a martyr, blessed with eternal life and so are you." He offered her an envelope. His hands were red and cracked. "He's arranged for you to keep the apartment. You're lucky. It's one of the nicest."

Zeinah blocked the door, not wanting him to come inside.

"We expect you to remarry. It's your duty to the caliphate."

"The mourning period is four months."

"Not during war."

Zeinah struggled to understand. "Remarry . . . ?"

"Another fighter."

"Another fighter? And when he dies?"

The man said nothing.

She noticed crumbs of food in his mustache and imagined an endless rotation of bearded men from different countries entering and departing.

"That is no life," she whispered.

He looked at her with compassion. "Yes, there's brutality, but there will also be free housing, food, and medical care. We're all part of jihad to create the Islamic State and defend our brothers and sisters."

She noticed dry grass and dust on his boots and wondered if he'd been with Omar when he died.

"Omar said you were a very good wife. Perhaps you'll be mine?"

She would not meet the man's gaze. A sourness formed in her mouth and she stepped inside, closed the door, and listened for his footfalls in the stairwell.

The adhesive on the white and wrinkled envelope was gummy with sand. Certainly, they'd taken some money, but what remained was still generous. She searched for a message but found nothing.

FLORA

At night, while the others slept, Flora suffered. Her breasts, red and engorged, tender to the touch, were swollen with milk. It would be so easy. Qadira Ibrahim could release her from this pain. She could go upstairs, no one would know. But it was too risky. She needed to stop. Instead, she leaned her naked and inflamed breasts over the small bathroom sink and squeezed her glands dry, sprayed her milk across the shallow basin and guided it down the drain with palms full of water. Private nights bent over a sink would be her last moments with Datu, her final goodbye.

JUSTINE

The security control room was located on the second floor in a remodeled studio apartment. Justine and Leo sat at a desk in front of two large monitors. He'd arrived early and queued up the surveillance footage for them to screen. The footage was on pause, each monitor a grid of six images featuring different views of the entrance, car park, elevators, and apartment hallways.

On the wall in front of them were four large screens wrapped in plastic, cords dangling.

"What are those?"

"Part of the government security upgrade. You're lucky. A few months from now, feeds will automatically connect to the precinct. There'd be nothing I could do."

Justine nodded. She was anxious to begin, to see the girl again.

———

Time code: 00:17. Surveillance footage: green, grainy, and dark. Justine's car, the white Nissan, stops at the security gate. Her window goes down, and her face appears tight, apprehensive, when she swipes her card. The footage cuts from one camera to another as her car spirals down the levels to the sub-basement. Two cars pass her on the way up. Headlights blow out the frame. The events of the night in motion.

00:19. It's the couple down the hall. The clarinetist and his sad scales. Justine watches as he takes his wife's arm and they meander toward the elevator.

00:21. Justine's bad parking job elicits a snigger from Leo. The headlights switch off and Justine exits the car, straightens her twisted dress. She does not wait for the girl but walks in front of her toward the elevator bank. The girl pauses in the dim light, clutches her purse to her chest, stalls for time, and scans the dark corners and cars. The footage is silent, but Justine hears everything: the buzz of the fluorescent lights, water dripping. Justine watches herself beckon impatiently to the girl, sees the insistence of her own arm movements, her irritation, the implicit demand that the girl bend to her wishes. It's her mother she sees. Shame travels up her spine, and she leans against the chair, grateful for the man in the brown suit who seems not to judge her.

00:26. They watch the footage in silence as the girl follows her to the elevator. She remembered the moments not recorded: the girl's long limbs extending across the road in a sprint, their shared aloneness on the highway in a country not their own, the flashing hazards, the smell of gasoline and salt in the fogged air.

00:27. Justine and the girl wait for the elevator beneath the vivid light. The girl drags her heel across the beige tiles, maybe aware of the surveillance cameras. In the elevator, they stand next to each other, facing forward and uncomfortable. When they leave, the camera cuts to an image above Justine's apartment door. She fumbles for her keys. The door opens, but the girl hesitates and gazes directly into the lens. It's as if she's looking into the future, at Justine right now gaping back at her. Many times that night she'd wanted to let the girl go—on the roadside, in the car, in the basement—and yet she'd held on.

"There are about five hours where nothing happens. I'll fast-forward to the last bit."

Justine watched the footage blur by. She never realized how recorded her life was, never considered the vast archive of dull human movement stored in the cloud.

04:54. The girl leaves Justine's apartment with the blue water jug. She closes the door with care and waits for the elevator, pressing the button several times, impatient to leave. She enters the elevator, her gaze resolute and calm as she descends and then exits through the dark tunnel of the parking garage. The footage stops.

"There she is. That's the last of her."

She wondered when the girl had decided to set herself on fire. On the side of the road, in the car, when she reached for her birthmark in the kitchen, when she'd talked about the embassy?

"What was her name?"

"No name. Not a real one, anyway. Fake passport. Ethiopia. No more than sixteen. Maybe younger."

She wanted to know the girl's real name. She could not bear the idea of her body lying in the sand beneath a numbered stone, in a country not her own . . . Everyone deserves a proper burial. The double helix of these impulses, of wanting to both erase and honor the girl, was not lost on Justine. U.S. drone strikes. Americans bombing civilian homes and then wanting to pay modest reparations to families whose children, wives, and fathers they'd killed. The U.S. lied about civilian casualties, took down drone coordinates initially posted on YouTube for transparency, doctored numbers, and then offered families compensation: $224.

"What do you wanna do?"

"I don't know, I . . ."

Leo regarded her and frowned. "She was a migrant worker on an illegal passport."

The man was repugnant to her now. She imagined a transistor radio by his bed, folded undershirts beside worn dress socks in a top drawer. And yet he knew things, talked to Callum, and worked with the government. This was the system she was a part of. And those blue water jugs loaded onto trucks, roped to roofs, traveling across highways, delivered to lobbies, stacked in hallways, flipped upside down and dispensing water to the entire population of the United Arab Emirates—this blue plastic container, a daily part of everyone's life, was now tied to this horrific act, the girl's protest. Such an innocuous object, no one had even thought to ask where the jug came from. No one suspected that the jug belonged to Justine; no one knew except the man sitting next to her. And Callum. Justine and Wren drank water from that jug, and that was not a crime, but her proximity to the girl, to her act of protest when the region was unstable, could be tricky for the Emirati partners, the government, and the British Museum.

The file waited for her on the desktop. Her mind teetered, and she felt unsure. Justine regarded Leo, and his gaze shifted toward her with reproach.

Justine nodded, unsure of what to say, of whose side she was on.

"There'll be time code gaps due to maintenance issues. It happens all the time. This old system is crap."

Justine imagined the girl's remains, someone collecting the chunks of ash, the soot on the fountain floor. Somewhere was proof of her existence, if only in a police report or a morgue ledger, a date, name unknown. The girl was archived somewhere, if only in a series of numbers. And that was a form of care, however small and bureaucratic: an acknowledgment by the state that the girl had existed.

Justine dragged the file across the screen and into the trash. She emptied the trash and listened to the electronic sound of paper crumpling, ones and zeroes colliding. Her proximity to the girl vanishing and then gone.

ESKEDARE

Fifteen, a time that lingers.

III.

III

DOUNIA

After the honey, a cold front descended on the concrete house. The air conditioner throttled through the night and blasted a wintry chill into Dounia's bedroom. She sat alone in the dark, the blue light of the computer screen illuminating her cheeks as she watched winter storms on YouTube. Snow flurries dusted green lawns and matured into sieges of white. The fuzzy headlights of snowplows illuminated empty streets: work suspended, schools closed, there was nothing to do but wait.

High winds flung branches into electrical wires, eighteen-wheelers slid across six-lane highways, and plastic kiddie pools tumbled over white fields. Gales distorted the sound of sirens. People documented storms, their excited voices narrating images of blight: "I'm going to walk just to show you the accumulation. Look at this!"

The camera panned to a car buried in a snowbank.

Flora came and went, brought and cleared her food, but Dounia did not acknowledge the woman or speak to her. She would not forget the humiliation she suffered after the honey, and an imperious ire took hold, refusing to cede to any kindness.

———

Online, spring snowstorms folded over swing sets and settled on bike baskets, daffodils, and bulbs. Kids sucked on long icicles picked from rooftop gutters.

———

In Chamonix, a woman filmed a snowfall while waiting for a bus. Middle-aged in a soiled car coat, she panned upward to the sky, over branches, the brown leaves dowdy, like the woman herself. Down the street, a truck beeped in reverse.

———

In Buffalo, a man's meaty hand opened the front door to reveal more than thirty inches of fresh snow. A dog barked at his feet.

"Go on, girl. You can go."

But the dog whimpered and refused to budge.

"Here we go . . ."

The man grabbed a leather work glove off a hook and threw it out into the yard. Dounia watched as the dog leaped off the porch and disappeared beneath the snow, tunneling through the cold in slow motion and then, to the man's delight, emerging with the glove in her jaw.

"Good girl. Come on back now. C'mere."

The man laughed as the dog struggled through the snowdrift toward him. Dounia pressed pause on the owner's smile and contemplated the man's satisfaction derived from the dog's obedience, the dog's desire to please.

———

And then there were the videos from Japan—addictive and strange. A man carved into a snowbank with an electric saw. In another, a boy set up a camera at a low angle beneath his rooftop. From up above, the sound of banging, and Dounia watched as a colossal block of ice inched closer and closer to the edge, until it finally collapsed to the ground with a hollow and resounding thud.

The anticipation and release were cathartic, and Dounia watched the video many times, and she was not alone: 846,063 other people felt the same way.

———

Blizzards cradled Dounia to sleep. She sipped ice water and dreamed of frigid zones: Alaska, the poles, Greenland, Iceland, and the arctic circle. In her dreams, she slept in igloos and traveled on ice floes. Wet snow collapsed wooden bridges and seeped between the seams of her imagined leather boots. She trudged through whiteouts, ice gnats bit her face, but the howls of laughter at her expense were all obliterated in the storm. It was the kind of squall that initially made a person frantic for friends and family, then stung the mind cold.

JUSTINE

The dollhouse had been ransacked and looted. Panicked, Justine scampered from room to room assessing the damage: mattresses overturned, plates shattered, chairs broken, cabinets plundered. The open refrigerator cast a dim light over the chaos and trampled flowers. In the distance, she heard the *thump-thump, thump-thump* of wingbeats. She opened the door, and a cloud of falcons flew across the sun, felling the world into darkness and propelling Justine up the stairs, where she clambered beneath the bed, scraped her bare knees on the floor, and choked on dust and loose feathers. On the dresser, a ceramic pitcher rattled in its saucer and shattered on the floor. The heavy thump of wings drew near. Birds in search of carrion. In the air, she smelled tobacco burning and heard the shouts of men. Downstairs someone banged on the door, the hinges rattling with every blow.

Justine awoke disoriented, unsure of where she was. Her breastbone ached as her mind spun like postcards on an airport display until she landed on Abu Dhabi, of course she was in Abu Dhabi, working for the British Museum. But the pounding from the dream continued, someone was at the door, and she stumbled down the hallway, arms outstretched, reaching for the walls, trying to catch hold of her dream.

"Coming."

Justine squinted into the overhead light of the hallway. Flip-flops, the loose sash of a flannel bathrobe belted across a distended belly, white briefs. Her neighbor, the clarinetist with his sad notes climbing up and down the scales on late afternoons, stood at the door. He'd been in the car garage that same night. In the surveillance footage, she'd watched him take his wife's hand.

"You all right?"

She imagined a balsam reed damp with his saliva and felt embarrassed.

"Your screaming woke me up."

"Screaming?" She laughed. "God, how awful. I'm sorry."

"You okay?"

He still had the soft curls of a child, and she wanted to reach out and touch them. Justine felt awkward in her t-shirt and underwear, at their shared state of undress, and avoided his gaze.

"You should've heard yourself."

Pieces of the dream emerged. The ransacked house. She leaned against the doorjamb for support. "Really, it's nothing." The shattered pitcher.

"I was worried. If you hadn't come to the door, I would've called the police."

"No, no, I'm fine. Night terrors. I used to have them when I was a kid. I'd sleepwalk and my mother would find me talking nonsense in hallways and closets." Justine shrugged and smiled weakly, disquieted by the memories. "I'm fine, really. Sorry to have woken you."

Justine backed into her apartment, sensing the clarinetist was not convinced. The latch clicked shut and the darkness folded around her as she recalled the cast of falcons, the rasping and choking on feathers. She dared not move, immobilized by her nightmare and memories of her childhood antics in the dark—

something her mother said was a phase but for Justine was a phobia of sleep. Night after night, her mother repeated a slate of lullabies, but it was the beauty of objects, the arranging and categorizing of things—forks, buttons, coins, skeins of yarn, and needles—that created a fortress, a security system, that finally kept the terrors at bay. She needed to return to Shema: the details of her training, the facts.

In the semidarkness, Justine shuffled down the hallway toward the kitchen. The overhead light flickered to life, hummed above the cucumber shavings curled on the cutting board, a dry tea bag stuck to the counter, her yogurt gone soupy. Tomorrow her family was coming home.

She removed the stems of rotting blue hyacinth from a vase and poured the mildewed water down the drain. The apartment was quiet except for the occasional burp of the water cooler, reminding her of the girl, the gas station, the fire, and in the laundry room she scooped dried feces from the litter box, swept stray granules from the tiles, and removed lint from the dryer. In the living room, she fluffed pillows, watered the plants, and emptied figs from a paper bag into a wooden bowl.

She mopped the kitchen floor, sprayed down the counters, and cracked the windows. In Wren's room, her bed remained untouched, the sheets taut and clean. She scanned the surfaces for remaining clues. Nothing. Her eyes fell on the mess of Wren's art table. She could organize the paints, models, and brushes. No, everything should remain as Wren left it. Her arms trembled as she drew back the curtains, slid open the door, and forced herself outside and onto the terrace.

The sun burned through the haze, and there was a forgiving

breeze coming across the Gulf. She swept up sand and debris, removed gaffer's tape, and reset the furniture, noticing brown stains
on the terrace where the iron legs of the chairs had been. She
sank into a chair, stretched her bare calves beyond the shade, and
closed her eyes. Far below she heard the distant bangs of sanitation
trucks. The sidewalks would be clean. She'd buy a fern, and flowers for the fountain too.

FLORA

Flora was stealing things, tucking items into her bra, the waistband of her uniform, the pockets of her apron. It started with the honey she'd rescued from the shards of broken glass, and then it was the gold shears from Basma's bottom drawer and a pair of silk stockings from Dounia's closet. Every night she cut a pearl from the wedding dress hanging in her shower stall and dropped it into the leg of the stocking. She knew they were real because Joenard gave her a pearl necklace for her birthday from an uncle who harvested pearls in Palawan. Before going to bed, she picked a white stone from the knots and threads of the dress, and like recycling days, the pearls marked time. She didn't know what she'd do with them once she was done. Maybe string a necklace to replace the one stolen by the storm and sell the rest. But did she really want Dounia hanging around her neck? She knew she'd get in trouble for what she was doing. The dress was a gift, but taking the pearls was stealing, and she kept the disfigured portions of the dress hidden, a secret she needed to keep from herself, because the pearls opened a future in her mind: a departure, the store, a return to Pia.

But tonight, after dropping a pearl into the silk stocking, Flora fumbled through her bras for a clementine she'd picked from the garden and then reached beneath the bed for the honey. Honey saved in a canister she'd found beneath the kitchen sink, gathered for a moment just like this. One hundred pearls. She wasn't sure how much money they were worth, but it was something. This time she'd sell fresh produce from a small garden. Peas, squash, and tomatoes. She'd invest in a refrigerator with a freezer for Popsicles. And once a week she'd cook a meal, and people could gather on the benches outside. She sat cross-legged on her bed and spread a linen napkin across the sheet. Her thumb peeled back the skin of the clementine in one continuous spiral. She dropped the corkscrew in the center of the starched napkin and then poured some honey into the lid beside the orange rind. Lists formed in her mind: school supplies, lottery tickets, Bibles, rosaries, beer.

She tore the fruit apart section by section, dipped the membranes in the thick honey, and savored each one, sometimes chewing, sometimes sucking, and sometimes catching a seed of glass between her teeth. It did not matter; her mouth ached with pleasure. And when she was done, the rind waited for her. And for the first time, her thoughts wandered to Joenard; she missed him. She could not forgive herself, but he was the kind of man who went easy on people, on her especially. His great sympathy for her had spurned distrust, but now she saw it for what it was: love. He would've kept Datu safe. She was sure of it. But still, he'd welcome her back, and in the middle of the night, he'd hold her belly and whisper about another child. She scraped up the remnants of honey with the rind. Bitter. Sweet. In this basement: pleasure.

ZEINAH

Ever since the dried grass on the boots, ever since the wrinkled envelope, ever since the countdown to a new husband, Zeinah could not sleep. She'd thought of nothing but leaving. The only man she may have loved was dead. But had she even known him? In retrospect, his martyrdom was like a cross-fade in a film. She'd felt her future expanding while his life was coming to a close, a send-off he'd imagined and executed without her. When he stole the Qur'an from his family, his death already had a shape, a structure. In his mind, Zeinah never threatened the narrative, she played her part perfectly.

She lived in a city no longer her home, in an apartment building where tenants disappeared. The old neighbor and his belabored breaths on their landing had vanished, the blue bike outside the building was gone, and the low roll of explosions intensified and reverberated through the sidewalks and streets. Fighter jets and aircraft carriers crossed the skies. Her life had been reduced to headlines, her country "liked" in endless taps, heart emojis, and flag banners on Facebook. And the people in Raqqa either reveled in its ruin or believed the old streets and playgrounds would return. Afternoons of coffee in the square were just months away. People were unwilling to accept defeat or become revolutionaries. Their loyalty to Raqqa was once heroic, but the city they'd defended was now a prison. She envied her brother; he'd died for a city, a country he believed in.

She wondered what smuggler would trust her after she'd joined the Al-Khansaa Brigade. She needed to maintain her outward commitment to the caliphate to roam the streets, and she'd have to celebrate Omar's martyrdom with her "sisters" in the brigade. There had to be someone from her old life, someone connected to her brother, who could help, but she could not be naive: the past was over.

———

"Alḥamdulillāh."

Everywhere Zeinah went, people blessed her, and every hour she was more of a stranger to herself. Greetings from male fighters came with flirtations and the threat of remarriage. She was good luck, a coveted talisman, an expensive bride, and people speculated about who would be the fortunate man.

Next to the old firehouse was a bakery, a place where smugglers were rumored to make deals. When Zeinah entered, customers scattered, and the man behind the pastry glass gave her free loaves of bread and escorted her out the door, pulling down the metal grates so he could head out early for prayers.

She ambled into a dusty internet café with clunky computers and listened to foreign women, now ISIS wives, reassure family and friends they were safe and doing the holy work of Allah. She knew there were online networks that helped people escape, but she didn't dare do the research here.

She could request border patrol and disappear, but what about her parents? If she went home, would her parents open the door, or would they turn off the lights and pretend to be asleep?

———

After the call to prayer, people crowded into the pharmacy. A man in the back corner offered up his stool for Zeinah, and she sat down and waited for her mother's prescription. A young man wiped dust from shampoo bottles and toothpaste boxes with a rag. The overhead fan blew across Zeinah's veil, cooling her face. She closed her eyes and allowed the familiar sounds to comfort her: the rattle of the bell as people entered and departed, pills dropped into plastic bottles, the slide of the register drawer, the counting of coins, the familiar names called out by the pharmacist.

She may have nodded off to sleep, but murmurings awoke her. She kept her eyes shut, as her ears brightened and strained toward the counter, where a conversation in a different frequency unfolded between a man and the pharmacist. As a child, she'd always known when grown-ups were telling secrets.

"We're all out of heparin. Tomorrow at our other store. Around closing. We'll have it then. I'll ring you up here."

"Thank you."

"How many refills does this say?"

There was a formality, a tension in their voices.

"Three."

"Ah, yes, that's a three," said the pharmacist.

Zeinah's eyes fluttered open, and she witnessed a meaningful glance between the two men. They were sharing a secret—the medicine and refills were a code.

———

Her parents weren't home. Zeinah stood alone in the kitchen. A pile of coats covered the box of plates in the corner, her attempt at reparation snubbed. Tokens of intimacy marked the house. Undergarments hung on a cord across the living room: yellowed and torn bras, cheek-stained pillowcases. On the kitchen table: a card game left unfinished, two juice glasses, pulp stuck to sides. Her parents had each other. She had herself. Sultan had nothing.

She wanted to eat but couldn't. Cabinets of canned beans, bags of flour and rice. On the counter: a couple of cucumbers and an unripe melon. Everyone hoarded. Prices kept going up. Hungry people with empty bowls waited in soup lines in the roundabout. Last week, she'd ladled broth alongside her sisters in the brigade and avoided eye contact with her neighbors. She was relieved when she scraped the last potato from the dented pot.

In the fading light, she wandered down the hall to her bedroom and lay on the mattress. Her feet rested on the bedspread folded at the end of the bed. Perhaps she should remove her shoes, but it didn't seem to matter. The last time she'd been in this bed she was a virgin. Now she was a martyr's wife.

Zeinah rolled onto her side and scanned her collection of ceramic animals on the bookshelf. Like Sultan's stamps, they belonged to a Saturday ritual. A weekly allowance of coins she held in her palm and traded for painted creatures glued to cardboard squares. In this room, she'd built worlds out of upended books, stacked blocks, and crushed pillows. A streetlamp came on and cast the familiar shadow of a vent across her floor. This would be her last time here.

The voices of her parents echoed on the stairs. They were laughing, talking, something about dinner. It was all so familiar, she could've been five or fifteen, but when they discovered the open door, the conversation stopped, and they listened into the darkness.

"It's me," shouted Zeinah. "I'm in here."

They shuffled through the rooms and appeared in Zeinah's doorway. She sat up and smoothed the covers in an awkward welcome. They joined her on the mattress. Her mother traced the pattern of the floral bedspread with her finger.

"I don't know if you heard . . . Omar is dead."

She waited for a response—anything—but neither of them said a word.

"It's strange, but I think I may have loved him. I imagine you don't want to hear that." Her gaze fell upon a childhood picture on the wall: she and Sultan locked in an embrace around the trunk of a fig tree. "He killed himself. And others. Maybe even Muslims. Some say he's a martyr."

Neither of her parents would look at her.

"They say I must marry another fighter. And after that, another. There will be no end to martyrs seeking wives."

Her mother's hand trembled, and Zeinah watched as it searched for her father's grasp.

Guilt seeds cowards, buries people and blinds them, but instead of feeling angry, she felt brokenhearted, and tears stood in her eyes. "Tartus Pharmacy, where I get your prescriptions, arranges departures. I'll explain what to do. There's a truck leaving tomorrow night."

Her mother began to protest, but her father squeezed her hand and silenced her.

"The code is 'heparin.' Three refills are the number of people. I can't make the arrangements; people know I'm in the brigade."

Zeinah removed the wrinkled envelope from her pocket.

"Omar left me this. It's enough for us to leave."

ESKEDARE

She boards the bus before dawn. No one sees her off. There's no luggage roped to the roof, no lips quivering when she leaves. On her way out of town, Eskedare notices the stacks of tires on the sidewalk, her uncle's tuk-tuk stand, the stalls selling lions with crowns of stars.

On the bus ride to Addis Ababa, she does not see the old churches. Not Debre Birhan Selassie, Lalibela, or the Church of Saint George with its cross sunk in the ground. Instead, she falls asleep, her forehead knocking against the glass with every pothole, stop, and start. A metal spring digs into her leg through the torn seat, and she dreams, dreams of Astroturf unrolling across the desert, rocks blooming into soccer balls in her hands.

She awakes as passengers gather their belongings. Buses park haphazardly along the street, sometimes three-deep from the curb. Through the glass, Eskedare watches people claim their luggage and then disappear into the shadows of buildings and street stalls. She's the last person off the bus, and a tall man wearing slacks and a yellow sports shirt approaches, an unlit cigarette dangling from his lips.

"Why keep me waiting like that?"

He walks in long strides and occasionally tugs up his pants from his narrow hips. Eskedare follows him through a crowded open-air market offering everything a person could want: apples, beans, rakes, wrenches, tires, t-shirts, towels, and toothpaste. People clutch their purchases in red plastic bags. Rotting fruit, wrappers, and bottle caps litter the ground. The man nods to someone, tucks his cigarette behind his ear, and smooths his hair back. He disappears down an alley. The streets tighten. Homes of cardboard, tin, and dirt. Laundry hangs across alleys, children run in and out of open doorways, and, on the corner, men place bets with a man in a yellow chair. Beneath a window box of plastic flowers, a cat licks another cat clean.

The man stops at a place no different from the rest. Tangled bedsheets on the floor and girls not unlike herself. At the table, a woman cuts tomatoes, her ribs spread across her back like lines in a notebook. Her body is muscled and strong, and she seems neither ashamed nor proud but more like a fact, like an equal sign connecting two sides of an equation.

DOUNIA

Cleaning videos inspired Dounia to order wipes, sprays, towels, and tools online. Boxes of pine-scented products arrived; the air smelled of evergreens. Flora wiped down every surface—floors, walls, counters, appliances, stairs, banisters, and doorknobs—until the scent of cedar hung on the house like sap on trees and the whispers and giggles from Basma's room hushed and then vanished.

Q-tips. Dounia insisted that Flora clean the floorboards, moldings, doorjambs, and refrigerator drawers with cotton swabs, the perfect tool for precision. "Q" for "quality." Objects she marginally regarded while cleaning her ears but admired in glass jars. Cotton teardrops that cleaned smudges off walls, dirt from shoes, dust from computer keyboards, hair from vents. A swab to reach all those niggly places. Perfect for polishing silver: fork tines, spoon hollows, the curved indentations of monograms. And don't forget the dust lodged between tiles and baseboards where a mop could never reach. On hands and knees, a Q-tip stretched into grooves and wiped corners clean.

Dounia scrutinized Flora's progress from the second-floor landing. One project per day. Best to keep things simple, keep things focused and moving. Sleep was prohibited until tasks were completed. It was important to stay on schedule. Precision was a balm. Management, a hierarchy. Flora no longer looked Dounia in the eye and addressed her only as "ma'am"; a formality Dounia once rejected held boundaries and the wisdom of historical relations.

Flora wilted on the stairs as she wiped down the rungs on the banister, her neck wobbling, her half-lidded eyes closed in mid-spray.

"No. No. You need to stand. Sitting makes you tired," announced Dounia.

Qadira stirred, animating Flora's limbs, calling her away from her post at the stairwell.

"Oh, the baby! The baby!" said Dounia in a jeering singsong voice before she disappeared into her bedroom, the nexus of her revolt.

———

Dounia read from a stack of newspapers while buried under the covers.

"Housemaid Found Dead, Employer Claims Suicide."

The headline neither shocked nor surprised her. These incidents were the subject of international outrage. Outrage from Western institutions whose power was predicated on genocide and slavery but who now signaled virtue by policing the world for labor infractions and human rights violations. But Saudi Arabia was a major employer of labor in the world, sending more than $46 billion a year in remittances abroad. Children were fed, clothed, and schooled because of this arrangement, houses built, and families sustained, but sensationalist headlines persisted, always focusing on the negative.

Flora's care for Basma and the baby perturbed Dounia. It was the small things: Basma's perfume bottles dusted, her sheets ironed; Qadira's lullabies at naptime, warm milk tested on the tender inside of Flora's wrist. Dounia received the bare minimum, as if she were the burden. None of them was to be trusted; all of them wanted her to submit, to stop her resistance, to accept her role of mother, wife, and daughter-in-law. Her behavior was viewed as a drawn-out, overdramatic performance that needed to end. They all believed conquest was inevitable; her resistance was a nuisance requiring more troops and time in the field, but they never doubted victory. It was as if they wanted her to live in a thorn garden, to stop complaining about the brambles, to ignore the constant sting of needled plants and abandon the girl whose hand was once raised high in classrooms.

Dounia circled the article with a red pen and tossed the newspaper on the floor. Let it be a warning.

JUSTINE

As the sun dropped into the Gulf, Justine heard familiar voices in the hall. She listened to the key in the lock and hesitated in the living room, not wanting to hover at the door.

High energy and laughter burst into the foyer and ruptured her days of silence and distress. Wren ran to her and held her tight while Sean encircled them both in a huge hug. Cornelius meowed at their feet, and she felt dizzy in the downpour of love and family smells.

"Mom, it was so awesome."

"Honey, you would've loved it!"

Justine noticed their laced boots caked with mud as Sean rummaged around in his bag. His body had regained its strength and his confidence had returned. "The place looks great."

Wren picked up Cornelius and led Justine to the couch, where a vase on the coffee table overflowed with white lilies. Wren pressed the fallen petals between her fingers, and Justine noticed bites covering her daughter's neck and hands, and she reached out to touch the scabs.

"It looks worse than it is."

"What happened?"

Wren yanked up her sweatshirt and flashed her naked stomach. Red splotches and scabs covered her torso. "Leeches! Mom, there was even one in my belly button."

"Oh my god."

Sean and Wren laughed, reveling in her horror.

"At first, everyone freaked out. It's not that big of a deal."

They both seemed different, loose-limbed and breezy. Wren grabbed her phone and scrolled through pictures of kids posing with leeches on their necks, arms, backs, and feet, but what Justine saw was her daughter smiling, her arms around new friends, a world without her. Wren scrolled to a row of hiking boots.

"Mom, blood was coming out of our shoes. While we were walking."

Together, they bent over images of teahouses, cooking over open fires, hiking trails at night, a sunrise over the Annapurna range. There were pictures of Sean with the other moms, and she felt pangs of jealousy and regret for prioritizing the falcon over her family. Everything would be different had she gone to Nepal.

———

Wren's laughter spilled from her bedroom into the apartment. Darkness fell across the living room, and Sean reached for a fig, searching Justine's face in the dim light. The paths between them were overgrown, and Justine awkwardly tumbled toward Sean, landing across his body in a clumsy kiss, the bitter taste of millet in his mouth.

Sean poured himself another glass of raksi and noticed her glass untouched. "You don't like it?"

She took his hand and traced his fingers. There were things she wanted to say.

"And what about the famous falcon . . . the fastest and fiercest hunter?"

He was teasing her, and she wanted to join in, but she was unable to find the words, to articulate a single thought or insight about Shema or the exhibition. She'd been unable to focus on the falcon or her presentation since she'd left the farm.

A shout of glee came from Wren's room: "Mom, I love it!"

Wren ran into the living room, her hair wet from the shower, pajamas on. The same ones she'd left out for the girl.

"Look what Mom left under my pillow."

Sean put the lamplight on. Wren beamed and held out her hand to display a red agate ring set in an elaborate silver design.

A coldness seized Justine's chest. She'd seen that ring before—on the girl's finger.

Wren bent down and covered Justine with kisses. "I love it."

Justine's mind was awhirl. She'd searched the room. The bed was untouched.

Wren dropped the ring into Sean's palm, and he held it close to the light. "Looks like those rings we saw from Yemen. Beautiful. Where'd you get it?"

Wren smiled up at her, and Justine's mind faltered. "I . . . A town near the falconer's farm. An unexpected find." She flashed an anxious grin but could not meet her daughter's gaze. "It reminded me of you."

The girl had left it there like a summons.

Wren slipped the ring back on her thumb. "I'll wear it every day."

————

Sean fell asleep fully clothed on top of the covers. Justine unrolled his mud-stained socks and traced the bites along his calves, admiring his elegant arches, his long toes.

She hauled their backpacks into the laundry room. Their clothes were damp and smelled of smoke and insect repellent. Socks, shirts, and underwear were stained brown with blood, and as she unrolled pant legs, dead leeches fell into her hands and onto the floor. She sprayed down the clothes with disinfectant and stain remover, Cornelius regarding her from his litter box.

FLORA

Numbered lists greeted Flora each morning: refold linens, steam sofas, mop floors, polish silver, iron laundry, wipe glasses, dust shelves, wash china, bleach whites. Sometimes Flora had to refold towels four times before Dounia was satisfied. From the videos: coordinate by color, fold into thirds, edges in. Dounia sharpened her mind on Flora's back; she prowled the property, assessed her every move, and stalked her progress. Dounia spotted every bit of dust, crumbs in kitchen cabinets, food beneath the counter, missing socks, water stains on faucets, the dirty microwave plate.

A strange sickness, thought Flora. The woman is unwell. Dounia tested Flora's rigor in unseemly ways, leaving toilets unflushed with defecation around the rim, bloody tampons between the sheets. Flora was on trial, and she felt anxious, unable to sleep, and at night she'd review her chores and often go upstairs to disinfect the sink and clean the strainer.

But Flora knew more about work than Dounia ever would. Folding napkins was nothing. And the more the woman tried to break her, the more placid Flora appeared. The truth was Flora could scrub for years, and still Dounia's mind would hitch on to Flora's uniform hugging her body and insist she wash her underwear in a separate sink.

———

One night, a bell awakened Flora and then rang again. She put on her slippers and climbed the stairs in the dark.

"Flora?!"

"Coming, ma'am."

Cold air stung Flora's cheeks as she entered Dounia's room.

"Yes, ma'am."

"Close the door. I can't sleep. I need you to stay in here tonight."

Flora hesitated in the darkness. "Where, ma'am?"

"Use the blanket at the end of the bed. You can sleep on the floor."

Flora stumbled over shoes in the dark and found her way to the bed, but when she reached for the blanket, it wasn't there. She patted the rug around her, and when she found nothing to keep her warm, she hugged her arms around herself and listened for Dounia's breath to settle. Soon she'd be asleep. Her eyes adjusted to the dark, and she thought about the shattered jar of honey. Ever since Dounia called her into the hallway to pick up the mess of broken glass and sweetness, it seemed that something had splintered in the woman too. And when Hamed returned, would he ignore Flora and restore order to the home? Flora wore a path through the house attending to one woman and then another to a constant incantation of "Flora, Flora, Flora." Qadira Ibrahim was the least of it. Basma blamed Dounia, said her refusal to breastfeed upset the natural order of things. And Flora did not disagree. Dounia pumped and pumped and pumped, but still she refused to feed or even hold the child.

———

The next night, the bell rang again.

"Come and sleep beside me. Here, on the floor."

Flora lay down as instructed, but as she settled onto the floor, she heard wind and rain. "What's that?"

"An app that helps me sleep. A storm."

And as Dounia slept, Flora suffered. Water pelted rooftops; wind cracked limbs. Sounds she'd not heard since Joenard floated away. Since she tipped over in a bus crammed with people. Since she released Datu into a stew of slick limbs and screams. And each time she thought Dounia was asleep and it was safe to leave, Dounia would protest: "No. Stay. Don't leave."

Dependence edged around her. I must hold on to myself, she thought. Draw a distance between us. Reread the instruction manual. Be the best helper I can be. Make no mistakes. She recalled the picture her teacher drew on the board in black marker: a gas hose filling up a tank. "You are the driver. Remember that when times are hard. You are the driver." At the time, Flora did not understand what the teacher meant, and even now, it remained a riddle.

I am the driver. I am the driver. I am the driver.

Maybe she had it wrong. Maybe she was the gas. What did it matter? Either way, she kept the home in motion. But she was reliant on them as well. Her pay, her phone, her passport—all promised to her when she completed her contract. She needed to fold into bedsheets, crawl into the crevices of sponges, slip between the bristles.

At dawn, Flora heard construction trucks on gravel: time to boil water.

ZEINAH

Zeinah arranged the pastries and cookies on platters. Cups and saucers waited on the kitchen counter. She hated to spend money on a party, but she owed it to Omar and to her sisters in the brigade. As much as it was a celebration of Omar's martyrdom, it was her own private goodbye. No one would suspect she'd leave after the event.

She selected the selfie Omar had sent her on WhatsApp the day after they'd first had sex. At the time, his eyes seemed gentle and invited her inside, but now she recognized a sadness in his upturned face—the traces of departure. She uploaded the photo to Kik:

> My husband @OmarAlSulani is a shaheed. He's in paradise,
>
> in sha' Allah—a time of joy and celebration <3

Hugs and predictions about her future threaded through the afternoon.

"Omar has bought a house in Paradise and is waiting for you."

"Together, you'll be green birds in Jannah."

"Don't be sad. In sha' Allah soon you'll be together again."

Zeinah wondered how many of them really believed these sentiments; they felt more like reassurances for themselves. She supposed it was different for the women coming from margin-

alized Muslim communities in the West, who were victims of
hate crimes and verbal slurs, especially since 9/11. For them, the
caliphate was a kind of homecoming, but for her as a local, it was
an invasion. She felt abandoned by the West, but not just the West,
the world. How could they watch and do nothing? And it wasn't
just about politics and the war—what about the historical monu-
ments, world heritage? Didn't Iraq and Syria mean anything to
human history? With technology connecting the globe, still no one
cared. The brigade women were here as a dress rehearsal, preparing for their own husbands' martyrdom. She was thankful Omar
had forced her to get the IUD. Birth control was a gift for them
both.

The desserts were gone, but the women lingered. They'd all
dressed up for the special occasion, and Zeinah admired the as-
sortment of prints and styles from different parts of the world. A
shadow of how Saturdays used to be, women talking, not about
martyrdom, but about books, classes at the university, love.

She recalled something Umm Humra had said during training: "You must do everything for Allah, otherwise you will be
disappointed." It was true. Belief would protect her from disillu-
sionment, but Omar's martyrdom had ripped the lining out of her
coat, and she was resigned to the cold.

Women brought dirty dishes to the kitchen; she heard the
water running, the clank of china plates and cutlery dropped into
the sink. Outside, the blue tarp expanded and deflated with wind.
She'd remember this view.

"How about a picture?" said one of the women, and like a cho-
rus, they all chimed in.

"Yes, yes. Great idea."

The women put on their cloaks and niqabs and piled onto
the couch. There was much excitement, and it reminded Zeinah

of the times when she and Sultan had performed skits for the family.

"Zeinah, get your gun and kneel here in the front. Raise it to the ceiling."

They set up several phones on the windowsill, adjusted their stances, and waited for timers to go off.

———

Later that night, when the lights were out and Zeinah's bag stood by the door, Little Monster pawed at her pillow and curled into a crown around her head. She'd told Omar it was the smell of her shampoo that folded Little Monster into a hat each night, but he told her cats always protected their queens. She'd miss her four-legged subject.

"What to do with you?" she whispered into the dark.

Little Monster buried her nose in Zeinah's neck and reached for her cheek with her paw. The image of the photograph taken earlier on the couch lit up her phone.

> These sisters used to be strangers and now we're one. 5 Star Jihad. Chillin in Raqqa. This is the Caliphate the Prophet Promised #makinghistory.

ESKEDARE

"Come closer," says the man behind the camera. "If you come closer, you'll look older."

A room on the ground floor near the Addis bus station. A blue sheet sags against the wall while a printer spits out photos of young girls to a man on a stool. He cuts pictures into squares. The place smells of burning plastic and sweat.

Eskedare steps forward.

"Beautiful."

The bulb flashes and she feels important, like she's about to be somebody.

Twenty minutes later, Nyela Tekle, twenty years old, departs the studio with a warm passport in her hand. Eskedare, fifteen, is gone.

———

Nyela. Nyela. Nyela. Eskedare tastes her new name, lets it roll around her tongue, travel to the roof of her mouth, crouch, and then open into song—*ahhhhhh*. She did not choose the name. It was the name they gave her, and she likes it.

Gold letters on a burgundy cover: Federal Democratic Republic of Ethiopia. Below, a gold star with beams of light and the word "passport" written in English and Amharic. Inside, her picture and, beside it, a smaller black-and-white version of herself hiding beneath text of her name, date of birth, and birthplace—all

false, but true. The passport belongs to governments, the world of
roll-down maps, globes, and borders, and it all feels official, more
real than the life she's lived. She flips through the blank pages
and imagines them full. The expiration date: ten years from now.
Nyela, her new self, will be thirty.

❧

FLORA

Paper. Plastic. Glass.

Ever since Dounia caught Flora talking to the neighbors' maid, she'd insisted the trash be removed at dawn, but this "punishment" was Flora's reward, the one moment of independence in her week, the only time she left the compound. The cool air of daybreak, the smell of damp plywood and sawdust, the occasional headlights in the distance. She took her time, relished every breath, every footstep, every property line sagging between stakes. These walks to the red, blue, and green containers:

> Cardboard, paper: blue
> Red: aluminum, glass, tin
> Bags and plastic: green

It was a Thursday morning; the wind was strong and dusted her face with sand. The newspapers flapped against her chest and ink smudged along her forearms as she inhaled the smell of newsprint. She felt Dounia's eyes on her back, watching from her second-floor bedroom window. At the recycling station, she stuffed the newspapers through the chute, only vaguely registering the articles written in English, but a headline circled in red caught her attention: "Housemaid Found Dead, Employer Claims Suicide." Flora scanned the article.

Early morning, rope.
Iron bar, hammer wounds. Filipina
housemaid dead. Hammered,
hanged, beaten, marks
on maid, Filipina maid,
her body. The court
heard the woman:
she never ever used
a hammer at home.

Flora's heart banged in her chest, and she steadied herself against the blue bin. Above her, out of reach, a plane streamed across the dingy sky, already smudged between the clouds. She faced the lonely expanse of sand, and in her mind, she heard Dounia calling.

DOUNIA

Dounia sipped black coffee at the kitchen island and scrutinized Flora ironing Basma's sheets in the adjoining laundry room. Flora swept across the linen with the steady arm of a metronome, her skin still moist from the shower. Dounia had stripped Flora of everything—hair, jewelry, makeup, her lace underwear—and still, her beauty remained an indignant affront, especially in her yellow polyester uniform. She thinks she's better than me. Her straight spine tells me so. Flora pumped a spray bottle across the sheet. The scent of eucalyptus hung in the air.

"I circled that article and put it on top of the recycling. Did you see it? I don't know if you know her . . . the maid."

The iron sighed across the fabric.

"There was a picture."

Flora rotated the fabric on the board.

"Two and a half million domestics in the Gulf. Almost a million in Saudi! Not everyone's from the Philippines, of course, but you never know. I thought you might recognize her from home. Or that training program I paid for in Manila."

"No, ma'am."

"I bet they tell you how horrible we are. How we still eat with our hands and cover ourselves."

Flora folded the sheet and removed a pillowcase from the pile.

"You're one of the lucky ones. You know that, right?"

"Yes, ma'am." Flora spread the fabric across the board. "It's just..."

Dounia traced the rim of the saucer and waited for Flora to complete her sentence. "What?"

"I'm wondering about my pay, ma'am."

"You know how many stories there are of women sending money home to their husbands, their children. You know what they do? Spend it. That's right. Spend and spend. They keep women like you away and working forever. Your money is safe in a bank account, and you'll get it at the end of your contract."

The legs of the ironing board creaked. Flora's slippered feet moved across the tiles—back and forth, back and forth—unfolding a memory in Dounia's mind. She was maybe six. Younger.

"Something about you standing there ironing makes me think of this green dress. It had red flowers embroidered on the sleeves. Always dust around the hem. They had to wash it while I was sleeping. Must've been July. It was hot. I spent my summers at my grandmother's date farm. The doors and windows were always open. No air-conditioning, and always the sound of sweeping. Maybe it's your feet across the tiles that reminded me. It was Ramadan. Everyone was excited about the harvest. The dates were big and hung down in clusters from the trees. The trucks rattled up and down the long driveway—back and forth, back and forth, from our farm to Mecca. The clatter of those trucks woke me up in the morning and put me to sleep at night.

"In the afternoons, I'd spread out beneath the arms of the ironing board and wait for the sheets and laundry to become my fort. The maid moved beside and all around me—back and forth— the metal legs shifting and creaking." Dounia paused and listened to the varied sounds of the ironing board beneath Flora's weight. "Just like that."

And for a few moments, the ironing board joined them together; Dounia and Flora listened to what it had to say, its shifts
and creaks, as the smell of steam rose from the cotton and settled
between them.

"I'd watch her bare feet move across the tiles, her long and
narrow calves. The skin beneath her toenails was pink. I always
thought of her as older, but she must've been fifteen, sixteen. From
the Philippines, like you. It felt so safe under there, with the iron
going back and forth, back and forth, her body circling and hovering all around me."

Flora ironed into the elastic corners of Basma's fitted sheet.
Dounia sensed she was listening, waiting for her to continue, and a
part of her wanted to stop, but a cruelty compelled her to proceed.

"Outside, my grandmother bent over wooden flats of dates,
palming the ripe ones and packing them into mesh bags for market. She called out for the girl. Lea. But Lea didn't respond, and
I didn't say anything. I didn't want her to leave, for the back and
forth to stop. I don't remember if we were talking or not. She may
have been singing. She used to do that. Like you. My grandmother
called for her again, her voice sharp.

"I heard the screen door slam, my grandmother's flat-soled
shoes approaching. It happened so fast. The sound of a slap and
then something much worse, Lea's scream. The hot iron tumbled
to the floor, the yellow fort vibrated around me, and I watched
the thick electrical cord twist across the tiles. The screen door
slammed; my grandmother was gone. I scrambled out from my
fort. Lea was crying, and when I tried to hold her, she hid her face
from me. But I'll never forget what I saw: nine sinkholes. Like the
ones in your hand, branded into Lea's arm."

Flora's iron paused over the cotton. Nothing moved.

"My grandmother called me outside, away from Lea. Together, we bent over screens and sifted for sweet dates. I remember the bees landing on the fruit, searching for torn and broken skins, sweet syrup, and meat. The sun went down. Neither of us said a word, but looking back, it was my grandmother's way of claiming me, securing an alliance."

Dounia regarded Flora's slippers traveling across the tiles.

"I wonder, am I what you imagined?"

"I don't mind, ma'am."

"It's easier to take the maid's side. Like that one who was tied to a tree in midday heat. That went viral. But no one asked 'What did the maid do?'"

"No, ma'am."

"Can you guess?"

Flora folded a pillowcase into thirds.

"She left the cushions to dry in the sun and the fabric faded. The employer wanted to teach her a lesson: this is what happens if you leave something out in the sun."

Flora took another pillowcase from the pile and spread it across the board.

"What do you think about that?"

"She shouldn't have left the things drying in the sun, ma'am."

"Right. And I wonder, was that the first time she'd done something stupid like that? They don't write about that in the paper. They don't mention all the careless things she did day after day. Or how she was stealing from her employer, talking about her private life to her friends, or texting rumors on her phone. They don't talk about how she did her job with a nice smile, just like you, but really, she hated her employer. No one writes about how every day, the person you're paying, the person you trained, the person you sponsor, the person who you're responsible for, witnesses your life and judges you. That's a torture all its own. No one writes about that."

"Yes, ma'am."

Flora finished folding the laundry, unplugged the iron, and left Dounia alone in the kitchen. Dounia fixed her gaze on the pale desert landscape where nothing moved. The Dream Development echoed around her: hammers tapped on the new house next door, an electric saw mewed, and from upstairs, the muffled coos of Flora's breath on Qadira's ear. Basma called for them. Through walls, hallways, and ceilings, Dounia heard the rustles, murmurs, and reverberations and felt very much alone. She brought her legs up onto the chair and wrapped her arms around herself. There's intimacy in violence, she thought. Contact. The way it yokes you to a person.

JUSTINE

Justine parked behind the cars waiting in line for pickup at the American Community School. All of them mothers or drivers with snacks and plans for playdates or afternoon activities. Across the street was the American embassy, the reason she'd chosen the school over the more rigorous British School near Khalifa City. In a crisis, she'd imagined students being led there to safety, Wren returned to the States on a secure flight home. She was early and switched off the ignition. Outside, whistles called kids off the field, and the high-pitched voices of children radiated from the courtyard.

For hours, she'd worked on her presentation on the biological history of the falcon and its evolving relationship with humans. She'd included religious texts, bird as hunter, bird as sport, traditions in the royal courts of the East and West, rituals between fathers and sons (and now daughters and female falconers), and new conservation practices. She'd added slides with links to media: paintings, photographs, movies, novels, songs, and spoken word. For over an hour, she'd listened to bird calls ricochet off the walls. The discordant chirping, kacking, and squawking of the peregrine, saker, and kestrel had pecked at her brain. And then she'd sat in silence. Reframing evidence had always been her métier, but now she found her mind inflexible, unable to pivot to the falcon and locate even a simple through line. Her approach was anemic, a bore.

Wren knocked on the rear window, startling Justine. Her arms were full of blooming pink azaleas, and she was with a friend. Justine unlocked the doors, and the girls scrambled into the back.

"Can we go to the Mina Port? Her mom can pick her up. This is Aleyna. She was on the Nepal trip."

The girl held out her hands. "Scabs to prove it."

They erupted in laughter, injecting an atmosphere of bliss. She could feel the energy between them, the early days of girlhood love.

"You can call me Justine."

"Cool." The girl had a ruddy complexion, and her thick hair hung in knotted strands across her face. She wore FREE PALESTINE and rainbow pins on her shirt, and her intense eyes, almost black, regarded Justine. A watcher.

Aleyna mumbled something to Wren.

"And yeah, is it okay if we stop at the roundabout near our apartment on the way? We wanna leave these flowers in the fountain."

Justine headed east along the corniche as the girls sang together to music in the back. Past the Emirates Palace where she'd had her drink at the bar, past the palm trees lining the shore, past the bike rental vendors, the public beach where people sat fully dressed beside the sea. Sean was out kayaking in the mangroves, sightseeing, and searching for the best Lebanese and Pakistani restaurants. They were both avoiding unstructured time, and neither of them seemed eager to discuss their marriage.

She'd wanted to believe that his troubles on the job market and subsequent depression were responsible for her move to the Emirates, a narrative that cast her as the hero, but the events over the last couple weeks drove her to question her motives and ask if she even had the capacity to be a good partner. Perhaps her desire to maintain her own welfare, to bury what was ugly, was at the heart of her marriage, her entire adult life. But she did not know what to do with these thoughts or if she could even trust them, and so, for the first time, she found herself grateful for Sean's evasive nature.

Wren paused the music. "Mom, why didn't you say anything? The kids were all talking about it on the bus. It happened right outside our building."

Justine glanced in the rearview mirror; the azaleas now felt menacing in the girls' arms, and she sped toward the yellow light and saw the surveillance camera only as she sailed beneath the red signal. She wondered if the ticket would go to the rental car company. There'd probably be a stack of infractions waiting for her when they left the country.

"Mom . . . ?"

"Yeah . . ."

"Did you hear about that girl?"

Justine tried to appear neutral. "Alex mentioned something."

"Everyone's talking about it."

Aleyna chimed in: "Someone said she might have been in your building."

"Well, we don't know what happened," said Justine.

"My mom says the hospitals are filled with women workers trying to escape. Women with broken ankles who've jumped from high floors. Last month a woman was killed walking down the middle of the highway with her hands up. Lots of them are trafficked."

Justine felt protective of Wren. Aleyna seemed precocious, the kind of kid who probably knew about nuclear weapons and sex before everyone else, who'd discovered the power of knowledge in friend groups early on.

Justine double-parked on Airport Road near the roundabout.

"Mom, aren't you coming?"

"No, you go. It's hard to find parking."

Justine watched the girls cross the street. Besides a lone police officer, they were the only people there. Late at night, from her bedroom window, Justine had watched workers remove the flowers from the roundabout below. In the morning the fountain was empty, and every day the pile of offerings grew smaller, and in a few days, a week, the incident would be forgotten. But Wren wore the girl's ring, twisted it around her thumb in a new nervous tic that seemed to yoke Wren to the girl in an indictment, making it impossible for Justine to move on or forget.

The girls ran back to the car, winded and solemn.

"I'm glad we did that."

"Yeah, at least we did something," said Aleyna.

Justine pulled away from the curb. "Next stop, Mina Port." But the mood was gloomy, and the girls would not shift away from the fountain and what had happened there.

"I can't imagine . . . ," said Wren.

"What?" asked Aleyna.

"Setting myself on fire. I could never do that."

"I wouldn't say killing yourself is exactly heroic," said Justine.

Aleyna piped in: "I don't know. It's like a message, a sign. My mom said it's a form of protest. These are women saying it's not okay."

"Yeah, I see that," said Wren.

Justine was aware of the impulse to stifle the conversation, the dawning of her daughter's consciousness, but Aleyna's mother wasn't wrong. These violent acts—jumping out of windows, running into traffic, setting oneself on fire—transcended language, sent up a flare, cast out a line for deeper understanding. She supposed they were acts of rebellion. Just yesterday, she read in the paper how five women had collectively murdered their trafficker in Abu Dhabi.

"Yeah. Like the vegetable cart guy in Tunis," said Aleyna.

"Or those Tibetans we heard about on our trip," said Wren.

Justine pulled into the parking lot. "Okay, let's not go too far down this road. It's a beautiful afternoon."

They laughed and then decided to get bubble tea before jumping on the trampoline.

ZEINAH

It was a little past eight p.m. when Zeinah locked the door for the last time. Already the apartment felt like an artifact, like a photograph of herself she didn't recognize. She thought she should bring something of Omar's to wear during the mourning period, but she also wanted to leave him behind. He was gone. Not true. A version of him lived on in her mind, the minds of his family. And friends. There was pre-Omar, an Omar who extended backward into an inscrutable past. She wondered if he was from Iraq or if that too had been a lie.

She left her home as if she were about to return, windows open, bed unmade, milk and leftovers in the fridge. She even left her lipsticks lined up at attention in the cabinet and dropped a tea bag in a mug by the stove. She headed down the staircase and crossed beneath the flickering light in the foyer. Buildings were a comfort. People would say Raqqa was once ruled by the Byzantines, the Romans, and ISIS. Once it was the capital of the Abbasid Caliphate. History goes on and on. Eventually this era would end, and the bombed-out structures would become the foundation for the next iteration of itself.

Even in the midst of war, the night smelled of honeysuckle, but she did not feel nostalgic, and she did not feel afraid. Her resolve cleared a path through the city, and she dared to consider a life outside of Raqqa, beyond the loss of Sultan, Omar, and these streets. And she did not feel guilty. She disappeared into the shadowed back alleys and passed no one. She timed her walk across town with the call to prayer. The yellow glow of house lights and women in windows kept her company. Now was a good time to say goodbye to Little Monster, and she stopped in a doorway, rubbed the cat's head with her chin, and let her loose. But as she walked away, Little Monster followed her.

———

When Zeinah opened the door, she found her parents at the kitchen table drinking tea and listening to the radio. Night gathered around them, citrus peels lay scattered on the table, and her mother's apron still hung around her waist.

The van would not wait.

The newscaster spoke of impending U.S. air strikes. Her father opened the window and did not bother about the screen. Bugs flew in and joined them. Zeinah pulled the string of the overhead light and felt the button Sultan had knotted on the end when he was a child. An orange button that had fallen off one of her mother's favorite skirts, from a time when she wore nylons, shirts with fringe, and chunky heels.

"I don't expect you to understand what I'm about to say," said her mother. "But I have more in common with those pines outside our window, the soil they're rooted in, than with my own children. I am not young. I see my life from afar. My place is here, I'm part of this city, this history. I'm not a person who moves."

"Ma, he's never coming back."

"It's not about your brother. This beautiful city has blessed my life. The end has been difficult, with Sultan, with Assad, with revolution, with ISIS . . . and with you."

Zeinah watched as her mother hid her face in her hands, and it took Zeinah a moment to realize that her mother was sobbing and her body trembling.

"I'm so sorry. What we've done to you."

Zeinah heard a car door slam. "I know it's difficult to leave."

"It's just . . . we're too old to start again."

"Anything could happen," said her father. "We might be shot or killed in an explosion. Starve."

"All of that is already happening here," said Zeinah.

"This is home. I want to die where my family is buried. I want to be in my own bed, beside your father. That is how I wish to die. In sha' Allah."

Zeinah dug out Omar's Qur'an and set it beside the orange peels on the table. Instinctually, they reached for the worn engravings of the leather cover, and Zeinah opened its pages, but the words were blurry from the water in their eyes, and so they huddled together, holding each other close in the dim kitchen light.

ESKEDARE

A Sunday in late August. Not the promised plane, but a truck. Girls cram into the back, sit on each other's laps, sleep in each other's arms, squat over a communal bucket. Headed to Fantenero, or something like that, a coastal town where they sleep in t-shirts on the sand between seaweed and sticks, waiting for something or someone. They're not told what.

During the night, Eskedare hears a man crying on the shore, and from the darkness voices shush him. A wooden boat arrives, and in the black water, they navigate the shadows of one another, hike up their skirts, and wade past the once-crying man on the edge of the sea. As the girls load into the boat, he stands at the water's edge and watches the foam gather and recede around his ankles, then waves weakly from the shore. The arms of other men lift the girls onto wooden seats. They grab for wet life jackets covered in sand, and when there aren't enough to go around, Eskedare gives hers to a bony girl whose body seems like it will drop like an iron pipe to the ocean floor.

A tall and narrow man wades out to the boat. His fingers skim the surface of the water, leaving a gentle wake behind him. He leaps and lands lightly in the back. The boat barely rocks. He snaps the motor cord toward his chest. The engine rumbles, and the boat slaps across the darkness, misting cheeks and clutched fingers. The air smells of salt and fumes, and Eskedare peers into the vastness around her, an old and ancient darkness offering comfort. This is me, she thinks. Me taking on the world.

The narrow man peels an orange and drops rinds into the sea. He splits the fruit in half and tosses it over the sleeping bodies and into Eskedare's lap. In the dark, he cannot see her smile; he's already looking beyond her, to a horizon she cannot see. The taste of bitter rind and sour juice bursts against her tongue. She spits seeds into the salt air. Afterward, the smell of burning tobacco. She watches his orange ember singe the night. They travel through the next day and into another night, passing boats carrying cattle, crops, and people.

Before dawn, a hazy rim appears and unveils a smudge of land. Yellow lights smear the fog. The man at the motor lets out an aching groan and shouts, "Jump! Jump!" The girls wake in a flurry of pounding hearts and panic. The boat rocks as the men grab legs and arms and dump them overboard. Eskedare dives beneath the kicking chaos toward the echo of rivers and stones—Amara. The water is cold and she can feel her bones. She holds her breath, muscles through the current, and falls onto the shore, belly down and breathless.

FLORA

On a Friday morning, Flora entered Dounia's icy bedroom and found the woman overlooking the garden, her forehead on the glass. Dounia was on the edge of something dangerous, and Flora tamed her breath to disappear, to be invisible.

"Good morning, ma'am."

"Come here."

Flora joined Dounia at the window.

"Notice anything?"

Flora saw the empty lots. The plastic mesh of orange fencing.

"The leaves. The clementines. Don't you see them? There. In the dirt."

"The sprinkler is still broken, ma'am."

"Water them by hand."

"There's no hose or watering can, ma'am."

Dounia rolled her forehead along the glass and rested her numb gaze on Flora. "Is there water in the faucets?"

"Yes, ma'am."

"Then use a cup if you have to."

———

Qadira Ibrahim lay in the Moses basket watching the blue tarp flap in the breeze as Flora traveled down the dead garden rows with a cooking pot and ladle. The soil gulped down the water, but the surface remained parched. Dounia watched from the bedroom window, and Flora stepped over the plants, turning her back against the woman. Gardens lived inside her, bitter with the stench of marigolds, wild with mint and marjoram, potatoes that pulled up like stones from the ground, and fat toads napping in the shade of melon leaves; where hay spread between rows and, at night, embers burned. Flora recalled all these gardens as she swept the dead leaves into piles and stuffed plastic bags, but the fallen clementines she kept. The stink of dirt, citrus, and sun stained her fingers, and she folded the soft oranges into her apron and traced their leather skin with her thumb.

Not that long ago, Flora felt sorry for Dounia. Wanted to help. Hoped they might even be friends. That was impossible now. Dounia was a broken woman. But I am broken too, she thought. I am selfish and claim people for myself: Qadira Ibrahim. Basma. Datu. She pictured Joenard with his arms outstretched, reaching for their son. I wanted Datu for myself. But I also give myself to people. Dounia does not give herself to anyone.

Qadira Ibrahim cried, and Flora picked her up. The baby's wet cheek slid across her sweaty chest. Flora wrapped her arms around the child and paraded the baby between the withered rows, back and forth, back and forth, beneath Dounia's window. And she hummed a song from home, hummed all the longing for Pia, Datu, and even Joenard into that melodic tune. But underneath she was also singing, *She is mine. Your daughter is mine.* She wore the child as a shield, and she knew that was a kind of torture too.

JUSTINE

Justine didn't recall getting up from her desk, but she was now lying in Wren's bunk bed contemplating the floral pattern of oranges and yellows in the mattress above her. Sean was at Wren's swim meet. Tonight would be their last night together.

Setting yourself on fire. She hadn't allowed herself to contemplate the details. There was the physical component—the pain of burning flesh, the killing of nerve endings, the leaking of fat, the rupturing of inner organs, the asphyxiation—but what she was considering now was how a person got to that place psychologically. It was radical, defiant, and desperate. A person who self-immolates is a siren of refusal: *I refuse to accept the conditions of my situation. I refuse to negotiate. And you (audience, spouse, family) will bear witness to my refusal and the depth of my anguish. You might look away, but on an animal level (because we are animals), you will register the seriousness of my act and depth of my despair. You may choose to do nothing, but I'm acting in accordance with my conviction. I'm incapable of living with this lie. I hope to be a siren for change, but there's also the acceptance of non-change.* Self-burning marks the witness. She thought about women setting themselves on fire: the Hindu widows burning themselves with the corpses of their husbands, Tibetan women self-burning to protest Chinese rule, the Pakistani and Sri Lankan women setting themselves aflame in response to domestic abuse and arranged marriages. The Afghani women. The Iranians.

What was so threatening about her connection to the girl, to her radical and tragic act? What was Justine protecting with the girl's erasure, her own silence, her lies to Wren and Sean? Since coming to Abu Dhabi, she'd been confronted with an engagement and connection to the world she'd not experienced at home. The acts of the United States abroad had become personal, knowable, and felt. She saw how this proximity activated Wren, made her stronger, while Justine wanted to withdraw, disappear into the shadows—hide. She was ashamed of her cowardice, terrified that Wren would find out, that Wren would see her for the weakling she was and never forgive her. She was complicit with these structures and had benefited from them. The alliances were antiquated and unjust, but she was unwilling to change.

———

Since childbirth, pee leaked from her crotch during workouts. Not that anyone noticed. Stairwell runs were a solitary journey. For years, she'd made a point of knowing the end before beginning. Back-channeling and strategic, she'd been confident of outcomes. And yet here she was, paralyzed on all fronts. She pounded up the stairs between floors, her skull damp. Air conditioners on the blink. She sucked dank air into her lungs. Lemon-scented chemicals. She was nothing but jellied limbs on concrete.

Her inspired breakthrough for the exhibit had seemed revelatory. A virtual reality spectacle featuring the falcon. Visitors would experience flight, training, the hunt, and even comradery. Both falcon and falconer. No. Everyone was trying to sell the UAE innovation. Khadijah wanted an evergreen exhibit, not some hyped-up technology that would be dated in a decade.

She'd lost her ballast and no longer trusted herself.

Leo's grip on her shoulder in the control room, the presumption of their likeness clutched her mind. She wanted nothing to do with him, but he was the only person who knew the truth of what she'd done, and complicity was a powerful form of kinship. She now lived in an imagined bunker, a place her family could not see but that was now her home. She'd given Leo the promise of secrecy, but her loyalty was a destructive oath jeopardizing her connection to the people she loved most in this world.

She needed to tell Sean. She craved his forgiveness, his counsel, but swearing him to secrecy bullied him into her lies, and she couldn't bear more selfishness. Her foot slipped and she caught the hand railing, her fingers grasped a hardened piece of gum beneath the banister. Sweat plastered her t-shirt to her chest, and she wiped rivulets from her brow with her damp forearm. Her thoughts were jumbled. She needed to keep going. If she gave up, she'd create a pathway to failure in her brain, and from now on, every time she'd reach this step, quitting would always be an option. She reached the thirty-ninth floor and surged forward, sprinting up the final flight. She heaved and paced on the top floor, her legs trembling as she hobbled down the five flights to her apartment. Yes. She would tell Sean and surrender to the havoc of confession.

———

Later that night, they lay together on the bed, her thigh across his stomach, and he held her hip in his hand. She wanted to speak, to say, *Something terrible has happened*. The words formed in her mouth. Sean searched her face. She would say them.

"I never told you. After we Skyped that night, I went to Hakkasan."

She could hear the eager tone and tension in her voice, but he seemed not to notice.

"I went alone. Had a martini at the bar."

"Really?"

She detected a flirtatious tone in his voice but continued. "I met an Iraqi man who was looking for a wife."

Sean traced her jaw with his fingers and then slipped his hand between her thighs. She meant to go on, to tell him she knew the girl who'd set herself on fire. Instead, they made love, but all she could think about were her lies, her life of hiding in dark rooms and archives. And as he slid inside her, she imagined leading him through a grove of thick cypress trees to her bunker, and, as she opened the door to share the worst of herself, Sean climaxed. He tried to touch her, but she refused, insisting he watch as she pleasured herself. It was difficult, mechanical, but finally she found a way in, and she rubbed herself hard and fast until she convulsed and a shock ran through her body.

Afterward, it felt nice to be naked, to overlook a city and the sea beyond with the man she'd made a child with. And yet, when he left to go to the bathroom, all she could smell was the stink of herself, and she felt hollow and alone. She'd never tell Sean because somewhere, deep inside her husband, lived the best version of herself, and she was unwilling to forfeit that promise.

ZEINAH

Little Monster was still waiting for her outside her parents' apartment. Zeinah scooped the devoted cat into her arms, planted a strong kiss on her belly, and tossed her to the ground. Around the corner, a van waited, and as she approached, a man got out and opened the back.

"Where are the others?"

Zeinah hugged the bag to her chest and climbed inside. "They're not coming."

The man grabbed her arm. "The rest of the money."

She shook him loose. "When we get there."

The man snagged the back of her abaya and hurled her to the street. She watched from the ground as he got in the van. The engine coughed to life. She could stay. Go back upstairs. Give the rest of the money to her parents. Marry again. Be here till the end.

The van shifted into gear and rolled forward. Zeinah scrambled to her feet and banged on the bumper.

———

Heartache fogged the windows as she watched her city dissolve from the back of the van. Debris shredded the sky, littered the streets with sand and lint, coated shoes with dust. People gathered under awnings, and she heard the murmur of men outside the mosque. She burrowed beneath the blanket and curled around the spare tire, inhaling wet wool and gasoline as the van moved like an old person through the streets.

The van stopped. A checkpoint. Zeinah heard the glove compartment open. The driver spoke to a man in a familiar tone, but the talk was just an excuse for money to exchange hands. The van rolled forward.

———

The back door opened, and the driver pulled off the blankets. "You can come out now."

Her limbs were numb, and the driver caught her as she tripped out of the back. She shook him loose and got in the passenger seat. He handed her a bottle of water, and as they drove down the dark road, the headlights opened a narrow tunnel for them to follow— an artery leading away from her heart. Zeinah rolled down her window and breathed into the night.

The time between towns grew longer until there were no more houses, just burned olive groves along the empty road. No cars passed in the opposite direction.

"You ever get nervous?" asked Zeinah.

"How do you mean?" He was Syrian, and she wondered if he was from Raqqa.

"Doing this."

"ISIS needs the money. Civilians want to leave. I'm just the middleman."

Pebbles sprayed against the undercarriage of the van. Zeinah wondered whose side he was really on and decided it was best not to speak.

DOUNIA/FLORA

Dounia stood at the kitchen island. Dawn brightened the steel counter. The bedroom had grown tiresome, and she skulked about the house, searching for places to settle during the day—perches for scrutiny and complaint. Flora padded up the basement stairs in her slippers and her heart quickened. She hated that shuffle; small feet coming to serve. Flora drifted through the swinging door and gasped, startled by Dounia's presence.

"Sorry, ma'am. You scared me. Good morning."

Dounia ignored her and flattened the crease of the newspaper spread out before her.

Flora lit the stove, and a blue gas flower bloomed as she searched the cabinets for a saucepan and filled it with water from the sink.

"It's best to fill the saucepan, then light the stove."

"Yes, ma'am."

Flora retrieved a bottle of Dounia's breast milk from the refrigerator.

"Tea or toast, ma'am?"

Dounia did not answer.

Flora lowered the bottle into the boiling water and dropped in a nipple to sterilize.

Dounia hated all the accoutrements: tubes, suction cups, bottles, nipples, lids, and caps. All these things to extract, monitor, and preserve her milk. Basma and Flora fulfilled Hamed's

wishes in his absence; he didn't even have to ask. Flora removed
the silicone nipple with a slotted spoon and deposited it on a
paper towel.

Dounia sighed into the crushing atmosphere. Flora did not
seem to notice or care. The woman was sealed off, a private park
closed at all hours; Dounia wanted to break in. Flora removed the
warm milk bottle, placed it beside the nipple, and unscrewed the
top with her slender fingers.

From upstairs, Dounia heard Qadira stir. "The baby's awake."

"Yes, ma'am."

Flora searched for something in a drawer.

"What are you looking for?"

"The nipple attachment, ma'am. It's not here."

"If you put things back in their proper place, things don't get lost."

"Yes, ma'am."

"You hear that? Qadira's crying."

Flora's elbow caught the edge of the milk bottle. Dounia
watched her breast milk tumble to the ground and splatter across
the tiles. All that inane pumping and time squandered, her misery
dumped on the floor as if it were nothing. Flora fell to her knees
with a dish towel.

"I'm so sorry, ma'am."

From upstairs, Qadira howled. Dounia approached the stove.
Flora stooped beneath her, and a desire to imprint her presence,
to mark, to smite Flora's skin, took hold. Her fingers grasped the
handle of the saucepan, hot within her palm. The hiss of simmer-
ing water. And with one stroke of the arm, one flick of the wrist,
Flora's face and neck were doused in boiling water. Scalding heat
slapped against her cheek, filled her ear, and a red mark bloomed
across her face.

Flora writhed across the floor below her like a crustacean,

splayed out in pain, stuffing her palms like mittens inside her mouth to silence her screams. Dounia felt herself release the handle. The pan clattered and rolled across the tiles, and when she left, the door swung back and forth, back and forth, behind her.

———

Flora could not move. She could barely breathe.

Her cheek burned and her ear imploded with pain. Boiling water melted through ear wax, tunneled through tubes and small bones, flowed down her throat, and she gagged and choked on the dislodging of herself. Everything melted inside her, unmoored, and floated away. She could hold on to nothing, and her bladder released a warm stream of urine between her legs. Her face and neck were on fire.

Flora crawled to the freezer, opened the door, and her hand fumbled inside, searching.

Frozen peas. She cupped the cold pebbles to her ear and face.

She felt woozy and weak, nauseated, her mind curdled and sour.

She groped for the vertical handle of the refrigerator and twisted on the metal rod as if it were a mast out at sea. Dizzy, she closed her eyes, and not unlike the day of the storm, Flora forged a path in a series of short lines: refrigerator to chair, chair to door, door to couch, couch to banister.

She stumbled forward, eyes barely open, pain radiating through her skull like branches of lightning against a black sky. Qadira wailed as Flora clung to the railing leading to the basement, and she half slid, half tripped down the steps and into her room, where she collapsed on the mattress, her body in trembles, a ringing and thrumming in her ear.

———

Basma waited in bed. She fluffed her own pillows and listened to Qadira cry herself back to sleep. She watched the black arms of her bedside clock make the rounds and listened for the ding of the elevator, the rattling of her teacup on her tray. She refolded the sheet across her lap, clasped her hands, huffed, and sighed. How quickly she felt forgotten and assumed the pout of a child. By 9:15 a.m., the baby's screams echoed through the eerie silence of the house and Basma's eyes darted about the room. At 9:20 a.m., she decided to get out of bed and investigate.

In the corner was her cane, a present from Ibrahim upon his return from Turkey years ago. A handcrafted item by a man he'd befriended on the streets of Istanbul. A gift that hurt her feelings as she watched Hamed open presents of leather books and lanterns. The cane was insulting, and she'd felt embarrassed. He now thought of her as an aged woman. They'd argued. But now, she felt the loving hand of her husband waiting for her across the room.

She took her time walking to the elevator and called out to the baby on the floor below: "Shhh. Shhhh. I'm going to find out what's going on. Don't worry."

The elevator carried her downstairs, and the doors opened onto a dark living room and a shameful silence. The curtains had not yet been drawn, and dread flocked around her.

"Flora? Dounia?"

She trudged toward the kitchen and crossed the threshold. The freezer was ajar, and a cold light spilled into the dim room. The tic-tic-tic of the burner, the air smelled of propane. A paper towel waited on the counter while an overturned bottle lay discarded on the floor. There was a puddle of water and the smell of urine, and beneath the table, a saucepan rested on its side. But most concerning were Flora's slippers, haphazard and abandoned on the tiles.

ESKEDARE

The girls collapse on the beach and heave into the sand. Trucks rumble toward them, headlights swell in the fog, and when the men in uniform arrive, they pin the girls beneath their bodies, stuff their fingers into small, contorted mouths so they can have pleasure and still hear the seagulls' coo. Afterward, the girls are herded into trucks, onto highways, and dropped like schoolchildren onto an airport curb. No tickets. No money. No plane.

The sun, a naked bulb in a dirt sky above them. Eskedare eases into the shade of an overhang and watches as the girls search through wet bags and wallets. Watches as the girls scan the parking lot for answers. And the answers come. Men get out of cars and saunter toward them. Soft-shouldered men offer the comfort of wrinkled cigarettes and water, employment, and sleep. Eskedare recoils as the girls disappear into cars and vans, sometimes in groups, sometimes in pairs, until it's just her, alone beneath the airport overhang.

As the shadows lengthen, Eskedare creeps along the darkness of the building to view the planes. Men pull carts of luggage out to the tarmac and hoist suitcases, duffel bags, and boxes into the open belly. A metal staircase rolls into place, and a flight attendant leads passengers toward the plane. Eskedare watches as they file up the stairs and disappear inside. She tries to imagine the seats, the view through the small windows, but she's never been on a plane. The pavement and pebbles imprint a pattern on the backs of her legs. Her spine stiffens against the building wall.

The metal staircase pulls away from the plane, wing lights flash, wheels roll backward. The cabin glow clicks off into darkness. The nose of the plane follows the blue runway lights, the engine surges as it sprints down the tarmac, and in seconds, the plane hovers above the ground and ascends into the sky. Eskedare watches the flashing wing lights disappear into the night. The eager men and the plane have vanished. Her stomach aches, orange peels and pith a distant memory. Eskedare has no money, no plan, and does not know what to do.

FLORA

Flora awoke to Dounia hovering above her in the dimness. Flora thought, Please, God, don't let her touch me.

"You need to get up. Raj will take you to the doctor."

———

Her uniform drooped on her limbs like clothes on a wire hanger. A safety pin cinched the elastic around her waist. She tried not to shamble, tried to lift her feet and head, to raise her eyes from the tiles, while passing Dounia at the door.

Dounia's hand grazed Flora's fingers. "She's an excellent doctor. I've known her since I was a child."

Flora flinched at Dounia's touch. She was terrified of the woman now, did not want to upset her, and nodded in thanks.

The sun stunned her eyes and she squinted. Her neck was raw and blistered where she'd been burned, and she felt disoriented, did not know what day it was, and the world seemed strange. Raj waited in the car, the engine running, and when he saw her, he got out and helped her into the back. His touch was kind.

It hurt to hold her neck upright, so she slid down and rested her head against the seat. Out on the highway, Flora cracked the window. The air felt good, and the light formed a kaleidoscope of dots inside her lids—yellow and orange circles swayed to the sitar and flute of Raj's music. Heat radiated through her ear canal, and

she listened to the sound of crackling wood, dry and hollow timber, splintering deep inside her eardrum.

Her thoughts wandered back to when she was a child, to a time when a whale was stranded in the bay of her village. For hours, they battled the outgoing tide that threatened to beach the poor animal. The whale flapped and fought, but in its last hours, she'd watched it float like a jellyfish, barely breathing, bobbing up and down in the diminishing swells, until it rested, unmoving, on reeds and sand.

———

The doctor's office was in a residential neighborhood. Raj helped Flora inside, guided her to a seat, checked her in, and then waited on the other side in the men's area. They could see each other through the glass, and he kept watch over her.

A door opened and the nurse called out her name. Flora followed the woman to an examination room where she was told to wait. A diagram of the ear canal spread across the office wall. Flora followed the path as if it were a children's illustration. The tube led down to the eardrum's purple mushroom underbelly, then into the green inner ear that connected to the eustachian tube that bloomed upward like a tulip. A grey snail curled on top of the belled flower, and a spongy layer of yellow fat surrounded tunnels in a froth of white.

"Flora, right?" A doctor in an abaya entered and washed her hands at the sink. "Dounia told me you'd be coming in today. She's concerned about you. Something about a fall in the kitchen. Boiling water. A burn on your neck?"

Flora remained silent and met the doctor's gaze.

The doctor rolled toward her on a stool. "Do you mind if I take a look?"

The doctor inserted a plastic nozzle into Flora's ear, and she retracted in pain.

"I know it's sensitive, but I need to look inside." The doctor reached for a Q-tip. "I'm just going to clean your ear."

The doctor's breath stung her raw neck as she gently dabbed the crust around her ear with a warm cotton swab. Flora's eyes began to leak, and she squeezed them shut, but tears rolled down her cheeks anyway. The doctor rested her hand on Flora's leg. "It's going to be okay. The blisters and swelling are a sign of healing." Flora nodded, but she dissolved beneath the doctor's touch and her shoulders began to shake.

The doctor rolled away from her and threw the bloody Q-tip in the garbage. She busied herself at the counter and waited for Flora's breath to steady before continuing the exam.

"I want you to hold your nose and blow gently."

Wind blew through her left ear like an open window.

"Feel that? That's a punctured eardrum." She peeled off her plastic gloves. "You're lucky it's not worse."

Flora memorized everything on the counter: the glass jars filled with tongue depressors, the misshapen stack of paper towels, three plastic cups.

"I'm going to give you some antibiotics and bandage your neck, then send you down the hall for a hearing test. It's a second-degree burn. In a few weeks the skin should heal, but you don't want to get an infection."

Flora hoped the tests would last all day and end in a hospital bed with starched sheets and a bell she could ring for help.

————

The brown listening booth felt confessional. On the ledge above her, a stuffed elephant played a tambourine. Remnants of tape dot-ted the walls. Flora sat still as a woman with delicate fingers adjusted spongy headphones around her ear with care, avoiding her bandaged neck and tender cheek. A pink skirt spilled out beneath the technician's robe, and her shoes were fuchsia.

Flora's ear throbbed.

"I know this must hurt, but is that okay?"

The woman smiled, and Flora noticed the gap between her teeth.

"Hold this." She handed Flora a cord with a jump rope handle. "When you hear a sound, press the button." She closed the door, and Flora was alone in an underwater kind of quiet. The woman took a seat outside the booth, and they faced each other through a small glass pane.

The technician's measured voice came through the headphones: "You'll hear a series of beeps, low and then high. Press the button when you hear the beep."

Flora froze, barely breathing, and strained into the silence. She heard nothing. Finally, in the distance, a low bullhorn. She pressed the button. The high tones were easier to detect, but the lower register felt far out to sea, mysterious, and sometimes she pressed the button randomly because the technician must've been playing something, and she didn't want to fail.

"You're doing great. Now, repeat the words after me." The woman held up a folder to cover her mouth.

"Water."	"Water."
"Salt."	"Salt."
"Sunshine."	"Sunshine."
"Mangrove."	"Mangrove."
"Falcon."	"Falcon."
"Shore."	"Shore."

"Jump."

"Lipstick."   "Lipstick."

"Cat."

"River."

"Stone."

"Honey."   "Honey."

Like a swing in summer, back and forth they went. Caught up in the game, she was unaware of missing words and only enjoying how they tumbled in her mouth and spread out like blankets between them. But before she knew it, the game was over, the door opened, and the technician removed Flora's headphones and smoothed down her hair before attaching a metal contraption diagonally across her head.

"Last one. This measures the sound registered by your inner ear."

Vibrations rumbled through her right ear, but in her left, nothing but silence. The technician smiled at her through the glass as if to say, *It's okay. It's normal to feel nothing.*

———

Flora sat beside the technician with a printout of a graph between them.

"Here." The woman pointed with a pen to a dip in the red line. "The blue is your right ear, and the red is your left. You've lost eighty-five percent of your hearing in the left ear."

"Will I need to go to the hospital?"

"No. No. It will heal on its own, but you'll never get all your hearing back in that ear."

Flora's throat constricted; a fog rolled in. The technician thought Flora was upset about her hearing, but really, she was terrified of leaving, getting back in the car, and going home.

"You smell good," said Flora.

The woman extended the inside of her wrist to Flora's nose: summer shade, sweetgrass. The technician took out a small bottle from her purse and held Flora's arms, dabbing it on the tender insides of her wrists, but her eyes looked away. She knows, thought Flora. Dounia had sent her to a place where Flora could never tell the truth, where doctors and technicians would treat her but never say a word. A place where everyone knew her accident was a lie.

JUSTINE

It was a Friday when Justine found herself setting off for the bus station. Not to buy flowers, but to go to the ladies' room. She wasn't sure what she'd do once she was there. Maybe just pee and come home. Maybe talk to the bathroom attendant.

As she walked through Little Bangladesh, she felt a blister forming on her heel. On weekends hundreds of men from the labor camps gathered in the superblock behind Electra Street to play soccer, drink tea, and talk on their phones. Today, a crowd gathered around a television propped up on a high stool outside the barber shop to watch cricket. Usually, men would smile when she passed, but today no one noticed, and as she walked through the entrance of the bus station, she heard jubilant cheers. Someone scored a run.

Again, the refrigerated air holding the scent of cinnamon and sugar, the magazine shop, her favorite florist. She aimed for the ladies' room.

A middle-aged woman wearing a cardigan over her uniform emerged from a stall with a trash bag. Justine smiled and slipped into the adjacent compartment. She latched the door and, not knowing what to do, stood foolishly in the stall listening for other occupants. A woman entered and used the toilet next to hers. Justine perched on the john and listened to the shuffle of fabric, urine hitting water, the unspooling of toilet paper, the flush, and then the refilling of the bowl. Beneath the partition she saw thick ankles in white tube socks, black slide-on sandals, a long green skirt with a dirty hem. The stall door closed, hand soap pumped, water rushed, a towel dispenser rotated, and then paper tore. Sounds of the girl's work life. Finally, the woman departed, and now it was just Justine and the attendant. Justine approached the attendant at the sink and waited as the woman wiped down the counter. She caught the woman's eye in the mirror.

"Excuse me. Do you speak English?"

The woman clutched her spray bottle. "Ma'am, what do you need?"

"I was wondering about the woman from Ethiopia."

"I don't know, ma'am."

"She used to work here."

"Not anymore, ma'am."

"Yes, I know."

The woman spritzed down the mirror, obscuring their reflections. "She was trouble."

"Trouble? What kind of trouble?"

"She did bad things, ma'am." The woman swept across the glass in large arcs. "She stole our money."

Justine stopped pumping soap into her palm as her mind flashed to the money the girl had left on Wren's bedside table. Dirham notes in fives, tens, and twenties that she'd thrown down the garbage chute.

"All our savings. She was supposed to be our friend."

Stunned, she lingered, but the woman ignored her, clearly wishing she would leave. The same lemon chemicals from her stairwell runs permeated the bathroom. Justine pulled on the paper towels and dried her hands. She thought about retrieving her wallet but only had a few bills.

"Where do you live?"

"Far away, ma'am. I go one and a half hours on the bus, work twelve hours, and then one and a half hours back to camp."

"Do you have a day off?"

The woman's eyes shifted to the door. "Tomorrow, ma'am."

Justine dumped her used paper towels in the trash. "What will you do?"

"Sleep, ma'am. I will sleep."

Justine exited the bus station through the revolving doors and found herself back on the superblock. The crowd around the television had grown, and as she walked to the ATM, she considered how much money to withdraw. She'd never even bothered to count, to even look at the bills she'd discarded. How many women had lost their savings? Let's say it was ten women (probably less, but just to be safe) and each had saved 2,000. Let's say 3,000, if you round up. The girl had stolen their money, but was that even true? The attendant had no reason to lie. And it made sense: the girl had left the money for Justine to return. Recovering their losses was the least she could do.

In the Etisalat lobby, bank machines stood ready and waiting, a place where customers paid phone bills and purchased calling cards in cash. Justine took the escalator to the third floor, where she'd have privacy for the sizable withdrawal. She stood in front of the ATM, her bank card in hand. She'd take out the maximum withdrawal amount, ten thousand dirhams. She did a rough calculation to dollars in her head: $2,700. It was better to be generous, but was it too much? In the past she would've been concerned about the withdrawal showing up on their joint account, but Sean would never know. Maybe five thousand dirhams—a school fee, a splurge on a pair of shoes. The withdrawal should not attract suspicion and incur a call from the bank. But it was her money. She slipped the card into the slot. The withdrawal options flashed on the screen. She'd need an envelope. She could stop at the stationery store. She'd seen a surveillance camera in the bathroom. She wanted to remain anonymous. This solution seemed risky. What if the attendant told the authorities? Someone at the labor camp? The other women whose savings had been stolen would know. She could leave the envelope in a bathroom stall. But it was possible someone else might discover it, keep it for themselves. The machine flashed. Cancel. This was a bad idea. The machine beeped, a reminder to retrieve the bank card and return it safely to her wallet.

ZEINAH

The van stopped. The lights snuffed out, and whatever tenuous connection Zeinah and the driver had vanished.

"We're here."

Zeinah strapped on her backpack and headed down a path of broken grass that led to the Euphrates. The air smelled of humus and brine, and the driver's eyes, malevolent now, watched her go. She located the shadow of the boat, a hump overturned on the rocky shore, and grasped the metal rim to flip it on its side. Wooden oars lay beneath the hollow, and she started the awkward journey to the water. Because of drought, the shore was wide and the water at a distance. Anxious about the sound of the metal scraping against stones, Zeinah grabbed the edges of the boat with both hands, rested it against her hip, and trudged a few steps forward before setting it down, taking a break, and repeating. She was thankful for the camouflage of her cloak. At the water's edge, she pointed the boat toward the black swath of trees across the river and waded out into the muck until the boat was firmly afloat. The van had not departed, and she knew the driver was watching.

The oarlocks clanked and the boat rocked as she climbed inside. She recovered her balance, dropped in the oar pins, dipped the blades in the water, and drew away from shore. The worn grooves of the handles in her palms held the memory of people who'd rowed this same crossing: tight-shouldered men with measured strokes; older women sharing this seat, perhaps one on each oar; children splashing blades in crooked lines.

She heard the cry of an eagle owl, saw it swoop several feet above the water, its orange eyes reflected in the surface before it ascended into the sky and disappeared. The current moved beneath her, pushed her downstream and off course. She tugged the left oar and was thankful for her forced fishing expeditions with her father—afternoons spent with her rowing as he pointed out shadowed pools behind rocks where carp gathered. And while he fished, Zeinah sank into the bottom of the boat, swallowed by the orange life preserver, and gazed into the movie screen of sky. Branches, birds, and clouds floated in slow motion across the frame, a frame transformed by light, from grey to orange to black.

Boom.

A gunshot echoed across the river and hit the water just feet away from her.

Zeinah lunged, belly forward, into the bottom of the boat.

More shots fired and splashed nearby.

A bullet hit the top of the bow and ricocheted into the water. She fumbled for her gun as the river carried her downstream. She heard a car door slam, the van engine trill and finally fade. She caught her breath, allowed her heart to steady, and thought about the driver, a half-hearted traitor, serving both sides to eke out enough money to survive. As she crossed the river, his chameleon existence occupied her mind, and she imagined a part of him wanting to accompany her, his gunshots the wails of a child left behind.

DOUNIA

Qadira's screams echoed in the stairwell and traveled across the marble floors. Dounia hesitated outside her daughter's room, afraid to enter, fearful of her daughter's gaze and what she might find there. But she yearned to see her, and so she sat in the rocker beside the crib and watched Qadira cry. The baby regarded her with a red face wet with tears, her hands in small fists, her legs kicking, and still Dounia could not bring herself to hold her. An anxiety, an inexplicable terror of the child, seized Dounia, and all she could do was watch. In time, Qadira gave up, and exhausted from all the shrieking, she now slept on her belly, her legs bent up beside her like a frog, her fingers curled around her nose, thumb in mouth. The steady rise and fall of her back created a sense of calm, and a part of Dounia wished she had the courage to murmur a lullaby, to say something.

She thought of Flora and recalled the soft topsy-turvy dolls of childhood, the ones with a head on either side, hiding in each other's skirts; she and Flora shared the same waistband but were unable to see each other. The fear of contamination goes both ways, she thought. From the beginning, I felt entitled to the woman's body. That was the agreement, the exchange. For money, Flora gave her body and labor. And once again, she replayed the events of Ibrahim's death, Hamed's allegiance to Basma, and Basma's merciless gaze upon Dounia as she relinquished her own life to inhabit the Dream house on the outskirts of nowhere.

Outside, a gardener arrived with a new pallet of tomatoes.

On YouTube, she'd watched a video about the trauma of plants. Scientists had subjected tomatoes to stress by withholding varying degrees of water and light and discovered the harvested seeds had learned to tolerate the suffering of the "parent" plants. Trauma, even in plants, had genetic memory, they said. Dounia rocked back and forth in the chair, studying Qadira Ibrahim in the crib, contemplating her own legacy and, if the scientists were right, her daughter's future strength and resilience.

ESKEDARE

Eskedare follows the desolate highway in the dark, far away from the shoulder and the sweeping headlights. Her mind branches off in different directions, her mouth parched, her limbs weak. She follows the blue signs with white buses posted along the road. Finally, buildings in the distance: a bus station, gas pumps, a mosque.

She walks to the back of the gas station, hidden from view, and rests against the building. Trucks stop for gas; men emerge from the canteen with Coca-Cola and cigarettes. Drivers park their white vans and buses, gather outside on a haphazard collection of couches, drink coffee and smoke. Occasionally, one of them stands up and shouts the name of a destination: Qawah, Ta'izz, Zinjibar. It takes only a few passengers for them to extinguish their cigarettes and depart.

She cannot say what time it is, only that it's morning and her stomach aches, but she does not dare to make herself known. The call to prayer echoes through a metal speaker. Taxi drivers stop, wash their hands and feet in a broken-tiled fountain, and pray on a large, faded rug unrolled in the parking lot. One by one, they return to their cars and drive away.

Weak in the knees, she slides down against the building, her eyelids sag, and soon, she's asleep. She awakes to a big-bellied man with a gentle touch speaking Amharic above her. He leads her to a bathroom in the back, opens the faucet, and watches as she drinks until she can drink no more. He leads her into the canteen:

white coolers against the wall, bread rolls behind glass, and half-empty shelves of candy and chips. A fan rotates in the corner, its broken blade clicking as it spins. She ignores the man appraising her behind the counter. The big-bellied man asks for a pack of cigarettes and coffee in a language she does not understand, but then in Amharic he says, "And get her what she wants." Eskedare holds up three fingers and points to the rolls. He pays for the coffee, cigarettes, and bread, and the men on the couches watch as he leads her across the parking lot to his white van.

She keeps her eyes to herself and follows the sound of his flip-flops slapping against the pavement. His hems are frayed, and a rope cinches his pants below his belly. He sweeps wrinkled newspapers from the passenger seat onto the floor. Blue dice hang from the rearview mirror. He might be five or ten years older, she can't say.

He tosses the brown paper bag with the bread rolls into her lap. She bites into the crust. Crumbs scatter across her chest. The dough is stale and tough, but that's no matter. She eats, chews, and swallows. Eat, chews, and swallows. No one says a word. He twists a ring with a red stone around his pinky. The heads of weeds knock against the broken curb, and she thinks about Qatar and Amara and supposes that a bus station is a good enough place to be. She finishes eating and wishes she had more.

When the driver finishes his coffee, he rests his arm on the seat beside her, takes Eskedare's hand, and, not knowing what to do, traces the tail of her birthmark with his chafed finger and presses against the bloom. His eyes remind her of home, her mother.

He rolls up the windows, locks the doors, and leads her to the back. He smells like soap and tobacco; his hair is curly, his belly soft. She thinks he wants something more, but instead he slides away from her and gazes out the window at the blue nettles growing in the patchy soil. He twists the ring on his pinky, his leg bounces, and she watches as he gulps tears into his big stomach. She doesn't move. Men call out the names of cities. Engines start and stall. He offers her the dregs of cold coffee from his cup.

"My sister," he says. "She was killed in the war."

Round and round, the ring.

"You look like her."

"War?"

He looks at her. "You're in Yemen."

"My grandmother's from Yemen."

"Then you should know."

All she knows of Yemen is that jug and broken shards of clay.

"The Saudis. The UAE. The Americans. The Houthis. Al-Qaeda. Everyone's aiming at us."

"Al-Qaeda?"

He waves his hand. "You don't wanna know."

For a long time, it's just the two of them breathing. Eskedare tries not to think about her mother. A man bangs on the back of the van. Neither of them moves or says a word. Eskedare's lids droop, and she falls asleep.

When she wakes, it's dark. She's lost track of his face, but she feels comfort in his sadness. She smells the sweetness of a banana and finds its softness on the floor. It's almost rotten; juice spills on her leg as she peels the limp skin back between her fingers. It's strange how my grandmother comes from this place, she thinks. How I look like this man's sister.

He pulls out a wrinkled cigarette from his shirt pocket and lights a match. Sulfur lingers in the air.

"You need to get out of this country. Cross a border. Any border."

Eskedare folds the banana peel into her palm.

"Do you have a passport?"

Eskedare removes the wrinkled and water-stained document hidden in her waistband. She watches as he flips through the pages in the dark and then slides the book into his pocket.

Eskedare walks beside the big-bellied man across the parking lot to the broken-down mosque. He twists off the ring with the red stone from his pinky and places it in her palm.

"It should belong to the living."

It was his sister's ring, Eskedare knows this. He does not say goodbye. Eskedare watches as he returns to his van, his ragged hems dragging along the ground, and she knows from the shake in his shoulders—he's weeping.

Inside, women and girls sleep on the ground. Someone hands her a blanket, and she squeezes between strangers. She feels nauseated, shivers and sweats through the blanket until she's too hot and tosses it aside. She thinks of the crying men, the one with his ankles in the shore, the one inside his van, and she imagines draping herself across their bellies in the field of blue flowers and blue stars.

The next morning, a woman calls out names from a stack of passports.

"Nyela Tekle."

Eskedare raises her hand, and she's brought into a room where she's told to sign papers that promise part of her wages to the man behind the desk.

❧

JUSTINE

Wren was standing on a step stool with her arms extended for the tailor when Justine entered the shop.

"It looks beautiful, Pavara. Thank you."

He nodded and smiled, a piece of chalk between his lips.

The middle school semiformal dance was weeks away, and Wren had wanted to design her own dress. She'd spent hours drawing sketches and pulling reference images, landing on a one-shoulder design cut on the bias.

Justine put her bag on the counter. "Happy? I brought you a snack."

Wren was unresponsive and would not meet her gaze. Justine looked to Pavara for a clue, and he shrugged.

Last week they'd visited Pavara's shop and gone through bolts of fabric. It was a cozy afternoon. The cluttered shop held a collection of gold-handled shears, rolls of ribbon and lace were displayed on the shelves behind the counter, and bolts of fabric lined the walls. Pavara and his wife, Anika, who ran the business, served them white Ceylon tea from Sri Lanka sweetened with honey and pine. The couple had moved to Abu Dhabi fifteen years earlier with Pavara's mother's sewing machine, a black metal Singer with a foot pedal that now stood in the center of the shop. They'd shared stories and laughed about the suits, dresses, and alterations made for members of the royal family, ambassadors, and professors. Just last week the director of the Louvre had ordered a grey silk suit.

In the middle of their conversation Anika remembered a bolt of cream taffeta in the back, left over from a gown they'd made for a cellist performing at the Emirates Palace. It was perfect.

"You can put your arms down," said Pavara.

"Honey . . . ?"

Wren clasped and unclasped her hands, tugging the ring on her thumb, and Justine could not discern if Wren was on the verge of tears or outrage.

"What is it?"

"Just now—on the bus—this kid told me how there's a school in Dubai where they removed all the chapters on the Holocaust. Just ripped them out."

"Is that even true?"

"Mom, Dad's family was exterminated in the Holocaust. His grandmother and nine great-uncles. Their children."

They'd agreed not to discuss Sean's Judaism in public while in Abu Dhabi, and Justine felt on edge. "Okay . . ."

"No, Mom, not okay. Have you lost your mind?"

Justine's eyes darted to Pavara. She felt embarrassed by Wren's insolence and wondered how much of the conversation he was following.

"It's just, like, *poof*, the Holocaust never happened. *Poof*, no queer people."

"My friend, please keep your arms still."

Anika entered from the back. Pavara spoke to her in Tamil, and Justine suspected he was relaying the conversation to his wife.

"We know plenty of queer people here. Besides, we've talked about this. Different country, different rules." Justine heard her officious tone, her desire to pivot.

"Oh my god. No."

Silence descended. Nothing but the ruffle of Pavara's hands

hemming the taffeta at Wren's feet. Justine felt chastened and hoped the moment would pass, but Wren pushed on.

"It started this morning. I saw that guy in the elevator. You know, the one you jokingly call 'the man in the brown suit' . . ."

Justine stiffened.

"I asked him about the girl who set herself on fire. Someone at school said she was seen leaving our building. They said the gas station guy filmed the entire thing, but the video's gone. They swear they saw it, but I searched online . . . There's nothing. Nothing in the newspaper. Not even a police report. Nope. *Poof.* She disappeared."

What was her daughter doing? None of the other kids were interfering. It had to be Aleyna. Wren had joined her friend in a budding rebellion, but for what? And Wren kept twisting that ring round and round. Justine felt her mother in her mouth, sharp and callous. "It's enough. You need to stop meddling and move on."

Wren regarded her, stunned.

"I'm sorry. I didn't mean that." Justine's face flushed as she rummaged in her bag for a Kleenex.

"Seriously? You're going to cry?" Wren's tone was mocking and unforgiving.

Pavara stood with the tape measure around his neck. "My friend, that is your mother."

"And you're going to defend her?" Disgusted, Wren tugged the dress in jerky and violent strokes above her head, holding back tears and ripping the seams.

Justine turned to Pavara and then Anika: "I'm sorry."

"You're apologizing for me?!"

———

They waited for the bus in silence. In the bus shelter, there was no graffiti, no expressions of outrage or lust, just an ad for Yas Waterworld featuring a family on a raft careening down a water slide. The bus was delayed, and when it finally arrived, they had to squeeze between the standing passengers. Justine welcomed the forced intimacy of the crowded bus, her daughter's body leaning into her with every lurch and stop, but she could feel Wren tightening, resisting contact, wanting to be rid of her, and when they returned home, Wren disappeared into her bedroom and closed the door.

———

Justine had been awake for hours. Silence does not heal wounds.

She got up, put the kettle on, and wandered out into the living room. Cobalt walls surrounded her, Old Glory Blue, a color she'd requested. Outside an orange belt of sky cast across the horizon. She stood in the blue room, in her sheer nightgown, and caught her dim reflection in the glass. She approached the wall of windows overlooking the Gulf and stood nearly naked in the long exposure of emerging light revealing her ugliness.

All her life she'd engaged the world from a pedestal behind glass. Her desire for safety and well-being was brutal, insatiable, an inheritance going back generations, a security that came at the expense and exclusion of others. Daybreak flared through the windows, highlighted the cellulite around her hips, the wrinkles around her knees, the folds beneath her stomach, and she regarded herself in the reflection—a diorama: *American Woman in Abu Dhabi.*

FLORA

Raj parked outside a single-story mall.

"Why are we stopping?"

"You need to eat."

Flora wasn't sure she'd be able to get out of the car, but Raj opened her door and offered his arm. "You're going to like this place."

"I don't have money."

His arm hung in midair, waiting. "Come on."

Together, they walked down the wide hallway, past stores selling luggage and gifts, electronics, perfume, and cheap jewelry. They waited at the entrance of the restaurant for someone to seat them. Filipinos clustered around red tablecloths and bouquets of plastic sunflowers. She heard Tagalog and laughter and imagined removing her abaya and joining in, but then she remembered her uniform, her bandaged neck, and felt ashamed.

Raj waited in the buffet line and brought Flora samplings of all the dishes: kare-kare, tocino, chicken adobo, humba, and rice. There was even tamarind and green mango in the sinigang, her favorite. Her hand shook as she brought the food to her mouth, and she used the red napkin in her other hand to hide the tremor. Raj watched and ate nothing.

"Good?"

Young men in baseball caps and t-shirts sat at the table nearby. Across the room, young women in floral dresses, printed scarves,

and lipstick laughed loudly. These other worlds—her world—
just feet away. Black eyeliner, hoop earrings, tamarind. She caught
a glimpse of herself in the tilted mirror above the buffet and was
alarmed by her appearance. In addition to the bandages, she was
gaunt, her cheeks sunken, her eyes vacant.

The woman with the hoop earrings headed to the bathroom.

"I need to use the restroom," said Flora.

"You okay?"

Flora steadied herself on the edge of the table and nodded. The
illuminated sign of the ladies' room was not far away. She could
make it.

Flora leaned against the bathroom wall and caught her breath
as she waited for the woman to exit the stall. In the mirror, she
inspected the red blotches and new blisters. She was afraid to remove the gauze from her neck and see what was beneath. A toilet
flushed and the woman joined her at the sink. Flora pumped soap
into her palm.

The woman glanced at her, then looked away.

Flora's throat tightened and she smiled. "I wonder, could I borrow your phone? My battery is dead. I need to text my daughter."

The woman rummaged through her bag and handed her
phone to Flora. "You know, you can report your employer."

Flora stared at the keypad, unable to recall Pia's number. "Oh,
no. No, thank you."

The woman stepped closer and spoke in a hushed tone. "I can
take you. Right now, we can go."

"I'm okay. I'm with my friend."

"You're not okay. I'm worried about your face." The woman
lifted Flora's cloak from her shoulder. "Your neck."

"We just came from the doctor."

"My boss will help you. She works with domestic workers."

Flora felt scared. How did this stranger know so much, this person who saw her only for a moment? If someone saw them together, they'd think she was trying to run away, she'd go to jail. And even if she dared to think about escape, what about Dounia? She'd never forgive her. And the way this woman looked at her with alarm was frightening. And Raj, he was waiting for her. He was right outside. She'd never get past him.

Flora rested the woman's phone on the sink. "I'm fine. Really. But thank you."

Flora returned to the table.

Raj left money for the bill. "I'm going to the bathroom and then we'll leave."

The waitress came by to collect the check. "Pack this to go?"

Flora looked at all the remaining food on her plate. "Yes, please."

She watched the woman across the room rejoin her friends. They were stealing glances and talking about her. The leftovers arrived, and she slipped them into her bag. Flora recalled Pia's phone number and repeated it in her mind. Maybe Raj could text Pia, let her know that she was okay. It'd been weeks since they'd been in touch, and she didn't want Pia to worry.

On the highway, she watched the light leave the sky.

Raj eyed Flora in the rearview mirror. "What's that smell?"

His lips drew together, and she knew he was angry.

"You want to get me in trouble?"

"No."

"You think Dounia wants me to take you to dinner? I was doing something nice for you. I can smell the food. Don't you think she'd find out? You want to get me fired?"

It was true. She hadn't thought of Raj. Only of herself.

"I'm sorry." She slid the leftovers onto the console beside him. The glass rolled down, and he threw the food out the window. The container flew past her, and she imagined the crunch of Styrofoam beneath speeding tires—mango, tamarind, and rice stuck in the treads. Raj would never text Pia.

ZEINAH

Zeinah suspended her oars above the Euphrates and listened: wind swept through branches, a cadence of katydids, her heart beating like a fish. Rocks scraped against metal, signaling the shore. She rested the oars inside the boat and crawled out, hiking up her cloak and clumsily stepping into the mud as she held the bow steady and guided the boat to a rooted bank, where she disguised it beneath the low-hanging branches.

She found a secluded spot to spend the night; at daybreak, she'd leave to find the camp. Above her, pine branches, cragged and raw, stripped naked from a storm. She removed her damp clothes and hung them on the splintered limbs to dry. The pebbles and sand were cold and stung her bare feet, the water colder still. She waded into the black and greenness and cupped handfuls of soft water between her palms before surrendering to the river, stretching across the muddy bottom as she swam out to a rock where she wrapped her arms around its slippery base and allowed the current to lift her belly and legs behind her.

This river revealed the hiding places of salmon, fish suspended above the crush of decomposing twigs and leaves. In the yellow fractured light of childhood, she used to dive into the roots of tall grasses and emerge with handfuls of mud. On laundry day, Tita led her down to the river in the predawn light, and together they watched black cede to grey, the shoreline and trees appear out of nothing. She drank warm milk from a thermos, caught small fish with the cap, and when the sky turned pale and herons skimmed the surface of the water, it was laundry time. Tita assigned Zeinah small items that belonged to the future: underwires, slits, and pouches smelling of grown-ups and sex. Later, they spread wet sheets across cypress branches to catch the smell of pine and riverbanks drying in the sun that would later lull her to sleep. But some mornings the sky did not clear, a gloomy darkness lingered, and Tita watched in silence as memories floated past her in the Euphrates. Zeinah recalled her grandmother's words of warning: "When the river dries and a palace of gold appears, do not take the treasures found there, as this is a sign of the second coming."

Zeinah stepped out of the river and dried herself on the shore. She dripped into the brittle moss. Wind swept across her thighs and left a pattern of goose bumps. The bends and depths of the river felt close, its heartache and violence familiar. The Euphrates could hold her and bring her back and back. Back to a place before cities, before villages, before farms, before hunting; back to a beginning. Above her, a white seed of moon dropped into a cloud and the sky went dark.

DOUNIA

It was early evening when Dounia heard the tires on the gravel. Headlights brightened the window and swept across the bare walls of Qadira's room where the baby slept. The infant startled awake. Dounia regarded her with a dim aggression, and before lolling back to sleep Qadira's eyes answered, *I don't like you either.* The engine died, car doors slammed, and she watched as Raj escorted Flora across the driveway. In the house she heard the rustle of paper bags and Flora's labored descent into the basement.

Liberation comes from accepting things as they are, she thought. Flora was a better housekeeper, daughter-in-law, and mother. Flora possessed things that Dounia never would; she was kinder and knew how to love. Some women were never meant to be a wife, mother, or caretaker. I cannot serve in that way, and every effort to domesticate me makes me wilder still. But if I do not perform these roles, what am I? I am obsolete. I serve no purpose, and I hate Flora for it. I cannot tolerate the sound of her breath.

Resentment spored savage thoughts. She resented them all: Basma, Hamed, her sister, her mother. All of them pitied her and made themselves the master. Flora and her martyrdom most of all. But they were superior, better in almost every way. Her sister's warnings and her mother's suggestion about running the date farm stalked her mind, and she felt ashamed of her imperious stance, her rejection of the people she loved; her self-loathing wrecked all hope.

Earlier, the doctor had called and said Flora could not work and needed to rest. Afterward, Dounia had swayed back and forth in the rocker, contemplating her future. She'd surrender to the violence within her and suffer the consequences. The feeling of freedom that accompanies catastrophe uncoiled within her. The time for second thoughts had passed.

ESKEDARE

Women face forward on a bus heading north through Yemen, then across the border into Oman, and then across another border into the United Arab Emirates. Two men share the driving. They pause at rest stops and hand out paper bags of food at appointed times: eggs, sweet grapes, and water. The mood is jovial, but Eskedare curls up inside herself, twists the ring around her thumb, and presses her ear against the glass, straining to hear her mother's breath and rolling rivers, everything she loves, further and farther away.

After the second sunrise, the bus signals off the highway and heads across a sandy road toward a cluster of beige barracks enclosed by a chain-link fence. A guard opens the gate. When Eskedare climbs out of the bus, she shields her eyes from the sun as she crosses a vacant lot to an open door. Inside: a room with metal folding chairs. The manager, a middle-aged woman from Bangladesh, introduces herself as "Ma," collects passports, records names, and assigns rooms. She's led between cinder block barracks. Thick electrical wires dangle overhead. Blue uniforms and white sheets drape across clotheslines stretched between buildings. Shelving displays the shoes of women sleeping inside on metal bunk beds shared in shifts. Three hundred women on two-year contracts. Care work, they say. Those who clean bodies; those who clean floors.

IV.

VI

ZEINAH

Zeinah walked beneath the sky and headed east. The wind sounded like the ocean, the dunes formed waves, and she followed a path of discarded and half-buried abayas toward the camp. She'd read about women shedding symbols of the caliphate as they walked to the tents, but Zeinah held on to her own, tying the length around her waist so she could move freely. The weight of the pack pinched her shoulders, and the fragile crust of sand cracked beneath her feet as she trekked forward. She half expected to see others, but not a single person appeared against the horizon.

I am leaving everything behind, she thought. But as she crossed the new terrain, her mind returned to familiar places: her city, the women in the brigade, her parents. Omar. Even Little Monster. Little Monster thriving on the streets with her fang, finding food in forgotten corners. She recalled the pink-petal tongue scratching against her hand, the whiskered cheek nudging against her palm, encouraging a rub. Little Monster wasn't thinking about Zeinah, but what about her parents? She imagined them in silence sitting at the kitchen table, their children gone. It was a relief to detach from that sorrow. She confronted the expanse of sand and scrub, her fingers tight around the knot of her abaya, her lips dry. She stopped and took a thermos from her pack, poured water into the tin top, and drank slowly, one sip at a time, thinking about Omar and what it would mean to return to herself without him. She'd heard of a female militia up north in Rojava, the YPJ, a Kurdish liberation movement that believed a country could be free only if its women were free.

Midday. The sun without a shade, naked and white, a compass pointing her east. She dropped her head to the sand and prayed. God superseded and preceded. Afterward, she felt at ease and a part of things.

———

A collection of tents with UNHCR logos appeared in the distance, and she recalled her uncle's goat farm in Jordan, recalled screaming songs into the wind from the back of a truck with her cousins as they raced across the red and rusty desert of Wadi Rum, hours beyond tour buses, to a place that was their own: three tents and a makeshift fence for goats. Inside, striped camel blankets in reds, pinks, and browns covered the floor, and a central fire simmered meals. The cousins slept together on blankets, and the smell of apple shisha hung around their dreams. During the day, they freed the goats from their enclosures and marched them around the base of rocky hills in search of tall grasses, only to find stubs of stalks, and as the sun went down, they climbed the mountains and watched the desert basin transform into a sea of black, the distant hills, humpback whales.

But as she approached the canvas tents and the blue UNHCR logos, a sense of apprehension and unease began to stir. Someone would demand her gun, papers, identification numbers, and address, and she decided to bury her weapon beside a scrub of sagebrush taller than the rest. She dug a hole with her hands and wrapped a cotton scarf around her AK-47 before covering it with dirt and sand. Some people plant seeds, others bury bodies. I hide a weapon, she thought, and then marked the spot with three twigs wrapped in grass.

FLORA

Flora awoke to a tomb-like silence. The room was dark, and the doors to the bathroom and bedroom were closed. She got up to relieve herself and found the door locked, and in a half-wake state she headed for the bedroom door to use the toilet upstairs, but the handle would not budge. She felt dizzy and delirious, and in a fevered sweat she collapsed into bed, convinced she was dreaming.

Later, when she awoke, she could not tell how much time had passed; only small patches of light slid beneath the bathroom door. She ran her palm along the baseboard to check the air-conditioning and found no circulation, only heat. The woman has created a cell and will wait for me to die, thought Flora. When it's over, there will be no evidence, only blisters from boiling water, confirmed by the doctor's report—a body in bed. The doors will reopen, the air-conditioning and refrigeration will resume, no one will know.

She had to use the bathroom and once again tried the doors. She was not getting out, at least not now. Her eyes fell on her suitcase. Flora unzipped the sides and squatted above the opened luggage; urine streamed and sprayed against the plastic, and a soft stool tailed around itself in the bottom. An Adidas t-shirt from home wiped her clean. Her ear and neck stung, and she searched for the bags of medicine and ointments to heal her wounds, but they were beyond the door, locked in the bathroom.

The heat mingled with the stench of her waste, and the throbbing pain sent her back to bed. Her stomach lurched, and she found herself vomiting onto the floor. Exhaustion poured into her body, her thoughts softened, and her muscles, tendons, even her bones, went limp. She doubted she had the strength to fight or that anyone would come to her rescue. They'd all seen her go to the doctor, and Dounia would tell them she was on bed rest. Maybe Raj, but he no longer trusted her. He had his own needs and a family to support.

JUSTINE

Driving out to Saadiyat Island, Justine avoided the fast lane and checked for cars in her rearview mirror. Presentations terrified Justine. Her father had stoked rivalry during dinners with her mother, her mother who had gone to Teachers College but was no intellectual. He was a tyrant who barked out world events, names of people, and locations, and he expected dates and explanations in return: causes of World War I, Ty Cobb, the longest river in America, recite "Jabberwocky" by Lewis Carroll. She feigned ailments and homework and abandoned her mother at the table, but as she matured, dates and poems stuck, and her father pronounced Justine a genius with a photographic memory.

The highway followed the shoreline of the corniche, and she noticed kayakers paddling toward the distant mangroves. Her thoughts returned to the falcon. Her interest in framing natural history through human experience had expired, and she felt her tight grasp on knowledge, her obsession with dates and order, loosening. She once knew a sculptor in his eighties, a man who had a daily practice of submitting to the ocean. Every day at low tide, he'd walk across the sandbars, wade into the waves, and float—not a gentleman's float with his stomach to the sun, but more of a loll, like a seal getting tossed, lifted, and rolled by the waves—until he was slung back onto shore, and he'd wade back into the sea again. She'd asked him once on the beach what he was doing. "Preparing for death," he said. "Submitting to the sea is my practice."

———

She signaled off the highway and stopped at a construction gate where she presented her ID to the guard, who handed her a hard hat.

"You need to put this on."

Justine nodded and waited for him to raise the security gate.

"Everyone needs to be wearing them on-site."

The helmet slid on easily, and he waved her through. The museum was years out, just breaking ground, and as she drove along the dirt road, past pilings and cranes, she doubted she'd contribute anything to the project. Khadijah, the director, was skeptical, the kind of person who conjured silence and then observed how people filled the void. Today was Justine's opportunity to prove that she was worthy, but already she felt an ennui that bordered on being reckless.

She parked on the sandy lot in front of the metal trailer, and as she stepped out of the car, her heel sank into the sand. Several drivers waited in air-conditioned town cars, seats reclined, eyes closed: a long day of waiting ahead of them. She wondered what they thought about, these drivers paused in parking lots across the Arabian Gulf for hours on end.

DOUNIA

In another story in the Dream Development, in another version of herself, duty and civility might have taken hold. With Flora bedridden, Dounia might have found purpose with everyone now dependent on her: the child, the mother-in-law, the maid. The domestic role she'd rejected might've become a lifeline to love and human connection. She could've moved Qadira's crib into her own bedroom, offered her breast tentatively in private, and in hushed purrs of reconciliation, mother and daughter would resume their conversation where it had left off.

But Dounia refused this version of herself. Instead, she implemented her plan to desiccate Flora in a gradual fade, like sun on fabric. She watched the sky move from black to pale grey, the barren landscape and half-formed houses a sedative on her psyche. She completed the domestic duties of the home with a regimented competency. Every exchange with Basma, the baby, Flora, and Raj was transactional. She was a zookeeper tending animals in stalls. She visited their bedrooms, cleaning the shit out of Flora's suitcase, and tended to their hides: chapped lips, diaper rash, chafed skin. This one has a broken wing, this baby needs to be fed and warmed, this old one has arthritis. She returned to the competency of her school days. She did not feel stress or anxiety. She was without emotion or attachment to any of them. Her mind demanded complete silence and focus. Everything was in its place. It was strange how little she had to do. In fact, her weapon was inaction—waiting and doing nothing. She'd done her research and nothing came as a surprise. An eerie calm pulsed through the concrete and steel beams. She was prepared for it all. A person cannot survive without water and food for more than four days. She was halfway there.

The Dream house was collapsing under a complicity of silence. Dounia told Basma and Raj that Flora was on bed rest and needed a break. No one questioned her authority, and they seemed relieved to see Dounia taking on domestic responsibilities and giving Flora a break. But Dounia believed they all knew what was happening and chose to do nothing. The only one refusing to accept the loss of Flora was Qadira. She was inconsolable, and Dounia wore headphones to silence her screams.

ESKEDARE

Eskedare works as a bathroom attendant at the Abu Dhabi bus station. She walks through the atrium of carts selling cell phones, stuffed animals, and cut flowers and heads toward the blue sign with the icon of a woman in a headscarf.

The female restroom: a windowless room, beige tiles with a border of green, a mirrored wall above three sinks in a counter of fake marble, five metal stalls, and a storage closet stocked with paper products, cleaning fluids, a mop, a pail, cleaning rags, and a folding chair. Women leave things: sunglasses, headphones, and shopping bags filled with postcards, magazines, and snacks. She keeps the valuable items in a box for a week, and if unclaimed, she brings them back to the camp and stores them beneath her bunk. Taped to the wall of the closet is a faded photograph of a small boy, maybe two years old, playing a plastic piano at a birthday party. Eskedare asks the women on the bus if they know who the kid belonged to, but no one knows. The tape has curled and yellowed around the edges, but Eskedare likes the photo and keeps it up in her office—that's how she refers to the closet, her office. In the morning, she hangs her bag on the hook on the back of the door.

At first, she likes working alone: the bathroom is like a house to clean and take care of. But it doesn't take long for the window-less room, the cleaning of urine and shit, and the endless hours of watching women preen in front of the mirror for misery to settle in. The days are lonely; she's a witness to women and their private lives in the restroom—diarrhea, vomiting, prayers, tampons, and tears. Occasionally someone nods hello, but mostly she's ignored unless a toilet doesn't flush or the paper's out. But worst of all are the women with their luggage, their rolling carts and tickets, taunting her with freedom, seducing her to escape.

Calculations in dirhams crowd her days. Monthly pay minus money for the man who arranged her travel. She needs three hundred for a cell phone and one hundred for a phone card. After that, everything will go to getting to Qatar. Someone shows her where it is on a map, a thumb of a country, 550 kilometers west of Abu Dhabi. A bus might take a day with transfers, but she needs her passport to get across borders and it's locked away in Ma's office for the next two years. Besides, it's an illegal passport, and she's afraid to use it. She could walk, maybe sneak across borders. Fifty kilometers per day. In ten or eleven days she'd arrive. Or maybe she could take a bus to the border and pay someone to get her across. How much? More calculations. She can't think about her mother or going home. She's come this far, crossed the sea and three countries. Everything is about Amara and Qatar. But first, the phone.

The phone.

At night, gas lines connect hot plates, and women spread newspapers out like tablecloths and gather to eat tomatoes, onions, and rice as their minds disappear into the images of shoes, cars, and vacations beneath their plates. Dirt falls from the ceiling, mildew grows on the walls, and Eskedare imagines living with Amara and her mother in a concrete house with a tin roof.

Later, the women race each other across courtyards in rolling office chairs. With the reckless passion of a teenager, she unrolls across the asphalt in spins and howls, the winner by yards, falling into the embrace of these mothers, sisters, and daughters who want to claim Eskedare as their own.

And later still, whispers and confessions from bunk beds in the dark. Voices float away from their bodies and speak in their home tongues. Bengali, Tamil, Arabic, and Urdu translate into broken English of what cannot be uttered during the day, like about Mahia from Bangladesh who was found dead in the courtyard before Eskedare arrived. Heart failure, says Ma, but they all know it was a suicide. Some say it was a protest. She tried to organize the workers and they docked her pay. Some say she was brave; some say she was a rebel; some say she had no brains at all. But Eskedare understands how a place like this could stir someone mad, could slant a mind in directions it'd never gone before.

Nipuni, Mahia's best friend, fills the silence that always accompanies talk of Mahia: "In my village in Sri Lanka, three women set themselves on fire. They were all abused by their husbands. Families and the village court did nothing. The three of them attended an arranged marriage of another friend. During the reception, they set themselves on fire. Two of them died. The other has scars all over her body and no longer speaks. Everyone called them crazy. But they just wanted people to listen. To see."

"None of this makes a difference," says the woman in the top bunk. "If we stopped coming, then we'd see changes. But if we can't make money in our own country, they've got us. Imagine if Bangladesh could pay us for all the labor we're doing here. Can you imagine . . . If we were building and cleaning in Rangpur the way we do here, we'd have one fine city."

"But look at that food cart guy in Tunisia. He set himself on fire and started a revolution."

"Yeah, he's a hero. The women are crazy."

Laughter tumbles into the darkness, but Eskedare thinks about Mahia and the women who set themselves on fire. Women who are fighters and believe in things.

The women form "banks" and manage living expenses. Collectively, they ration. With the support of the group, they spend less and save more. Eskedare is good with numbers and people see how she saves. Every stem and peel goes back into the pot. One Saturday, she cuts a deal on bulk quantities of flour, onions, and garlic with a market owner near Electra Street. Her bunkmates insist on giving her their money, and they share the expense of a notebook, where Eskedare keeps perfect records of every deposit and withdrawal. But Eskedare keeps her own money separate, squirrels it away in different spots: hidden behind a shelf, buried beside a gas tank, stuffed in a gutter, away from these women tied to contracts and countdown days.

*

JUSTINE

The receptionist wiped down her phone with disinfectant and did not look up from her task when Justine entered.

"They're waiting for you."

In the reception area, a haphazard circle of metal folding chairs surrounded the museum model unveiled for His Highness, Sheik Mohammed bin Rashid al-Maktoum, and Her Majesty, Queen Elizabeth II. Foster + Partners won the design bid with its five thermal towers, each one in the shape of a falcon wing. In the museum pitch, the firm had promised a live display of hunting birds to welcome each visitor. Minutes away from the Louvre and the Guggenheim (yet to be completed), the Zayed National Museum would be the "jewel in the crown" of Saadiyat's cultural district, a monument to honor the country's founder and a comprehensive history of the region starting with the arrival of people hundreds of thousands of years ago. Extensive loans from the British Museum would highlight the UAE and its important connection to world heritage.

Justine used to feel archives mattered. She'd watched CNN and cried as world heritage sites were destroyed: the Buddhas of Bamiyan, the Great Mosque in Aleppo, and, just recently, the Temple of Baal. World heritage felt personal, humanity's family album. But destruction was inevitable. Everything moved toward entropy, it was a law of physics, and archiving was just humans grasping at permanence. Curating now felt like a fancy form of accounting, logging inventory into a ledger with "indelible" ink that inevitably led to conflicts over ownership and display. The only archive that truly mattered was the Svalbard Global Seed Vault—a collection of the world's seeds to be opened in the event of a global disaster. That one was worth saving.

She spotted Callum through the glass windows of the conference room and braced herself for a day of presentations to "the partners," their Emirati employers. The Sheik would not be there; Khadijah al-Dhaheiri would preside. Callum told Justine this would be her chance to win her over, to prove that a Western woman with no falconry experience could curate the exhibit. Justine joked about how she was on probation, and Callum had let her laugh linger above the wineglasses at dinner.

Justine took a slice of pound cake from a white cardboard box and poured a cup of coffee into a Styrofoam cup. There was no milk, only powdered creamer—a far cry from their initial meeting at the Sheik's palace. The pleasantries were over.

FLORA

Flora surfaced in and out of consciousness, each time waking to a different hue of dimness reaching out to her from beneath the bathroom door: pale blue, bronze, purple black. Her limbs were wooden spoons, her throat a hollow reed. But there was comfort in the dark and the muffled sounds from outside—men and their machines, the call to prayer—measured the hours and called her home. It was strange how she entered this basement room and might never emerge again.

She prayed. She thanked God for the world He created, and she asked that He protect Pia and keep her safe. Please provide for her daughter in all the ways she could not. May Pia have a blessed life. She stretched her chapped lips across her teeth in gratitude. It was not a desperate prayer (she would not beg) but a conversation that moved closer and further away, like tides throughout the day. At low tide, she accounted for her life, walked the exposed shore, and gathered broken shells, discarded netting, bottles of detergent, and twine. She assembled the collection on the beach and considered them.

She discovered the tangled brown threads of her mother's cassette tapes spread across the beach and wound them back inside their casings. Numbered cassettes that had arrived in padded envelopes from her mother in Japan when she was a child. Brown tape that, when rotated around plastic pinwheels, delivered the disembodied voice of her mother, a voice cutting into the absence, a voice she now welcomed and recalled. Her mother murmured in her ear, and while in the past Flora had rolled away, she now curled around the voice like a snail and cherished it.

All these mothers, left and gone, picking up the abandoned homes and children of other mothers, left and gone. So many women entwined, tangled together in fragile knots of absence. Nets of women mending holes. A labor force of women forfeiting connection for survival and the promise of economic freedom. Freedom: pistachios jumping loose across the ferry bow, nut salt on her tongue, purple skins stuck between her teeth, an in-between time, suspended between here and there.

But neither she nor her mother was a modern-day hero, and if the women in the domestic training center could see her now, she'd tell them not to come. But she knew they'd come anyway.

Hope is a rebel.

———

She felt Dounia's presence in the room. The woman sat beside her on the mattress and applied the medical ointment to her blistered scar, held the edge of Flora's ear between her thumb and forefinger, an unsettling affection that held the promise of cruelty.

"Does it hurt? It's getting better."

Flora could not speak, but she felt her eyelid twitch.

"Trust me. I'm being kind."

But her kindness comes only because she's won the battle, thought Flora.

ZEINAH

The camp was not large, maybe a hundred tents. Hard to say how many people. An armed guard directed Zeinah to a table where a woman in a blue uniform entered her name, address, and age into a computer.

"Passport and birth certificate?"

Zeinah eyed the tables piled with official documents.

"Don't worry. They'll be returned in a few days."

Zeinah handed the woman her information and was given a bottle of water, food coupons, and a map. The woman marked the tent where Zeinah would sleep with an X and sent her on her way.

On the central street, women lugged blue water containers back to their tents. People bent over drying clothes scattered on tarps, and the smell of detergent and smoke hung in the air. She walked across a soccer field with tree limbs hammered into the sand as goal posts toward the food canteen. Two girls played on a makeshift seesaw, a wooden plank strapped across the side of a plastic bucket, and two toddlers sat in a broken cooler, pretending it was a boat. Zeinah followed the scent of rice.

Three men were cooking in a caravan. They'd created an assembly line of platters: piles of rice topped with chicken, peas, tomatoes, and lemons. The plates were wrapped in foil and then stacked on a cart. There were boxes of Turkish Delight and sweets topped with pistachios and honey. The festive atmosphere was unexpected, and Zeinah felt wary.

"A wedding?"

"Yes," said the man stacking platters.

"Noor and Hashem! You don't know?" said the man at the small stove.

"I just got here."

"In an hour. Everyone's invited."

Zeinah reached for a piece of chicken on a platter.

The man at the stove slapped her fingers, and she pulled her hand away, embarrassed. He looked at her sternly and then laughed, scooping a portion into a bowl and giving it to her. He nodded toward the tent across the way. "Go! See for yourself."

Inside the mess tent, women unrolled a rug and hung a blanket as a backdrop for the ceremony. Another group gathered around a girl, maybe fourteen or fifteen, playing on her phone as they painted her eyes green and cheeks red. The women looked askance at Zeinah and then ignored her. She hung back by the entrance and watched, knowing her niqab created discomfort and signified what they'd escaped, but many of the refugees were from Raqqa, and she wanted to remain anonymous. A young girl with lights entered and strung them above the bride, who seemed oblivious. Maybe it's better that way, thought Zeinah, and she slipped outside in search of the groom.

Zeinah heard hollering, and through an open flap, she saw a young man balanced on the shoulders of men. The groom struggled to button his white shirt as men danced around him, but when Zeinah entered, the jubilation stopped, and they returned the groom to the ground.

"The women are in the mess hall," said one of them.

Zeinah pulled on the fingers of her left glove and removed her ring. "I have a ring to sell." She extended the ring in her palm.

"What's happening?" asked a man just beginning to pay attention.

"A wedding ring. A beautiful diamond," said Zeinah.

The groom stepped forward, and the others circled around. The groom took it from her palm. "How much?"

"It's worth five million Syrian pounds. I'll take five hundred thousand."

She heard them scoff. The groom replaced the ring in her palm.

"You could go in on it together," she said.

"What do I get helping him buy a wedding ring? Half of his wife?" The tent erupted in laughter.

One of the men who'd been carrying the groom swiped the ring from her palm. She suspected it was the groom's brother. He turned the ring in his fingers. "That's a nice ring. I'll give you one hundred thousand."

Zeinah took the ring back.

"Let's see it here," said an older man sitting on a low stool behind them.

The men parted, and Zeinah went to the man, placing it in his cupped hands. He felt the weight in his palm.

"You sure you want to get rid of this?"

Zeinah watched as he held the ring up to a slant of light between the tent's uneven seams.

"That's my son," he said. "One hundred eighty thousand."

"Three hundred fifty," said Zeinah.

"Two hundred."

Zeinah took the ring back and placed it on her finger. She watched his face as the ring disappeared beneath her black glove.

"Two hundred fifty thousand. That is all I have," he said.

"Cash."

The man nodded.

Zeinah weighed her options. Another opportunity like this might not arise.

DOUNIA

A faint light. Flora's open jaw. There were bouts of rapid breaths followed by silence. Dounia dabbed Vaseline on Flora's chapped lips. I'm like a mother or a lover to her, she thought. I sit beside her and trace the nub of bone at her wrist, her caretaker and tormentor.

Dounia listened to Flora die, listened to the sound of her breath, and was reminded of the veil exhibit she'd seen at the Emirates Palace while visiting Abu Dhabi with her grandmother as a child. The room was dim, and the walls were painted black. They might have been the only people there. Spotlights illuminated freestanding glass cases and mounted frames, and her grandmother gathered Dounia into her arms and stopped in front of each display, pointing to the fabric, embroidery, and jewels. But the sight that arrested her grandmother, the marvel that rooted her for long moments in the dark, was the ovals of threadbare cloth marking each veil where women's lips and breath once had been, the evidence of life. "Beautiful," said her grandmother. And Dounia had whispered back, "Beautiful." Now, she watched Flora's breath, more curious than upset, waiting to see what would happen.

———

While the temperature rose in Flora's room, blizzard videos accompanied Dounia's daily chores. Now that she'd learned how to change diapers and feed the baby, now that she prepared Basma's tray and rubbed her legs without resistance, now that Flora was not eating or shitting and lay unconscious in the basement, the challenge was one of anticipation and endurance. Basma announced Hamed would be returning soon. Let him come, she thought. Like the camera steady beneath the ice block inching across the Japanese shingled roof, she was watchful and unmoving, a mere witness to the inevitable collapse. Flora will die, she thought, and with any luck, I'll be taken away to live in a prison with other women like myself.

ESKEDARE

Thursday: payday. Eskedare waits in line at the bank to cash her check with other foreign workers. But afterward, she does not follow them to Western Union to wire money home. Instead, she returns to the bus station, to Saif and his cart, where she's lingered over cell phones and Hello Kitty cases. When he sees her coming, he reaches for the Nokia, and she watches as he unwraps the box, removes the phone, inserts the battery and SIM card, and punches credit into the keypad.

A Cinnabon to celebrate. Eskedare carries the warm dough wrapped in pastry paper to the table beside the power outlet. She plugs the phone into the socket and watches NOKIA appear on the screen. The green charging light blinks, and Amara's phone number hums along in her mind. The smell of sweet cinnamon, butter, and sugar. She licks the white icing. This is me, she thinks. This is me eating a hot cinnamon roll with my cell phone. The raisins, soft and sweet, my companions. On the way back to the camp, Amara's number picks up tempo, and the Gulf spreads out like a carpet for her to cross. Tonight, she thinks, tonight she'll call. She wants the moment to be right, to have privacy.

After the evening race across the courtyard, Eskedare hangs back and slips behind one of the buildings. Weekends, a time of hushed tones and family updates in shadowed corners. The screen illuminates her cheeks, and her hands tremble as she presses numbers into the keypad.

Ringtones dash across the dark sky—shooting stars connecting time. She leans against the building, still warm from the day, her heart pounding. Ringtones puncture the silence all around her. She sits like this until the building grows cold against her back. It doesn't matter no one answers. Ringtones are enough.

That week, ringtones thread through her days and nights, stitch her closer to Amara, mend the expansive sky above her, and return her to the vastness of forever. This moon is also Amara's moon. The sun is theirs. Sometimes she cradles the phone between her ear and pillow, the chimes lulling her to sleep. To and from work, she leans with her head against the window, the phone to her ear, and at night she hides in the shower stall with the strongest signal.

A Monday, after work. Eskedare, alone in the back of the bus, her eyes closed, listening to the tolls.

"Allo?" a man's voice answers.

Eskedare clutches the phone. "Amara?"

"Huh?"

"I'm looking for Amara."

"No Amara."

"Is Amara there?"

"No Amara. Sorry."

She repeats the number.

"Yes, but no Amara. This is Ahmed. What is your name?"

The line goes silent between them.

"If you tell me your name . . ."

She presses the phone to her ear, listening to the man talking about what he can do for her, unable to hang up, to set her hope loose, to feel the world without it. It's impossible, but it's true: that

string of magical numbers holding her future is dead. The ringtones, her riverbed to Amara—gone.

———

Shadeless days of sweat-stained sheets, black flies, and melted
tar. Sorrow weighs her down, her limbs droop, and her thoughts
tilt homeward, toward her mother, but she cannot return empty-
handed, with nothing. Regret tightens her days. If only she'd
called Amara earlier—from Addis, from the mosque, from someone's phone at work. She waited too long, disgraced her mother
by leaving. She cannot bring more shame upon her, become a girl
gone mute. She must complete her contract. But even if she does,
people say it's impossible to leave on an illegal passport.

Without Amara, her job is torture. Wet toilet paper on the
floor, shit on rims, women entering stalls like livestock. I work in a
windowless farm, she thinks, without the smell of manure in dirt,
sun on thick hides, or field stones. The cleaning fluids turn her
stomach. One day, she removes the photo of the boy taped to the
wall, tears it into pieces, and throws it in the trash. This is a closet,
she thinks. Call a thing what it is. She watches the women regard
themselves in the mirror—the lipstick, the blush, the mascara. The
overheard phone calls as if she's not there at all. The consideration
and then snub of the tip jar. The tampons, the smeared blood on
toilet seats, the hoses, the sweat of water on porcelain. The lonely
days. Witnessing pockets of life between friends and children, the
aging women who remind her of her mother. Cinnabons—hot
butter, cinnamon, and sugar—aromas now twisting her stomach
sour. She no longer visits Saif at his cell phone and Hello Kitty
cart. All of that was a before time—a hope time.

Now, as the bus travels along the corniche on her way to and
from work, the Gulf appears wrinkled, and the women she works

with, sad. She's joined the herd of white vans rolling across desert highways—slack-jawed, head-on-the-glass journeys. Bodies
roped to endless contracts living in countdown days. Eskedare
avoids the lifers and switches bus seats, moves tables when they
get too close. I am fifteen, she thinks. These women are mothers
and sisters. Their thoughts are not her thoughts. Their concerns
are not hers. I am not like them, she thinks. This is not a life. I
must find a way out of here.

And like the black fly with iridescent blue wings that moves
slowly and lands on the wall beside her pillow, in the sink where
she brushes her teeth, on the pocket of her uniform, buzzing in
her ear, the notion takes form and follows her from bus to bathroom and back again: the collective savings tucked safely in the tin
beneath her bed. At first, she just counts the money, organizes the
bills from smallest to largest. Later, she admires the illustrations of
falcons, mosques, and forts. Her plan is soft around the edges, but
with every flush of a toilet, every squeeze of the mop, every spray
across the glass, her escape takes form.

FLORA

Flora's body clattered in the last slugs of revolt. The walls watched. The mattress waited, and Flora's breath, a tattered leaf on a limb, held on. Outside, the pounding and echoes of hammers, the growl of a drill, the shouts and footsteps of men.

She heard the bedroom door open and then close. Dounia stood against the wall, and for a long time the women listened to each other's breath. The air shifted in the room, and Flora felt Dounia coming toward her. She lingered at the foot of the bed and finally sat down beside her, once again tracing the bone on Flora's wrist, carpeting her hand with a warmth she did not welcome. And in the darkness, she heard Dounia grieving. Let me be alone, thought Flora. It took all her strength, but Flora slid her fingers free from Dounia's grasp and went in search of her own heart and found it beating.

The room held its breath.

Flora fell from the branch.

The mattress braced her; she was still alive.

There are clementines in my bra, she thought. Datu's blanket in the drawer.

JUSTINE

Justine was one of two women in the room, the only American. The lead architect was from Canada, and his building plans were impressive: a 3D model with Emirati and expat figurines inhabiting the galleries, restaurants, courtyard, and rooftop gardens. The design integrated local architectural traditions in a vision of glass, blond wood, and bending metals. Interactive exhibits included textile lounges, video kiosks, and design labs.

The architect ended his presentation and stood at the lectern as Khadijah raved about his design: a building that would celebrate the UAE as a nexus of cultural heritage and innovation in the region and beyond. Everyone in the room wanted her validation, it was all that mattered. When Khadijah finished speaking, everyone clapped politely, envious of the architect's good favor with the royal court. Justine was up. The architect handed her the projection cord; she plugged it into her USB port and opened her computer.

A news headline about the burning girl appeared on the projection screen behind Justine and silenced the room. Callum shot Justine a look, and she quickly X-ed out of the article. But the image of the girl inked her mind, spread across her thoughts like dye on porous paper. Another search tab appeared: a domestic worker jumping from her employer's high-rise window. She apologized and unplugged the USB port while she located her presentation.

Khadijah waited, her hands folded in her lap.

Sensing she was on the edge of a dangerous precipice, Justine clicked through her slides before connecting to the projector. The presentation was a feeble and predictable attempt to chronicle the material culture of falconry, of conjuring Shema.

Khadijah checked her phone.

"One second."

"Should we take a break?" asked Callum.

"Nope, here we go." But she was stalling for time.

"Technical difficulties?" asked Khadijah.

"Yes," said Justine, closing her computer.

"It happens to the best of us," said the architect.

"Forget about the slides," said Khadijah, leaning forward. "Tell me, in your own words, your vision for the falcon wing."

"Or she could present at our next meeting," said Callum.

"No, no. I can do it," said Justine. "I'm happy to share my thoughts. In fact, I prefer it this way."

Other than the whir of the air conditioner, the room was silent, and Callum assessed her with a baffled gaze.

Khadijah turned her phone face down on the table. "Please."

Justine's mind went numb, a crater opened, and she tripped down the craggy chasm of knowledge she'd accrued. About the falcon, she knew many things, and it all came tumbling out in no particular order, a manic stream of consciousness that included quotes from Egyptian queens, poems, observations from naturalists, the number of species, average weights and lifespans, statistics of hunts, the minute details of hoods, gloves, jesses, and bells, and her personal insights and links between falconry, domination, freedom, and culture. The room disappeared, and no one interrupted her as she slid down the dusty sides of her gorge, reaching for roots and rocks on the chasm walls. She was inside the books, the images, the databases—shedding knowledge, cycling through topics.

She posed questions and wondered things aloud in an untethered rant that did not pause for answers. "What does it mean to create an animal exhibit in the twenty-first century? Is it possible to create something that does not continue the colonial project of the imperial archive? What if we were to banish nostalgia? If we agree to reject the colonial tradition of preserving nature behind glass, what do we have? Or perhaps there's an important experience inherent in creating and witnessing taxidermy, crossing the chasm where the lived and living meet. And who can deny the ritualistic, experiential, almost religious experience of dimly lit rooms populated with animal shrines where an osmosis between human and creature crosses between glass in an almost Deleuzian animalness. And what about museums as spectacle? Virtual exhibits that take visitors inside the relationship between humans and falcons. Guests could become the falcon, inhabit her wildness. But is imagining and trying to conjure the falcon's experience a form of erasure?"

Justine spread her arms and demonstrated flap patterns, glided around the room simulating flight, before hurtling downward and landing at the bottom of a dry ravine, an injured bird, her heart heaving in the rubble.

———

Justine's eyes fluttered open as she returned to the conference room. The uneasy onlookers averted their gazes. Circles of perspiration soaked her silk shirt, and her hair was damp like a tuft of feathers.

No one said a word.

Callum shuffled his papers and looked at the floor.

Khadijah regarded Justine and surveyed the room. "Questions?"

Everyone felt the density and volume of the director's thoughts and waited to see what would happen. Justine stood at the front of the room—a natural disaster on mute.

Khadijah's reaction to the presentation was inscrutable. Not one of them dared to speak.

"Very good," she said. "Let's take a break."

DOUNIA

In the dream, her uniform was pink, and the guards wore green. Concertina wire cut across a clear sky. Dounia stood in a dirt courtyard watching weeds knock their heads against the fence. A torn blue tarp shaded a doorway and slapped against a wall. She was in a long line of women for the bathroom. There was only one toilet, and her bladder pressed against her pelvic floor. A hose snaked across the cracked courtyard toward a cluster of blue jugs in the laundry area, beneath prison uniforms drying on clotheslines in the sun. She ducked out of line and followed the hose across the courtyard, where she pulled down her pants and positioned the neck of the jug between her legs. A thick flow of urine streamed into the bucket, echoing across the square, and when she looked up, all the women were watching.

Dounia awoke to a wet mattress, her underwear soaked. She lay alone in the darkness of her bedroom, stunned. She stripped the sheets, piled them in the bathtub, and sat on the rim in shock. The sting of Flora's revolt lingered: she'd removed her hand, backstroked away, and rebuked her. In her final hours, Flora broke the links of ownership. Dounia recalled Flora's delicate fingers fumbling across the sheet, her palms landing on her chest in an oath indicting Dounia: "This is me. You are you."

Never had Dounia felt so frightened of herself; she felt small and ashamed of the woman she'd become. Her contempt for Flora was built on what? Skin a darker shade of brown, a rounder face, a

hing. I'm a sad and cruel person, she thought. I'm so desperate;
amost killed a woman.

kindness and humility she'd never have. A willingness to work for
what she wanted, even if it might not come to pass. Faith. Marking the woman, containing her, extinguishing her, accomplished
nothing. I'm a sad and cruel person, she thought. I'm so desperate;
I almost killed a woman.

She searched through her drawers and retrieved Flora's passport and phone. The phone was dead. She opened the passport
and lingered on Flora's photograph. She did not want to part with
the passport and was aware of her envy, her mind contracting, her
desire to hoard the woman's freedom, to deny a life that existed
outside the boundaries of her own. Dounia's sighs echoed through
the concrete house. She felt afraid of Flora's absence, the silence
waiting for her, the persistent hush of the structures determining
her life and the choices she had made.

———

In the same saucepan that scalded Flora's neck, Dounia heated
soup. On a tray, she arranged a plate of crackers, butter, and a bowl
of dates. She slipped the passport beneath the napkin, and as she
crossed the living room to the basement stairs, she heard her own
feet shuffle.

ZEINAH

Zeinah thought she might sleep, but images of the bride and groom appeared between the seams of her tent, and she decided to attend the wedding. When she arrived, the ceremony was already in progress, and she slipped between back flaps and found a seat in the corner as the bride said, "I accept, I accept, I accept."

The bride and groom sat apart on the couch, and the officiant stood above them. Zeinah shifted in her seat to get a glimpse of the girl in her stiff white napkin of a gown. A dress shirt sagged across the young man's shoulders and his pants were baggy, probably borrowed. The air smelled of rosewater and sweat.

"Noor, you have known Hashem to be a believer and worshipper of God alone, and you are entering this marriage to him with trust in him to be your husband by your own free will?"

"Yes," said the bride.

"And the dowry payable to you by Hashem and his family has been mutually agreed upon and you are satisfied with it and the terms of execution?"

"Yes," said the bride.

Zeinah wondered if it was possible to call what these girls were doing consent. Child brides were saving families from financial ruin and creating ways to survive. Weren't they also martyrs who deserved a special place in heaven? The groom slid her ring onto the girl's finger, and Zeinah uttered a silent prayer: May she wear it in good health. May she prosper. May she sell it, if she must.

"In the name of God, Most Gracious, Most Merciful: inasmuch as you have pledged to each other your lifelong commitment, love, and devotion, and with God as a witness, I now pronounce you husband and wife." Everyone began to recite the Surah al-Fatiha. The mood in the tent was gloomy, and Zeinah did not feel encouraged.

The bride reached for her mother, and even though no one could see her face, they all knew she was weeping. Not that long ago, Zeinah had clung to her own mother beneath the kitchen door, and she was overcome with the desire to be held by those arms again, to smell the onions and talc, to feel the faded flowers of her mother's apron against her cheek. Despite the girl's tears, this young wife was no coward.

A small crowd followed the couple to the groom's family tent, and the mother-in-law placed a Qur'an on her new daughter's head and everyone clapped as she entered. Zeinah's chest tightened as she imagined Omar's mother placing the weight of the family Qur'an on her own head, a reception of extended family. Maybe even a sister-in-law or a niece. To imagine how things might have been was both a comfort and a torture, fictions she needed to abandon if she wanted to survive.

ESKEDARE

Women step around Eskedare's sorrow; anyone can catch the blues. After dinner, she no longer races across the pavement in rolling office chairs but sits alone on steps, against walls between buildings. At night, as the other women murmur and chortle into the darkness, Eskedare wraps herself in a blanket, faces the wall, and considers Mahia, the woman who'd killed herself before Eskedare's arrival, who maybe slept in this very same bed, and she feels Mahia hanging around, urging her to leave before it's too late.

Tomorrow is the day. She gathers the money from her hiding places: the oil tank, behind the shelf of shoes, the gutter. And when she hears the women laughing in the courtyard, below the clotheslines stretched between buildings, sagging from the weight of their wet uniforms, she reaches for the tin beneath her bed, the communal bank, and she feels Mahia urging her to take the bills she's lovingly arranged by color and illustration—pale yellows, reds, and blues; falcons, mosques, and bridges. She won't return to her village empty-handed but as a hero. She knows she'll never pay it back, but she does not leave the box empty. She deposits all the jewelry, sunglasses, lipsticks, and items the women have left behind in the bathroom as a parting gift.

On the bus in the morning, Eskedare sits alone, avoids eye contact, and in her mind, she says goodbye. This is the last time I'll see these women. I'll never board this bus again.

On the way to work, they pass the blue bench on the corniche.

Soon, she thinks. It's too risky to catch a bus from the station where she works, but there's that bus stop with the blue bench; she can catch a late bus to Dubai, where she'll disappear and find the world of men and border crossings. She'll slip out the side entrance at the end of the day. Women will worry, perhaps look for her, but eventually, they'll return to the camp. At first, they'll say she was a wicked girl who stole their earnings. But they'll use the sunglasses, lipsticks, and scarves. In time, she'll become a story. That's all. A story about the girl who got away.

———

At the end of her shift, she stocks the toilet paper, wipes down the sinks, and props the mop inside the closet for the last time. She waves goodbye to Saif at his atrium cart, passes the gold stores selling rings, pendants, and chains, and pushes through the side doors spilling out onto the supermarket parking lot. Women load groceries into trunks and leave shopping carts askew. She aims toward the green cross of the pharmacy and disappears down a narrow street populated with cobblers selling refurbished shoes, a bakery, a typesetter. At the corner, she slips behind a row of dumpsters and changes out of her uniform and into the dress she bought during her lunch break. She'll wait for night to swallow her.

A high and humid wind blows loose wrappers and paper cups across the superblocks and streets. An orange hue tinges the edges of the sky as Eskedare disappears into the shadows of buildings, trees, and construction sites on the way to the corniche, to the blue bench and the bus to Dubai. It begins to rain, the first rain she's felt in months, and in the thick dust and fog, headlights bloom like daisies, reminding her of home. I am free, she thinks. Soon,

I'll hold my mother's head in my lap, rest my stomach on the backs of cows.

But the underpass to cross the highway is closed. Tall grasses and wild roses cover the meridian, and even in this rain, the sprinklers arc above the foliage and glisten beneath the streetlamps. A couple blocks away, she sees the bus stop. The blue bench.

She's a good runner.

In the shadows of palm trees, she waits for cars to pass and straps her purse across her body. The traffic is sparse this time of night, the pattern irregular, and when there's an opening, she sprints out onto the highway. Her dress blows in the wind behind her as she crosses lanes. She leaps with ease onto the meridian, runs through the thorns of roses and itch of high grasses, and without slowing down—her limbs outstretched, her torso tilted forward, the fog misting her skin—she emerges onto the other side, aiming for the blue bench now in view.

A horn blows, white headlights swerve and flare. Eskedare dodges the collision but loses her balance; she feels her body giving way as she hits the pavement face down, inhaling the smell of salt air and gasoline. Pebbles sting her broken skin. Dazed, she stares into the red hazard lights of the stalled car on the shoulder of the road in front of her. Dizzy, she closes her eyes, and when she opens them, she sees the blue bench and hears the rumble of the bus approaching.

A woman stands above her, a silhouette in the dark night, her voice anxious, on the edge of hysteria. "You terrified me. I worried you were dead."

Eskedare brushes herself off. But when she stands, a pain radiates through her ankle, she stumbles, and the world begins to tilt.

"We need to go to the hospital." The woman insists that she's been hurt, which she has, but not badly.

"No . . . no hospitals. No doctors."

The bus stops—she's sure of it—and she believes she sees a figure departing. It's not too late. She sees herself on the blue bench,
boarding. The bus door closes, the engine sighs, and the taillights
fade. But she's not on the bus, she's on the ground, sobbing into the
pavement. She feels the woman's gaze on her back, her ankle throbbing, and there's a stinging in her shins and palms, and it seems it's
just her and this woman, alone, on an abandoned highway.

"You shouldn't be out here in the middle of the night. You can
come home with me or we can go to the hospital. I can't just leave
you here."

Eskedare turns over on the asphalt and sees a flock of birds
drifting above her in the high winds and fog. She meets the woman's gaze and knows her journey is over. Eskedare wills the woman
to leave, but instead the woman bends down and joins her on the
pavement. The way this woman hovers makes her nervous, and
she twists her ring round and round, and even though Eskedare
does not understand every word the woman's saying, she knows
this woman will never let her go.

In the car, the woman goes on and on about the embassy. The
embassy this. The embassy that. If she only knew what the women
at the camp say about the embassies: runaway women sleeping on
stairs; workers sent to jail, returned to their employers. Eskedare's
an illegal runaway, a worker who's broken her contract, a thief.
If she goes to the embassy, she's going to prison. Panic vibrates
through her body, and she reaches for the door handle, seized by
a desire to fling herself out of the car, to land on the tarmac, for
the tire treads to mark her body, but the door is locked. It's one of
those fancy cars that accounts for the impulse in children to jump.

≈

FLORA

In the dimness of her room, Flora smelled broth and salt. She could not say if she was dead or dreaming. She sensed her stomach rise and fall, felt wisps of air around her nostrils. To open her eyes took effort. The light in the room had changed. The doors were open, and somewhere there was food. She let her arm dangle over the bed; her hand searched the floor. A tray. Her fingers in soup. Crackers. It took all her strength, but Flora brought a cracker to her lips and held it in her mouth until she felt the edges dissolve. It took a day to eat one cracker. Dounia did not come down to check on her. Tomorrow I will roll over, roll over and see what else is on the tray.

Water. Dates. Passport. Soup.

She recalled her reflection in the bathroom mirror at the restaurant, how afraid she'd felt to leave Qadira, Basma, and Dounia. She wanted to be good. Guilty of nothing more. When she'd first awoken in this makeshift cell, she had permission to die. But something had shifted. It was not her mind propelling her forward but an energy beyond thought, a current lifting her up, and while she slept, an undertow dragged her further and further away from what she thought to be herself. She smelled the salt rolling off the soup, tumbling forward out in front of her, making plans. *You can stay here,* it seemed to say, *but I'm leaving.*

The call to prayer, a siren five times a day, nagged at her to submit and forgive. And in this way, with food and prayer, an uprising gathered around her and gave her strength. She bit into the delicate skin of the dates. Dates she'd promised to never eat, not now, not ever, but there they were in her mouth, the violence and sweetness of life. This is not about forgiveness, she thought, but accepting what is.

———

In the darkness before daybreak, Flora held on to the basement banister and climbed the stairs. She stood in the silence of the foyer, heard an ice cube drop into the freezer tray, and slipped out the front door unheard and unnoticed. But in the driveway, she stalled.

The sky was still black, and as she caught her breath, a yellow light switched on in the garage. Raj was up, watching, waiting to see what she would do next. He's another person I'll never see again, thought Flora. Would Qadira Ibrahim ever know her name? Probably not, but that did not erase their time together.

She stood in the driveway, not in her uniform, but in the clothes she wore on her arrival, and she did not hold a trash bag, a newspaper, or a child. Next door, she heard sprinklers coming on, rotating their heads, nodding to her in the stillness of the not-yet-dawn, and she felt the warmth of the previous day trapped in the pavement beneath her feet, prodding her forward.

JUSTINE

Justine was the first to leave, retreating to the ladies' room, a one-room stall where she could be alone. She sat on the toilet shaking. In the hall, she heard hushed voices, the first whispers of rumor. She'd displayed her mind and paraded all there was to see. She doused her face in cold water, avoiding her reflection in the glass.

Khadijah waited for her outside the bathroom. They were alone in the narrow hallway.

"Justine, you may not be aware, but there are organizations that help migrant women in the Emirates. I wish you'd called me." They stood awkwardly across from each other, and Justine leaned against the wall, unable to meet Khadijah's gaze. "I want to thank you. You've amassed an impressive amount of research, and I appreciate your efforts. Your bag and computer are waiting with the receptionist. Callum will follow up regarding the details of your termination and return home."

Khadijah skipped the niceties of a hug or handshake and headed back to the conference room. Her heels tapped against the industrial carpet, her abaya swished against the corridor walls, and there was even an air of kindness in her wake.

The receptionist handed Justine her things with a lazy stare and did not say goodbye. Outside, the air was humid, and her shirt clung to her skin like flypaper. She got into her car and left the sandy parking lot and sleeping drivers behind. I've been fired, she thought, and without a work visa it's impossible to stay. All of this will go on without me. The drivers will keep driving, the museums will open, the falcon wing will unfold. She couldn't recall a single thing she'd said, but then a realization snagged her mind: it was all recorded.

Heading west on the E12, Justine recalled her first days in Abu Dhabi, a time when she'd mapped New York onto the city. For the longest time the corniche was the West Side Highway, Electra Street was Canal Street with its cell phone stalls and lighting stores, Rashid bin Saeed al-Maktoum Street was Broadway with the bus station and taxi stands, Mussafah was Queens with all its car dealerships, and the Upper East Side was Saadiyat Island with its museums and the St. Regis hotel. But eventually that changed; Justine no longer compared the palm trees lining the highways with LA, or Abu Dhabi with Casablanca, or Jones the Grocer with Dean & Deluca. Abu Dhabi became itself, and she opened into its heat, its monochromatic landscape, her weekend drives to the health food store in Dubai, and the half-finished bridge that was built by a sheik and suspended midsentence. The half-finished bridge she'd come to admire. Not all projects need to come to fruition. She committed the street names to memory, knowing she'd never return: Khalifa bin Shakhbout, al-Falah, al-Nasr, Sheik Khalifa bin Zayed.

DOUNIA

Even after Flora left, Dounia continued to gaze out the window, and she noticed the weeds knocking their heads against the compound wall as they had in her dream. The necks of tomato vines bent toward their dropped leaves on the ground, and a corner of the blue tarp snapped loose in the wind. Already, she could not recall Flora's face in her mind, but the stone of the woman's wrist remained, a hill Dounia had traced with her finger and wanted to own, and again her heart seized as she recalled Flora's hand slipping away and finding freedom.

———

Dounia stood motionless in the dank basement room in a silence so absolute that Flora might as well be dead. Flora had left everything behind. In the top drawer was her lingerie, the cheap lace underwires she'd forbidden, a wrinkled clementine tucked inside a padded cup. The second drawer held clothes she'd never seen: dungarees, slogan t-shirts, a purple ruffled dress. The bottom drawer kept her uniforms and a baby blanket, neatly folded.

Dounia lay on the bed and considered Flora in a way she'd never done before, the whole of her. On the wall was a postcard of a faded beach and palm trees. Black cursive in the bottom corner spelled "El Nido." Dounia peeled the postcard from the wall, curious to read the back, but it was written in a language she did not understand.

She reached for the remaining date in Flora's bowl and imagined herself sitting in her grandmother's wooden chair in the clearing of the date farm, Qadira Ibrahim in her arms, her lids like moth wings falling open and closed. A pile of dead palm fronds soaked up the slanted sun like kerosene. And the smell of honey. She imagined the sunlight warm against her back as it had been when she was young. Her push outward, living inside marks on a page, moving toward who she was really meant to be. Her mother and sister would take her back, her bad behavior could be forgiven, but as these naive thoughts of renewal seeded in her mind, she heard the compound gate open, and Raj greeted Hamed in the drive.

The front door opened, and she listened to Hamed's footsteps above her in the foyer. The air conditioner switched on, and a cold draft blew through the vents, pimpling her skin. Flora's employment would be tracked to her sponsorship. To avoid shame, Hamed could pay a diyah, blood money to Flora in exchange for dropping charges. Dounia would not go to prison or shame her in-laws with divorce; she and Qadira Ibrahim would remain here, in the Dream Development.

ZEINAH

By two o'clock, the party had migrated to the soccer field, where men banged on buckets alongside a boom box. Zeinah stood outside the circle. She should leave, go back to her cot, but it had been so long since she'd listened to music and seen people dancing.

The bride and groom arrived, and Zeinah found herself inching closer, wanting to reacquaint herself with what was forgotten. The guests joined arms, formed a line, and then peeled off into two circles: one for the men, one for the women. The mother of the bride guided the line of women and hooked Zeinah's arm, insisting she join. Another woman grasped her hand, and she was linked into the chain. Her arms rose and fell in a wave of elbows and hands, and as her feet stamped and her legs crossed, she struggled to keep her niqab in place. The steps carried her into childhood. The drumming pumped into Zeinah's heart, and she forgot herself as she joined in the ululations and high-pitched cries of home, allowing her niqab to shift and slip. It seemed everyone was smiling, lulled into the dream of the past. Zeinah danced, surrendering to the music traveling through bodies linked in joy, and in a celebratory gesture, she stripped the garment from her head.

The mood in the circle shifted. One woman murmured to another. A cluster broke loose from the line, and the woman beside the bride pointed at Zeinah: "That's her." Anxious whispers scattered through the crowd.

"She was in the brigade," said someone.

"That's Zeinah. The one who flogged Rima."

"Biter!"

Zeinah looked at the crowd, read the women's faces, and felt their judgment upon her. The circle broke, and they shoved her forward, down the alleys lined with tents, chanting, "Biter. Biter. Biter, be gone."

She heard the stamping of feet. The crowd pressed against her; she stumbled on a stake, lunged forward, and let out a wild cry before grabbing hold of a tent rope to keep from falling. At the toilets, she smelled human waste and her stomach lurched. The wrath of the wedding party lifted them all up, united them in adrenaline and a purpose to reject the woman who'd brought shame to family members and ruin to Raqqa. They drove her out of the camp and expelled her like a stray dog with raised sticks.

It was true; this camp was no place for her. She walked away with no papers, no water, no food, and aimed in the direction of her buried gun. Marooned now, beyond the margins of life, Zeinah's heart sank into an empty hollow and her legs trembled. I am alone, she thought, and the breeze blew up her cloak, exposing her bare ankles.

ESKEDARE

She explores the girl's bedroom, opens her closet, touches the stacks of t-shirts and jeans. She lingers over the art table, a mess of thread, sewing needles, jars of buttons and sequins, scraps of paper, brushes in a jar of cloudy blue water. She leafs through a large sketchbook of drawings: winged creatures, small animals, and dresses. The mural on the wall taunts her, the woman with her blue dress swirling around her legs, the words above her head: NOT ALL WHO WANDER ARE LOST, and in cursive across her skirt: WILD & FREE.

Her entire life, she's been pushing outward, further and farther away. There's no coming back from the humiliation of prison. She twists the ring around her finger and thinks of the man in Yemen, his belly stifling tears, bobbing in the dark, the sweet juice of a rotten banana, his dead sister. She knows what she must do, but his sister cannot come with her. She'll leave the ring behind, for another girl.

———

Now, a Sunday before dawn, when her underwear with the stretched elastic and black rubber-soled shoes are all she has from home. Now, when the fields of ringtones are dead and the Gulf feels impossible to cross. Now, when she tucks the stolen money beneath the water glass. Now, when she opens the terrace door and steps through the sheer curtains drifting into the room. Now, when the sand stings her cheeks, when the brown sky of the city fades. Now, when she sees the white fluorescent falcons of the gas station below—ADNOC. She doesn't know what those letters mean, but the gas stations, their falcons and blue pumps, are everywhere, and without really thinking, maybe in a dim sort of way, she grasps the neck of an empty five-gallon jug and steps back from the terrace edge.

Her arms wrap around the blue jug, and she carries it close to her chest like a toddler. Her gait is slow and awkward across the parking lot, and despite the pain in her ankle, her resolve is strong as she considers the path before her. The gas station. The roundabout. The fountain. She's deciding something for herself. She's not going to the embassy, she's not going to prison, she's not going back to the labor camp, she's not returning home with nothing. Sometimes that's the only freedom a person has: no.

She pays for the petrol and takes a book of matches from the counter. The man at the register regards her, suspicious, but she does not make up a story, say thank you, or even offer a goodbye. But the bells on the door jingle when she leaves.

The bays are empty. The falcons watch from the gas pumps, their eyes upon her. The plastic and metal handle feels warm beneath her palm. She inserts the nozzle into the neck of the bottle, squeezes the metal lever, and as the gasoline fills the jug in a low, hollow stream, the bitter scent of oil walks her back to the abandoned truck below the warka tree. She's filled up that tank many times in her mind, but right now, this is real, and she's overcome with sorrow. She'd wanted to roll out her heart for someone, get kneaded, and rise. The jug is full. She clicks the nozzle into its cradle. The man steps away from the register and watches her from the window.

Morning, on the brink of breaking, a grey fog awash in orange. She squats beneath the pumps and falcons, wraps her arms around the jug, and rises. The jug is heavy, the journey slow. She heads across the empty street and steps off the high curb. The roads are quiet, the air humid and moist upon her skin, as she walks past the electrical stores selling bulbs, fixtures, and wires. She passes a dumpster overflowing with trash, the dawn full of rot and rinds stewing in the heat.

At the roundabout, she crosses the street and heads into the central plaza of broken tiles that once formed a lotus in the weeds. Her arms and legs shake from the weight of the jug, and she nearly trips as she steps into the bowl of the defunct fountain. Sweat coats her scalp as she places the jug on the ground. Her dress sticks to her back, chest, and legs, and she holds the fabric away from her skin to catch a breeze. Occasionally, white headlights approach and then pass, but it's still early and she mostly has the city to herself.

She recalls Miss Eshe at the board, mathematical equations, the arrows indicating greater and less than. She always saw herself in those growing arrows, life getting bigger, but her life is getting smaller, funneling into a point that's no life at all. There are the things she thought she'd do: work in Qatar with Amara, rescue her cows, return to her mother. Everything in her body refuses less than. Eskedare feels a surge of energy and righteousness, a feeling from when she was young and tripped on field stones in the dark. A feeling of wildfire outrunning rain.

She stands in the middle of the fountain facing Electra Street and tries not to be afraid. She thinks of Mahia who killed herself at the labor camp, the brides in small villages, the Gulf-return girl gone mute, the bus driver's little sister. She raises the jug, pours the contents over her torso, legs, and arms; down her back. She rubs the gasoline over her skin, feels the dryness, and then douses her head, hair, and chest. Before she strikes the match, she allows herself a moment to recall other things. The caw-caws of birds in the trees and the dust they leave behind. Rock pigeons. Mourning doves. Nubian nightjars. Amara. They'd been girls together, in and out of each other's laps, holding hands down riverbeds, and making wishes on a plane. She imagines wrapping her limbs around her mother's body, bringing home the stench of sweat and trampled roses, pressing her cheek against her soft shoulder and shrunken breasts.

She strikes the match; blue flames lick the hem of her dress, the nylon catches, and in an instant fire spreads and sparks along her legs, torso, chest, and back. She screams as her skin and body burns, closes her eyes, and smells the singe of flesh, her hair a curtain of fire. She chokes on fumes, the reek of gas. Soon, she'll no longer breathe. She feels her neck shrinking. All her life she's struggled to make her urges real. She doesn't feel bad about dying, only that the worlds within her will die as well.

That milky stalk of pulp.

Those blue stones.

And blue stars.

❧

FLORA

Flora sat with her back against the blue recycling bin, unsure of what to do next. She listened to her own breath, the whoosh of wind in her ruptured ear. Not a single shadow lingered or emerged.

In the distance, the green lights of the mosque switched off, and in the hollow of her chest, Flora felt her aloneness. But God had not left her, and she began to envision things, like pushing on an old screen door and joining Pia in a dirt courtyard, like weaving wigs and pouring condensed milk into teacups, like sipping on a beer and sitting open-legged in front of Joenard, like singing in a church and sweeping her feet across the floor, like spooning mango relish into her mouth at an open window as boys played basketball below, like swimming above a red coral reef in her favorite cove, like unpacking boxes of Bibles and blue Popsicles, like flying in the dim cabin of a plane surrounded by women heading home, like Pia in her arms.

Aluminum siding flapped in the wind, banged, and echoed through the neighborhood. Stacks of golden lumber waited for construction. She drank water from the container she'd hidden under her bed and tasted the last remnants of honey along the rim. In her pockets: passport and pearls. In her mind: Pia's phone number. She watched the cars pass on the not-so-distant highway. She closed her eyes, listened to waves of traffic, and imagined strangers at the wheels of vans, trucks, and cars. She walked herself across dirt and sand and stood on the side of the road, her arm raised to people she did not know and who did not know her. It only takes one, she thought. One person to press the brakes, slow down, and stop.

DOUNIA

Dounia slept in the nursing chair beside her daughter's crib. No one had spoken to her since Hamed's return, and she'd been quarantining with Qadira, pledging a promise for today. Not because it was demanded of her by law, by her family, or because she was a woman, but because it was her desire.

Outside it was still night and nothing moved. Her breasts felt heavy and full and her stomach queasy as she watched the horizon line appear in the purple-grey dawn. She lifted Qadira from sleep and brought her to the chair, not a mourner's chair, but something else, something she did not yet understand or know how to name. She fumbled with her buttons, her hands trembling, feeling insufficient and fearful that her daughter might reject her, bite at her breast in retaliation for all the ways she'd failed. Qadira awoke and regarded her, wide-eyed in the dimness. She's scared too, and I don't blame her.

She brushed Qadira Ibrahim's lips with her nipple, waited for her mouth to open wide, and then placed the nipple in Qadira's mouth and pulled her close. Her eyes stung; never had she felt so vulnerable. A small foot kneaded her belly. A mouth latched on. A jaw moved, and there was a deep tugging in her ducts. Milk released and let go. The hardness in her breast softened, and she closed her eyes in relief. Qadira's hands reached for her face and pulled her hair in a painful tug. This is what we have: each other and a chandelier catching sunlight and throwing red pebbles across our foyer. And as she looked out at the rising sun, she recalled the oil spills from Kuwait, how they'd streaked rainbows on the water.

———

People will say, and say, and say.

People will say she is vicious and step backward in their minds upon greeting her. People will say she is unwell and look upon her with concern. People will say she is a girl who always needed attention. People will say she's a victim of larger structures and wonder what can be done. People will say she should divorce and run the date farm. People will say the country is changing and the future belongs to their daughters.

Dounia bent over a tomato plant she was tending and held a delicate yellow bloom between her fingers. At the end of the row, Qadira slept in the shade of the blue tarp.

Let them say, and say, and say.

JUSTINE

Wiped out from packing, Justine waited in the car at the Mina Port while Wren and Aleyna had their farewell jumps on the trampoline. She pushed back her seat, propped her calves up on the dash, and let her elbow hang loose across the open window. She never realized how much comfort she took in asphalt, how her childhood was embedded in tar—waiting in the car outside supermarkets, laundromats, and hardware stores while toggling the dial for her favorite song. Rubber tires rolling over a black hose, the gas bell ring. Bike wheels on blacktop amid green graves and oaks. Like tar, she rolled over weeds and wild plants, flattened uneven ground. She could repave and repave.

She slipped on her shoes and got out of the car. The lot was desolate, not even a shadow to keep her company, but in the distance, she spotted the outdoor produce stands. She bought figs and yellow star fruit, and while waiting for her change, metal speakers amplified the call to prayer, and she watched as gates and awnings fell across stalls and storefronts. A trail of men walked toward the old mosque carrying flattened cardboard boxes on their heads, and when the mosque was full, the cardboard morphed into prayer rugs, and the men knelt on the ground and bowed their heads to the pavement. A grey taxi parked, and a man got out and rolled out his rug on the asphalt.

———

In the kitchen, Justine wrapped dishes in newspaper and packed boxes marked FRAGILE. Wren was organizing her artwork, deciding what to keep and what to let go. Justine imagined the empty apartment, what she'd leave behind: hangers in closets, the litter box, bleach.

"Mom. Mom . . ." Wren called for Justine from her bedroom.

Justine walked down the hall with a damp dish towel swung over her shoulder.

Wren stood at her art table examining a picture. "Who was in my room?"

"No one, why?"

"Who painted this?"

Justine approached the desk. Wren held up a watercolor of blue stones and blue stars in shades of turquoise, navy, and indigo. Gold letters stretched across the sky: ESKEDARE.

That is her name, thought Justine.

Eskedare.

Wren regarded the picture, twisting the ring round and round her thumb. "Mom, I saw the photo online. My macramé was on the jug." Wren traced the blue stones and blue stars of the painting. "She was in our apartment, in my room."

It was not a question: her daughter was demanding something.

Justine had been dreading this moment, and she did not want to allow it, but she was defenseless, a tree in a winter wind losing all her leaves, and she stood bare before her daughter. Wren searched her face like a friend, a sister; like the daughter she was, hoping with all her tender limbs that her mother would meet her gaze and surrender.

ZEINAH

It was past midnight. The moon cast Zeinah's shadow before her, narrow and long, a stronger version of herself. Her expulsion from the camp was now a relief, and she clung to her gun as if it were her infant.

She found her way back to the Euphrates, and instead of charting the river south to the Gulf, she surprised herself and aimed north, following the dignified firs toward unknown towns and places. She'd seen it over and over again, the Euphrates, the same river since childhood, but it was not the same, and her thoughts returned to her brother and the people who had fought for the revolution. Even if you lose, she thought, resistance makes a mark. And in this way, her mind carved a way forward.

———

During the day, she sought shelter beneath the shadow of brush or the makeshift tent of her cloak and sticks. When the sun was high, she tried to sleep, or she sat for a long time and saw nothing while she smelled flinty rocks bake in the heat and watched the blue iridescent wings of flies as they landed in the sandy dirt and sparse clusters of grass.

At night, the Euphrates was a generous host, welcoming Zeinah into her scrubland, loamy banks, and knotted roots. Zeinah drank from the river. Even the water bugs and sandflies seemed to accept her presence, and she felt her dependence on the charity of the land for her survival and was thankful. The land is not guilty, she thought, only the humans who press themselves against it. But who can blame us? We're animals as well.

That night, she slept while walking, delirious with hunger, shuffling across the sand. She walked until she could walk no more, until she sucked wind and lunged toward the ground, until she could barely keep her balance, and her thoughts dropped like stones and she stumbled over them. Nothing moved, everything seemed the same, and sometimes it felt like she was walking in place. She heard a rumbling in the distance, followed by lightning that shattered the landscape into pieces. The sky that just yesterday held so much promise now felt vast and threatening, and she decided she needed to leave the river and search for cover.

Beyond a belt of willows, Zeinah discovered a cluster of abandoned shelters, all of them ransacked, most reduced to stumps, but one retained a tin roof above splintered walls. Light spilled inside in broken patches, and dried herbs hung from nails on the wall. The leaves crumbled in her hand: oregano. She could not say how long the place had been deserted. Months maybe, not a year.

Zeinah curled into a corner that was dark and cool and smelled of rot. Wrinkled potatoes sprouted roots. She bit into the soft barnacled skin and tasted chalk and dirt. Fabric, pink and frayed, hung across the door and ballooned over the threshold, lulling her to sleep.

She awoke to rolling booms in the distance, and she could not tell if they were artillery or thunder. She lay in the dark and listened. Wind whirled through the shelter, knocked on the walls. Rain thrummed against the metal roof. Her black cloak hung on a nail like a frayed umbrella, and the air, full of dust and sand, blew across her body, prone on the floor as she recalled those afternoons searching for her brother beneath the metal rods and fabric. The roof banged, and her hand found a ceramic shard to cling to.

When the storm was over, her breasts rose and fell, and in the gulf between them was a dark, expansive quiet where she dared to feel the shape of things. And like a fresh-caught fish in the bottom of her father's rowboat, Zeinah wondered if she'd be hurled back into life or perish.

The wind shifted out of the north, and she believed she heard voices on the horizon. Maybe the shadows of female fighters, their hair tied back in braids. Zeinah closed her eyes and sent a prayer across the scrub, tumbling into what she hoped might be the ears of women.

> Tulip,
> Cherries in Snow,
> Dare to Bare,
> Bruised Plum,
> Russian Red,
> Revival.
>
> Intense Nude,
> Violet Femme,
> Viva Glam,
> Heroine,
> 999.
>
> Jungle Red,
> Lady Danger,
> Fire and Ice,
> Black
>
> Honey.

ACKNOWLEDGMENTS

It's a full moon in November and the marsh tide has flooded the field. For years I've sat at this desk and looked out the windows of my shed, a gift from my husband, my best friend, Matt. Your desire to see me thrive, your generosity of mind, your love, stand at the foundation of this novel and my life. And for Zibia and Dove, thank you for accompanying me on this journey, for enduring my absence, and for always leaving the porch light on.

Gulf would not have been possible without the support and resources of New York University and my work on the NYU Abu Dhabi campus where I served as both the Associate Dean of the Arts and the Director of FIND, a creative lab researching the transnational heritage of the UAE. These experiences introduced me to extraordinary artists and scholars who were thinking globally. I want especially to thank Hilary Ballon for her extraordinary mind, and for modeling a rigorous scaffolding for examining big ideas across history, cultures, and mediums, and for the team at FIND and their commitment to including transnational voices in the narration of national identity.

For Yasmeen Hassan, a remarkable friend and activist, who called me when I was living in Abu Dhabi about five women who had murdered their trafficker in the UAE. That case sparked the initial research for this book, and throughout the writing process Yasmeen's insights and the people and organizations she's recommended have guided my thinking. Her work on legal reforms has been a beacon for women's rights globally.

For Tisch School of the Arts: my students, colleagues, and Dean Allyson Green, who awarded me two research/travel grants. The first was to the Philippines, where I spent time at a domestic training center with forty women being deployed to Saudi Arabia. Thank you to Karla Delgado, a friend of decades who shared the extraordinary natural beauty of her country and who introduced me to Lila Ramos Shahani, who generously connected me with women and organizations devoted to the welfare of domestic workers. The second grant brought me to Ethiopia, where I traveled and interviewed Gulf-return girls, young women who had been illegally trafficked through Yemen. Thank you to Lisa Woodward, who generously hosted me in her home and introduced me to Habtamu Demele at the International Labour Organization, who arranged interviews and read the manuscript with care. Thank you to the Ethiopian Education Fund and the students who welcomed me into their school.

For my teachers. In midlife I became a student again at the NYU Writers Workshop in Paris. I will never forget those magical afternoons of writers sharing their work and insights on craft; thank you Ocean Vuong, Ishion Hutchinson, Robin Coste Lewis, Catherine Barnett, and so many others. For my mentors: Katie Kitamura and her brilliant reading list, particularly Elfriede Jelinek's *Wonderful, Wonderful Times* and Marguerite Duras's *The War*, and Sasha Hemon for encouraging me to take formal risks. For John Freeman, my thesis advisor, who saw early pages as a novel and kept me swimming across the gulf with a mantra of character and scene. For Elizabeth Gaffney and her singular novel manuscript workshop. For Jacques Menasche, who saw me in ways I had never seen myself and boldly declared I was a writer.

And finally, for Jamaica Kincaid, J.M. Coetzee, Michael Ondaatje, and Svetlana Alexievich—their books, enduring companions on my desk.

For the following organizations and individuals who nurture artists in idiosyncratic and profound ways: the Sharjah Art Foundation, Fine Arts Work Center, Castle Hill, A Public Space, Aperture, ICP, the 24-Hour Room, Geoffrey Nutter's poetry seminars, and David Naimon's podcast, *Between the Covers*. These institutions never failed to inspire and replenish me during this long journey.

For keen insights and first reads: Colette Burson, Pam Koffler, Janet Grillo, Laura Rosenthal, Cyndy Sperry, Anita Naughton, Gail Segal, Ella Martinsen Gorham, Luke Fiske, Iman Qatani, and Nour Malas. For Bill Spindle, who connected me with journalists to fact-check the manuscript. For Scotti Parrish and her essay "The Female Opossum and the Nature of the New World." For Maura Condrick and her hand-drawn map that opens the book. For Winky Lewis and the wonderful afternoon in her studio talking about motherhood as she took my author photo. For Jade McGleughlin and her insights about vulnerability and becoming visible. For Susan Arena, our weekly studio visits and mutual devotion—a shimmering throughline for decades.

For the people who brought this book into the world. Jordan Pavlin, for your structural insights, unflagging interest, and support when it mattered most. For Anna Stein, you are a force. I am so grateful to have your instincts and brilliance in my life. Thank you for your steadfast belief in this book. For my editors, Judy Clain and Jocasta Hamilton, thank you for encouraging brave edits, for loving these women, and for stewarding *Gulf* into the world. Thank you to the outstanding team at Summit Books, for your dedication to excellence and attention to detail. Everything

22ACKNOWLEDGMENTS

from the beautiful cover designed by Keith Hayes, to interior design, to copy edits, to publicity and marketing has been executed with such thoughtful care and expertise. Thank you Josefine Kals, Anna Scrabacz, Kevwe Okumakube, Luiza De Campos Mello Grijns, Kimberly Goldstein, Kayley Hoffman, Amanda Mulholland, Lauren Gomez, Jackie Seow, Carly Loman, Lexy East, Beth Maglione, and Alexis Leira.

This book is dedicated to my mother, a woman who encouraged me as a child to explore the fields and rivers of South Williamstown while also showing me the beauty of tunneling inwards. When I was fifteen, she liberated me from a situation that took her many more years to leave. This act of love, of pushing me outward, further and farther away, has made all the difference.

New York City
2024